# LAST PRISONER OF THE LITTLE BIGHORN

*Smokey River Suspense Series*

Joseph M. Marshall III

LUCID HOUSE
PUBLISHING

# LU☾ID HOUSE
PUBLISHING

Published in Marietta, Georgia, United States of America by Lucid House Publishing, LLC
www.LucidHousePublishing.com.
©2024 by Joseph M. Marshall III
All rights reserved. First Edition.
This title is available in print and e-book form.
Cover design: Troy King
Author photos: Kevin Garrett
Interior layout: Jan Sharrow, The Design Lab Atlanta, Inc.

This novel is based on the author's heritage and knowledge as one of the leading Native historians and writers in the United States. Lakota is his first language, and he was born into a traditional Lakota household on the Rosebud Reservation in South Dakota. The characters and events in this novel spring from the author's imagination, and any resemblance to a person living or dead is coincidental. Names of some places are fictionalized.

No part of this publication may be reproduced, stored, or introduced into a retrieval system or transmitted, in any form or by any means (electronic, mechanical, photocopying, recording, or otherwise) without the prior written permission of both the copyright owners and the publisher. The scanning, uploading, and distribution of this book via the internet or via any other means without the publisher's permission is illegal, and punishable by law. Please purchase only authorized print, electronic, or audio editions, and do not participate in or encourage electronic piracy of copyrightable materials. Brief quotations or excerpts in reviews of the book are the exception. Your support of the author's rights is appreciated.

Library of Congress Cataloging-in-Publication Data:
Marshall III, Joseph M., 1946-
Last Prisoner of the Little Bighorn: Smokey River Suspense Series/
by Joseph M. Marshall III–1st ed.
Library of Congress Control Number: TK
Print ISBN: 9781950495559
E-book ISBN: 9781950495658

1. Lakota 2. Kidnapping 3. South Dakota 4. Battle of the Little Bighorn
5. Custer's Last Stand 6. Family drama 7. Indigenous 8. Murder mystery,
9. Native families 10. National Museum of the American Indian
FIC030000 FIC059000 FIC022080

Lucid House Publishing books are available for special promotions and bulk purchase discounts. For details, contact info@LucidHousePublishing.com

## Dedication

*For my Grandparents*

*Annie (Good Voice Eagle) Two Hawk
Albert Two Hawk and*

*M. Blanche (Roubideaux) Marshall
Rev. Charles J. Marshall*

*Thank you for telling me stories*

# LIST OF CHARACTERS
## (IN ORDER OF APPEARANCE)

Note: In the Lakota culture, cousins (male and female) are considered the same as brothers and sisters, any older person may be called Aunt or Uncle, and there is no distinction between great-grandparent and grandparent in public references, although the status is known to family members.

**Red Shawl** – Sicangu Lakota, wife of Lone Wolf and matriarch of Lone Wolf family, present at Greasy Grass Fight (1876 Battle of the Little Bighorn)

**Lone Wolf** – Sicangu Lakota, husband of Red Shawl and patriarch of Lone Wolf Family, participant in Greasy Grass Fight (1876 Battle of the Little Bighorn)

**Little Shawl** – Sicangu Lakota, daughter of Red Shawl and Lone Wolf, with parents at the Greasy Grass village (Little Bighorn River) in 1876.

**Dr. Gavin Lone Wolf** – Sicangu Lakota and Scottish, twin brother of Gerard Lone Wolf and brother of Loren (Lone Wolf) Hale, professor at Smokey River University, primitive archer, historian and anthropologist, PhD

**Darrell Berkin** – Sicangu Lakota, son of Henry Berkin, student at Smokey River University

**Arlo High Crane** – Sicangu Lakota, graduate assistant at Smokey River University

**Thomas Hale** – Sicangu Lakota and Winnebago, son of Morgan and Loren Hale, university senior at Smokey River University

**Patrolman Jason Singer** – Sicangu Lakota, member of Smokey River tribal police force

**Justin Primault** – Mniconju Lakota, Lieutenant and criminal investigator (CI) with Smokey River tribal police, BS

**Annie Little Turtle** – Sicangu Lakota, daughter of Maud No Horse and Victor Little Turtle, one-hundred-year-old grandmother of Gavin, Gerard, and Loren, who passed on to her descendants a map of where to find a family legacy

**Loren (Lone Wolf) Hale** – Sicangu Lakota and Scottish, sister of Gavin and Gerard, director of nursing at Smokey River Indian Health Service Hospital, RN, MS

**Morgan Hale** – Winnebago, husband to Loren, father of Thomas and Theresa, principal of Kincaid County High School, BS, MS

**Andrew No Horn** – Sicangu Lakota elder, uncle to Loren, Gerard, and Gavin, traditional healer (medicine man)

**Dr. Gerard Lone Wolf** – Sicangu Lakota and Scottish, brother of Gavin and Loren, retired Marine colonel, Iraq and Afghanistan combat veteran, owner and chief executive officer of Washington DC-based security firm, PhD

**Teresa Thibodeaux** – Sicangu Lakota and Winnebago, daughter of Loren and Morgan, sister of Thomas, niece of Gavin and Gerard

**Dr. Clayton Lone Hawk** – Sicangu Lakota, husband of Veronica Streeter (Lone Hawk), retired school administrator and president of Smokey River Sioux Tribe, PhD

**Joby Bone** – Sicangu Lakota, cousin to Lone Wolf family

**Veronica (Streeter) Lone Wolf** – Wife of Clayton Lone Hawk, foundation executive

**Henry Berkin** – Sicangu Lakota, father of Darrell, rancher and tribal councilman

**Dr. Caleb Hightower** – British national, professor at Smokey River University, archeologist

**Esther Red Thunder** – Sicangu Lakota, elder and grandmother, chosen relative of Gavin Lone Wolf

**Katherine Hill** – Sicangu Lakota, former fiancée of Gavin Lone Wolf, also called Soldier Woman, environmental attorney based in Washington DC, JD

**Agnes High Crane** – Sicangu Lakota, mother of Arlo High Crane

**Raymond High Crane** – Sicangu Lakota, father of Arlo High Crane

**Ben Avery** – Choctaw, chief of Smokey River tribal police, BA, MS

**Mel Triplett** – Sheriff of Redoubt County

**Special Agent Bryan Dempster** – Agent in charge, Pierre FBI field office

**Dr. Douglas Eagle Shield** – Sicangu Lakota, president of Smokey River University

**Dr. Theodore Wells** – Historian, assistant director of research and development, National Museum of the American Indian

**Jacob Galbreath** – Wealthy collector of historic artifacts

**Antonio Caruth** – Friend and former business associate of Caleb Hightower

# PROLOGUE

Night of June 25, 1876
Little Bighorn River, Montana Territory

The sound of drums rumbled and boomed like thunder among the tall cottonwoods on the flood plain west of the river called Greasy Grass by the Lakota. Songs of celebration rose into the warm, early summer night among the thousand lodges interspersed with the trees. But not everyone was celebrating. The resounding victory against the Long Knives had come at a price. Many Lakota and Northern Cheyenne fighting men had been wounded, and almost as many had been killed.

Inside a lodge in the Sicangu Lakota camp, a worried young woman waited with her mother and daughter, hope rising each time voices and footsteps approached outside. Red Shawl had not seen her husband since he had grabbed his weapons and jumped on his horse, riding off toward the first sounds of gunfire from the south. She and her mother could not help but hear the wails of grief from a lodge nearby where an Oglala family had lost one of their men.

According to the news that came like dry leaves on the wind through the village, the attacking Long Knives had been utterly defeated. Only those hiding in the holes they dug on the hill to the south and behind barricades of saddles and dead horses were still alive.

Red Shawl was familiar with waiting. During long hunting trips her husband was gone for days. But this was different. Long Knives had attacked the village, guns had been firing, and the entire village was a frenzy of confusion, activity, and noise, with Lakota and Cheyenne men being killed in front of their families. Red Shawl's lovely face, framed by her raven-haired braids, was clouded with uncertainty.

She heard someone approaching and recognized the tattered moccasins and bare legs just outside the low, oval doorway.

"Can you throw me the gray blanket?" asked her husband, Lone Wolf.

She took the blanket out to him. He was clad only in his breechclout and moccasins. His bow and empty arrow quiver were in one hand, and a rifle and his rolled-up leggings in the other. He put the weapons and leggings on the ground near the doorway and took the blanket, wrapping it around his waist to cover the scratches and dried blood on his legs.

Red Shawl looked him up and down. She saw no wounds other than the scratches. He reached for her and held her in a long embrace, his hands trembling on her back. She held him tight. After a long moment, she spoke against his chest, "We have food ready for you."

He nodded and waited for her to enter, then stooped through the doorway to follow her in, glancing at the tiny form sleeping next to his mother-in-law. Holding the blanket tight around his waist, Lone Wolf walked wearily to the back of the lodge, sat down in front of his chair, and leaned back.

"She just fell asleep," Red Shawl said, pointing at their daughter, Little Shawl.

Blue Corn, the old woman, rose slowly to her feet. "I will make some tea over the outside fire," she said softly.

Lone Wolf was a tall man of about thirty, slender though his shoulders were broad and his arms were muscular. His face was long and narrow with a strong jaw, a thin, straight nose, and a wide mouth. Red Shawl could see that he was exhausted, but it was the haunted expression in his eyes that worried her.

She placed the elk meat roasted on wooden skewers and a tin cup full of water next to him and sat down.

"What will happen now?" she asked.

He lifted his eyes from the cold ashes of the inside fire pit where he had been staring and drank the water.

"Long Knives are still on the ridge to the south, across the river," he said, putting down the cup and reaching for the meat. "We have them surrounded. Crazy Horse and the war leaders are with Sitting Bull and the old men, talking about what do with them. Many of the war leaders, and the younger men, want to kill them all. Nothing will happen until tomorrow, after the sun comes up."

She pointed to the pistol he had tucked into the belt that held up his breechclout. "That is new."

He nodded. "I found it in the dust. We killed the Long Knives Crazy Horse blocked from the north, then surrounded the ones that made it to the end of the ridge. When I got near the top of the hill where they all lay, I found this six-shooter. But I could not find any bullets for it."

"I'm glad you're home," said Red Shawl. "And your brothers?"

"They are on the ridge with the men surrounding the Long Knives," he replied. "They were both wounded, but they are alive."

He reached up and touched her face. Despite his smile, and her knowledge of his unquestioned bravery, she again noted his haunted eyes, as if he were trying to shake off something he had seen.

# ONE

A red-tailed hawk's piercing cry greeted Gavin Lone Wolf as he exited the Lakota Studies Building. Looking up, he spotted the dark profile of outstretched wings soaring over the campus of Smokey River University. Snared in the hawk's talons was a large, writhing snake. About two hundred feet above the ground the hawk released the reptile, then folded her wings into an arrowhead and dived toward the ground, matching the speed of the plummeting snake. With a sharp SPLAT the hapless reptile hit the ground in the tall grass south of the SRU Administration Building as the raptor flared its wings and tail feathers and landed, wasting no time tearing into the flesh of her lifeless prey.

Such was life on the northern plains—some were hunters, and some were the hunted. Gavin had watched this life and death drama play out in less than ten seconds, knowing that he was part of it whether he liked it or not.

Walking to his dark blue Jeep Wrangler he unlocked the door as an older model tan sedan entered the parking lot and found an empty space. He recognized both young men in the vehicle, though unaware he was the topic of their conversation.

"Hey, there's Dr. Lone Wolf," Darrell Berkin said, pointing at Gavin about to get into his Jeep. "I think you should talk to him. Do it now."

"Ah, I don't know. I think he and Hightower are pretty tight," the other young man said.

"So? I think he's a straight-up guy. I think he'll listen to you. Do it."

Arlo High Crane looked at his friend. "Maybe you're right. I just don't know."

The two young Lakota men stepped out of the car. One had two long black braids, and the other was dressed like a ranch hand. The long-haired boy waved at Gavin.

"Dr. Lone Wolf," he called out. "We found something in the Big White."

"Are you serious?" He knew Arlo High Crane and Darrell Berkin were helping the university's resident archeologist, Dr. Caleb Hightower, with an exploratory dig near the White River, or the "Big White" as some local people called it. The Lakota had called it *Maka Ska Wakpa* or the White Earth River.

As Darrell Berkin headed toward a pickup, Gavin walked to the sedan. Arlo High Crane opened the back door and extracted a long object wrapped in towels.

"What is it?" Gavin asked.

The boy laid the object on the trunk and pulled aside the towels, revealing a long tube covered in dried black mud and river silt.

"Maybe a musket barrel," Arlo replied. He pointed toward his companion who had climbed into the cab of a newer pickup. "Darrell and I helped Dr. Hightower dig this out of a sandbar. It was buried deep, at an angle, in the mud," he said, tapping an encrusted curved shape on the side of the end. "Dr. Hightower thinks this might be the striker."

"Well, he's been insisting that there are artifacts there from those French trading camps in the 1730s," Gavin said. "Maybe he's right, maybe he's found something this time."

Arlo High Crane shrugged. "It might be a musket barrel, but the question is its age. It looks too intact to be from the 1730s. I think it should be a bit more rusted through and deteriorated. What do you think?"

Gavin leaned in close and looked. Dried silt and black mud made it difficult to get a good look. With a master's degree in anthropology and a doctorate in history, Gavin was asked many such questions, having taught both at Smokey River University for years. However, he did not consider himself an expert on old firearms.

"You may be right," he said. "Generally speaking, it does seem intact. By the way, where is Caleb?"

Arlo rewrapped the tube and then turned to wave at Darrel Berkin in the pickup truck as he drove by. "He's coming. He had to break camp and load up his stuff."

"He camped?"

"Oh, yeah, just west of the Little White, and south from the Big White where he found the musket barrel. He's obsessed with finding something. Maybe he has, finally. Anyway, he asked me to put this in warm water. Then I've got some work to do before I can call it a day. What time is it?"

Gavin glanced at his watch. "Ten to four."

The young man paused, a shadow of uncertainty on his face. "May I ask you a question, Dr. Lone Wolf?"

"Sure, what's on your mind?"

"Well," the boy said tentatively, "how long have you known Dr. Hightower?"

"As long as he's been here. I was on the search committee. Your friend Darrell's dad was on the interview committee. That's when I first heard of Caleb and saw his vitae and resume. I met him after he was hired in the Lakota Studies Department four years ago. Why do you ask?"

The boy shrugged. "So, he was vetted, thoroughly?"

"I assume so. I'm sure Human Resources did."

"Yeah, okay. Dr. Lone Wolf, is there a chance we can talk tomorrow?"

Gavin saw the worried expression in the boy's eyes. "How about now?"

Crunching whispers of tires rolling on pavement interrupted the moment. An older light green Ford pickup drove into the parking lot and pulled up behind the Jeep. A tall young Lakota man with a runner's build jumped down and hurried over.

"Uncle Gavin!" Thomas Hale called out.

"Thomas, what's up?" Gavin asked, noting his nephew's expression of anxious concern.

"Mom just called me; she wants everybody to get over to Grandma's house."

"What happened?"

"The doctor is there. Grandma is getting weaker. I'm on my way there now. Uncle Gerard is flying in from DC tomorrow, and Theresa's coming up from Denver."

"Okay. I'm right behind you." He turned back to Arlo High Crane as Thomas jumped into his truck and drove away. "I guess it will be tomorrow. Is that okay?"

"Yeah, no problem. Sorry to hear about your grandma."

"Thanks. See you tomorrow." Gavin watched as the young man turned and walked up the sidewalk toward the entrance of the Lakota Studies

Building. Something about the boy's worried expression gnawed at him, but it would have to wait.

# TWO

At just past six the next morning, tribal police officer Jason Singer saw his first dead body that was not in a casket. The body was found in the sparse grass about thirty feet from the water's edge. Singer assumed the two men standing next to a pickup truck twenty yards to the south were the fishermen who had called the police dispatcher. At this hour there was no one else at Flat Butte Dam. According to the dispatcher, the call about a body had come in around 5:20 a.m., not quite an hour ago.

This was the first homicide for Singer, a tall, lean, and studious tribal member who had been on the job nearly six months. He pulled a small notebook and a pen out of a side trouser pocket of his dark blue uniform. The two Native men were something past sixty, he guessed, and appeared nervous.

"Good morning. I'm Patrolman Singer with the Smokey River Tribal police. Can you give me your names?"

They nodded. "My name's Ken Brown Otter," the shorter of the two replied.

"Max Prior," the other man said.

"When did you get here?" the officer asked.

"A bit after five," Brown Otter answered.

"Where'd you come from?"

"Red Table. We both live there," said Prior. "This is one of our favorite places to fish."

"Yeah," affirmed Brown Otter. "It's kind of a party place, though, so we sometimes come to pick up beer cans and bottles and stuff."

Singer pointed toward the body. "Did you see it right away?"

They both nodded grimly. "We were here four days ago until sundown. It wasn't there then. This morning we noticed something and drove around to this side. Turned out to be that body." Prior pointed. "Those are our tire tracks, along the shore."

"Okay." Singer took their phone numbers. "The criminal investigator is on the way. He'll want to talk to you. Just, ah, maybe wait in your truck."

They nodded and climbed into their truck.

Singer, who had pulled a camera out of his backpack before exiting his vehicle, began snapping photos, starting with several wide shots. Then, climbing onto the roof of his cruiser, he snapped a series of shots, each with the body at the edge or in a corner of the shot. From that perspective, he noticed a set of vehicle tracks that followed the worn car trail from the gate and curved around the dam. The tracks turned off from it and ended about ten yards from the body. From there the vehicle had apparently reversed in a semi-circle turn to the left, then likely backtracked on its own trail.

Singer spotted what he guessed to be footprints near the vehicle tracks. There were two sets. One set was adjacent to the vehicle tracks and stopped just inside of them. The other prints obviously belonged to the dead man. It appeared he had walked about five yards before he fell, around ten yards from the water's edge.

Singer jumped down and circled wide to the north of the deceased man's footprints. A sense of sadness fluttered in his stomach. He approached the body and knelt, snapping close-ups of it, focusing on feet, hands, and face. An extreme zoom through the camera revealed that the back of the man's head was covered with coagulated blood and appeared crushed. There was no other way to describe the unnatural, deeply concave angle. Moving closer he saw that ants were swarming over the blood as Singer reached and waved away flies from the face, knowing it was a futile gesture.

The face looked young, turned to the right, eyes partially open. The hair was in two long braids and coal black. No doubt the man was Native, probably Lakota, and almost certainly a local tribal member.

The right arm was angled down to the side of the torso, and the left arm was beneath the chest. Singer moved closer and took extreme close-ups from head to toe. His glance kept going back to the obvious cause of death—the wound on the back of the head. Singer leaned down to the ground to see as much of the face as he could, which looked very young. There were no other marks or wounds. There was dried blood on the ground below the upper part of the face.

Singer's shoulder radio crackled.

"Primault for Singer. Come back."

Singer keyed the mike. "Singer here, Lieutenant."

"Roger, just checking. I'm about five minutes out."

"Roger that. The scene is secure. No one's here but the two people who called it in. Sir, I would advise going left or right of the car trail. It goes south of the water from the gate. There appears to be fresh tracks on it."

"Copy that. Ambulance is behind me. I'll advise them. See you in a few."

Nearly thirty minutes later Lieutenant Justin Primault, calm and thorough, the only criminal investigator (CI) on the tribal police force, finished interviewing the two fishermen. He pronounced his name *pree-moe*, the same as relatives here on this rez, though they spelled their name Primeaux. The EMTs with the ambulance had a body bag ready as well as a litter.

Primault stopped about fifteen yards from the body, as Singer pointed out the footprints he had spotted.

The CI pointed to the vehicle tracks. "Those tracks aren't deep, so maybe they were made by a mid-sized or smaller sedan. It looks to me like someone got out of the vehicle there, just to the left of the track, and went about five steps. That's where the other footprints occur."

"Yes, sir," Singer agreed. "The first set of prints are bigger, definitely a male, with lug-soled shoes. The other prints are lug soles as well, but they're narrow."

"Right, and the bigger tracks double back to the vehicle. The question is where did they come from?" The CI looked around the immediate area of the tracks, noticing the remains of other footprints, and pointed them out.

"The two men who found the body said this is a party place, so maybe those prints are older. And people do come here to fish."

"Right, that is a possibility." Primault reached for his camera, which was hanging from his shoulder.

"I took photos," Singer said, scrolling through them for the CI.

"Great, we'll go with those. Time to get up close and personal," he said, somberly.

Primault squatted next to the body and put on latex gloves, his dark eyes scrutinizing it from head to toe. "Gunshot wound, likely the entry," he commented, and bent low to the face. "I can't see an exit wound, though."

Singer had a thought. "Maybe it's a puncture wound, with the tip or end of something that had a blunt point, you know, like a club or a hammer." He winced at his own words. "And there's no exit wound."

"Autopsy will shed some light, hopefully." Primault reached gently into the left hip pocket and pulled out a three-fold leather wallet with a driver's license and tribal identification card. He shook his head sadly.

"Arlo High Crane," he said, softly. "Twenty-four years old, from Gray Grass."

Primault studied the wound at the back of the victim's head. It was the fatal wound because there was no other intrusive mark on the body. Something had caved in the entire lower third of the back of the skull. It looked a bit like a broken clay pot. Pulling out his cell phone he called police dispatch.

"Rhonda, this is Justin. Got a prelim on the body at Flat Butte."

"Go ahead, recorder's on."

"Okay. Body is a Lakota male, Arlo High Crane, age twenty-four. Could have been here a few days. It is probably a homicide, fatal wound to the back of his skull. Victim will be transported to cold storage at the hospital morgue, and we'll need to request an immediate autopsy. Pass this on to the Chief."

"Yes, sir."

Primault had used his cell phone to prevent any information leaking out to the airwaves. There was always someone listening in on the police frequency, and he didn't want the victim's family to find out inadvertently that their son or brother or husband was dead.

He looked up at Singer. "I'll need your help once we get back to the station. We need to find out who this young man's family is. And later someone has to tell them."

Singer nodded. "I can help with that."

Primault motioned to the EMTs. "Let's turn him over," he said when they arrived.

They turned the body over carefully. There were no indications to change the original assessment; certainly no exit wound. Primault examined the hands, especially under the fingernails. They looked clean, and then he saw marks on the left palm and leaned in close.

"Here," he said to Singer, pointing to the marks. "Take shots of those."

"Those are numbers," Singer noted as he took extreme close ups. "And some kind of a design, I think."

Primault wrote the numbers in his notebook.

Minutes later the two officers watched as the EMTs skillfully maneuvered the bag beneath and over the body and then lifted it onto the litter. A few minutes later it was secured inside the ambulance for the trip to the hospital morgue.

Primault gazed at the landscape around the 30-acre dam. "This is the fourth homicide this year," he said. "But this is the only one where we don't know who the perpetrator is. Someone, maybe just one person from the footprints, brought that young man out here and killed him. From the tracks, the fatal wound was inflicted after he got out of the vehicle. Once that was done, the perp got back into the vehicle and drove out."

"No tire tracks," Singer said. "Wind took care of that. My cruiser's tire tread marks are plain." He pointed to the trail left by the unknown vehicle. "The incoming vehicle tread marks are gone. I guess that's because it was breezy or windy while that vehicle was out here, or since."

"Right," Primault agreed, nodding. "Not many clues there. Let's just you and I check around and see what we can see."

They separated and began combing the area. After half an hour of walking and visually scouring the ground, they found only a few discarded beer cans, plastic water bottles, and a broken carbon fishing rod. Fifteen yards from the gate, Singer found tire tracks in a slight depression. He called out to Primault, who was kneeling and examining a track of some sort.

Primault hurried to the young officer and saw what could only be called a strange track in the depression. "It rained a few days ago," Singer recalled. "And this spot probably held a bit of water, then dried out. A car came across it while it was still damp. But I've never seen a track like this. It looks like there's tread in the middle and bald on the sides."

Primault leaned down, looking closely. Overall, the track was not much over a foot in length. The strange part was the two-inch wide and well-defined tread marks down the middle.

"Yeah, you're right," he agreed. "Those are clear marks in the middle and bald on the sides. I've never seen a track like that. Well, let's take close-ups. And when you're done with that, there's a track over there we should photograph as well. I'll show you where it is."

Twenty minutes later they finished taking the close-ups. Primault's print was a horse hoof, obviously made by a shod horse. Like the tire marks, it was in a small, dry mudhole.

Singer leaned down to look closely at print, and then brought up the photos on his camera. "What does that look like to you, sir?" he asked.

Primault gazed at the very distinct image in the photo. "That is a medicine wheel symbol," he said.

"I thought so," the young officer agreed. "I didn't know farriers did that sort of thing, use Lakota symbols, I mean."

"Well," Primault mused, "there's at least one who does, and I'll bet he's Lakota, which narrows it down a lot. That should help us identify who was riding a horse with that shoe, and, hopefully, when he, or she, was here. Maybe it's unrelated to our homicide, but we need to determine if it is or not."

"Sir, what are the odds we'll ever find who killed that young man?"

Primault shrugged. "Statistically, not very high," he said. "There are eleven unsolved homicides on the books, cold cases on this rez since the 1960s." He looked toward the gate. "Let's put some tape across the gate."

# THREE

Annie Little Turtle was a month shy of her one hundred and first birthday. A petite and feisty Lakota woman, she was born to Maud No Horse and Victor Little Turtle during the height of the 1918 influenza outbreak and the end of World War I.

A few minutes past 10 p.m. on Thursday, Gavin, his sister Loren, her husband Morgan Hale, and their son Thomas were sitting in Annie's room. They had been with their gravely ill grandmother since late Wednesday afternoon, and much of that time she had slept periodically. There was no sense of dread, but definitely a heavy sadness. Loren had combed Annie's long but thin snow-white hair and was gently braiding it.

Loren was nearly six feet tall and slender. Her eyes were dark, and her attractive face was medium brown, leaning toward her Lakota bloodline, but her auburn hair was unmistakably from her mother, Molly McLean, who had been born in Edinburgh, Scotland.

Gavin nodded at his uncle, Andrew No Horn, as he stepped into the room and took a seat by the wall. Andrew was tall and wiry with long salt-and-pepper braids nearly to his belt. He was approaching seventy-five, a practicing medicine man—a traditional healer—for most of his life. He and Gabriel Lone Wolf—Loren, Gerard, and Gavin's father—in addition to being first cousins, had been lifelong friends. It was Andrew who had stepped in to assume the role of father to the twin brothers and their older sister after their parents had been killed in a car crash. Andrew had never married and had no children of his own. Now he sat quietly, his face with its long nose, wide mouth, and dark eyes the very image of inscrutable.

A minute later Annie slowly turned her head and leveled a gaze at Gavin. Her voice was weak but clear.

"Grandson," she said, "reach into my nightstand and get that leather pouch."

Gavin retrieved the pouch. He had recalled seeing it once when he was a teenager.

"Open it," she instructed. "There's a big brown envelope. Tell me what you find inside."

Gavin took out three sheets of folded heavy bond paper. Carefully unfolding them, he saw even, neat handwriting in faded ink on two pages and a hand-drawn map on the other.

"Ah," he said, "there's a map and then something written on the other pages."

"Good," Annie sighed as she glanced knowingly toward her nephew Andrew. "Put them back in and keep it. I want you and Gerard to look at them."

Gerard Lone Wolf arrived just after midnight. Theresa Hale Thibodeaux, Thomas's older sister, was only a few minutes behind him, after a long drive from Denver. Dr. Amanda Wiest was sitting with Annie, who was sleeping. Gerard and Theresa stepped quietly into their grandmother's room. Each bent to gently hug the sleeping woman.

Then everyone gathered in the small living room, speaking in hushed voices as Loren and Morgan brought in freshly brewed coffee from the kitchen.

"There's food," Morgan Hale said. He was a member of the Winnebago Tribe from Nebraska and the principal at Kincaid County High School, the largest public school system on the Smokey River Reservation. He and Loren had met at the University of Kansas. "Some soup and the makings for salad. Just help yourselves."

Gerard's short hair was the opposite of Gavin's long single braid that hung to his belt. Otherwise they were as identical as identical twins could be. Both were six feet four inches tall and weighed exactly one hundred ninety pounds. Gerard was the owner and CEO of Wolf Star, a security firm based in Washington DC and had retired from the U.S. Marine Corps as a full colonel at the age of forty-three, seven years ago. After two tours in Iraq and one in Afghanistan, he was ready for civilian life.

"What do you think, Uncle?" Gerard asked Andrew, acquiescing to his uncle's status and vast experience as a healer. "Is this her time?"

Andrew No Horn nodded somberly. "It is," he replied honestly. "The pneumonia will take her, but—she's ready. You should all know that. There's no fear in her because her spirit is strong. She's ready to make the journey. We Lakota know that death is the end of a cycle, a transition to the next dimension, not an enemy to be fought and feared. That's why we say death is the beginning of the next journey."

All the men nodded while Loren and Theresa unabashedly wiped away tears.

As a contemplative silence fell on the room, Dr. Wiest walked up to the table and put a hand on Gavin's shoulder. "Your grandmother is awake, and she's asking for all of you."

# FOUR

Andrew No Horn smudged Annie's room with sweet grass, filling it with a soft, sweet, comforting scent. This ritual welcomed the benevolent spirits of Annie's ancestors to guide Annie's spirit from the physical realm to the spirit world.

Everyone perceived a difference in the old woman's demeanor. Only hours ago, she had been alert despite being weak. Now she seemed to be looking beyond those in the room.

Just before four in the morning her breathing became noticeably shallow. Dr. Wiest turned a questioning glance at Andrew, who nodded almost imperceptibly. The doctor quickly placed an oxygen mask over Annie's mouth and nose. Her eyes opened; her gaze cleared as she glanced around the room, then became distant and moved to the foot of her bed, to the left. She smiled for a moment. And then she stopped breathing.

Andrew stood and went to the bedside. Dr. Wiest gently placed her stethoscope on the old woman's chest; in a moment she nodded at the medicine man, glanced at her watch, and removed the oxygen mask. Andrew reached out slowly, gently closing his aunt's eyes.

"Death is one of the great truths," he said to the those in the room. "Death gives life meaning. Though we know this truth, we will still weep.

There will always be emptiness in the air where this precious woman was because we loved her and she loved us."

Wiping away tears, Andrew leaned down and kissed Annie on her forehead. "*Toksa ake wancinyankin ktelo* (I will see you again)," he said softly. After he stepped aside everyone did the same, giving their beloved grandmother and great-grandmother a loving farewell.

According to her wishes, Annie Little Turtle was not embalmed. The funeral director's only tasks were to bathe her and put her in her favorite dress, wrap her in a star quilt, and place her in the simple cedar casket that she had ordered to be constructed.

After one night of wake, Annie's funeral was conducted by no less than seven medicine men. All prayers were offered in Lakota. Clayton Lone Hawk, the Smokey River Sioux Tribal President and close family friend, delivered the eulogy, first in Lakota and then in English. Then six young men carried her, walking behind traditional singers with a drum as they sang an honoring song, to the family cemetery on the hill west of her house. She was buried next to her children and last husband.

After the funeral a meal was served. As sunset approached the crowd of two hundred or so had dwindled to family and a few close friends helping to clean up and put Annie's house in order. Joby Bone, a cousin to the Lone Wolf family, was among them. Joby, in his late forties, was a lifelong bachelor, living alone in his house in Lower Horse Creek.

"*Tahansi* (Cousin)," Gavin said, stopping next to Joby. "Thanks for helping and I hope you had plenty to eat."

Joby nodded. "I did, Cousin, I did."

"Plenty of leftovers, too. Take some with you, and I'll give you a ride whenever you're ready to go."

"Sure thing. I think Auntie Esther needs a ride, too."

"No problem. See you later."

President Lone Hawk and his wife Veronica, an attractive green-eyed blond of Norwegian descent, were among the helpers. Gavin and Gerard chatted briefly with them.

"I appreciate what you had to say, Clayton," Gerard said. "And no one could have said it better."

"My thoughts exactly," Gavin echoed.

"I'm honored you asked me to speak," the president replied. "Especially since your grandma stood by me in my time of need."

"Mrs. Lone Hawk," Gerard said, "I'm sure a Lakota funeral is unlike any other you've experienced."

"Definitely," she affirmed. "And very meaningful."

Caleb Hightower was among the people clearing a table. The Englishman nodded affably at Gavin, though he turned away at the appearance of Henry Berkin, the tribal council representative from Fast Creek, resplendent in a gray suit, white Stetson hat, and expensive western boots.

Berkin's presence was frankly a surprise to Gavin. The councilman, who styled himself as "progressive," was a frequent critic of traditional Lakota beliefs and ways, often accusing Gavin of being nothing more than a highly educated "half-breed progressive" trying to pass himself off as a traditionalist.

Berkin approached, a solicitous smile on his face, evoking the image of an Old West snake oil salesman rather than a Lakota man. Though he was married, Gavin had never seen the man anywhere with his wife, Mavis. "Hey, my friend," Berkin said, "your grandmother was a great lady. My condolences."

Gavin nodded and shook the man's hand. "Good of you to come, Henry."

"Not at all, not at all. I thought Father Jones would be here. He admired Annie a lot."

Gavin could only assume the remark was a jab at the Lakota funeral conducted by medicine men, since Berkin was an avowed Episcopalian. "We invited him, since he and Grandma were friends, but I think it's a long drive from Rapid City for a ninety-two-year-old man," he commented.

"Right. Anyway, good to see you."

Gavin shrugged off the encounter as soon as Berkin was out of sight and sat down next to his Aunt Esther under the shade of a tree. "Auntie Esther, thanks for coming. Did you get enough to eat?"

The woman took his hand in both of hers, her wrinkled face smiling. Her hair was almost totally gray and hung in two long, neat braids. She wore a simple black dress, a usual sign of mourning by older Lakota women. "I did," she said, and pointed to a plastic container full of leftovers. "And something for my grandkids."

"Oh, good," he said. "Joby said you might need a ride."

"Yeah, I came with my cousin, Cora," she replied. "But she left already. It's a nice day, so I was thinking of walking."

"No," he said. "Let me give you a ride."

Hightower approached, looking a little wan. "Just had a nice chat with Loren," he said. "And wanted to check with you before I left." His blue eyes squinted at Gavin.

Hightower's Midlands English accent was still distinct, even after twenty plus years of living in the United States. "You're looking a little tired, my friend," Gavin told him.

"Late nights," the Englishman replied. "Grading papers. Anyway, you take care and I'll see you Monday."

"Hey, thanks for helping. What's the situation with that musket you dug up?"

Hightower shook his head. "Good question. It's still in my workshop. I'll check it out first thing Monday. Anyway, didn't mean to interrupt." He waved and walked away.

Gavin turned his attention back to Esther Red Thunder. "I'll get Joby and we'll get going," he said.

Esther, who was over seventy as far as Gavin could remember, also lived in Lower Horse Creek, a housing cluster two miles south of Cold River. All the houses were the same, though the paint on some was more faded than others. Even in the summer the place looked worn and bare. Gavin waved back at brown children playing in the yards or on their bikes skillfully dodging potholes in the street. Their youthful exuberance and excited voices momentarily pushed aside his sadness.

"Thanks, *Tunska* (Nephew)," Esther said, as they pulled up in her driveway. "Your grandma was a good person, a strong woman. I'm gonna miss her."

"Me, too," he said. "Do you have a phone, Auntie?"

"No," she said. "Them things are too expensive." She pointed to the street. "There's a phone line though, they said, in the ground. And I have hard time with those little flat things that are s'posed to be phones."

The old woman smiled as she carefully stepped down from the pickup. Two kids, a boy and a girl, came out to meet her. She turned to hug them. Gavin watched them walk across the bare yard to the door. The little family had suffered their own losses. Nora and Christopher's parents—Esther's daughter and son-in-law—had frozen to death two winters ago in a minus twenty-degree night after running out of gas on a little-used reservation back road and trying to walk out. Now Esther Red Thunder, for all intents and purposes, was a parent again. She paused at the back door and waved.

A minute later Gavin pulled up at Joby's house. "You doing okay, *Tahansi?*" he asked.

"Yeah, yeah, I'm good." Joby held up his containers of leftovers. "Won't have to cook for a few days," he grinned. Joby had no car and barely got by on a part-time job. He had no electricity, and his water came in by a hand pump in the kitchen.

"Sometime this summer," Gavin said, "I'm replacing some barb wire with light barbless cable, because of my horses. I need some help if you want to earn a few dollars."

"Sounds good," Joby nodded.

Twenty minutes later Gavin was back at Grandma Annie's house.

"It seems a shame to leave," observed Loren. She was with Gerard and Andrew in the living room when Gavin walked in. "But I know we must. Life goes on."

"True," agreed Gerard. Twelve years had passed since his wife had died. To assuage his grief, or perhaps to avoid it, he had volunteered for another combat tour in the Gulf War, and a third in Afghanistan, much to his family's anguish. "Now it's time to think about the necessary and ordinary things we're left with. Such as her will," he said.

Andrew nodded. "She appointed me executor, so I suppose I'll see that it gets to probate. She wanted it done as quickly as possible."

"Maybe I can help with that."

The low, husky voice familiar to everyone came from the front doorway. They turned to see a woman standing in the last glow of sunset, that transitory moment before dusk. All the men rose to meet her.

Katherine Hill stepped forward into the room, and those few steps were not unlike a slow dance. She was a family friend and had once been engaged to Gavin. Her initial glance was directed at him.

"I'm sorry to be late," she apologized. "I was out of the country when I got the news. I came as fast as I could manage."

She was not as tall, but Katherine Hill could have been cut from the same mold as Loren. She was slender and carried herself with confidence and grace, qualities that accentuated her natural beauty. A nearly full-blood Lakota, her skin was a deep brown, and she had the obvious markers of high cheekbones and raven black hair. Her eyes were large and brown, and gazed at Gavin for several long seconds before she turned to greet the others. She went first to Andrew.

"Uncle," she said, embracing him warmly. "It's good to see you. I'm so sorry about Grandma Annie."

"She wouldn't want you to be sad," he replied. "She lived a long life, and she passed peacefully."

Gavin escorted her to the cemetery on the rise west of the house. In the fading light of day, they stood at the fresh grave. Katherine took his hand.

"I was thinking of coming to see her last fall," she said. "She sent me a card, I promised to come back for a visit. There are always regrets at a time like this."

"Yes, but don't hang on to them. Just remember that she was so proud of you. She's the one who started calling you Soldier Woman, because you were the first Lakota woman lawyer from this reservation."

Katherine nodded as she wiped away a tear. Gavin handed her his clean handkerchief. "Ever the gentleman," she said. "Thank you."

"So, how's life these days?" he asked.

She laughed softly. "It's fine, if life would stop interfering with my life."

"How long can you stay?"

"A few days. My return flight is on Monday."

"If you need a place to stay, you can stay here," he said, pointing to the log house. "And I think Loren and Morgan have a spare room."

She squeezed his hand. "I was hoping for your couch, actually."

He squeezed back. "If you're not joking, it's yours."

"I wasn't and thank you."

The reluctance to leave Annie's house overwhelmed them all. Loren and Theresa made coffee and later served leftovers from the funeral feast. Chairs were arranged in a circle in the small living room, and more stories were shared. Annie Little Turtle, it seemed, had not completely left the building.

# FIVE

Katherine followed Gavin to his log house along the Little White River. He had built it nearly five years ago, after they had last seen one another. Ten long years had passed since she had called off their engagement.

"I can't see you living in Washington DC," she had told him. "Although I know you would try, you would be miserable. You belong on the prairies with the wind in your hair." She was a rising star in environmental law, having graduated in the top three percent of her class at Arizona State University. The offer from the firm in Washington DC was her dream job, with very little room for marriage and children.

By the time she had arrived in the District of Columbia and signed her employment contract, Gavin was in the wilds of the Brooks Range in Alaska, hoping that the pristine wilderness and a mountain goat hunt would help heal his broken heart. It didn't.

He had had no contact with her for a year, until a serendipitous encounter at the Seattle-Tacoma Airport. They were going in opposite directions. She had seen him having coffee in the main terminal and joined him at his table. The first thing he had noticed was the pewter friendship ring with the jade setting on her left hand, third finger, which he had given her before they were engaged. She was wearing it still, but he didn't allow himself to speculate as to why.

He shook off the memory and made up the bed in the spare bedroom, which was small but cozy. He had never imagined that the woman he almost married would be sleeping in it.

"Let me guess," she said, looking around at the interior of the two-bedroom, two-bath log house with the open kitchen-dining-living area below a cathedral ceiling. "You built this yourself?"

"Not entirely," he told her. "I bought the logs and Thomas and Morgan helped me put up the exterior and interior walls and lay in the floor. I did the wiring and the plumbing. A friend helped with the fireplace."

She stepped up to the stone fireplace, admiring it. "A new house. Congratulations."

"Thanks, but technically it's not new."

"It looks new."

"All the logs were mistakes—cast-offs—from sawmills that made house logs. Morgan and Thomas helped me recut and reshape them. All the windows and doors are recycled from old houses; so are the floor joists, roof rafters, and every piece of wood and lumber. The only things new are the bathroom and kitchen fixtures, the wiring, and the plumbing, doorknobs and locks, and the concrete for the foundation and partial basement. You're standing in a mostly recycled house."

Katherine looked around at the interior. "As I said, it looks new. Not as big as your old house."

"Well, it's just me."

"I hear you have a place on the Wind River Reservation as well. Is that off the grid, too, like this house, with a wind generator and solar panels?"

He chuckled. "I'm not there as often so there's only a wood stove and a gas generator. I guess that means that either rumors fly really far, or you've been checking up on me."

"A little of both," she admitted. "Is that a log house, too?"

"A small frame house," he told her, "insulated with straw bales. Would you like some water, or tea, maybe?"

"You wouldn't happen to have some wild peppermint, would you?" she asked, her eyes twinkling.

"As a matter of fact, I do."

In the time it took for the water to boil and her tea to steep, she had changed into black silk pajamas. Perhaps owing to a sense of self-preservation, he took the leather recliner on the opposite side of the coffee table since she had curled up on the couch, a mug of tea in hand.

"It's hard to come home, sometimes," she said. She looked up at him for an instant. "Sometimes life gets in the way. Or maybe I've just become too colonized, as you like to say."

He sighed and sipped his tea, his insides fluttering a bit. "Well, your life is your life, and I know you're good at what you do. It's just that, the last thing I expected was you sitting in my house in silk pajamas sipping wild peppermint tea."

She smiled. "I'm surprised you're still single."

"I thought you would be—well, at least spoken for, by now. Or maybe you are."

She shook her head. "No, you're a hard act to follow."

"Well, likewise."

A moment passed, and then a few. They looked at each other nervously, almost shyly.

"Ah," she finally said, "do you suppose Uncle Andrew will let me have a look at Grandma Little Turtle's will?"

"Of course, won't be a problem."

His phone chirped. He went to the dining table and picked it up, glancing at the incoming number on the screen. "Hi, Loren," he answered.

"Morgan and I want to invite everyone to breakfast at our place tomorrow."

"Great, thanks."

"Gerard is staying with us and said Katherine might be at your place. If so, can you tell her?" There was a curious and hopeful tone in his sister's voice.

"I'll tell her, she is here."

"Thanks, and maybe you can call Uncle Andrew."

"What time do you want us to come over? And can we bring anything?"

"Oh, by nine, and just bring yourselves."

"Okay, we can do that."

Gavin could imagine what was now swirling around in his sister's head. She had been just as heartbroken as he when Soldier Woman had called off the engagement.

"Loren and Morgan are inviting us to breakfast tomorrow."

"Lovely," she said, an inquisitive look in her eyes as she gazed at him over her teacup. The question he was expecting didn't come.

There was, however, a question in his mind. *Why is she still wearing the jade ring?*

"I've had a long day, and you must be more tired than I am. I'm going to turn in," she said.

"Of course. You should be comfortable. Theresa and her husband slept there."

"It'll be just fine," she assured him, standing up.

She took her tea mug to the sink and rinsed it. On the way to the spare room, she stopped and took his hand. "Thanks," she said, "for letting me stay here."

He nodded. "Good night," he said. It was all he could think of to say.

"Good night," she echoed. "I'm looking forward to your coffee in the morning."

Forty minutes later he was still awake. Coyotes were barking somewhere out in the night. Their voices sounded mournful.

Soldier Woman was no more than twenty feet away on the couch, and his heart was breaking all over again.

## SIX

Sunlight poured in through the east-facing window of Gavin's bedroom. In the first instant of wakefulness, he remembered everything that had happened the day and the evening before. He could hear every word and feel every look. He took a deep breath and sat up, remembering her words: *I'm looking forward to your coffee in the morning.*

Donning sweats he slipped on sneakers and hurried to the kitchen counter and put on coffee. He heard the whisper of the shower from the small bathroom as he hurried out to the barn to check the water in the horse tank. His two geldings were on a rise in the north pasture. He checked them over with binoculars. One was a gray and the other a bay, both mustangs from a rescue ranch in the Black Hills. He swept the glasses over the expanse of the verdant pasture, a peaceful scene on a Saturday morning with a light westerly breeze.

He looked up at the briskly spinning three-bladed wind generator atop a twenty-foot pole behind the barn. Two panels of photovoltaic cells were in front of the house, one angled south-southeast and the other south-southwest. The storage batteries were in the partial basement of the house. Everything seemed in order. After four years the generator and solar panels had already paid for themselves.

Like the house, the barn was constructed of used and recycled materials. Whatever he didn't use on the house was relegated to the barn. Only the wiring was new. He had stained the wood siding to match the color of the logs on the house.

Back inside the house he took two mugs from the cupboard and set them on the table. The enticing aroma of coffee filled the room. Katherine emerged from her bedroom, dressed in loose sweats, and rubbing her hair with a bath towel.

"Good morning," she said cheerily.

"Morning."

"That coffee smells so good."

"It's done and there's plenty of it."

She shook out her hair. It was longer than the last time he'd seen her. "Are we late for breakfast?"

Gavin glanced at the clock on the wall. "No, plenty of time. I'll jump in the shower. It's about a twenty-minute drive to Loren and Morgan's place."

By the time he was dressed, she was at the table sipping coffee. Clad in blue jeans and a form-fitting white sweater, her hair was tied back in a long ponytail. Try as he might, he couldn't ignore any of it, the white sweater and the ponytail swaying with the slightest movement. This was going to be an interesting day.

"Your coffee is delicious," she complimented him. "But then again you always were good at making coffee."

"A man's got to be known for something."

She laughed softly.

"I'm not sure what your plans are after breakfast," he said, "so you can follow in your rental or jump in with me."

"Later I want to go visit my mom's grave, but if you don't mind, I'll ride with you."

It was the answer his ego wanted to hear but the one his heart was dreading.

"Great," he heard himself say.

Gavin chose his four-passenger pickup truck. Though not new it was newer than the Jeep and had a smoother and quieter ride, not to mention the Bose CD player and speakers. He put in *The Best of Abba* as low background music, a necessary distraction.

"Ah, still you and Abba, huh?" Katherine teased. "Kind of far afield for a traditional Lakota, don't you think? You do know there were other musical groups out there."

"Yeah, I suppose" he countered, "but no one came close to Anni-Frid Lyngstad and Agnetha Faltskog for pure talent and sex appeal. And Benny Andersson and Bjorn Ulvaeus weren't bad either, as partners go. No one was as good in their day, from 1970 to 1982 and since, in my opinion."

The smile she gave him, with a slight tilt of her head, sent shivers up his back.

Loren greeted them with long, warm hugs and immediately noticed the jade ring on Katherine's hand, shooting Gavin a quizzical look.

Uncle Andrew was the last to arrive as Morgan put on a grand spread. The heaviness of the past three days was beginning to lift. Even the comments and stories about Annie Little Turtle were more lighthearted. Life was moving on.

Loren and Morgan's house overlooked the Soldier Creek valley to the west. They had bought it from a retired rancher soon after Morgan had been hired as principal at Kincaid County High School. From here Loren's drive was five minutes to the Indian Health Service hospital near Agency

Village where she was director of nursing. Like many Native males, Morgan Hale had chosen to live among his wife's people.

For Gavin, home was where he and his siblings had grown up. For Gerard on the other hand, the death of his wife, Marilyn, was affirmation that he didn't belong here. All in all, when it came to the brothers Lone Wolf, Gerard leaned to his Scottish half and Gavin to his Lakota half. Gavin spoke Lakota fluently, but Gerard had lost some of that ability. Gavin was a traditional dancer, to the point that his entire dance regalia was made of natural materials—brain-tanned hides, dyed porcupine quills, and elk hooves—eschewing cloth, glass beads, and brass bells. Gerard's closet held Armani suits, tailored shirts, and Italian loafers. Yet for all their outward differences, they were close, as twins usually were.

As Morgan refilled coffee cups, Loren glanced at her brothers. "Guys," she said, "I would like to see what's in that envelope Grandma gave you. Did you happen to bring it?"

Gerard and Gavin exchanged a smile and a conspiratorial glance. "Does the pope take a… stroll in the woods?" Gerard teased.

As Loren stared at them in exasperation, Gavin reached into the side pocket of his cargo pants, pulled out the brown envelope, and handed it to Gerard. "I've had a look at it," he said to his brother. "I think you should do the honors and read it aloud for us."

"Sure, ah, just give me a minute to glance through." After looking at the map, he passed it along. After nearly two minutes with the handwritten pages, he cleared his throat. "You know, this document is ninety-four years old. Bear with me. I am going to insert prepositions and transitive verbs here and there, so it'll be a slow read. This is dated February fifth, nineteen twenty-four."

*Brother to my husband ask me write My name Maud No Horse Husband Victor Little Turtle end son [of] Lone Wolf [and] Red Shawl He die killed 1918 war [in] France I learn read write words carlile school brother in law ask me do this This begin [with] father to my husband Lone Wolf he my fatherinlaw [and] warrior at greasy grass fight june 25 [and] 26 white man winter 1876 Lone Wolf there [with] wife Red Shawl [and] little daughter Little Shawl He do fight by brothers Black Wolf [and] White Tail Feather They all live [and] two wounds Brothers fight many long knifes [and] two long knife chiefs one called Custer long hair Lone Wolf draw story use pencil colors [in] book have green sides I see book Story many drawing pictures Lone Wolf make pictures winter my father be born 1880 Green sides book give by black robe live agency Lone Wolf take sixshooting gun from dirt [by] dead long knifes [and] keep many winters Boss farm man smoke river agency want [to] give Lone Wolf six silvers [for] six shooting gun Lone Wolf say no boss farm man say Lone Wolf ride iron road to levenwert jail [for] take six shooting gun Lone Wolf hide gun tell boss farm man six shooting gun put [in] blacksmith fire Boss farm man bother Lone Wolf many years [and] he die Lone Wolf brothers know [of] six shooting gun Lone Wolf hide summer 1924 [at] place pick [by] him Annie my daughter help They dig [and] put six shooting gun [and] green sides book [in] stone pot [in] far down hole east hill horse creek Black Wolf draw land picture show where far down hole Black Wolf talk indin word [to] wife Esther she pass words me turn Indin words [to] white words My honor [to] do this [to] help good man Lone Wolf.*

A deep and reverent silence hung in the air after Gerard finished reading. All eyes were on the pages in his hand.

"This is one hell of a story," he said.

"I'm trying to visualize the setting," Gavin said, looking at Uncle Andrew. "I mean, according to the last sentences, it was Black Wolf, Esther, and Maud. Grandpa Black Wolf did the talking to his wife Grandma Esther, and Grandma Maud translated and wrote it all down."

Andrew nodded.

"Amazing," Loren said.

Theresa Thibodeaux leaned forward to gaze in awe at the pages in her uncle Gerard's hands. "This is history," she said. "Not only for our family. This is Lakota history. What do you think we should do with it?"

Gerard smiled at his niece. "We need to talk about this, that's for sure." He turned to Andrew. "Uncle, you knew about this and said not a word all these years."

The medicine man nodded slowly. "Yes, so did your father, and he kept it a secret, too. It was Grandpa Black Wolf's wish for us to be cautious about the story."

Loren cleared her throat softly. "I've never heard anything about Great-Grandfather Lone Wolf finding a pistol at Little Bighorn," she said, gazing intently at Andrew. "And what was the reason to be cautious?"

# SEVEN

All eyes of Annie Little Turtle's descendants turned to Andrew No Horn, expectantly. The old man, who had kept the contents of the envelope secret all these years, cleared his throat and glanced somberly at everyone.

"Well," he began, "two reasons to be cautious about this story. There were rumors all over the place about the government punishing anyone who fought at Greasy Grass. They were mostly rumors, but the threat of Fort Leavenworth prison was downright scary. Lakota people were sent there before. So, years after the battle when *wasicus* (white people) came to interview combatants, Lakota people were leery. Some told about what they did or what they saw. Others refused to talk or just told tall tales."

"Dad said many times that Great-Grandfather White Tail Feather wouldn't talk to any white man," Gerard recalled.

"Right," Gavin said. "And what was the second reason, *Leksi* (Uncle)?"

Andrew took a deep breath and looked around. "That's a tougher story," he said, almost hesitantly. "It has to do with the government's sub-agent for the Horse Creek district. Boss farmers, they were called. The one assigned to Horse Creek, Jens, heard about a pistol that Great-Grandfather Lone Wolf had found. He did find it on Last Stand Hill, by the way. Jens knew just enough Lakota to get the gist of a conversation he overheard between two friends of Grandpa Lone Wolf. That was around 1912. They mentioned the six-shooter.

"Jens went to Grandpa Lone Wolf, and of course Grandpa denied having the gun. That didn't stop Jens. According to what Cousin Gabe told me, that guy was relentless. And as Grandma Maud wrote, he threatened to send Grandpa Lone Wolf to Leavenworth if he didn't give up the pistol."

"I guess it's a good thing the guy died," Loren observed.

Andrew chuckled wryly. "Grandma Maud didn't say how he died. Grandpa Lone Wolf came home one day and found Jens in his house. They lived on the flats above the river, west of where I live. The guy had Grandma Red Shawl terrified, tore up the house looking for the pistol. Well, Grandpa Lone Wolf was having none of that. He was in his sixties but still a strong man. He grabbed the man and hauled him out to the boss farmer's buckboard. Jens pulled a pistol and shot Grandpa in the hip. Grandpa took the pistol away from him, shot and killed him. Then hauled the body out somewhere and buried it."

"Oh, my!" Loren covered her mouth in astonishment.

"So, then what happened?" Gerard asked.

"Well, Grandpa came home," Andrew continued, "and Grandma treated his wound. He went to Grandpa White Tail Feather and told him what happened. Sometime later they drove the buckboard to the issue station and told the other boss farmer they had found it and the horse. There was a search, of course, for Jens, but he was never found."

"Oh, my god," Loren said. "You mean that son-of-a-bitch's body is still out there?"

Andrew nodded. "It sure is."

"This land holds a lot of stories," Gerard mused. "So, Uncle, that's what Grandma Maud meant when she wrote 'and he die.'"

"For sure."

Gerard chuckled. "And where do you think Great-Grandpa Lone Wolf and Grandma Little Turtle buried the book and pistol?"

"On the edge of the plateau east of Horse Creek," Andrew replied. "Grandma Little Turtle took me there when I was fifteen and had me mark the spot."

Loren was incredulous. "Uncle, you've known about this for what—sixty years?"

Andrew slowly nodded. "Your father knew about it, too."

"That's simply amazing," she went on. "And what's in the book with green sides?"

"I'm guessing it's a ledger book," Gavin interjected.

"You're right, *Tunska*," Andrew said. "A Catholic priest gave it to him, and colored pencils, I heard. So, Grandpa Lone Wolf drew sketches of what he and his brothers did in the Greasy Grass Fight."

"That's a priceless historical record," Gerard pointed out. "Not to mention what the pistol would be worth. What kind was it?"

"A six-shot revolver," Andrew told him.

Morgan let out a low whistle. "I think this information stays here. It should go no further than all of us here, in this house. Do you realize what would happen if word got out that you all own a 7th Cavalry pistol from the Battle of the Little Bighorn? That could be a lot of trouble. Do you realize the kind of people would want it?"

A contemplative silence fell on the room.

"What are we going to do about this situation?" Loren asked.

"I think we should dig them up," Thomas suggested. "The ledger book and the gun."

Once more all eyes turned to Andrew, who nodded as he gazed at his coffee cup.

# EIGHT

Gerard said his good-byes after breakfast in order to catch the evening flight from Sioux Falls to Minneapolis and then on to DC. "Uncle Andrew let me read Grandma's will last evening. It's all good by me. Let me know when you dig up that stone pot," he said to Gavin. "Better yet, send pictures. That's a piece of our history I want to know about."

"You got it," Gavin promised.

By midafternoon Gavin and Katherine were back at his log house. Katherine changed and drove away in her rental sedan but left behind her roller bag and brief case in the spare bedroom. Through the partially open door he saw her makeup bag in the second bathroom.

Gavin heated water and made a cup of green tea, then sat at the table to think. In another day or two, she would be gone, flying back to her life and job in Washington DC, fifteen hundred miles away. He should have anticipated that Katherine Kay Hill might show up for Grandma Little Turtle's funeral, but he hadn't. After all, there had been no word from her in years. A long time ago he had accepted that he and Katherine were no longer a couple, and that she had chosen, instead of him, a world far removed from his, culturally and geographically.

Two years after she had broken off their relationship, he had turned down an offer from Dartmouth. There was plenty of prestige and challenge to be had as department head of indigenous studies, not to mention a salary befitting the position. But for him Dartmouth was too close to DC and—at least where his shattered heart was concerned—the odds were too high that he would bump into her somewhere, somehow. He had no desire to manifest Rick's heartbroken line from *Casablanca*: "Of all the gin joints, in all the towns, in all the world, she walks into mine."

The encounter at Sea-Tac Airport in Seattle was by pure chance. Though he had soaked up every millisecond of it, his heart had broken again when she walked away toward her gate and the plane taking her back to the world she preferred.

Part of the reason he had built this log house on the river was to have something not associated with her. She had lived with him in his old house. There was no part of it that did not hold some memory of her. She had cooked in the kitchen, showered in the bathroom, studied for her bar exam on his desk, and curled up on the couch. Her laughter, her voice, her essence, and her vitality were ingrained in every molecule of that old house. He had sold it to a rancher with the stipulation that he had to move it. Now after years of wind, rain, snow, grass, and weeds, the site was mostly erased—but not the memories.

Gavin sighed and reached for a spoon to stir the honey he had poured into his tea. And now she had imprinted herself in this house as well. How was he to keep her memory at a safe distance now when she had said, *Actually, I was thinking of your couch,* in her thrilling voice. He sipped his tea, absently staring out the window.

He almost didn't hear his phone chirping. Feeling strangely apprehensive, he was on the verge of not answering until he saw a number on the caller ID that seemed familiar.

"This is Gavin Lone Wolf."

A polite but insistent voice spoke. "Dr. Lone Wolf, this is Lieutenant Justin Primault with the tribal police. I need to ask you a question. Do you know a young man by the name of Arlo High Crane?"

"Yeah, I do. He's a graduate assistant at the university. Why do you ask?"

"Because his body was found by Flat Butte Dam."

Gavin gasped. There was no sense in the words. They were absurd. "What? That can't be right."

"It is, I'm afraid. It appears he was shot, Dr. Lone Wolf, in the back of the head."

"That's—I mean, I just saw him four days ago, on campus." He paused. "And how is it you're calling to tell me?"

"We talked to his parents. They gave us a list of people he knew, some connected with the university."

"I see."

"What was Arlo's connection to the university?"

"He was doing an internship here as a graduate student at the University of Nebraska. He was assigned to my department."

"I see. And you last saw him four days ago?"

"Yes."

"That would have been May sixteenth?"

"Yes."

"Thank you, Dr. Lone Wolf. I will be in touch again."

"Of course."

Gavin disconnected the call, put down the phone and stared out the window. "*Tuweni!* (This can't be true!)," he said out loud. The last conversation with Arlo came to mind. The boy had wanted to talk.

He retrieved his phone and placed a call. Uncle Andrew answered after four rings.

"Hello?"

"*Leksi, akicita kin lecala masapapi.* (The police just called.)"

"*Ohan.* (Yes.) Was it about Arlo High Crane?"

"Then you know already."

"*Atkuku kin lecala masamakipe.* (The boy's dad called me.) *Ekta mni ktelo, Peji Hota ekta.* (I'm going to their place in Gray Grass.) *Toksa ciciyuhla kte.* (I'll call you later.)"

A few minutes later Gavin decided to go to Gray Grass himself. He picked up his cell phone to text Katherine a message and realized he didn't have her number. With a sheet of paper from the printer, he wrote a note and taped it to the front door:

Went to Gray Grass. Will inform why later. Key in usual place.

Gavin was certain she would remember that, at the old house, the spare key was tacked to the top of the back door sill, as it was here. Another part of their past.

In a lonely hollow surrounded by low hills in the Gray Grass district, a grove of tall cottonwood trees encircled a small frame house. Nearly a dozen vehicles were parked around it. Gavin found a spot for his truck and made his way through the crowd of people outside. Most were students or university staff. He recognized Darrell Berkin, standing alone along the wood rail fence. The young man looked up at Gavin's approach, shadows of shock and grief on his face.

"I'm sorry about Arlo," Gavin said, putting a hand on the boy's shoulder.

"Me, too," Darrell said, in a near whisper. He shook his head. "I should've stayed with him."

"What do you mean?"

"We took that thing we found in the river back to campus. I left when he was talking to you. That's the last time I saw him. I should have stayed with him."

"Darrell, what happened isn't your fault. That's not your burden to bear."

The young man shrugged dejectedly. "Can I ask, did he talk to you?"

"For a minute or so. Why do you ask?"

"Ah, I—I think he had a question for you."

"Yeah, maybe. We were going to talk the next morning because I had to leave."

Darrell Berkin nodded but said no more. Gavin stood with him for another moment.

Smells of beef soup simmering and coffee brewing met him when he stepped into the house. Agnes and Raymond High Crane were seated against a living room wall, looking lost and vulnerable. Gavin never knew what to say at moments like this. There were no words, in any language, to assuage grief. Only the presence of those who truly cared came close.

Agnes was petite and thin with salt-and-pepper hair tied back in a low ponytail. Her face was lined, and her dark eyes rimmed red from tears. She wore a simple black dress. Seated next to her, Raymond was in a quiet conversation with Andrew. He was, as far as Gavin was concerned, an older version of Arlo. Finding a space against a wall, Gavin waited for a break in the conversation to approach. On the opposite wall he saw a photo of Arlo resplendent in traditional dance regalia, smiling broadly for the camera. He suddenly recalled the conversation they had had and the questions.

Arlo had seemed somewhat tense and anxious, the opposite of his usual cheerful disposition.

Gavin stayed for a couple of hours, accepting a cup of coffee and a bowl of soup before he left. As he drove the back roads home, the lump in his throat wouldn't go away Who killed Arlo?

## NINE

The question of who killed Arlo High Crane was still roiling in Gavin's mind the next morning as he finished filling the horse tank. Just as mysterious was the question of why.

Stepping through the back door into the kitchen he saw that Soldier Woman was dressed in white exercise sweats, her long hair tied back in a ponytail. His eye was drawn once again to the pewter ring with the jade stone.

On the table were two plates of scrambled eggs and two bowls of steaming hot oatmeal. She brought sourdough toast to the table and poured freshly brewed coffee from a dark blue ceramic decanter. Like the ring, the food was a reminder of their past. They both preferred a simple breakfast.

"Thanks," he said.

Gavin's cell phone chirped as she joined him at the table. It was Loren.

"Good morning, sis," he answered. He gazed at Katherine as he listened. "Yeah...sounds great...okay...see you then."

Katherine looked at him with a smile in her eyes. "Sounds like schemes and plans," she teased.

He nodded, reaching for his coffee. "Big time," he said. "Loren and Morgan want to buy us lunch at Edna's, in Cold River. They want to see you before you leave. Theresa's leaving today as well. I hope you don't mind; I accepted, for both of us."

"No worries. It would be good to see them again. What does Theresa do?"

"She's an RN like her mom, works at a hospital in Littleton, I think. She's going to school, too, to be a nurse practitioner. And her husband is a civil engineer. They intend to come back here, one day."

Katherine nodded. "A family with strong women," she observed. "I'm sorry to hear about that young man, Arlo. Whatever words we use to try to describe it fall short, don't they?"

"Very true," he agreed. "His parents are in shock, and his sister couldn't stop crying."

"I'm glad you went to be with them."

Gavin nodded, staring into his coffee. "It's the fourth homicide on the reservation already this year and another funeral. Ironically, within two days I saw two human beings for the last time I would ever see them in this realm. One was to be expected, and the other—a total shock."

"Mom said 'death is a part of life, you'd better get used to it,'" she said softly. "But that's not easy."

"She was right and so are you. The television station reported it as another murder on an Indian reservation. Just something the Indians do to one another, sort of an 'I told you so' attitude. The only good part of it is all the people who were there with Arlo's family."

She reached and took his hand. "Maybe that's the best part of who we are," she said.

"It has to be. You'd think the world would pause, at least for a heartbeat or two to acknowledge the bottomless sense of loss, to admit there's suddenly a hole where that young man was, but it didn't and it won't. The sun still rises and sets, the wind still blows, stars still shine. So, it must be us. We pause, we weep, we question the universe, and we shoulder the burden of grief."

She squeezed his hand.

A few minutes after noon Gavin carried Katherine's bag to the rental car, then called Uncle Andrew and asked him to meet everyone at Edna's Restaurant. He drove behind Katherine, alone with his thoughts.

Edna's was a bar six days a week and a restaurant seven days of the week. On Sunday no alcohol was served, and the liquor and beer signs were not turned on. It had the usual Sunday after-church crowd. It looked to Gavin like there was an equal representation of Methodists, Lutherans, Baptists, Nazarenes, Catholics, and Congregationalists. Yet all that added up to three dozen people, mostly families, and all white. Some nodded politely, some stared at the newcomers.

Gavin helped Morgan and Thomas pull two tables together in the middle of the main dining area and rearrange the chairs around it.

"I stayed with Arlo's folks until after midnight," Andrew told Gavin. "He was a good boy. His family was proud of him. He's not the kind to go out to Flat Butte Dam. He doesn't smoke, drink, or do drugs."

"Yeah," agreed Gavin. "I can vouch for that. He had plans. As soon as he was done at Nebraska, he was going to come back here and teach."

"I'm going out to see his family again this afternoon," Andrew said quietly.

Sheriff Mel Triplett was just standing up from a booth, a tall thin "drink of water," in white Western vernacular. In his sixties and finishing his last term in office, he didn't carry a gun and was as pragmatic a man as there ever was. He waved a hand at Gavin, who waved back. Then he turned and headed slowly to the front door.

An hour passed quickly. Most of the other customers had departed. Loren linked arms with Katherine and walked to the rental car with her. Katherine hugged everyone in turn, Uncle Andrew and Gavin last.

"Come back again, my girl," Andrew said. "We all miss you."

"It is definitely in my plans," she told him.

She moved to Gavin, smiling nervously. "Thanks," she said softly as she handed him her business card. "If your travels ever take you to DC, these are my numbers."

He smiled, nervous as well, and took the card.

"Thank you. I'll keep that in mind." He leaned down and kissed her lightly on the cheek, a move duly noted by Loren.

All too quickly, the white rental car made a right turn at the stop sign and disappeared. Gavin's body involuntarily slumped as he let out a big sigh. Loren stepped over and hugged him without saying a word and drove off.

Only Gavin and Uncle Andrew were left in the restaurant parking lot. Nothing was moving but the dust stirred up by a lonely, errant breeze.

"I'm heading to Gray Grass," the old man said.

Gavin watched his uncle's old Ford pickup heading west out of town. He stood for a moment and stared out at the distant hills, not wanting to return to his log cabin, knowing his house was now filled with memories that would haunt him.

A mile out of Cold River Gavin pulled off the road as his cell phone chirped.

"This is Gavin Lone Wolf."

"Dr. Lone Wolf, this is Chief Ben Avery with the tribal police. Got a minute?"

"Of course. I'm guessing your call is regarding Arlo High Crane."

"We'd like about an hour of your time, perhaps tomorrow."

"Yes, of course. What time?"

"Ah, you tell me."

"Is ten good for you?"

"Absolutely."

"Okay, see you then.

With a sigh, he pulled back onto the road and continued home. The instant he walked into his house the lingering smell of recent cooking ambushed him. The door to the spare room was open. She had taken off the sheets and pillowcases and left them neatly folded at the foot of the bed—another reminder of her presence.

## TEN

Stars were visible through the bedroom windows as Gavin lay gazing out at the incredibly clear night. The house was utterly silent. Even the coyotes were silent. Sometime later he felt himself drifting off.

Waking with a start, seemingly only a moment later, he saw the dawn through the windows. Soldier Woman was probably at the airport by now or already on the plane. It had been years since she had been the first thing on this mind when he awoke, and he had worked hard to make it that way. Tossing the covers aside, he sat up, annoyed with himself.

Chief Ben Avery of the Smokey River Sioux Tribal Police was not a Lakota. He was a Choctaw from Mississippi. He was into his twelfth year at Smokey River. Like Gavin he was over six feet and physically fit. At the other end of the table were the department's only criminal investigator Lieutenant Justin Primault, and FBI Special Agent Bryan Dempster, looking more like a rumpled professor than a federal agent.

"Dr. Lone Wolf," Primault said, "did Arlo High Crane talk with you on a regular basis?"

Gavin shook his head. "Not regularly, but often, in the course of work and school. Though we did have a conversation the last day I saw him."

"I see. Where and what about?" the CI followed up.

"In the parking lot of the Lakota Studies Building, just before five. He asked me about Dr. Hightower, and we were going to talk about something else that was apparently on his mind, but we never got the chance. I had to leave."

"I see. Who is Dr. Hightower and what did Arlo ask?"

"Dr. Hightower, Caleb, is Acting Department Chair of Lakota Studies, teaches history, and he's been at SRU for four years. Arlo asked how well I knew him."

"Any idea why?"

"No. He had helped Caleb with a dig that day, on the Big White River."

"Dig?"

"Yeah. Dr. Hightower is an archeologist. He was apparently looking for artifacts along the Big White River."

"I see. Anything else?"

"No."

Avery shot a glance at Special Agent Dempster from the FBI Field Office in Pierre. The man's only involvement thus far had been to turn on his digital voice-activated recorder and take a few notes. "Special Agent Dempster, do you have any questions for Dr. Lone Wolf?"

"Yes, as a matter of fact, I do. Dr. Lone Wolf, how would you describe your relationship with the High Crane boy?"

"Oh, cordial, friendly. He was a very polite young man."

"The two of you never had a difference of opinion?"

"No."

"He wasn't in any of your classes?"

"No. He was an intern assigned to our department from the University of Nebraska, sort of an intern exchange program. He wasn't taking classes; he was helping to teach a couple. He was doing his practicum under Dr. Hightower."

"One last question. Do you believe that Arlo High Crane was as straight-laced as everyone says he is—was?"

Gavin stared at the agent for a few seconds, his unwavering gaze on the edge of anger. The man reminded him of a coach he had at Cold River High School, a man who hadn't bothered to hide his bigotry.

"Yes, he was," he said, controlling his tone. "After finishing his master's in history, Arlo was coming back here to teach at the university. His parents are on a limited income, and his older sister has multiple sclerosis and is in a care facility. He was coming back here to teach so his sister could spend more time at home with her family. If you're trying to imply that he somehow brought this down on himself because of some character flaw, you're barking up the wrong tree. He had the right kind of character in spades."

Dempster was somewhat taken aback but not about to show it. He turned off his voice recorder, and avoided Gavin's cold stare, clearing his throat slightly. "Just doing my job."

Gavin glanced at Avery and then Primault. "This meeting is over," he said.

Avery leveled his own hard stare at the agent. "Yes, it is. Thank you for coming in."

Avery walked Gavin out to his truck. "Dr. Lone Wolf, my apologies for Agent Dempster."

Gavin looked toward the window of Avery's office. "No worries. An FBI agent on an Indian reservation is a not always a good mix."

Avery nodded. "No argument here. They come here, to what they call 'off the grid' field offices. Some of them come with an intent to make a reputation for themselves so they can go back to the real world and strut like a bad ass, sometimes over the rights of Indians. The John Wayne complex, I call it. Some of them don't care about justice or fairness for us, for Natives. Unfortunately, we have to work with them."

Gavin nodded. "Of course, this is a capital case."

"Right. I assume the best place to find Dr. Hightower is in his office on campus."

Gavin nodded.

A nearly new Ford pickup entered the parking lot and drove up to them. A familiar voice called out after the driver's window slid down. "Gentlemen." Henry Berkin pushed back the front brim of his Stetson hat and focused his gaze on Chief Avery. "Just the man I want to see," he called out.

"What can I do for you?" the Chief asked perfunctorily.

"Well," Berkin replied, "as chairman of the Law and Order Committee, I was wondering if you're looking into that shooting, you know, the High Crane boy."

Avery nodded and leveled a noncommittal gaze at Berkin. "We are."

"Glad to hear it, Chief," Berkin said, flicking a glance at Gavin. "Any idea how it might have happened or who might have done it?"

Avery shook his head. "We're in the preliminary phase," he said. "Just gathering information. Nothing definite yet."

Berkin nodded. "Damn tragic," he said. "He and my boy were friends. Would appreciate it if you kept me in the loop."

The Chief nodded without reply. He and Gavin watched the pickup drive out of the parking lot. A glance revealed to Gavin an expression on the police chief's face somewhere between puzzled and annoyed.

## ELEVEN

On campus the murder of Arlo High Crane was very much the buzz. A wreath had already been hung along with an enlarged photo of him in the lobby of the Lakota Studies building. Ramona Red Star, the department secretary, greeted Gavin with a hug as he walked in. She clasped her hands to her mouth and looked up at Gavin. "You know about our Arlo, I take it?"

He nodded somberly.

"I still can't believe it," she said. "I saw him last Wednesday, just before I left for the day. He brought something in, something they found in the Big White."

"Yeah, that's the last time I saw him, too, out there in the parking lot."

"It's just so hard to think about. I heard about your great-grandma, too. I'm so sorry."

Gavin shook his head. "Thanks, but these are two different situations. My great-grandmother was almost one hundred and one, and she lived a long life. Arlo was twenty-four, and he didn't really get to start his."

Ramona wiped away a tear. "Yeah, I know. I hear there's going to be an autopsy. We've reached out to his family. We offered to have his wake and funeral service here."

"That would be appropriate."

Before his first class he used the department's copy machine to make two copies of Great-Grandma Maud's letter and the hand drawn map, putting one set in an envelope in the file drawer in his desk. After his last class, a little over three hours later, he returned to his office to wrap up the day. He logged onto the Internet to check his school-related email. As usual there were a few questions from students related to coursework. He answered them, then checked his private email, typing in his screen name, Wolf Bow. The third screen name he saw for incoming emails sent a chill through him; it was from Arlo High Crane. He clicked it open.

**Dr. Lone Wolf, I have something to tell you.**

There was no heading, or sign off, only the message. He stared at it for several seconds, noting the time stamp: 5:37 p.m., over an hour after they had spoken in the parking lot. Whatever the boy had wanted to talk about must have been important. He logged off, strangely sad to break that last connection to Arlo High Crane.

As he stepped into the house, Gavin's house phone was ringing, a call from Uncle Andrew. Gavin answered in Lakota.

"*Hau, Leksi. Toka hwo?* (Hello, Uncle. What's the situation?)"

"*Hau, Tunska. Koskalaka kin hunku na atkuku ob wowaglake.* (Hello, Nephew. I spoke to the young man's mother and father.)" Switching to English, he said, "As soon as they get his body back, they'll know when to have the funeral."

"Yeah, the university offered facilities on campus for the wake and funeral."

"They're okay with that. Listen, I got a healing ceremony for some folks from Cross Creek. I have to get ready. Come over in the morning, around ten. I'll fix breakfast. We need to talk about a couple of things."

"I'll be there."

Gavin put down the landline phone and pulled out his cell phone. He found the tribal police number and placed the call, asking for Lieutenant Primault when the dispatcher answered.

"This is Primault," the CI answered.

"Good afternoon, Lieutenant," Gavin said. "This is Gavin Lone Wolf and I have a bit of information regarding Arlo High Crane. He sent me an email last Wednesday evening at 5:37. I just saw it a little over an hour ago. It went to my personal email."

"Wednesday," the CI said. "That's the last day anyone saw him alive. What was the message?"

"Short and vague. It said, 'Dr. Lone Wolf, I have something to tell you.'"

"That was it?"

"Yes, that was it."

"Okay. Can you forward it to me? I'll give you my email address."

"I will, as soon as I hang up."

"Thanks. And do you have any idea what he was referring to? Something school related, maybe?"

Gavin stared out the front window. "I couldn't tell you. Likely school related, I would guess."

"Right. Okay, well, forward me that email."

A few minutes later he finished the task and stayed at the desk looking again at the time stamp on the email. How many hours did that young man have left to live beyond 5:37, he wondered. He stood and walked to the fireplace and grabbed a braid of sweet grass from the mantle. From a small bowl he took a match, struck it, and held the flame to the braid.

The aroma that wafted up with the smoke was soothing, subtle, and sweet. He watched the smoke curl upward and said a prayer for Arlo High Crane.

After changing into light running sweats, he put together a chef's salad and took it out to the back yard along with a big cup of peppermint tea. It was a quiet place to sit, eat, and contemplate without the ever so subtle hint of perfume that still lingered in his house. His cell phone chimed. Pulling it from his pocket, he saw the reason for the scent of perfume had sent a text.

> *Fondly remembering the endless prairie.*
> *Thank you for a lovely visit.*
> *Seriously, let's not let it be four years until the next time.*
> *Love, Soldier Woman*

Gavin gazed at the words. How should he take the meaning of the message or what he thought was the meaning? Or perhaps he was attaching too much weight to what she had written.

Soldier Woman, Katherine Kay Hill, had sweetly manipulated her way into his house (*Actually, I was thinking of your couch*).

He didn't want to wait four years to see her again either. Yet this was a fact his common sense was not ready to allow. What would "seeing" her amount to—a dinner, a sweet kiss goodnight or good-bye and nothing more? On the other hand, he had frequently—more times than he would care to admit—considered what had to be the ultimate regret. It should have been different.

## TWELVE

Set on the east side of a gently sloping hill, Andrew No Horn's house was round and insulated with straw bales. The south half of the interior was entirely open. The closed portion comprised the bedroom, bathroom, furnace room, and utility closet. Gavin had helped his uncle build the straw bale house.

Behind it was another round structure, though smaller, constructed from used lumber, and two used doors, one to the east and the other to the west. The building had no windows because it was his ceremony house. Beyond it sat a sweat lodge, like an inverted bowl, framed with willows covered with heavy canvas. A few yards beyond that was a four-foot deep and wide walk-in fire pit for heating stones.

Andrew's home was minimalist but comfortable. There were the usual amenities, a refrigerator and a gas cook stove. Pots and skillets hung from wall hooks. He called his four settings of chinaware his "uppity stuff." On one side of his upright 1950s style cupboard was a full set of blue-speckled metal plates, cups, and bowls. He had brewed the coffee "Indian style," as he put it, in an old, blue-speckled pot on top of the cook stove. He had no interest in using a percolator or a modern drip-style coffeemaker. Those things were the epitome of "uppity."

In the living area were a single leather couch, two leather chairs, and two lamps—gifts from Loren and Morgan. Against the west wall was a stone fireplace, in front of which were two traditional Lakota chairs, now called *backrests* by those ignorant of pre-reservation culture. The Lakota chairs were four feet high tripods made of sturdy willow, chokecherry, or dogwood poles. To the front of two poles was tied an elaborate horizontal lattice of thin stalks. The bottom portion extended beyond the end of the front two poles on the tripod and was the seat portion of the chair. Of course, to use the chairs, one had to sit on the floor or on the ground. Two other traditional chairs were rolled in bundles and stored next to the fireplace.

Breakfast was sautéed vegetables—red onion, green and red chili peppers, diced potato, and cucumbers—mixed with scrambled eggs with a side of buffalo sausage and plenty of coffee.

"Good ceremony last night?" Gavin asked.

"Yeah, a good one. We did a sweat first, forty-eight rocks. You should come the next time."

"I will," Gavin promised. "Oh, by the way, I'm going to pay the funeral home for Arlo's family. Don't say anything to his folks. I know they don't have the money."

The old man nodded. "Okay. Good, that's good."

"You mentioned you wanted to talk about a couple of things."

"Yeah. Auntie's will, for one thing. You read it so you know she left her house and land to all of us—you, your brother and sister, and me. And the important thing is she wants it passed down and kept in the family. Once the probate is done, how do we do that? Another will?"

"Yeah, that's one way, or a revocable family trust."

"Is that hard to do?"

"I don't think so. We just have to make sure it says what we want it to say."

The old man nodded and quietly sipped his coffee.

"So, what else is on your mind, *Leksi?*" Gavin asked.

"Something I been thinking about since we read Grandma Maud's note—Grandpa Lone Wolf's gun. I asked the Spirits about it last night," the old man said. "I asked about the ledger book and the gun. They said they were still there; and if you dig up that gun before the next new moon, it will bring forward the person who killed that young man."

"Arlo?"

"Yeah."

"That old gun will tell me who killed Arlo? How?"

"They didn't say it would 'tell' you. '*Nicau ktelo,*' they said. That means it will bring that person to you."

Gavin searched the old man's face. "*Nicau ktelo,*" he repeated. "He, or she, is implied and singular. *It* is the gun, and it will do the bringing. Is that it?"

"That's right," Andrew confirmed.

"But who did they mean by 'you'?"

"Whoever digs up the gun."

"Okay. You mentioned that you had put up markers."

"Yeah," the old man nodded. "But not up. The markers aren't standing. They're on the ground." He retrieved a dog-eared notebook from the coffee table and found a blank page. With a stub of a pencil, he drew a pattern. "I can put you in the area and this is what you'll find if they're still there. From each of the four directions, straight, there are four stones. Each of the outside stones is larger, about the size of a football. And they get smaller. They are about two feet apart. Like this," he pointed to the pattern he had drawn.

"The east stones are in line with the west stones," he went on, "and the north with the south. In the middle is a space about five or six feet. If you draw lines through the stones, where they cross in the middle is where the pot is buried."

Gavin studied the sketch. "Grass has been coming up each spring and growing each summer for sixty years. So, the rocks won't be in plain sight. But I think we can find them." He glanced at his watch. "Hey, I wonder what Thomas is doing today."

"What do you mean?"

"We need someone to help with the digging," Gavin replied.

"You call my grandson, I'll find some tools," the old man advised.

# THIRTEEN

Gavin was not surprised that Uncle Andrew had a pickaxe. With that and three spades and a heavy five-foot crowbar, he felt they were equipped to do the job. A twenty-minute drive took them five miles south of Cold River to an Episcopal cemetery on the east side of the highway. On the opposite west-facing slope, a road led to the top of a plateau. When they arrived at the top, the medicine man burned flat cedar and prayed. Then he took them to a slight rise.

"Look east," he said. "We should be able to see the top of a butte, which is about eight miles from here."

Using his binoculars, Gavin found the butte and managed to see enough of the top without them.

"Okay, now look to the west," Andrew instructed. "There, the Twin Buttes." Two tall hills stood about quarter of a mile apart and could be seen plainly with the naked eye, though they were over ten miles away. "Now, that's how your Grandma Little Turtle showed me how to find the place where the pot is buried." He pointed east. "It's in line with the middle of that butte and the middle of the south Twin Butte."

Line of site measurement was the best guess, but they were able to align themselves with the two points.

"Now, we walk from this spot, keeping that line with the south butte, until we come to the north side of a shallow gully. We walk into the gully and when the top of north Twin Butte gets even with our horizon, that's the area where my stone markers should be."

They walked about forty yards until the north Twin Butte dropped to their horizon, and Andrew jammed a wooden stake into the ground, and began looking for the stone markers. As he had said, because this was pasture for cattle it had never been mowed, so the older growths of grass were thick.

"It's in this area," he insisted. "Them rocks are buried by dirt and grass. If you step on anything hard, we need to see if it's a stone."

On the highway below them, a light green Ford pickup slowed and turned right onto the narrow gravel road. They watched it come slowly up the hill and turn off to park beside Gavin's truck. Thomas Hale stepped down, waving and smiling.

"Grandpa! Uncle! What's going on?"

Gavin quickly explained the task at hand and what they were looking for.

"Cool!" the young man said. "Let's get to it."

Each went in a different direction from the upright stake, taking short steps and feeling in the grass.

Nearly fifteen minutes of stepping slowly and carefully went by. Thomas was the first to find something solid. "Here!" He was five yards downslope from Gavin and Andrew.

Gavin pulled out the grass around Thomas's shoe, creating bare ground, and took out a hunting knife. "Okay, step back a bit." He scraped away the dirt until they all saw the top of a stone.

Gavin looked up at his uncle. "I think that's one of them."

Slicing and jabbing and digging again, he cleared away enough dirt to reveal the mostly round stone.

"That's the big one," Andrew pointed out. He turned and looked around at the slope and then back at the stone. "Now, let's look just to the east of it, a couple of feet or so."

"Here's another one!" Gavin announced.

"Ha!" Andrew exclaimed. "We lucked out. There should be another one to the east of that."

Working feverishly, they found and uncovered the corresponding line of stones up the slope. Owing to incredibly good luck, all the stones were undisturbed, thanks in large part to the fact that fifteen-year-old Andrew No Horn had the foresight to partially bury them.

Next they marked the spot where the north-south and east-west lines intersected. Gavin drove his truck closer. He set up the lawn chairs he had loaded and brought out the cooler filled with water and snacks. They started digging.

Gavin loosened the top layer of soil with the pickaxe, an area four feet square. His logic was simple. He wanted to cover a wide area. If the stone pot was not inside the four-by-four hole, then it would be simple to expand from each side.

"*Leksi*, how large is the pot, do you think?" Gavin asked.

The old man thought for a moment. "Grandma Little Turtle remembered it was about, oh, at least a foot wide. It was round and maybe almost two feet high. And it was heavy, she said."

"How deep?" Thomas wondered.

"I don't know. Grandma didn't say."

"Okay, well, we're going to work slow, and take plenty of breaks," Gavin decided. "I don't have class today, and by sunset we should know something about Great-Grandfather Lone Wolf's pistol and ledger book. Or at least what's left of them."

Four hours later, at nearly five feet down, Gavin's shovel touched something solid. Setting the spade aside, he grabbed his knife and scraped away soil, exposing an area roughly eighteen inches square.

Andrew knelt and helped scoop away dirt by hand as Thomas stood by, leaning in. Using the tip of the knife blade, Gavin loosened the soil until he revealed the hard surface, something round and approximately a foot in diameter, as Grandma Little Turtle had described to Uncle Andrew.

He knelt back. "*Leksi*, we found something."

The medicine man nodded slowly, his dark eyes glistening as he stared at the exposed object. "Yeah, it's the top."

## FOURTEEN

By 6:15 p.m. the round ceramic pot, about a foot wide and eighteen inches long, stood on a wooden bench behind Andrew No Horn's house. They had meticulously brushed away all soil from the sides and top.

Thomas snapped photos. "It's very possible," he said, "that at some point, the pot might crack or crumble. If it does, whatever is inside shouldn't be damaged, I hope."

"We have pictures," Andrew said. "That pot isn't as important as what's inside."

"Good point," Gavin agreed.

A few minutes later the round lid was loose enough to lift off, revealing a smooth layer of sand.

"What now?" Thomas wondered.

"Let's lay the pot on its side," Gavin said.

Most of the sand poured out. Leaning in they saw what looked like brown paper. After a couple of close-up snapshots, they leaned closer, Andrew with a flashlight in hand.

"Looks like waxed paper," he said, "the kind grocery stores used to wrap meat. Grandpa Black Wolf put a lot of thought into this. He wrapped the ledger book and the gun in waxed paper and then poured sand into the pot."

"Right," Gavin agreed. "Then he buried it below the frost line."

"So," Thomas pointed to the inside of the pot, "it looks like there are two distinct shapes in there. Which one of you wants to reach in and pull them out?"

Gavin looked over. "You do it, *Leksi*."

Andrew nodded and slowly reached into the opening, grabbing the flat looking object and tugging gently. It came out easily. The other object tipped down slightly.

"It has to be the ledger," Thomas said.

Andrew put it on the bench and reached back in. He wrapped his hand around what they all assumed was the six-shot revolver from the Greasy Grass Fight.

"Let's take them inside," Gavin said. They waited until Thomas snapped more photos.

They cleared a space atop the oak table for the paper-wrapped objects. The waxed paper around what they assumed was the ledger book cracked along the folds as Andrew slowly unwrapped it.

"Don't worry about it," Gavin assured him. "If it falls apart we have plenty of photographs of it."

In less than thirty seconds the "green sides book" lay before them.

No one spoke for several long seconds.

Thomas finally softly cleared his throat. "Since it's in the open now, will decay start to happen?"

Gavin nodded. "Good question. The short answer is 'yes,' so we don't open the book just yet. We need to put it in a closed container of some sort. *Leksi*, do you have any plastic bags?"

"No. I got some cotton cloth."

"That will do."

Wearing cloth gloves, Gavin placed the book on a half-yard square of red cotton material and then carefully wrapped it. But not before they all saw the faded image of a wolf paw print sketched on the cover and some lettering.

At a nod from his nephew Andrew carefully unwrapped the other object. There was no doubt, of course, that it was a pistol. As the waxed paper was pushed aside, they were all barely breathing.

## FIFTEEN

Gavin stared at the revolver that had to be about one hundred and fifty years old. But what the Spirits had told his uncle in the ceremony was pounding like a drum in his head. *Nicau kte lo. It will bring him to you.*

After a moment, Thomas noticed the puzzled expression on Gavin's face. "Something wrong, Uncle?" he asked.

"Ah, no." Gavin shook his head. "We know that Great-Grandfather Lone Wolf found this pistol, probably on Last Stand Hill. That's not open to debate."

"So, what is?" Thomas wondered.

"This does not look like the revolvers issued to the 7th Cavalry. They carried Army Colts with long barrels. This is not one of those."

"Is that significant?"

"Could be. Firearms from that historic period are outside my area of expertise. Still, I don't recall ever seeing a photograph of this particular weapon. It's about, oh, I'm guessing eight inches in length overall. The Army Colt is about thirteen inches long. I have a replica that Gerard gave me. I know that some officers used weapons other than standard issue. In any case, photograph it from all angles, if you would, please."

Thomas set about his task.

Andrew made an observation. "Long Hair was there, at the end. What other officers were there?"

"Probably his brother, Captain Thomas Custer, and a few others. Any of them could have been carrying this," Gavin recalled. "Or maybe a civilian. There were several with the Seventh. Seems like we need to do some research," he went on. "But let's keep in mind Morgan's warning. The fewer outside people who know about this, the better. People go nuts over things like this."

Gavin paused for a moment.

"We need a plan," he said. "Whatever is in that ledger book is an important historical record from our side. The gun, well, we'll have to think about that."

The old man pointed at the revolver. "That," he said, "could cause a lot of trouble. And remember what the Spirits said."

Gavin nodded. "There's a lot for us to think about. When I woke up this morning, I didn't think I'd be looking at this," he pointed to the wrapped ledger book and the revolver.

After a contemplative silence, Andrew looked toward the stove. "I'll make us some food. I think we should eat and talk about this thing."

As Thomas helped with the cooking, Gavin moved the book and the revolver to the coffee table in front of the couch. The revolver was not overly heavy, with a short octagonal barrel, perhaps no more than five inches with a large bore he guessed to be .44 or .45 caliber. The oval shaped trigger guard appeared large, the handgrip curved down, and the cartridge cylinder was round. Overall, it did not have a streamlined configuration.

There was one unavoidable fact, however. In May of 1876, someone, probably a soldier in the 7th U.S. Cavalry, had carried it from Fort Abraham Lincoln near what is now Bismarck, North Dakota, to the Greasy

Grass River in Montana—and probably fired it in the Battle of the Little Bighorn in late June. Perhaps he had killed or wounded a Lakota or Cheyenne warrior with it.

The pistol was an instrument of war, and likely a purveyor of death, but it was also in a sense a prisoner, having been captured by a victor. Many pistols and rifles had been captured during and after the battle. Not many had resurfaced in the 142 years since one of the most famous battles in Western American history. Considering that all the approximately 230 soldiers under Custer's direct command—five of the 7th Cavalry's twelve companies—had been killed, that added up to nearly five hundred weapons. Each soldier carried a revolver and a rifle. In the first attack, Major Reno's column of 120 had been routed, suffering heavy casualties. Pistols and rifles had been captured during and after that engagement as well. A conservative estimate, then, would be that around five hundred cavalry weapons had to have been captured by the victorious Lakota and Northern Cheyenne. Yet not many had found their way to museums or private collections.

But here was one. It had been buried for ninety-six years and now sat in the light of day. But to what end?

He suddenly realized that Andrew and Thomas were sitting in front of him.

"You look like you have serious thoughts, Uncle," Thomas said.

"Well," he said, "my gut tells me to put the gun away. The real story is Great-Grandfather Lone Wolf's ledger drawings."

At the table Andrew poured coffee for them as they sat to eat. "Some people say things happen for a reason," he said quietly, after he took a seat. "I don't know if that's true. But I do know that we can give purpose to things that happen."

"I think you're right, *Leksi*," Gavin agreed. "I don't know why Great-Grandpa Lone Wolf decided to bury the ledger and the gun. Maybe he was afraid it would bring his descendants serious trouble."

"Well, he had to kill a man because of that pistol," Andrew reminded them, nodding toward the gun on the coffee table. "So, maybe you're right. Maybe he wanted to protect us because he was afraid someone else would want it bad enough to kill for it."

"There are museums all over the world dedicated to weapons of war," said Gavin. "But that ledger book is more important, at least to me, because it tells stories. And stories are more powerful than weapons. I want to know more about Great-Grandfather Lone Wolf's story."

The old man smiled. "Me, too."

Gavin nodded. "So, here's what I think. The pistol goes into my safe. We need someone to help us with the ledger. Meanwhile, we have to find a way to store it safely. I think Caleb Hightower can help with that. At some point the university has to be brought in, I think. Tomorrow I'll drop in on President Eagle Shield."

Andrew stood to answer his phone and listened for a few seconds. "Okay," he said. "I'll pass the word." He sat back down, sitting quietly for a few moments. "Arlo's dad just said the funeral home will get his boy's body tomorrow. First night of the wake is Friday. Funeral Sunday."

Gavin nodded. "Did he say anything about the autopsy?"

The old man raised his eyebrows. "One shot to the back of his head."

By dusk the ledger book and the pistol—the "prisoner" of the Little Bighorn—were inside Gavin's safe, the gun wrapped in black cloth. The middle section of the floor of the master bedroom's walk-in closet opened to a space below. A three-foot-wide doorway slid down on garage door rails, making it easy to walk down the ladder to the six-foot-wide, eight-foot-long space, with seven feet of headroom. Several cardboard boxes were stacked neatly along one wall next to two full sized metal file cabinets. The safe itself was two feet by two feet by six and a half feet high.

Inside the safe were two muzzle-loading rifles on one side, one shorter than the other, and several narrow shelves on the other side, with small metal boxes on two of the shelves. Sitting on a narrow shelf was a wooden case with a replica Army Colt inside, a gift from Gerard. Gavin placed the ledger book on the highest shelf and the gun on the shelf below it.

He stared at the cloth-wrapped objects for several seconds, and for the briefest of moments he could have sworn that he felt something looking back at him.

## SIXTEEN

A beloved old woman dying after a century of life was to be expected. An intelligent, gifted young man losing his life at the hands of someone with a gun, before he had chance to find his place in the world, was gut-wrenchingly tragic.

After the funeral service, Gavin drove in the car caravan to a remote cemetery in the Gray Grass community, on the western edge of the reservation, one of more than sixty sedans, pickups, vans, and sport utility vehicles, some old and some new. Under a cloudless sky they laid the casket into the ground, as old and young women wailed their grief and heartbreak. The sad expression of grief triggered a memory, a story Gavin's father Gabriel had told him and Gerard.

> When I was a boy I crossed the river on my way home, and I heard a voice that sounded like weeping. It got louder and in the bushes on the rocky shore I saw a killdeer, that small gray bird that lives along rivers and creeks. It didn't run away when I got close. It was still crying, and it made me feel sad. Then I saw why it was crying, its nest was on the ground. Something had torn it apart, and there was blood on the rocks. Its babies were gone. Probably a fox got them.

That mother bird just ignored me. She was weeping, sobbing, just like Indian women do when anyone dies. That bird was grieving, too. Its heart was wounded.

As the last drum beat of the honoring song faded, Gavin took his turn in the ritual of men and boys shoveling dirt into the grave. After a dozen or so shovelfuls, he passed the tool to a solemn and stoic Caleb Hightower who was waiting in line. Hanging back in the crowd was Darrell Berkin. The young man took his turn after Hightower, finished, and stepped away. Though he looked, Gavin didn't see young Darrell's father Henry anywhere.

In less than an hour most of the people would leave and Arlo's family would face the stark reality that he was no longer here. Andrew No Horn told his nephew that he and a few other medicine men would stay with Arlo's family.

Gavin took the shortest route to the main highway, drove back to Kincaid, and parked in front of the coffee bistro where he had arranged to meet his colleague. Caleb Hightower arrived shortly after. It was obvious he was distraught and a bit distracted as they waited for their coffee.

"Caleb, we can do this another time," Gavin offered.

"No, no. I'm good, really. An FBI agent came to my house, and—and today the funeral. It's a bit much, you know? What's on your mind?"

"Something up your alley."

"'Fess up, bud. What is it?"

"Okay, short version," Gavin started. "Grandma Little Turtle gave us information about a long-hidden item belonging to my Great-Grandfather Lone Wolf. We used the information, some of it already known to my Uncle Andrew No Horn, and we found it."

"And that item is…?"

"A ledger book with sketches my Great-Grandfather drew of his involvement in the Greasy Grass Fight, what you call the Battle of the Little Bighorn."

Hightower's jaw dropped, his eyes shifted back and forth. "You're not jerking me around, are you?"

"Nope."

"Blimey! When can I see it?"

Reaching into his jacket Gavin pulled out two color printouts—one of the front cover of the ledger and the other of the back—and slid them to Hightower.

The photo of the back was of a plain, light green cloth covering, but the photo of the front was the kicker. There was a faint outline of a drawing, a paw print of a wolf, above faded printed lettering: *Atchison Accountants*.

Hightower was dumbstruck. "Have you opened it?"

Gavin shook his head. "No. We don't know if the pages are stuck together, and we didn't want to do any damage."

"Probably a wise decision."

"What do you think we should do now?"

"Well, you need an expert of some kind."

"That's why I'm talking to you."

"Right, ah, a specialist, like a—someone who knows how to protect—."

"A conservator? Is that what you mean? You've had training in that area, right?"

"Of course. And get the university involved."

"We are," Gavin nodded. "I have a meeting with Doug Eagle Shield tomorrow. I can bring that up, the conservator, I mean."

"Good move. Now, remind me, my friend, you had more than one ancestor in that battle, right?"

"Right. My great-grandfather Lone Wolf was already with the Crazy Horse people by late April of 1876, up in eastern Montana, and they had joined Sitting Bull and were heading west, eventually ending up at the Greasy Grass," Gavin told Hightower. "His brothers, White Tail Feather and Black Wolf were there, with their uncle, Fast Hawk. A few other families were living along the Big White. Not everyone was at Fort Robinson."

"Okay, and at some point the brothers traveled to Little Bighorn?"

"Yeah. They left here around the last part of May, probably. It took them over twenty days to get to the Greasy Grass. The day after they arrived, the 7th Cavalry attacked."

"Blimey! So do you suppose Lone Wolf's sketches show all that?"

Gavin shrugged. "I guess we'll learn that, depending on the condition of that ledger."

"Wonderful! What are the dimensions of the ledger?"

Gavin glanced at the photos. "It's about half an inch thick, oh, maybe eight inches wide and fourteen inches long. That's my best guess."

"Wonderful! When can I see the ledger itself?"

"Come on out for buffalo burgers, and I'll show it to you."

Hightower's eyes seemed to glow. "I'll bring the beer."

## SEVENTEEN

Gavin was in the yard practicing with his Lakota hunting bow when Hightower arrived. True to his word, he stepped down from the car with a six-pack of beer in hand. He watched as Gavin finished shooting, amazed at his pinpoint marksmanship. "You're scary with that thing," he observed. "How long have you been shooting?"

"Since I was five," Gavin told him. He unstrung the bow, retrieved his arrows, and invited Hightower into the house.

The ledger book was inside a cardboard box on the coffee table. Gavin had placed it inside a large plastic zip bag. Hightower's eyes were drawn to it the moment he stepped into the house.

Dinner was simple fare. Buffalo burgers, sweet potato fries, and a side salad. Gavin opened two beers as Hightower, wearing latex gloves, carefully slid the book out of the plastic bag.

"Oh, my!" he whispered. "Oh, my!"

He pulled a magnifying glass from his pocket and scrutinized every inch of the ledger, front and back, especially the front where the pages came together.

"This looks good. No damage that I can see."

"It was wrapped in wax paper inside a ceramic pot, filled with river sand, bottom to top," Gavin told him.

"Lucky for us," Hightower said. "This is simply priceless. Did you know about this, Gavin?"

"No. I knew the story of my great-grandfather at the Greasy Grass Fight. I didn't know he had drawn sketches in a ledger book."

"Just imagine," Hightower continued, "this book probably has forty pages, and if even half of it has sketches—essentially pictographs—I shudder to think of the possibilities. Of course, other people would call it ledger art."

"Pictographs or ledger art, they would certainly add to the Lakota side of the story," Gavin said. "And dinner's getting cold."

Hightower reluctantly stood. "Of course, of course."

After he finished his meal, Hightower cast a final backward glance as he went out the door to drive home.

Gavin used his landline to place a call to his brother. Gerard was in Canada, as far as Gavin knew, and had been for several days. He was prepared to leave a message and was pleasantly surprised when Gerard answered.

"Good evening. You're back in DC?"

"Yeah, since last night. What's up?"

"Are you ready for news that will knock your socks off?"

"Would that be Abba reuniting and going back on tour?"

"Don't I wish. Remember the letter you read? Grandpa Black Wolf's letter about the stone pot?"

"I do indeed."

"We found it, Uncle Andrew, Thomas, and I."

"You found the pot?"

"We did. Everything was intact, the pot and the ledger, the 'green sides' book."

"What about the gun, the pistol?"

"It was there and still in good condition."

Gerard's tone turned serious. "You're not kidding, are you?"

"Not for a second."

"Jesus, Gavin. That pistol is world-class trouble. Every legitimate collector as well as those in the black market will want it. What kind is it?"

"I don't know," Gavin said. "It's not familiar to me. I'm fairly certain it's not an Army issue Colt. Thomas took photos. I can fax a couple to you."

Three minutes later Gerard was staring at the photos, one in each hand. He dialed Gavin. "This is real, isn't it?" he said. "This weapon is definitely not 7th Cavalry standard issue. There's no mistake; this was in the stone pot?"

"Yeah, we pulled it out of the ceramic pot and unwrapped it."

Something stirred in his memory the longer Gerard stared at the photos. "You might think I'm crazy, but I think I know about this weapon."

"You do?"

"Yeah. I think this is an English-made revolver, a Galand and Sommerville."

"English, really? Then how did it end up at Greasy Grass?"

"Here's what I know, or what I think I know. An English lord might have given a brace of pistols, like this one, to Lieutenant Colonel George Custer, and another set to his brother, Captain Thomas Custer."

"Oh, hell."

"What are you going to do?"

Gavin quickly filled him in on his decision to keep the pistol hidden until Lone Wolf's ledger drawings had been studied.

"What steps have you taken?" Gerard asked.

"We'll contact conservators and find the money," said Gavin. We need the experts to come to the university because we don't want the book out of our control. It stays there."

"Yeah. This is big. A combatant's personal account of *the* most famous battle in Western American history in pictures." Gerard paused for a moment. "Didn't you write a narrative of Great-Grandpa Lone Wolf, from the stories handed down, from him to Grandpa Black Wolf to dad?"

"I did, as part of my dissertation."

"Okay, the drawings are corroboration. If those drawings match that narrative to any extent, historians are going to be falling all over themselves to analyze and dissect the book."

"Debunk it, discredit it," Gavin added.

"There's always that. Okay, so the conservator will go to the rez, to Smokey River University, and do what?"

"Perform two critical steps: one, determine the condition of the ledger, and two, open the pages. We're hoping and praying that the pages aren't stuck together, that they don't tear when we open them, and that the sketches haven't faded."

"Do you have photos of the ledger?" Gerard asked.

"Sure, but nothing spectacular, just of the front and back."

"Well," Gerard said, pacing. "Maybe that's all we need. I think I may have a way to get at least a query to someone at the National Museum of the American Indian."

"Damn, if you do, that would be great. I can get the SRU media department to make a video with a date and time stamp, if that would help."

"It couldn't hurt. Let me make some calls tomorrow and I'll get back to you."

"Hey, thanks, bro."

"Now," Gerard said, switching gears. "Is the pistol staying hidden forever?"

"I really don't know. Speaking for myself, I'm not sure; but this is a decision Grandma left to you and me."

"Well, I'm going to do some research into the story I told you, about the gifts to the Custer brothers. I can practically guarantee you, however, that they were each given a brace of pistols by an English lord."

"Galand and Sommerville?"

"I'm sure of it."

"And if our great-grandfather's captured pistol is a Galand and Sommerville, we have a tiger by the tail."

Gerard locked his gaze on the photograph of the revolver. "That's putting it mildly," he said. "I'll call you tomorrow."

## EIGHTEEN

Getting in contact with a conservator at the National Museum of the American Indian (NMAI) was a classic case of "I know a guy who knows a guy." One of Gerard's assistants took lessons in English riding with someone from the Smithsonian who knew a man who worked in the Preservation and Research Program of NMAI. A simple inquiry resulted in an appointment for Gavin at NMAI on Wednesday at 3:30 p.m. with assistant conservator Dr. Theodore Wells.

Gavin was encouraged, especially when he saw the man's reaction to the photographs.

Thomas had skillfully put together a booklet of the photographs of the "dig" that had unearthed the ledger. He had omitted any photos of the pistol. But it was the eight by ten color photographs of the front and back of the ledger, including close-ups of the edges and spine, that elicited the most attention. Not long after Gavin arrived for the appointment, the photos were in a perfect line on a conference table. He took a seat at one end of the table as Dr. Wells examined each photo with his magnifying glass. He was obviously intrigued but keeping his cool.

"Where is the ledger book now?" Wells asked without looking up. Not quite six feet tall and slightly built, he was dressed in tan slacks, a light blue shirt, and a bright red tie.

"In a locked safe."

"Glad to hear that. It needs to be in a humidity-free environment."

Wells finally reached the last photograph, taking just as much time with it as he had with each of the others. Putting his glass down, he took the chair at the end of the table next to a flat canvas case. "I would like to ask you some questions, for the record."

Wells positioned a digital recorder with a remote microphone between himself and Gavin and opened a notebook.

Nearly twenty minutes later Gavin finished telling the story of the ledger that started with Uncle Andrew's recollection of the burial site, although he did not reveal Grandma Little Turtle's handwritten letter because of its reference to the pistol. But as validation he produced a photocopy of the hand-drawn map.

Dr. Wells clicked off the recorder and took several minutes to study the map without the magnifying glass.

"Dr. Lone Wolf," he said, after turning on the recorder. "What do you have in mind to do with your ledger book? And, secondly, what role does Smokey River University have?"

"I would like expert assessment to determine its condition in order to open its pages and examine the sketches and then to produce a photographic record of all of the sketches that are accessible. Ideally, this endeavor will be done under my family's supervision in cooperation with Smokey River University and the organization providing the expertise and attendant resources."

"I will need to talk to one or two people, and then we would like to give you a proposal to define our probable role in this process as well as resources we can provide," Wells responded.

"Wonderful, Dr. Wells. I look forward to seeing your proposal. And I appreciate your making the time for me today."

"Yes, thank you, and my pleasure, of course. Can we schedule a meeting in two days? That would be Friday, late afternoon."

"I didn't expect this to move along so quickly," Gavin admitted to Gerard during their lobster dinner at a restaurant called Gemini.

"Take your victories where you can," Gerard advised. "Speaking of which, how are things with you and Katherine?"

"I don't know exactly. We're not, you know, starting up where we left off, if that's what you're asking."

Gerard nodded. "That's exactly what I'm asking, and there's a reason I'm asking. I've been in this town for almost seven years, and Katherine has been here longer. In all that time I've seen or heard from her only once, about four months ago. I happened to see her at an event at the NMAI, purely by chance. Two days later I get a call and she invites me to lunch. And, brother, the topic of lunch was you."

A shiver went up Gavin's spine. "Well, that's—that's interesting."

"Is that all you can say? And then, she stays at your house. I don't know what happened there, I'm not asking that. But damn it, little brother, don't ignore it."

Gavin nodded and caught their server's attention, a statuesque young woman with hazel eyes. Her nameplate said ALIXANDRA. "I'd like a Jack Daniels straight up, no ice," he told her.

"Make that two," Gerard added. When the server left he leveled a long, thoughtful gaze across the table at Gavin. "Look, I know what it did to you, when she called it off. And I wouldn't blame you if you don't want to go there again. All I'm saying is maybe she wants another chance but is afraid to ask."

Gavin thought for a moment. "Maybe."

Their server brought the drinks. "Gentlemen," she said, "may I ask you a question?"

They nodded.

"Are you twins?"

"Yes, ma'am, identical," Gerard replied. "But I'm the handsome one."

"Right. I ask for a reason. This establishment is owned by two sets of twins. Twin brothers married to twin sisters."

"Ah," Gerard went on, "hence the name of the place, Gemini. Are you a twin?"

"No. But there is a policy here. Since you are twins and this is your first visit together, your meal and drinks are on us. But there is a catch. We would like to photograph you and get your names and birth date."

"Don't tell me, there's a wall in the next room with all the photos."

"You got it."

Gerard grinned broadly. "In that case, snap away. But I must warn you, my brother is not very photogenic. I've got two good sides, he's got none."

"Well, you could've fooled me, but he has beautiful hair."

They posed, sitting and standing, for a young photographer, eliciting curious gazes from other patrons, and then signed a two-inch thick guest register already filled with decades worth of names. That done, they resumed their meal and conversation.

Gerard raised his glass. "Thank you, mom and dad, for free food."

Gavin joined the salute. "Thank you, mom and dad."

"Back to the topic at hand," Gerard said. "Here's my thought. It's not advice, I'm not telling you what to do—just a thought, from me to my twin. I lost the love of my life to cancer, and you lost yours to human nature. I'll never grow old with the woman I loved more than life. You still have a chance; please don't let it pass you by."

The words were still rolling in his head on an endless loop as Gavin brushed his teeth. He was in the bathroom next to the spare bedroom in Gerard's apartment. He heard his brother calling out from the living room. "There's plenty here for breakfast if you feel like cooking. I'll be up and gone by seven. A spare key is on the credenza. Do you have the security code? Remember, you have thirty seconds once you unlock the door."

"Yeah, I have it in my wallet. Thanks."

A short while later he sat propped against the headboard as he finished a long email to Caleb Hightower and President Eagle Shield, reporting the initial meeting with the NMAI research and preservation expert. He was surprised when a reply came back almost immediately from Doug Eagle Shield.

Gavin, give me a call if you can.

Finding his cell phone, Gavin placed the call.

"I have a thought," Eagle Shield said. "I'm going into DC on Friday. The American Indian Higher Education Consortium is having a weekend event. Would it help if I sat in on your meeting with NMAI on Friday? If so, I can move up my flight and get there tomorrow."

"That would be great, Doug. Your presence will likely seal the deal."

"Then I will be there. Email me the address and meeting location. And congratulations."

Gavin was up in time to have coffee with Gerard and see him off. After a shower and light breakfast, he had a second cup and considered how to spend the day. At just after eight he scrolled through the texts on his phone and found Katherine's to him. With a slight shiver of trepidation, he touched Reply.

> *Good morning.*
> *Got into town yesterday,*
> *staying with Gerard.*
> *Thought I'd ask about possibility*
> *of lunch or dinner.*

After a long moment, he touched Send. In the middle of reading an email from Caleb Hightower, his phone chimed.

> *Lunch would be lovely.*
> *Meet me at Red Oak Restaurant,*
> *3112 D St. near my office.*
> *I'll get us a reservation for 12:30. Okay?*

He didn't know how long he stared at her text before he replied.

> *Yes. See you there.*

As soon as it went he fretted that it was too terse, or too juvenile. But he was surprised at how quickly she had replied. Before he could contemplate and fret further, his phone chirped, showing a call from Caleb Hightower.

"Good morning, Caleb."

"Top of the morning to you, old boy. I just got off the phone with President Eagle Shield. Congratulations! You certainly managed to get some attention there, haven't you?"

"Thank you. One of the perks of clean living and being Lakota."

"Just wanted to let you know I'll help however I can, regarding the ledger."

"Thanks, Caleb. I knew I could count on you."

"Wonderful! You're a gentleman and a scholar, regardless of what anyone says."

"Right. By the way, what's the situation with your ancient musket?"

"Ah, well, I don't think it's from the time period I had hoped."

"At least it's not a '55 Chevy antenna like the last time, what?"

"You know, Lone Wolf, you are a savage through and through."

Laughing, Gavin disconnected the call and set about emailing information to Doug Eagle Shield. Then he called a car service to schedule a taxi to the Red Oak Restaurant, learning that it was a forty-minute ride, traffic contingent. A glance at the clock above the gas fireplace told him he had two hours to get ready.

As he was reorganizing his file with his copies of the photographs of the ledger book, as well as the handwritten note and map, his phone chirped again. He recognized the number.

"Gavin Lone Wolf," he answered.

"Dr. Lone Wolf, good morning, this is Justin Primault."

"Good morning. What can I do for you?"

"We found something puzzling, so I'm casting a wide net."

"What is it?"

"Ah, marks, written on Arlo's left palm, probably with a roller ball pen. I'm guessing he wrote them, mainly a set of numbers. Since you knew him, I'm just reaching out. Did you ever see him do that, or know of him doing that?"

"No, can't say I have, though I've seen students do that, write numbers on their hands, on their palms or forearms. What kind of a number? Are you talking about a date or a phone number, perhaps?"

"It doesn't seem to be either. Maybe if I give it to you, you might have some inkling as to what it might mean, or be?"

"Sure."

"Good. Thanks. Here it is. Zero-zero-one-one-four-nine-seven-capital C-capital R."

"My first thought is a serial number of some kind," said Gavin

"Has to be, and it identifies something. Trouble is it could be anything: a printer, a cell phone, or a car jack."

"Numbers aren't for nothing. My brother is in the security business. I'll ask him to check into it."

"Appreciate it."

Suddenly he could see Arlo High Crane's email. *Dr. Lone Wolf, I have something to tell you.* Was it connected to that number?

People sometimes wrote numbers on their hands when they couldn't find paper, or to hide them. What was Arlo High Crane's reason? Maybe both?

He placed a call to Gerard.

"What can I do for you, little brother?"

"I have a totally off-the-wall question. If I give you a number—a serial number, I think—could you determine what it identifies or represents?"

"Well, I don't know. If we assume it's a serial number, specific databases can be checked. Do you have a number or is this a hypothetical question?"

"I have the number."

"Okay, give it to me."

"Zero-zero-one-one-four-seven-nine-Charlie-Romeo. The letters are capitalized."

"Got it. Why is it important to you?"

Gavin sighed. "Because those numbers were on the hand of the boy, Arlo High Crane, who was found shot to death, back home."

"Damn! I'll see what I can do."

A text came in as Gavin exited the building to wait for the taxi.

> *Have narrowed number down to a few categories, including firearms.*

The second text came a few minutes into the taxi ride.

> *Assigned assistant to chase numbers.*
> *Will take time. In firearms category alone*
> *there are over 300 million damn guns in this country.*

Gavin could only shake his head, "300 million damn guns." And one of them had been used to kill Arlo High Crane.

## NINETEEN

Either that sneaky, low-down brother of his had told Soldier Woman that he was in town so she could look absolutely "take your breath away" stunning in a black Vera Wang pants suit for their lunch date, or she simply dressed to stun every day.

Gavin was waiting in the front alcove of the restaurant when she walked in. Her hair was tied in a ponytail and still reached below her shoulder blades. She removed the Gucci sunglasses and smiled. The shock went down to his toes.

Gavin reached out to take her hands, but she somehow managed to slide into his arms and hug him tightly for a long moment.

"I'm glad you're here," she said, looking up as the smile stayed in her eyes.

"It's wonderful to see you again, and sooner than four years," he said.

She guided him to the hostess's table and gave the woman their names. The hostess led them through the middle of the restaurant and into the back section with high-backed booths, style and privacy in one shot. Menus were already on the table.

"You look like you stepped out of a fashion magazine," he said. "Is that standard uniform for environmental lawyers, or simply your exquisite taste?"

"Thank you," she said. "This is actually my Thursday going to a meeting uniform. Now, I'm guessing you're here on business and not just to have lunch with me. So, feel like filling me in?"

"Sure. Remember the note written by Great-Grandma Maud that was in Grandma Annie's envelope?"

"I do."

"To make a long story short, Uncle Andrew, Thomas, and I found the stone pot and dug it up. In the pot were the ledger book—you know, 'the green sides book'—and the gun."

Katherine was astounded. "That's wonderful. So that's why you're here?"

He nodded. "Yeah, because of the ledger, not the pistol. I had an initial meeting at NMAI yesterday and have a follow-up tomorrow. I think they may help us." He spent the next fifteen minutes explaining the situation with the ledger and pistol and the investigation into Arlo High Crane's murder as well.

Food and drink were an afterthought, but they also talked about the food, the city, and airport security lines. Gavin had an inkling that there was much that wasn't being said, topics and thoughts still much too sensitive for this moment. Therefore, the ledger, the pistol, and even as difficult as it was, Arlo High Crane's murder were necessary to the current moment like pawns in chess game.

"This was the fourth homicide so far this year on the rez," Gavin pointed out. "But there's something different in his situation. With the other three, we know who did it and how it happened. One was a domestic argument, another was someone high on meth who shot someone else high on meth, and another was a jealous young man who shot his ex-girlfriend's new boyfriend. We don't know who shot Arlo in the back of the head. That's the scary part."

"Could it have been a random act?"

"I don't think so. He was found on the shoreline of a remote dam. Someone took him out there. The killer is either long gone or is still on the rez somewhere. And if he, or she, is still on the rez, that's scary, too."

"Any clues, any leads?"

"Yeah, oh, yeah. There was a number written on the palm of his hand. He likely wrote it. And he sent me an email at 5:37 in the afternoon on the day I last saw him."

"He did? What did he say?"

"It was one sentence, 'Dr. Lone Wolf, I have something to tell you.'"

Katherine flexed her shoulders. "That just sent a shiver up my back. And the number?"

"Seven numbers and two letters. Lieutenant Primault, the tribal CI, thinks it's a serial number to something. Anyway, I'd rather talk about the ledger, or something else."

"Right, I'm with you. You have a lot on your plate. The ledger, that has all the ear marks of a major project."

"Yeah, if the pages aren't stuck together. Nah, life wouldn't be that cruel."

"Even so, I think conservators have ways to mitigate problems like that." She glanced at her watch. "Well, I have to meet with my boss before I head out of town. Would you mind walking me back to my office? I'd love to show it to you."

A tiny warning bell was going off in his head. "Sure, yes," he said, ignoring it.

## TWENTY

The hustle and flow and noise of Washington DC was annoying, as Gavin walked Katherine back to her office. It was just past two.

"I'm sure I've told you this, or you maybe know already," he pointed out, "that the Lakota and Cheyenne head men who came here in the late 1800s referred to this place as 'Wash-ton.'"

"I did not know that. Who needs that middle syllable, right? White historians like to write that those 'chiefs' were impressed by what they saw."

Gavin shrugged. "Could be, but most of them didn't like the noise and the smells. It was the number of people—white people—that made the greatest impact and was the hardest reality to accept. That's what convinced many of them that it would be useless to fight the *wasicus* because there were too damn many of them with too damn many guns."

She nodded. "That would be a sobering reality. Reminds me of a line in a movie—'an endless supply of white men and only a limited number of human beings.'"

"That sums it up."

"Here we are," she said, pointing to some double glass doors. The building was old, a 1950s brick behemoth. Though it only had ten floors it seemed much bigger to Gavin. Out of the elevator they stepped into a décor that didn't match the behemoth. Although not as luxurious and sumptuously furnished as many law offices were, the offices of Lolley, Beamer, Hatcher, and Snyder were tasteful.

The ceilings and walls were light green with large photos of natural wonders from around the globe—waterfalls, endless desert vistas, the Amazon River, the oceans, and a sea of tall-grass prairie. Wherever he turned, the office was breathtaking.

The carpeting was indoor/outdoor and just a shade darker than the walls; and the entire staff—clerical personnel, paraprofessionals, and attorneys—were in two wings separated by a wide aisle. To Gavin's surprise there was not a single wood-paneled office. Even the attorneys were in glass cubicles.

Katherine led him to her cubicle, located on the east wing. After nine years with the firm, she had earned a cubicle with a window. Her desk without drawers was clear Plexiglas. She noticed Gavin's expression as he stared at the desk.

"It's made of recycled plastic," she explained.

He heard footsteps behind them and then a soft, almost sultry voice.

"Good afternoon."

Gavin turned to see a beautiful, dark-haired young woman with blue eyes.

"Margeaux, hi," Katherine said. She gestured toward Gavin. "Margeaux, this is Dr. Gavin Lone Wolf. Gavin, this is the person who really runs this outfit."

Gavin reached out his hand, "Margeaux, I'm pleased to meet you."

"My pleasure as well. I can finally see what the living, breathing version of you looks like." She pointed toward photos on the desk. "You're the adventurer."

A glance revealed the photos to be of Gavin. "Oh, I got it."

Margeaux's smile was genuine. Her gaze shifted to Katherine. "Jared is available any time you are."

"Great. I'll be there in ten minutes."

"I'll let him know." With a nod toward Gavin, the young woman turned gracefully and walked away.

Curiosity pulled his gaze toward the photos standing on one corner of the desk in a silver double frame, to match the silver desktop computer, he assumed. The left photo was of him standing with a primitive bow in his hands and gazing placidly at a prairie landscape. In the other his legs were dangling out the side door of a small plane, a parachute pack on his back, with thumbs up, apparently about to launch himself into the void. Gavin didn't know what to think of those photos having a prominent place in the workplace of a woman who had so unexpectedly called off their engagement ten years ago.

"Those are my favorites," Katherine said. "I have them just so I won't forget what you look like," she teased. "Thanks for walking me back. There's a taxi stand at the end of the block." She glanced toward the end of the long room. "Jared Snyder is the only active partner. He wants to go over some points for tomorrow's meeting in Atlanta. I'm going in his place." She pointed to the roller bag next to her desk. "I'm leaving for Reagan from here in about an hour. I'll be back in town tomorrow afternoon."

"Travel safe and knock 'em dead," he said. "I'll see you when I see you."

After a quick hug, he tore himself away and made it to the taxi stand. Her perfume was still teasing his nostrils when his phone chirped. It was Gerard.

"I have some interesting information for you."

"Okay. Lay it on me."

"After the computer narrowed our search to nine categories, I arbitrarily selected some that fit Arlo's environment—phones, desktop computers, laptop computers, copiers, printers, mobile WIFI receivers, DVD players, and firearms. A sub-category, if you will, was data bases for manufacturers of replica firearms, and there we found a match."

"You did? Damn, that was fast."

"Yeah, with a company called Cranston Replicas."

"Did you find out what type of a gun it was, with that serial number, I mean?" He could see the mud-covered object Arlo had laid out on the trunk of his car.

"Yes, we did."

"And was it some type of musket?"

"Yeah, yeah, but how do you know that?"

"I think I've seen it, or at least the barrel to it. What exactly is it?"

Gavin heard the rustle of paper. "Ah, here, Denise just printed it out for me, in living color, no less. It's a replica of a French smooth-bore musket called the Charleville from 1717. And you've seen it?"

"Yeah, I think I might have, and I think I know where it is. Listen, I've got to make a phone call. I'll see you back at your place."

Gavin backed away from the taxi stand and stood under the awning of a storefront. Scrolling hurriedly through the Call Log, he found Primault's number and placed the call.

"Justin Primault."

"This is Gavin Lone Wolf. I know what that serial number belongs to, and I know where it is."

"Are you kidding me?"

A few minutes later Gavin caught a taxi and gave the address to Gerard's apartment building. In his mind he could see the mud-covered tube on the trunk of Arlo's car. Were those numbers on that piece of rusty barrel?

## TWENTY-ONE

Eschewing a search warrant, Lieutenant Primault drove to the SRU campus. The department secretary led him to Hightower's office.

"Dr. Caleb Hightower?" Primault asked.

Hightower seemed surprised.

"Yes?"

"Good afternoon, I'm Justin Primault with the tribal police. I'd like a few minutes of your time."

Hightower blinked and nodded toward two chairs against a wall. "Ah, certainly. Have a seat. Is this to do with the Arlo High Crane case?" He leaned back and folded his arms.

"Yes," Primault replied.

"I talked to an Agent Dempster."

"You did, and we appreciate that; but I have a few more questions, just to clear up loose ends." Primault opened a small notebook.

"Excuse me, but do you have legal jurisdiction here, in this instance?"

Primault paused. "No, but if that's any issue I can call the Kincaid County Sheriff, or an FBI agent. It's just a few questions. You can answer them now, or later."

Hightower sighed and nodded. "Now's fine."

"Thank you. Dr. Hightower," Primault said. "Nearly two weeks ago, did you recover an artifact from the White River, the Big White as some people call it?"

Hightower cleared his throat. "Ah, yes, I did, with young Arlo's help, as a matter of fact. And a friend of his as well."

"I see. What was that artifact?"

"A gun barrel."

"I see. What did you do after you recovered it?"

Hightower looked puzzled, still blinking rapidly. "We brought it back here and put it in water. Actually, Arlo did that."

"I see. Then what happened?"

"He left after that."

"I mean to the gun barrel."

"Oh. It's still in my workshop."

"Would you mind showing it to me, Dr. Hightower?"

"No, not at all."

Hightower led Primault down a flight of concrete stairs and into the basement. In one corner past the building's furnace, central air conditioning units, and hot water heaters, was a room with a padlock on the door. He took the keys from his pocket, unlocked the padlock, and pushed the door open.

Inside the room he stood to one side and thrust his hands into his trouser pockets. Worktables stood against three of the walls. Rock samples, driftwood, hand tools, deer antlers and other various and sundry small items were scattered about on the tables. Cardboard boxes, both open and closed, were beneath two of the tables. On a center worktable was a long, black, narrow trough filled with water. Primault walked slowly to it. In the trough, completely submerged was a long gun barrel.

He slipped on a pair of latex gloves, reached into the trough, and lifted the breech end of the barrel. With a magnifying glass he pulled from a pocket, he searched the sides of the entire length of the barrel and then paused, looking at the engraved numbers.

"It's just a replica," Hightower said. "I thought we found something old, I really did. Arlo, and his friend, helped me dig it out of the riverbed."

Primault put the barrel back in the water.

"Thanks for your time, Dr. Hightower."

"Not at all."

Hightower didn't move as the officer walked to the door. He listened as footsteps went up the stair well to the first floor.

"What was that about?" he said, out loud.

And what "loose ends"?

## TWENTY-TWO

Fifteen hundred miles away at something past seven Eastern Daylight Time, Gavin was having Chinese take-out with Gerard. They were talking about the numbers written on Arlo High Crane's palm.

"Well, there's one likely possibility," Gerard decided. "The boy saw the number on the barrel and wrote it down to check it out for some reason."

"Avery told me that Caleb told Primault, the Criminal Investigator, that the barrel was from a replica," Gavin said. "I'd expect him to do that, so maybe Arlo was looking up the number for Caleb."

"And maybe his email to you has something to do with the man in the moon, or whatever. You'll never know. Bottom line is, this type of homicide on the reservation doesn't usually get solved, or it will take years."

"That's not encouraging."

"Movies and television shows are totally misleading. Murders aren't solved in days or even weeks."

Gavin shook his head. "Why is that?"

"Lots of reasons. Lack of manpower, inept investigators, budget shortfalls, smart criminals, little or no evidence or clues, reluctant witnesses, or just plain bad luck."

"Well, reservation police departments sometimes have to share criminal investigators. But really, where does one start an investigation into a homicide?"

"Gathering information," Gerard said. "Building a case file. I'd start with the victim and branch out to family, friends, acquaintances, and employment. His activities, routines, phone calls, emails, spending habits. In general, everything connected to the victim. Most murders are by someone who knows the victim. A very small percentage are random acts by a stranger. And speaking of friends and associates, tell me about your friend Caleb."

"Well, he came to the rez four years ago, after he was hired at SRU. He's from England, Liverpool, as far as I know."

"Education?"

"Doctorate in archeology, masters in anthropology, and undergraduate degree in history, all from the University of Durham."

"Damn. University of Durham, as in London, England?"

"Yes."

Gerard walked from the couch to the kitchen and brought back two bottles of Stella Artois.

"What's the matter? Budweiser not good enough anymore?"

Gerard responded with a grin. "Don't get me wrong, bro. I'm just wondering why a guy with a doctorate from the University of Durham is teaching at a small university."

Gavin shook his head and raised his bottle. "I'm just wondering if living among all these *wasicus* is spoiling your taste."

## TWENTY-THREE

Hightower was still bothered by the Indian cop's questions. Ramona had left over two hours ago so he was alone in the building. If he went back to his house, he would be alone there, too.

That Indian cop had come specifically to ask about the gun barrel. Why was that important?

Three people for certain knew about the musket barrel—himself, Arlo High Crane, and his friend Darrell Berkin. But Arlo had mentioned he had shown it to Gavin Lone Wolf. That was likely how the cop knew because Lone Wolf probably told him. But why would Lone Wolf mention the gun barrel to the cops?

Well, fair was fair. Hightower opened his file cabinet and found the key hidden in a file, the master key to all the offices in the building. If Lone Wolf had told the police about the musket barrel, there had to be a reason, and he wanted to know why.

Grabbing a small flashlight and a pair of rubber gloves, Hightower headed up to the second floor and the corner office—Lone Wolf's office. At the door he inserted the key into the deadbolt lock, turned the doorknob and pushed the door open. Stepping inside, he shut it behind him. Crossing the room, he closed the blinds and the heavy dark curtains, casting the room in dusky light. He didn't turn on any lights and used only the flashlight. Not knowing where to start, or what he was looking for, he paused at the desk.

For the moment Hightower decided to ignore the tall file cabinet next to the two bookcases full of books. He knew for the most part what was in those files was course materials because he'd borrowed some and Lone Wolf had let him look through the files several times. Any recent notes or scribbles would likely be on the desk.

He opened the desk's file drawer and saw file headings related to students and grades. Two headings in neat block printing caught his eye—Correspondence In and Correspondence Out. Five minutes of looking revealed only work-related letters.

One file was out of alphabetical sequence, the first file folder with the heading SOLDIER WOMAN. Inside he found a five-by-eight photograph of a stunningly beautiful Native woman. Behind that folder was a yellow clasp envelope with papers inside, by the feel of it. He put it back and shut the drawer and looked carefully at the top of the desk.

There was a plastic holder with pens and pencils, an old-fashioned Rolodex, a wire incoming mail tray, and the desktop computer supplied by the university. But there were no sticky notes or messages anywhere. Lone Wolf was annoyingly neat.

Hightower sat back and flashed his light across the top of the desk, and up to the bulletin board on the wall to the left. There was nothing connected to the musket. Putting the flashlight on the desk he opened the file drawer again and slipped out the clasp envelope in the SOLDIER WOMAN folder. Opening it he pulled out three sheets of copied material. There was a map and what appeared to be a letter written in cursive. He marveled at the neat, even penmanship and started reading. After he read the second to the last sentence on the first page, his heart started to pound. Bringing the light closer, he went on reading, sweeping the beam back and forth.

The hand holding the flashlight was actually trembling as he finished reading. He read it again and felt his face growing warm. Whoever had written it, a woman, he thought, didn't know English well, but her handwriting was elegant. Taking several deep breaths, he leaned back in the chair.

"You son-of-a-bitch!" he spat in a harsh whisper. "You didn't tell me everything! Ledger book, my ass!"

Grabbing the envelope and the pages, he stood and opened the door to listen and look. He was still alone in the building. Leaving the door ajar he hurried to the back stairs. Behind the door on the first floor, he listened before he pushed it open and hurried to his office. Without turning lights on he placed the pages one at a time on the desktop copier he kept on his credenza. It was slow, but unlike the department's large copy machine, it did not keep track of who made how many copies.

Pausing to listen again, he tiptoed up the back stairs to Lone Wolf's office. He put the papers he had copied into the yellow envelope and slipped it back into the file folder.

He was startled when the computer screen flashed on when he bumped the mouse. Lone Wolf had forgotten to log out and shut down the base, something everyone was advised to do before leaving for the day. Hightower grabbed the mouse, but after a moment, he decided the safe course would be to leave it alone. Grinning like the Cheshire Cat he looked at the copies in his hand. How much was *that* worth, the "*six-shooting gun?*" And where the hell was it?

He shined the light on the pages, moving the narrow beam until he counted how many times "six-shooting gun" was mentioned.

## TWENTY-FOUR

Ten minutes later he was driving away from the building with the distinct feeling that people were looking out from all the windows in all the buildings, though no one was. The campus was quiet at this hour, although there were several evening classes underway.

Hightower lived thirty miles from the SRU campus in a small town called Hilltop. Once it had been a thriving little farming town with a grain elevator. Now it was nothing more than a bedroom community. Most of the houses still left had been purchased for cents on the dollar and turned into rental properties.

The small house he rented was on the western edge of town. Letting himself in through the kitchen, he dropped his keys on the table, and stopped. It was nearly a full minute before he turned and flipped on the wall switch for the overhead light.

He grabbed a can of beer from the refrigerator, opened it, then reread the handwritten note, pacing from the living room to the kitchen and back. The ledger book was real. He had seen it, held it in his hands. Therefore, the gun had to have been in the cache, the stone pot, as well. Gavin Lone Wolf obviously had his reasons for keeping it close to the vest. That was not the bothersome reality.

"Where the bloody hell is it?" he said out loud.

He doubted if it was in Lone Wolf's house. A more likely scenario was a bank safe deposit box. Hightower looked at the note. It was the proverbial dangling carrot.

A "six-shooting gun" from the goddamn Battle of the Little Bighorn. Somewhere on this godforsaken reservation was a bloody six-shot revolver carried by a soldier of the United States 7th Cavalry.

He wanted nothing more than to get his hands on that weapon. The musket he had buried in the river had been a silly gamble—perhaps Lone Wolf had figured that out—but that six-shooting gun was the ticket for the rest of his life. Downing the beer, he opened another. From the top drawer of his desk, he yanked out an old address book and grabbed the landline phone from its base. Punching in the numbers, he chugged the beer as he listened to it ringing.

"Galbreath," said a scratchy voice.

"Greetings," Hightower said. "The reason for this call is about a one-of-a-kind historic artifact. There is an item that might be of interest to you. Therefore, I need some information, and I don't want to go looking on the Internet."

"So noted. What sort of information do you need?"

"I need to know what a six-shot revolver from the 1876 Battle of the Little Bighorn would be worth."

"Are you serious?"

"Yes."

"Do you have such an item in your possession?"

"Not yet. Until then I cannot provide specifics about the weapon or a photograph."

"Sounds somewhat far-fetched."

Hightower chuckled. "If you will be so kind as to provide your fax number, I will prove this is as real as it gets. Or if you wish no further involvement, I will take my inquiry elsewhere."

A long pause on the other end. "Here is a fax number."

Hightower carefully jotted down the number. "Thank you. A three-page document will be transmitted to you within the next half hour. If this information is leaked, I will take my business elsewhere."

"Understood."

"When you have the information I requested, please fax it to me."

He disconnected the call. Finding a felt-tip marker, he placed one of the copies of the handwritten statement on his desk. Working slowly, he redacted "horse creek" and "smoke river agency" to keep the exact location unknown. Finishing that, he placed the pages in the bin of his fax machine. A few minutes later the machine printed out a confirmation that the fax had been received.

Now one of two things would happen. Galbreath would pass this off as nothing more than a scheme, or he would state his interest. It didn't matter to Hightower if Galbreath took an interest or not. He was after a number, an estimate that would let him know where to start the bidding. That was all he needed, for now.

In the same small notebook that contained Jacob Galbreath's telephone number were a few other numbers—with no names. Hightower had committed the names to memory because he didn't want anyone else to stumble onto them. The names and the numbers were from a time when he had mucked about in the dark underbelly of the American criminal landscape.

Hightower stared at one of the numbers in the notebook. He could see this "anonymous" contact behind the number 2 clearly: not quite six feet tall and solidly built. But the physical attributes were not what made him scary. It was his attitude. The man was afraid of nothing and had been busting heads and a lot of other body parts since he was a teenager. He knew all the moves and methods to make people hurt, and he didn't give a flying rat's ass about anything or anyone—except money and women.

Hightower hesitated. He was afraid of Gavin Lone Wolf, who at age fifty was still a powerful physical specimen, and had been a champion long distance runner in high school and college. Hightower had overheard that he was a black belt martial arts fighter, and knew he was highly skilled with several weapons including bows and arrows.

But the man, "Number 2," who Hightower was thinking of would not be afraid of Gavin Lone Wolf, and Hightower needed help to find the gun. This was the answer. He would get Number 2 to do whatever had to be done in the shortest timeframe possible.

## TWENTY-FIVE

Gavin Lone Wolf's taxi was moving at a crawl. His focus, however, was on the voice on his cell phone, Chief Ben Avery.

"The fact remains," the Chief was insisting, "Arlo High Crane sent you an email and said he had something to tell you."

"Correct."

"So how do we take that? Where do we go with it?"

"You and Lieutenant Primault have more of an inkling than I do, Ben."

"Right, and we'll get on it. But that email is bugging the hell out of me, especially since Arlo said he wanted to talk to you about something. Anyway, I'll talk to you later."

Gavin disconnected the call. He realized he was frowning when the driver's question broke into his thoughts.

"Which entrance, sir?"

"Ah, the main one, on this street."

He entered the building and gave his name to the security guard. Five minutes later he greeted Dr. Theodore Wells, another conservator, and President Douglas Eagle Shield in an office. Ninety minutes after that Gavin and Doug Eagle Shield were having coffee in the arboretum and congratulating each other.

"So, in two weeks a couple of museum nerds—and I say that with utmost respect—will arrive on campus with equipment and take over our lives," Eagle Shield predicted. "And if all goes as well as we hope, the Lone Wolf family, the National Museum of the American Indian, and Smokey River University will make an announcement that will make old white male historians salivate."

"I like everything about that scenario," Gavin said. "I'm really hoping that the pages in the ledger book aren't stuck together, otherwise we will not experience the unforgettable sight of salivating old white male historians. But, I have a good feeling about all of it."

"Great. As soon as I get home Monday I'll get the ball rolling so the university can hold up its end of the bargain."

While standing outside waiting for their taxis, Eagle Shield brought up Arlo High Crane. "I know things happen on our rez, and any rez is a tough place to live. But that this murder is on our doorstep, the university's doorstep, really bothers me. I liked that boy, Arlo. I heard him do a presentation about the early reservation. I was impressed. What are we going to do?"

Gavin shook his head. "I don't know. I've talked to Chief Ben Avery, who was formerly a criminal investigator. Plus, he seems to have a lot of confidence in the CI he has, Justin Primault. And the FBI should be stepping in, too. I hope someone can pull a rabbit out of a hat and find Arlo's murderer."

When Gavin returned to Gerard's apartment, a nineteen-seventies high-rise in Georgetown, the brothers took beers out to the small balcony and sat down to enjoy the evening air.

"You've got to admit, all these lights are impressive," Gerard said, waving at the city's nightscape.

"Maybe," Gavin teased. "I'd rather see fireflies along the river, though."

Gerard chuckled softly. "Well, as they say, 'you can take the boy out of the wilderness, but you can't take the wilderness out of the boy.'"

"Really? Who says that?"

"I did, just now."

After a sip of his beer, he turned to Gerard. "Fireflies aside, or maybe because they are such a part of life, there's something that bothers me down to my core."

"And that is," Gerard said.

"Why? What was so important, so off-the-scale drastic that it outweighed the sanctity of that young man's life? What reason could possibly justify killing him?"

Gerard shook his head. "Sometimes there isn't any, bro. Here's what I think." He paused for a second, gazing out at the lights. "Combat is sanctioned violence, and combatants have permission to kill. However, only a small percentage of us are ever in combat. All other violence occurs outside that arena. Throw in fear, hate, desperation, jealousy, greed, and a host of other extreme emotions that come into play in the course of human interaction, and good and bad people are pushed to doing the deed, often during one moment of madness or weakness."

"In the arena of combat I've seen natural-born killers, bro," continued Gerard. "They don't bat an eyelash, during and afterwards. They're coldhearted, and just not bothered by killing; they don't hold anyone's life in high esteem. Some ordinary people in everyday life are that way. In the case of your young friend, it might be that someone's cold-heartedness, or need, fear, or selfishness outweighed the sanctity of his life." Gerard paused and sighed. "That is a long goddamn answer to your eminently necessary question."

Gavin held up his bottle and touched it to Gerard's. For a moment, he saw the pain of remembering in his brother's eyes. "Thanks, bro. Spoken like the warrior who's been there. Semper Fi."

"Oo-rah."

# TWENTY-SIX

Justin Primault was new to his job but not to police work. The Smokey River reservation was his third posting in his ten years as a Bureau of Indian Affairs officer, but his first as a CI. He had been born and raised on another Lakota reservation. He was Mniconju Lakota, but he had relatives here.

One bothersome fact in the Arlo High Crane preliminary autopsy report had grabbed his attention. Although the somewhat flattened lead round the pathologist had extracted from the victim's brain was large, likely a .45 caliber or more, there was no exit wound. The entry wound was big, essentially caving in the back of the skull.

But Primault was back at the murder scene for another reason. Arlo High Crane died thirty feet from the east shoreline of Flat Butte dam. Someone had brought the young man out here and killed him. There had to be some kind of overlooked clue.

This morning, two weeks after the murder, Justin Primault returned to Flat Butte Dam with a theory, a plan, and a drone. Stepping out of the large police SUV, he walked to the back and lifted open the window. As he was preparing the drone to fly, Jason Singer arrived in his cruiser.

"Morning, Jason. Thanks for coming out."

Singer was new to police work, having graduated from the federal academy at Artesia, New Mexico, six months before. As the first officer on the scene after the call from the men who had found the body, Singer had done a commendable job securing the crime scene and doing a preliminary investigation.

"Glad I could help, sir," Singer said by way of greeting. He pointed to the drone. "I didn't know we had that."

Primault grinned. "We don't. This is my personal property, and the high-resolution camera, too."

"Damn. That must have set you back a bit."

"Oh, yeah. I'm still explaining to Sandy why her new gas range is on hold."

The young officer chuckled sympathetically. "What's the plan, sir?"

"Nothing complicated," Primault replied. "I just want to prove a theory—a hunch, really—about whoever brought Arlo out here. We have that unusual track, but here's my theory. I think Arlo High Crane's killer knew this place. He, or she, had probably been here before, maybe more than once. So, I think he-she drove in, stayed on that well-worn trail, and didn't deviate. When we get the drone up I hope to confirm that the perp's vehicle came in and stayed on that trail."

"Got it."

Primault was satisfied that all systems were working and decided on a lift-off and a test flight. He handed the camera's zoom control to the patrolman. The sound of the four sets of six-inch propellers was a high-pitched, almost angry-sounding hum. In less than half a minute he was comfortable with the controls, though it took all his concentration.

"We have ninety minutes of battery power," he said, keeping his eye on the drone circling above them. "I'll fly, you watch the monitor and guide me and work the camera. We'll stay here, no need for us to get any closer. I'll take it across the water and we'll find our tracks, then go from there. Be sure to hit the record button on that thing."

It took five or six minutes until each of them found a comfort level in operating their devices. At the end of the nearly thirty-minute flight, Primault was more than satisfied with the results.

Three hours later Ben Avery finished watching the bird's eye view of the drone-mounted camera for the second time, after Primault managed to tap the feed into a large wall-mounted television screen in the conference room. Primault hit Pause to leave the image on the screen.

Avery leaned back in his chair. "Well, if those are the perp's tire tracks, I can see what you're saying. The car that made the tracks came into the north gate, and apparently did not deviate, didn't wander around. He knew where he was going. He shoots Arlo, then drives out, in the same tracks."

Primault shrugged. "Right, it's not much, I know. But here's what I think. We closed off the road so no one's been out there since we found the body, so no contamination. Maybe the perp had been out there several times before. So that might mean he's a fisherman. That dam is on tribal land, requiring a tribal fishing license, so we can get a list people with tribal fishing licenses from tribal fish and game."

"Works for me, Justin."

"Oh, and one more thing. Jason Singer, the first officer on scene, measured the tracks. The width of the tread area is seven inches, and the axle width, side to side, is seventy inches, tire to tire. And, by the way, the tracks were not made by Arlo High Crane's car. The axle width doesn't match."

"What about the tread marks? How close are we to matching those up with a brand of tire?"

"We're still searching but we don't have much to go on, just the one narrow print."

"Thanks, Justin. Anything else?"

"Where's the FBI?"

Avery shrugged. "I don't know. They're investigating a large embezzlement case, and I think there's some kind of personnel change in their office."

Primault shook his head and paused. "Right. I guess we'll see them when we see them. There is something else that bothers me, doesn't add up. We know there was no exit wound and yet the bullet the pathologist took out was a large caliber."

Avery agreed. "Yeah, bothers me, too. At close range, there probably should have been an exit wound. An interesting riddle."

## TWENTY-SEVEN

Gavin walked out of the amphitheater classroom toward the stairs to the first floor of the Lakota Studies Building. He had just given the final exam to his eighteen students.

Much had happened in six days. He had gone to DC because of the ledger, and now he and the University were joined at the hip with the NMAI. Gavin had expected at least some initial statement of interest and no more. So, to walk out of NMAI with a research and development contract in his pocket was just this side of mind-blowing.

He put the folder with the finished tests on his desk. A second before he grabbed his cup to walk down to the staff kitchen for coffee, a soft knock came at the door. It was Ramona Red Star.

"Hey, come in Ramona," he told her.

She seemed upset. "Hi. I just put on a fresh pot of coffee," she said. "But, ah, got a minute or two?"

"Sure," he gestured toward the overstuffed chair in the corner. "What's on your mind?"

"Well," she said pensively, "I guess everything that's been going on. First it was Arlo and now Caleb. He seems pretty shook up. I suppose you heard he might take the fall semester off. And he hasn't signed his contract yet."

"No," he said, "I haven't heard that, as a matter of fact."

"Well, I know he can do what he wants, but that seems kind of unusual to me."

Gavin shook his head slowly. "You're right. It's news to me."

"He's acting department chair, so what are we going to do, if he goes on leave, or just leaves?"

"Doug will appoint someone."

"You? I hope."

Gavin smiled. "No, I'm only part time. Jess No Horse, probably. He would be my recommendation."

"Yeah, I think that would be good. I guess all we can do is ride it out, whatever happens. Anyway, coffee should be done shortly, and I'll be here for a while."

"Thanks. I'm going down for coffee in a bit. By the way, where is Caleb?"

"He's probably home. He left here about an hour ago," she said.

Gavin took the desk phone and dialed Hightower's cell phone.

"Hightower," the man answered.

"Someone told me you're in the market for a good black powder musket," Gavin said. "I've got one, for a reasonable price."

"You know, Lone Wolf, anyone ever tell you that you have a mean streak a mile wide?"

"No, but I might have an old Chevy antenna lying around, too."

"Oh, Christ!"

"Sorry, old man, couldn't resist. Besides, just wanted to soften you up for the hard question."

"I can hardly wait."

"Want to borrow my pen, to sign your contract?"

"Well, now," Hightower said. "Is that your way of begging?"

"Nope, just trying to get to the bottom of a shady rumor I heard. Can you enlighten me a little?"

Hightower chuckled. "Funny thing, I was going to invite you over for some bangers and mash, but my cupboard's bare. And as far as that shady rumor, I am thinking of asking the boss for the fall semester off. Just need some rest, my friend."

"I hear you, but still sounds shady to me. Hey, why don't you let me twist your arm a bit, say over a steak at Edna's in Cold River?"

"I don't know. That's over twenty miles for me and only seven for you, but since you're buying, I accept."

"Well, as much as I don't like throwing effort after foolishness, I'll meet you there at seven."

"Oh, brother. You just don't let up, do you?"

"Said Custer to Crazy Horse. And, oh, let's make it seven-thirty. I want to stop off at Lower Horse Creek and check on Esther Red Thunder and her grandkids."

Gavin didn't notice the new pickup parked at the end of the Lakota Studies parking lot. The person inside it watched him get into his pickup and exit the lot. Darrell Berkin watched Gavin drive away, disappointment etched on his face. After sitting in the parking lot for nearly an hour, he couldn't build up the nerve. Now the opportunity was gone. Darrell slowly reached for the ignition key and started his truck. He didn't want to go home because it meant driving by Flat Butte Dam, but there were chores to do.

Edna's was busy for a Monday night. Hightower looked tired and admitted to not sleeping well. But his appetite seemed normal. He was halfway through a twelve-ounce rib eye in short order and chasing it down with a beer.

"So," Gavin said, "what happened to 'I'm here to help you with the ledger'?"

"What can I say? I'll be around to help how I can," he said. "Still, I must say, this situation with Arlo. It's got me by the short hairs."

"Couldn't disagree with you on that issue," Gavin told him.

"Have you heard anything? I mean, do the police have any leads, anything?"

"Not that I know of. So, are you serious about the fall? Are you really going to ride off into the sunset for a bit?"

Hightower shook his head. "You know, that's the first time I've heard you use cowboy jargon."

"You're a white guy. Isn't that what white guys do?"

Hightower chuckled. "Yeah, especially those of us from East Liverpool," laying on his accent thicker than usual. "I don't know. I've been thinking of going home. I've been gone a long time."

"Across the pond, you mean?"

"Yeah."

"I thought you didn't have family back there—home?"

"I don't. My parents died a long time ago. My brother's in the army, god knows where he is. We were never close. But home is home. You know?"

Gavin leaned back in the booth. "Well, my friend, I'm not one to talk a man out of a firm decision. I just wanted to hear it straight from you."

Hightower slowly nodded and lifted his glass of tap beer. "Truth be told, I'm tiring of reading papers and giving grades."

Gavin lifted his glass. "Hear, hear! So, if you're to cross back over the pond, how will you go? Risk the effects of jet lag and fly, or sip bourbon on a luxury cruise ship?"

"Boat, it's how I came some twenty odd years ago, on a container ship. Wasn't exactly luxury, but it was good. I hired on as a deck hand."

"Interesting. To add to your treasure-trove of experiences?"

"No, for the money. The ship docked at the Port of New Jersey. Found work after that in a warehouse. That was my entry into the land of the free and the home of the brave. And I had the callouses to show for it."

"Didn't see that on your resume."

"Yeah? But it's those experiences that teach you what's real in life, don't you think?"

Gavin was about to answer when he spotted Joby Bone bussing a nearby table. The disturbed look on his cousin's face caught his attention. Joby was staring intently at Hightower, frowning slightly. After a moment, he shook his head and finished his task, and with a backward glance at Hightower he disappeared through the door to the kitchen.

A few hours later, as Gavin was brushing his teeth before turning in, he was still trying to imagine Dr. Caleb Hightower, a three-time graduate of Durham University, working as a deckhand.

## TWENTY-EIGHT

Hightower handed his university car's key to Ramona. She hung it on a board in her office.

"How was the meeting?" she asked.

"Great," he said. "I know Pierre is centrally located, but I would have chosen Deadwood, in the heart of the beautiful Black Hills."

"Not to mention a couple of casinos," she replied.

"Really? Hadn't noticed."

"Yeah, right. So, we will see you the end of June?"

"You better believe it, toots."

Thirty miles and nearly forty minutes later, Hightower was re-reading the fax that had arrived while he was gone. His eyes devoured the note as he allowed himself a slight smile.

> Dr. Hightower: After several inquiries regarding the artifact in question, I have been able to determine a low and high estimate of its probable worth to collectors in Europe and the United States. At the bottom of the scale is 7 million US and the top is 12 million US. Once authentication has been made and independently veri-

fied, I will decide if an offer to you is in order. Advise when you have acquired it.

Cordially,

JG

Hightower tore his gaze from the note and glanced around at the small house. It was spotless, owing to days of cleaning as a consequence of nervous energy.

He looked at the note again. Seven to twelve million dollars was not all the money in the world, but it was a hell of a lot more than he had now. It was more than enough to set him up for the rest of his life in certain places in the world. He knew damn well that Galbreath's estimate was on the low end overall. There was one major flaw, however, in this picture. He didn't have that damn gun.

But he did have a plan He pulled out his small black notebook and dialed Number 2.

"Let me hear a name," a voice answered. "If I don't know it, this conversation is over."

"This is Hightower," Caleb said, trying to make his voice deeper.

"Hightower? Really? It's been years. What's on your mind?"

"A historic artifact worth a hell of a lot of money."

"Define 'a hell of a lot of money.'"

"Seven to twelve million."

"You have it, the artifact, I mean?"

"No, I need your help getting it. Interested?"

"Maybe," said Number 2. "First, what is it and do you remember what my percentage is?"

"The artifact is a six-shot revolver from the 1876 Battle of the Little Bighorn and, yes, your cut is twenty percent."

"So that means you are willing to pay me at least, let's see, one point four mil or more, for my help."

"I am. After it is acquired and sold, of course."

A hollow chuckle on the other end. "Of course. My decision depends on the details."

Hightower sighed inwardly. "Right. If you have pen and paper in hand, I can give you the details."

"Shoot."

Fifteen minutes later Hightower answered Number 2's final questions.

"Is this a good number for you?"

"It is, but there's one other thing."

"And that is?"

Hightower took a deep breath. It was worth a try. "Well, someone is blackmailing me, and it's cost me a lot of money. I want it to stop. It's made my life hell for the past four years."

"Really?" said Number 2. "Well, we can't have that, can we? Details, give me the details."

"Right, and if you can help, it's worth at least another one hundred K to me." Once again, Hightower filled him in.

"I have other obligations to take care of," Number 2 said. "After that I will make a plan and a timeline to do these tasks. I will take care of your problem and then acquire your artifact, in that order. Communicate by text from now on, and we'll talk about arrangements for payment when I have your historical artifact in hand."

"Understood."

"One last question. This Mr. Lone Wolf, is he also expendable, if necessary?"

Hightower didn't hesitate as an involuntary shiver coursed through him. "He is."

The call was terminated with a soft click and Hightower folded his phone. His hand was trembling.

He stood up from the chair at the kitchen table and looked around. On the table lay the fax from Galbreath. He read it again—seven to twelve million dollars.

He knew Number 2 had more than a good chance of finding the weapon and taking it from Gavin Lone Wolf. But what if the "less than a good chance" part happened? Lone Wolf was no pushover, that was for certain, and that could mean seven to twelve million dollars was no forgone conclusion. It wasn't that he doubted Number 2's abilities. He just didn't know the full extent of Lone Wolf's abilities.

In the meantime, he had to smile and make nice.

## TWENTY-NINE

Something past three o'clock on a Friday afternoon, Michael Marshall, the facilities manager for the university walked to the vehicle maintenance garage where Fred White Horse, the transportation supervisor, greeted him with a handshake.

"What's up, Fred?" Marshall asked.

"Oh, probably nothing," Fred replied, looking up at the much taller and bigger facilities manager. "Just thought I should let you know what we found while we were cleaning this car."

Marshall looked at the dark gray Chevrolet Malibu parked in the bay with its hood and trunk open. "This car?"

"Yeah." Fred grabbed the car's logbook from the front seat. "There's a slight discrepancy in the mileage. I don't think it's a serious thing, but I thought I'd run it by you. There's a gap between the starting odometer reading yesterday and the last entry before that, on the twelfth."

"A gap? What do you mean?"

"Ah, there's a little over forty-four miles unaccounted for."

The facilities manager took the logbook and looked at the entry, which was dated nearly three weeks past. "Whose car is it?"

"Dr. Carter, the head of the Math Department. He dropped it off yesterday for routine maintenance."

"Well, forty-four miles, that's not too bothersome. If it were a hundred and forty-four, then it would be."

"Gotcha."

"I will talk to Dr. Carter. There's probably some explanation."

Pulling out his phone, Marshall tapped a number in the phone log. "Rachel, could you find me Dr. Roger Carter's phone numbers?"

Roger Carter reached down into the burn barrel in his backyard and struck a match on the side. He and his wife lived a mile south of Kincaid. After thirty years at SRU he was contemplating retirement more and more. When the flame was steady he touched it to the pile of torn paper at the bottom. The pile caught immediately. Carter waited until there were only blackened ashes before he turned away. He felt his cell phone vibrating in his back pocket. A quick glance at the Caller ID screen showed a vaguely familiar number.

"This is Carter," he answered.

"Hello, Dr. Carter, this is Mike Marshall at the university. I'm calling about the car assigned to you."

"Oh, hello Mike. Okay. I believe it's in the maintenance garage."

"You're right, it is. There is a slight issue with the mileage log that's why I'm calling."

"Oh, ah, you know, I'm sorry. I'm always forgetting to do the logs."

"Yeah, we know, but you did make entries yesterday. You went to Black Pipe. But before that there is a gap of forty-four miles. Do you remember at all where you've driven it lately? That forty-four miles could have been one trip or a few into town."

Carter glanced toward his house as he tried to remember. "Uh, well, there were a couple trips to the high school."

"Alright, thank you Dr. Carter."

Carter closed his phone and took a deep breath, his eyes blinking rapidly beneath his bushy white eyebrows. "Forty-four miles?" That did not sound right but didn't seem that important.

# THIRTY

Bismarck, North Dakota, was far from being Liverpool, Jersey City, or New York, but it was big enough to meet Hightower's needs. Just as the sun rose he was checking into a mom-and-pop motel on the east side. He had been there before, a place that didn't mind cash customers. Taking his key attached to an oval piece of plastic with the room number stamped on it, Hightower trudged to his car.

He had decided to make the trip on the spur of the moment at two in the morning. He had an idea and an urge, and a man in Bismarck could help him pursue the idea and answer a few questions. As for the urge, he had satisfied it here before.

Driving his SUV thirty yards to the end of the building, he stepped out and gathered his backpack and almost stumbled to number nineteen. Once inside he locked the door and slid the chain latch in place. He wanted a bit of sleep before he worried about food and the rest of the day.

Hightower got out of the shower and dried off, then pulled back the bed covers and grabbed the TV remote. Piling pillows against the thin headboard, he turned on the television and was asleep in less than two minutes.

Two hundred and fifteen miles south as the crow flies, Gavin Lone Wolf backed his Jeep out of the parking area in front of his house, heading the back way toward Uncle Andrew's. Before he reached the gravel county road, he turned left onto another pasture trail, taking a longer than usual route to Uncle Andrew's. He had driven the pasture trail several times over the past four years, enough to leave a faint trace through the grass and soap weeds. The trail went up and then back down a couple of long slopes, though it was not much of a test for the Jeep. Several mountain back trails on the Wind River Reservation in Wyoming offered more of a test for his trail modified Jeep. But Gavin liked this trail for another reason. Except for the point where it crossed the gravel road, there was not a single structure, pole, or object that hinted at the presence of modern humans.

Perhaps Gerard had been right to rib him for being born two hundred years too late. No matter. This trail also evoked stories of the old times before the *wasicu*, the "fat takers," came. And it was those stories of simplicity, steadfastness, and adaptability that helped him navigate the world in the here and now.

Along the way he saw three Pronghorn antelope, *nigesanla* or "white bellies" as his father had called them. Overhead he saw hawks, and for a stretch of the trail a large jackrabbit exploded out of the grass and decided to hog the trail before he veered off.

Breakfast was a feast of roasted elk back strap and what was known among Andrew No Horn's friends and relatives as "slow-fried" potatoes, all washed down with hot, strong campfire coffee. They ate at the small table behind the house, beneath the willow shade. The coffee in the big, blue-speckled pot was kept warm on the grate over the low fire. Gavin was savoring every bite.

"*Leksi*," he said, "I've been meaning to ask you something ever since I was a kid. Never had the nerve to bring it up."

The old man chuckled. "What is it?"

"Did you ever think of getting married?"

The old man's face opened to a broad grin. "Yeah, I thought it about it a lot."

It was Gavin's turned to chuckle. "Well, wrong question. Was there someone you wanted to marry?"

Andrew nodded. "Yeah, there was, once."

Gavin nodded and sipped his coffee, hoping the old man would tell the story since he didn't want to be impolite and pry any further.

"I courted her in high school," Andrew said. "Her dad was from Pine Ridge, an *iyeska*, a mixed-blood. Her mom was from here. It was serious, her and me, but her dad didn't like us 'traditional Indians,' said we were too 'Stone Age.' They moved to Omaha, and she wrote me letters, even after I was in the Marines. And then, she got married."

"Whatever happened to her?"

"Oh, the usual stuff, I guess. Had kids, her husband ditched her for a while because he drank a bit, I heard. She's a grandma now. Still lives in Omaha, I think."

"There was no one else?"

Andrew shook his head. "Oh, I had a few girlfriends after that, but she was the one."

Gavin nodded his head and sighed. "Life is strange, isn't it? And sometimes it's outright cruel."

"It damn sure is, if you're talking about the boy that was killed."

"I am. It's possible he was killed a few hours after I saw him on campus. I don't know why it affects me the way it does," Gavin admitted. "He had an aptitude for teaching. He was good at it and knew his stuff. And someone took it all away from him."

"We really don't think of the meaning of anyone's life until after they're gone."

Gavin nodded. "That's so damn true, isn't it, *Leksi?*"

"Right. And there's nothing you could have done to change what happened. Life gets heavy if you take on things that are not your responsibility. Then you can't hang onto the good things."

"Yeah, I know, but I was thinking of Arlo's folks and his sister. Haven't they had a hard enough road? And it isn't as if meth, drugs, booze, car wrecks, and suicides aren't killing enough of us."

Andrew sipped his coffee and cleared his throat. "I saw something on the news at Loren's house a while back, about Africa, about some civil war over there, kids getting killed, women being raped. Black kids and Black women. A white reporter asked what could be done, and a woman told him 'nothing will be done, this is Africa, most people don't care about the Black people of Africa, only about the gold, the diamonds, and the lithium.' That was a hard truth."

"It's kind of like that here," he continued. "Life is tough for us. Meth, poverty, racism, diabetes, but no one cares. White America wants us Indians to behave ourselves, stay in line, stay poor, and stay powerless. We have to care enough about one another in order to survive. The whites killed off the buffalo to weaken us. They tried to kill us all because they believed it was their right to do that. It's still their thinking today. Look how white law enforcement reacted with the oil pipeline up at Standing Rock. Even though some white people were there with us, white authorities saw it as a Native thing. That's the same kind of mindset and the same kind of guys who rode into Sand Creek in 1864, and Wounded Knee in 1890. So why should we expect them to care? It's up to us. We have to care about each other. Enough of us have to care about Arlo's family and about everyone else who's having a hard time. We're all we got."

They both fell silent for a few moments.

"Well, that is our reality, isn't it?"

"Yeah," said the old man, "it is what it is. Get enough to eat?"

Gavin nodded, after a moment. "I always do when you feed me, *Leksi*. It's probably good I don't eat here every day."

The old man nodded, narrowing his gaze toward the eastern horizon. His expression was contemplative.

"What do you see, *Leksi*?"

Andrew shook his head slowly. "Nothing in particular. It's just that a lot of our troubles as Lakota people came from the east. Maybe that's what I'm feeling." In the next moment, his demeanor changed. "I'm putting two young men on the hill to do their *hanbleceya*, their vision quest, getting them ready for Sun Dance."

Gavin nodded. His uncle was conducting a Sun Dance after a four-year hiatus. Several young men had pledged to dance this coming summer, and strict traditionalist that he was, Andrew insisted on following the old way. A vision quest was an integral part of the process. Four days and four nights alone, on an isolated butte without food and water, in prayer and meditation, was not for the faint of heart.

"Need any help?" he asked.

"No, but we'll be over at Coyote Butte if you want to come by."

"Yeah, I can do that. *Wopila* (I'm grateful) for the breakfast."

Gavin played that last remark in his mind over and over again as he drove home—*a lot of our troubles as Lakota people came from the east*.

## THIRTY-ONE

Justin Primault stepped into the conference room with a thick accordion file under his left arm and a large to-go coffee mug in his right hand. The balancing act elicited a smile from Ben Avery. In the age when thousands of pages of information could be kept on one thumb drive, Primault refused to go with the flow. Thumb drives were strictly back-up, as far as he was concerned. He was a tactile person, preferring the touch and feel of paper to the glare of a computer screen. Which made his use of a drone a conundrum.

Avery pointed at the file as Primault adroitly maneuvered his loads onto the table without losing a page or spilling a drop. "So, all of that is the ongoing investigation into the death of Arlo High Crane?" the Chief asked.

"Yeah, definitely a work in progress," said Primault.

Avery glanced at his watch. "Good, but you have only fifteen minutes to enlighten me. I've got a meeting with the tribal council's law and order committee."

"I'll leave a copy of the file on your desk," Primault promised. "So, here goes," he said, opening a slim clasp binder. "We have, so far, a copy of the preliminary autopsy report, our research into the tire tracks, a printout of the files on Arlo's laptop—by subject—a list of all his relatives, friends, and acquaintances, a chronology of his movements from May sixteenth backwards, and, of course, photos of his car, the probable murder site, and so on."

"How many people have you talked to so far?"

"Ah, nearly two dozen, mostly relatives and university staff. Now I'll expand it to the names that came up in those interviews."

"Those partial tread marks you photographed," Avery brought up next, "have you confirmed or dismissed them as relevant?"

"Well, I think they're relevant," Primault replied. "We may be looking for a car with really bald tires and a weird wear pattern on one. A bit of a rain came through on the sixteenth and left the ground damp enough with a few mud holes here and there. The vehicle with Arlo in it had to have been out there after the rain, after the ground dried out a bit. Arlo was still at the university around 5:30 p.m. on the sixteenth, so he had to have been taken out to Flat Butte Dam after that. The fishermen found him around 5:30 the morning of the seventeenth. So, yeah, I think those tread marks are relevant."

"So, we need to find whose tire made the strange track," Avery concluded. "The proverbial needle in the haystack."

"Yeah, that track is every bit as relevant as the flattened round the pathologist took out of Arlo's brain," Primault asserted. "No matter how damn big the haystack is, we need to find that tire. I've requisitioned Jason Singer to help me. His shift supervisor is okay with that. I'm going to put him in front of a computer to search the Internet for that tire."

"Okay. What about our FBI friends?"

Primault shrugged. "Special Agent Dempster didn't sound very enthusiastic about this case. He's the acting supervisory agent, replacing Atkinson for a while apparently."

Avery nodded with a wry grin. "They'll take over, sooner or later. In the meantime, let's keep digging, and make copies of everything we can."

A second after the Chief left the room, Jason Singer entered and stopped in front of the table as Primault began to arrange papers. "You sent for me, sir?"

"I sure did, Jason. Thanks for stopping in."

"What can I do for you, sir?"

"Well," Primault said, "you strike me as the type of guy who's got his sights set high. I mean, you're sure not going to be a patrolman your whole career, right?"

"No sir."

"Great. So, I'm thinking you wouldn't pass up an opportunity to perfect your investigative skills."

Singer looked puzzled.

"This investigation is growing. I need help," Primault went on, "and I think you're just the man for the job."

"Sure. What can I do?"

"Well, we're going to use two very effective tools at our disposal as investigators—two wonders of technology—the Internet and the phone."

"When do we start?"

"Exactly the right question. We start now. Your first job is to identify that tire, the brand, and where it's sold." Primault rapidly thumbed through his thick file and pulled out a single sheet. "And I will start here," he said, "with the only Lakota farrier on this reservation."

"The hoofprint?"

"That's right. I'm hoping he uses the medicine wheel as his trademark, and, if so, to find out who he's shod horses for."

Gavin was home grading papers when the cell phone chirped. It was Douglas Eagle Shield.

"Hi, Doug. What's up?"

"Something mostly good."

"Okay, that sounds interesting."

"I just got off the phone with our NMAI partners. The mostly good part is that they want to move up the timeline for the ledger book project. Two technicians and all their equipment are on the road in a van as we speak. They'll be here in three days."

"Okay."

"The little bit bad part is that we're not quite ready administratively. We can provide the facilities they need; however, there's a problem. Caleb Hightower just resigned as department chair, and Jess No Horse just turned me down when I offered him the job."

"Okay," Gavin said, suspiciously.

"So, I'm asking you to be interim chair, but—but hear me out before you say 'no.'"

"Okay, I'm listening."

"Take the job as interim chair for the duration of the book project. It'll put you hands-on with it. And who better? It's your great-grandfather's story, after all. That'll give me time to find someone permanent."

"You always were a good salesman, Doug. I'll do it, but just for the duration of the project."

"Thank you, my friend. First item on your agenda is a meeting with the facilities manager and me tomorrow. The techs are bringing what they call an environmental cube for the ledger. We need to find a place for it."

Three hours later Gavin finished grading papers, wondering the whole time what he had gotten himself into. He could have entered the grades on a PDF file and emailed it to the registrar's office. Technology was not his forte, however, so he decided to drive the thirty miles to the university. After a brief conversation with the horses, he grabbed his paper file and jumped into the pickup, just as Uncle Andrew called.

"Hey, *Tunska*, Esther Red Thunder needs a ride to Agency Village. If you're going to Kincaid I thought maybe you can give her a ride."

"Yeah, I'll stop and pick her up. You know, I gave her my phone number so she can call me. Why does she call you?"

Andrew laughed. "It's just her thing. She doesn't have a phone and doesn't like using them. She asked a neighbor to call."

"Okay. I'm glad to give her a ride."

Esther didn't say much during the ride, only that she was going to the social services office to get help with the Medicaid card for her grandchildren. He let her off in front of the door to the tribal social services building with instructions to have someone call him when she was ready to go home. The old woman smiled and nodded.

"Thanks, *Tunska*," she said. "I'll ask the girl in the office to call."

When he arrived on campus twenty minutes later he dropped the grades off at the registrar's office. On a whim he stopped in to see Ramona, who had already heard from the president about the new development.

"Does this mean you'll be here full time?" she asked, hopefully.

"Probably, as much as I hate for that to happen," he teased.

Ramona smiled and waved off his verbal jab. "What do you think's going to happen with Caleb?" she asked.

"Well, I think he just needs a break. Teaching for twenty-five years can wear a person down. He'll be back."

After Gavin picked her up in Agency Village, Esther Red Thunder was no more talkative on the ride home than she had been on the ride in. She did say that the issue with the Medicaid card had been straightened out.

"*Tunwin* (Auntie)," he said, "*Yati el omasape wanji luha kta tka.* (You should have a phone in your house.)"

"*Han* (Yeah)," she said. "*Slolwaye. Eyas hena otehike.* (I know. But those things are expensive.)"

"How about you let me put one in? Things happen, you know? Kids get sick or injured. A phone can be helpful, especially since you don't have a car."

"Yeah."

"So, is it okay if we put a phone in for you, in your house?"

"I think so."

"Good. I'll take care of it. I'll come down and let you know what the phone company says about when they can come."

"Okay."

## THIRTY-TWO

Chief Ben Avery kept his annoyance in check as he gazed across the table at Henry Berkin, chairman of the Smokey River Sioux Tribal Council Law and Order Committee. In Avery's twelve years with the Smokey River Tribal Police Department, the members of the council's Law and Order Committee had changed with each general election. Two of the five members of the current committee were new. Nevertheless, Ben Avery was on a first-name basis with all of them. Meetings were always cordial, until today.

"You're a former cop," he said in response to Berkin's unexpected criticism. "You know every situation is different and you know investigations are, more often than not, a slow process. And sooner or later, the FBI will take over and take the lead and in some instances all we do then is help, although sometimes they don't want our help."

Berkin didn't relent. "I get that, I know that. But it seems to me you've not compiled a lot of evidence."

"Henry, you haven't been privy to what's happening with the investigation of Arlo High Crane's murder. We've gathered information and interviewed people. I can't say more than that." Avery paused and glanced around at the four other committee members, one of whom was a woman. "I assure you; this case is on our front burner."

Dora White Crow, the representative from the Turtle Hill District, nodded in understanding. "Henry," she said, turning to Berkin, "I don't see any reason for us to have a blow-by-blow report on this one case. Besides, there are other items on our agenda today."

Everett Gray Bull from Horse Creek leaned forward and glanced at Berkin. "Henry, the protocol is for Chief Avery to report generally on his department. Now you suddenly want specific information about a case? This is my third year on this committee, and I have never seen or heard you act like a bully. I think you need to back off about the High Crane case."

Avery could feel the air growing heavy with tension. Two of the committee members remained silent, though they were clearly uncomfortable. "Listen," he said, "here's what I can do. I will keep you all in the loop—generally—about any developments, progress, or setbacks with the case."

Jeremy Cane, from Black Pipe, chuckled and shot a bemused glanced at Berkin, who was glaring at Gray Bull. "Thank you, Chief, but I don't think that's necessary. Most of us know your department is doing its job, on this case or any other."

"Thanks, Jeremy. I will say this. There have been four homicides this year, and we know the victims and the perpetrators. We obviously know the victim in the High Crane case, but we don't know the perpetrator—yet. The perpetrator or perpetrators in this case hid their tracks well. That means we leave no stone unturned. That means this is a piece-by-piece investigation. I don't know how long it will take but we've given it our highest priority. And somewhere along the line the FBI will step in. Maybe the investigation will move faster then."

That seemed to satisfy Berkin. His expression softened as he nodded. "Works for me, Chief. I think we're all okay with that."

Avery closed his notebook and stood. "Thanks. If you'll excuse me, I'll get back to it." He could feel Berkin's gaze as he left the room. Recalling the brief encounter in the parking lot a few days after the boy's body had been found, Henry Berkin obviously had an interest in this case from the beginning. The man worked hard at coming off as a "man of the people." But Avery wasn't buying it. Never had.

## THIRTY-THREE

Justin Primault examined two tempered steel rods. One was eight inches long and had deep perpendicular grooves filed into the end that formed an equilateral cross. The other was nothing more than a tube about a foot long.

"I heat the horseshoe," Leonard Little Bird explained. "I do that to fit the shoe to the hoof, and while the shoe is cooling I stamp that cross into one end of it and then the tube that circles it. And that's how I put the medicine wheel in. I don't make the shoes; I buy them factory made, various sizes. That symbol is my trademark, so to speak."

Primault handed the round, quarter-inch rod back to Little Bird. "Yeah, I can see how that works."

"So, I'm going to need a list of everyone you've shod horses for—names and addresses if you don't mind."

"Yeah, no problem," Little Bird replied, walking to a battered wooden file cabinet against a wall of his garage workshop. Pulling up files he wrote names on a sheet of paper and handed the list to the CI.

"Fourteen names," Primault said, after a quick count.

"A lot of people and families have horses but not everyone puts shoes on them. I do this part time during the school year. I teach at St. Ignatius.

Most of my farrier and horse-training work is in the summertime. School's out, so I'll be busy now."

Primault liked the young man, who was pleasant and friendly, nearly six feet tall and slightly built. He read the list. The fourth name caught his eye: Henry Berkin.

"Are all these people fairly regular customers?"

Little Bird nodded. "Yeah, pretty much." He reached over and pointed to two names on the list. "They only have one horse. Everyone else has at least two. Berkin, Morrisette, and White Bear have several."

"And all the shoes you used on their horses, all of these people, have that medicine wheel stamp?"

"No," Little Bird replied, and pointed to two names. "Scherer and Garrison don't. They're *wasicu*. I just do it for my Indian customers."

From the addresses Primault realized that the twelve Native horse owners who used Little Bird's services were all over the reservation. It was his job to know as much about the reservation as possible and he certainly knew where all the twenty-one districts were. Two facts aroused his curiosity. Flat Butte Dam was in the Fast Creek District, and Henry Berkin, who owned horses shod by Leonard Little Bird, lived in that district. The obvious question was how far or how close was Berkin's place to Flat Butte Dam?

Berkin had a ranch, that much Primault knew. Back in Agency Village he stopped at the BIA leasing office to ask about Henry Berkin's operation. Within ten minutes of his first question, he was standing over a large table looking at a satellite map of the southwest part of the reservation. The BIA realty clerk pointed out Flat Butte Dam and a house with outbuildings and corrals several miles from it.

"That's Henry Berkin's place," he told Primault. He owns eighty acres and leases three adjacent quarters. He has five hundred and sixty acres all told. Sixty of that is for alfalfa and the rest is grazing land. He has almost two hundred head of cattle."

"So, part of the pastureland he leases is adjacent to Flat Butte Dam," Primault surmised, using his pen to trace a line from Berkin's place to the dam.

"Yeah," the clerk affirmed. "It's about six or so miles from his place to the dam."

In his office Primault reviewed his notes and sat back. The shoes on Berkin's horses would have the medicine wheel mark that Little Bird used. A print from a shod horse left a discernible image with that medicine wheel about fifty yards from the east shore of Flat Butte Dam.

What did that mean?

Probably nothing, Primault concluded. Maybe Berkin or his son was checking on cattle or simply going for a long ride. There was no way to know when that print had been made.

There was another consideration. Henry Berkin was the chairman of the tribal council's Law and Order Committee. And there were rumors he might be running for tribal president come the next election. He was a vocal critic of Clayton Lone Hawk, the current tribal president.

An instinct told Primault not to dismiss the significance of the shod horseprint, but for the time being to keep it to himself.

# THIRTY-FOUR

Hightower watched the woman step out from the bathroom and walk to the dresser where her clothes were neatly folded. She was no longer young, but she was still good-looking, even without make-up. Her reddish-brown hair was long and still thick. While she slipped on her panties and bra, she looked at him unabashedly.

"It's been a while for you, huh?"

He grinned and waved a hand toward the bills he had arranged neatly next to the television.

"Are you free this evening?"

"For you, sure." She glanced around at the room. "There are nicer motels," she pointed out. "The Roadhouse Inn up by the Interstate has a restaurant next door."

"Can you drop by about eight? We can go to dinner first."

She finished putting on her slacks and blouse, then her pumps. "Eight o'clock it is. I'll meet you in the restaurant." She scooped up the cash and slipped it into her bra. Putting on her sweater, she blew him a kiss and headed for the door.

Hightower reached for his phone and clumsily dialed a number, then waited impatiently for the man on the other end to answer.

"Del Conway," a scratchy voice said. "How can I help you?"

"Hey, Del, it's Hightower. Did you get my earlier message?"

"I sure did. Come on by if you can, and we'll talk."

"Outstanding, See you in about an hour."

Two hours later he finished a second bottle of water and cleared his throat, trying in vain to ignore the constant smell of smoke in Conway's small office cramped into a corner of the building. The space outside the office was filled with shelves, glass-top counters, and tables piled with everything from music CDs, DVDs, to clothes, guns, jewelry, electronics, and tools. To Hightower it felt like walking in the middle of a lifetime of last hopes. This was Conway's pawnshop.

Conway finished reading the letter Hightower had copied.

"You ain't shitting me, are you?" the man rasped, leveling a narrow gaze at Hightower.

"I give you my word," Hightower said. "I saw that ledger, the 'green-sides book.' It's real. I know the 'six-shooting gun' is real, and I have a plan to acquire it."

"I'm not giving you money for something you ain't got."

Hightower chuckled. "Not asking for that. I simply want your help in ascertaining how much that pistol is worth."

"You ain't planning on selling something you don't have, are you?"

"No, hell, no. I will put that genuine historic artifact up for bids after I have it in my possession. And I don't want some fast-talking broker or collector blowing smoke up my ass. I want an honest assessment of what a pistol from the Battle of the Little Bighorn would be worth."

"Okay, okay." Conway reached for another cigarette. "But what kind is it, exactly?"

"It is very likely an Army Colt because that's what the 7th Cavalry had as standard issue. So, if you can ask the people you know, I'd appreciate it. I'll gladly pay you for your time and for whatever expenses you might incur."

Conway nodded as he lit up. "Right, okay. I prob'ly could broker a good deal for you," he said hopefully. "For a percentage."

"My friend, I would gladly consider that," Hightower said. He took one of Conway's business cards from a holder and wrote down his cell phone number. "Here's my number."

"Okay. I'll get on it right away. Don't know how long it'll take though."

"Yeah. Keep moving on it and let me know."

As he finished checking into the Roadhouse Inn nearly an hour later, thinking of a shower to get rid of the smoke smell, he felt the vibration in his shirt pocket. He pulled out the phone and glanced at the number.

"Hey, Dr. Lone Wolf, how the heck are you?"

"I'm good. Just wondering if you have some time to chat."

"Ah, yeah. I'm in the middle of something. I'll call you back in a few."

A few minutes later, Hightower sunk down into a soft chair in his room. The woman was right. This place was much better. He grabbed his phone and placed the call to the man he had said was expendable, forcing himself to sound friendly.

"Let me guess," he said, "I'm gone a few days and the place is falling apart already."

"Actually, everything is going like clockwork, and Doug is thinking of advertising your job. So, asking for a raise may not be advisable. Just a word to the wise."

"Right. And they're cancelling Christmas this year. What's really on your mind?"

"If you're serious about helping with the ledger book project, the NMAI people will be here soon. Since you bailed out I've taken your job on an interim basis and that means I'll be involved on two levels. Just giving you a heads-up if you want to ride along."

"Right, okay. Ah, yeah, for the time being just keep me in the loop."

"I can do that."

Hightower leaned back and smiled after he disconnected the call. Here was an unexpected opportunity to get closer to the Little Bighorn gun. The esteemed Dr. Lone Wolf had apparently decided not to reveal the pistol to the NMAI, meaning he probably had trust issues; the fewer people that knew about the gun the better. Smart thinking. All Hightower needed to know was where the pistol was so he could pass that on to number 2.

Five hours later, panting a bit, he extricated himself from the woman and rolled to his side of the bed.

"Well," she murmured, "that was an inspired performance."

"Oh, darling," he said, breathing hard. "Life is good."

As he was falling asleep later he heard his phone vibrating on the nightstand.

Flipping it open, he allowed himself a smile.

**Plan is to be in your neck of the woods in two weeks.**

# THIRTY-FIVE

Gavin sat at Esther Red Thunder's bare wooden table with the coffee she had poured and finished buttering the fresh, hot bun she put on a saucer for him. Esther was known for her baked goods, whether it was bread or cinnamon rolls. The smell of fresh-baked bread filled the house.

The kitchen-dining space and the living room was a large open L-shaped area. The few pieces of furniture were old and worn. In one corner the technician from the phone company was finishing the installation of the phone line. Nora and Chris Janis, Esther's grandchildren, were watching with great interest even as they helped their grandmother with the baking chores.

"My grandma taught me how to sew, iron, cook, bake, and chop wood, and to take care of myself," the old woman said. "That's what I'm teaching them." She pointed to her grandchildren.

"Same here," Gavin affirmed. "My grandma taught us how to cook, sew, and iron."

Yesterday a narrow trench had been dug from the main trunk line, paralleling the street, to Esther's house, and a phone line spliced in. Gavin had bought a landline phone for Esther, charging the base for her before he brought it over, as well as a new flat-screen television. In addition was a cardboard box, which he put on the table.

Esther joined him at the table still wearing her apron.

"Thank you, *Tunska*," she said. "We sure needed a phone."

"You're welcome, Auntie," he said.

"And I know the kids will like the TV."

A few minutes later the technician joined them. "I'm done, Mr. Lone Wolf," he said. "The satellite dish is up, and everything is working. I just need to hook up the phone and see that it works the way it should." He put a piece of paper on the table in front of Esther. "Ma'am, this is your number."

"And everything will be billed to me?" Gavin asked.

"Yes sir, as per your instructions."

After a few more minutes the technician answered the ringing phone. "Thanks, Lola," he said. "Everything works."

After the man gathered his tools, he left with an entire loaf of fresh, unsliced bread, somewhat surprised at the gift. Gavin grabbed the cardboard box and motioned Nora and Christopher to join him on the couch. He opened it and pulled out two new smartphones. Both kids leaned forward. Gavin gave each of them a phone.

"Wow!" Chris shouted, his eyes wide. Nora simply smiled and glanced shyly at Gavin.

"Now," he said, "I know you know what these are and how to use them. They are now yours. I'm giving them to you mainly because I want you both to stay in touch with your grandma when you're away from the house." He handed each of them a charger and phone cover.

"I talked to your grandma and she's okay with you having them, as long as you follow her rules. And since I'm the one who bought these for you,

I get to make a rule. And that rule is you follow grandma's rules about the phones. Right?"

They nodded in unison.

"Good. My nephew Thomas has already put some blocks and safeguards on them, so all you need to do is put in a password."

"Thank you, Uncle Gavin," Nora said.

"Yeah, thanks," Chris echoed.

A few minutes later Gavin walked out of Esther Red Thunder's house with all the fresh bread she had baked in a bag under his arm. On his way out of the housing area he stopped at Joby Bone's house.

"Hey, cuz," the man said. "The coffee and soup are done. Come on in."

Gavin knew refusing the offer would be an insult. "Thanks," he said, putting a loaf of fresh-baked bread on the small table. Joby's house was a one-bedroom version of Esther's, though older. The few pieces of furniture were a mismatched collection. Gavin pulled a chair to the table and waited for Joby to ladle the soup into bowls and pour the coffee.

"*Tahansi*," he said. "I have a proposition for you."

Joby dipped soup from the small saucepan and set it back on the stove. Next he brought the coffee pot. "Okay," he said, taking a seat. "What's on your mind?"

"The north fence line to my pasture. It's about a half mile and right now it's barbed wire."

"Looked good to me the last time I was at your place," Joby replied.

"Yeah, but that's not it. I want to replace that barbed wire with some light cable. Don't want my horses cutting themselves."

"Right, that's what you said. When you want to get it started?"

"Oh, soon as the cable gets here. I haven't ordered it yet, but here's my proposition. I know I can count on your help, so, in return I'll hook up your electricity and take care of your monthly bill."

Joby nodded. "Seems like a lot of money for a little bit of work."

"I know how hard it was for you last winter, *Tahansi*. One of the times I stopped by you were out of wood."

"Hey, life is tough. It's how I grew up."

"Doesn't have to be all the time, and we're not getting any younger."

Joby smiled. "I appreciate it, Cousin. You order that cable and I'll put up your fence."

They ate in silence for a couple of minutes, tearing chunks out of the bread. "Auntie Esther sure can bake," Joby declared.

"That she can."

"Hey, cuz, there's something I been meaning to tell you."

Gavin lifted his bowl and drank the last of his soup. "Okay," he said. "Good soup, by the way."

"Thanks." Joby glanced away for a moment, and then sipped his coffee. "It might be nothing, but—but I saw something one evening, some weeks ago."

"Oh, what did you see?"

"Ah, your friend—you know, that white guy you had supper with in Edna's, the bald guy."

"Oh, you mean Caleb Hightower?"

"I guess. I know you work together."

Gavin pushed his empty bowl toward the center of the table, a gesture indicating that the food was good and appreciated. "Okay. So, you saw something, or saw him? He's been around for a while."

Joby nodded, his expression pensive. "Well, I saw him. You know me. I'm always on the road, and I was walking back from Kincaid one evening just before dark. I sat down to rest at the cut-off road, just before the junction. I was at the corner against the fence and lit a cigarette. Right then, a car turned in and went down the cut-off road. By the time I finished my smoke, it came back."

"Okay. So, what's that got to do with my friend?"

"It was your friend; he was the driver. I noticed because of the logo on the door—the university logo. It stopped and the door opened, the driver leaned out. When the light came on, I saw his face, his beard and bald head. It was your friend, fifteen feet away."

"Okay, I believe you, but why are you telling me this now? Caleb has that car assigned to him."

Joby shook his head and sipped his coffee. "I guess it was the way your friend looked."

"What do you mean?"

"He looked scared, really scared, like the devil himself was chasing him."

Gavin nodded. After a moment he realized Joby had spoken again.

"Hey cuz, if you're heading toward town, can you give me a ride to Edna's? I work this evening."

Nearly half an hour later Gavin finished a leisurely turn around his yard and then circled the barn, just to do a visual check. Both horses were in the two-acre paddock connected to the barn, grazing peacefully. Their mood was always a good indicator. If they were nervous or unduly alert, it could mean something or someone was nearby. He glanced east as Uncle Andrew's comment came to mind again: *a lot of our troubles as Lakota people came from the east.*

Entering the house through the kitchen door off the east deck, he stopped to put water on for tea. A feeling of wariness crawled up his back, pulling his eyes to the east window behind the table.

# THIRTY-SIX

Budgetary shortfalls were always a fact of life for reservation police departments, affecting everything from paying overtime to buying equipment. It was the reason Justin Primault was the department's only criminal investigator. The murder of Arlo High Crane was not his only case. Assaults, attempted rapes, sexual harassment, and even "white collar" crime were the dark side of life on every reservation, not unlike the rest of America. There was another even more disturbing and ugly, decades-old problem: missing Native women and girls. There were three active cases on Primault's desk, but those were only the ones that were officially known. He pointed at the files and looked at Ben Avery.

"One of these girls is eighteen, one is seventeen, and the youngest is fifteen. It's damn hard not to take all this personally, Chief," he admitted. "Women and girls started disappearing when all those oil-field workers started pouring into North Dakota

Ben Avery gazed thoughtfully at the younger man. "No progress?"

"No. Short of raiding those damn man camps."

"Not a bad idea, actually." Avery paused for a moment. "Anything new on the High Crane case?"

"No. Because of the hoof print of the shod horse we found at Flat Butte Dam, I talked to the farrier, the Lakota farrier, who uses those shoes. He gave me a list of the people he's done work for. There's a name on that list that might interest you."

"Who?"

"Henry Berkin."

Avery stared at the CI. "Damn."

"Yeah. I've located everyone on that list, as far as where they live. The interesting thing is that Berkin lives six miles from Flat Butte Dam. The next closest guy is over twenty miles away. Long way to ride a horse."

"What's your next step?"

"Berkin will have to wait. Singer and I are just picking our way through what evidence we do have and chasing a few leads. A lot of bleary-eyed tedium."

Heavy footsteps caught them by surprise as Primault was standing to leave Avery's office. Henry Berkin walked in without knocking. The two officers exchanged glances.

"Just the guys I want to see," he announced loudly.

"What can we do for you?" Avery asked, pointing to an empty chair against a wall. Primault gazed calmly at the man and didn't say a word. Something about Henry Berkin was annoying. Maybe it was his air of assumed authority.

"Is the High Crane case progressing? Any leads?" Berkin remained standing, not bothering to remove his white hat.

Avery looked up at Berkin with a noncommittal gaze. "Yes, to both questions," he said, and no more.

Berkin glanced at Primault and shifted his attention back to the Chief. "Well, tell me. What's going on?"

"This is an active investigation," Avery said, "and as such we are not at liberty to share sensitive information, Mr. Berkin."

Berkin's face flushed as he stared at Avery. "I'm the chairman of the Law and Order Committee," he pointed out.

Avery rose slowly until he was at eye level with the man. "Of course, I realize that, but you are not a law enforcement officer or an officer of the court. We've been over this ground before, haven't we, Henry? Rest assured, sir, we are doing everything we can, and making progress."

Berkin's mouth compressed into a thin line and from the side Primault could see the clenched jaw.

"I see. Well, you will keep me informed," he said, relenting somewhat.

Avery nodded. "Of course."

Primault saw an opening. "Mr. Berkin," he said. "I do have a question, unrelated to the investigation. Maybe you can help."

Berkin turned, eyes blinking, still holding a spark of defiance. "Ah, sure. What's the question?"

"Do you know a man by the name of Leonard Little Bird?"

The man's eyes continued to blink, and the defiance in his eyes turned to confusion. "Yeah, I do. So what?"

"I have a friend who's looking for a good farrier."

Berkin's tone was hesitant. "Ah, Little Bird is a farrier, and a horse trainer."

"Would you recommend him?"

Berkin nodded. "Yeah, I would." He shifted his gaze to Avery and walked out of the room. The two policemen listened as the footsteps faded.

"What was that all about?" Avery wondered.

"Just wanted to distract him."

"Well, Henry Berkin owns about two hundred head of cattle and leases a lot of land," Avery said. "If you're thinking of doing any more than that, consider this. He's been making noises about running for tribal president in the next election. He is a politician through and through, and he's learning all the tricks, including the dirty ones."

## THIRTY-SEVEN

Gavin and Douglas Eagle Shield watched as the two technicians from the National Museum of the American Indian, with help from two facilities management people, hauled large wooden cases into the SRU administration building. The large van was backed up to the main entrance.

"Once they've assembled the unit they're calling the 'environmental control capsule,' it will house your ledger book," Eagle Shield explained to Lone Wolf. "And once the ledger is in it, it will remain there, handled only by the conservator or a technician wearing protective gloves to separate the pages and take the photographs. A security guard and at least one of the techs or the conservator will be with the capsule at all times. At night the capsule will be wheeled into the university records vault and locked inside. I asked the university foundation people to give up their office space next to the vault."

"When will the conservator be here?"

"Late tonight. Mike Marshall sent a driver to pick him up from the Sioux Falls airport. He and the techs will be staying in our guesthouse for the duration. Tomorrow will be our first meeting to kick off the project. Once they assemble the capsule and do tests on it, they'll be ready for the ledger."

An hour later Gavin finished a meeting with the Lakota Studies Department staff. Of course, a van on campus with the NMAI name and logo on its sides raised a lot of curiosity. After Gavin filled the staff in on the discovery of his great-grandfather's ledger book and the research and development project in partnership with NMAI, the excitement was palpable. The questions were nearly endless.

"This is the biggest thing to happen here at SRU since we built the library," Jess No Horse opined. "This will really put us on the map."

Sandra Bear Runner had another opinion. "It's a chance to add to the Lakota account of that event," she said. "That's what we need, more of that. I went to the battlefield last year and, to me, it's still basically a shrine to the losers."

"Well, what can you expect?" Denise Archambault asked sarcastically. "The place started out as a shrine to Custer—Custer Battlefield National Monument. When the name change happened in 1991, the superintendent, who was Native, received death threats, I can only assume, from hard core Custer buffs. Your great-grandfather's story is another indisputable eyewitness account from our perspective. You need to write a book, Gavin."

Some minutes later Gavin returned to his office. He barely had time to sit down when his phone beeped.

Gavin answered, "*Hau, Leksi.*"

"*Hau, Tunska,*" Andrew No Horn said. "You got a minute?"

"Yeah. What's up?"

"I had a dream last night about your friend, the Englishman."

"You did?"

"Yeah, I saw him with a mask he kept putting in front of his face, but the mask had no features, no eyes, nose, or mouth. Then it turned into his face."

"That's strange. What do you think it means?"

"Well, maybe there's a side to him you have not seen."

Gavin stared at the bookcase in his office. "That's possible. How much do we know about anybody beyond what they reveal to us?"

"Yeah, we all have secrets," said Andrew.

## THIRTY-EIGHT

Whatever new responsibilities Gavin had as interim chair of the department, there were always chores to be done at home. After filling the horse tank, Gavin turned off the water and decided to take some firewood out to Coyote Butte where Uncle Andrew was supporting two young Lakota men who were doing their vision quest prior to participating in the Sun Dance

Gavin arrived at the camp as the sun hung just above the horizon. The long, flat butte rose a hundred and fifty feet above the prairie floor on the western border of the reservation, the highest point among a few other buttes and high ridges. For as long as the Sicangu Lakota had been in this part of the northern plains, it had been used by medicine men for vision quests.

A young man, who turned out to be the younger brother of one of the men on the south end of the hill, was with Uncle Andrew. The other young man was on the north end. Andrew's camp was on the south-facing slope halfway between them. The helper, whom Andrew introduced as Jimmy Ashes, unloaded the firewood.

Gavin was pleased to see that his uncle had pitched his twelve-foot, conical Lakota tipi, the smaller of two that he owned. He always liked to see the four-foot long red, black, yellow, and blue cloth streamers attached to the tops of the tipi poles as they fluttered in the breeze. A fire was already burning in front of the lodge and the entire appearance and atmosphere around the camp was straight out of the stories Uncle Andrew and Grandma Annie liked to tell. Around the fire were three Lakota chairs. Except for the two pickup trucks, the iron coffee pot atop the iron grate over the fire, the canvas lodge covering, and clothing worn by Gavin, Andrew, and Jimmy, the scene could very well have been two hundred years in the past, an empowering and tangible connection to ancient relatives.

Gavin joined his uncle by the fire, leaning back against one of the chairs. Gavin had been "put on the hill" on this very spot as a young man by his uncle Andrew, so he knew first-hand what the two young men currently on the hill were going through. Four days and four nights in total isolation—except for mosquitoes and snakes and sometimes an otherworldly presence—no matter the weather, in prayer and meditation, was an experience like no other.

"They have two more nights, after tonight," Andrew told Gavin. "So far the weather hasn't been too tough. Nights have been chilly."

"So, when is your Sun Dance this year?" Gavin asked.

"First part of July," the medicine man replied. He pointed to the north. "On the other side of the butte, where we usually do it. Would be good to have you there to help, especially with the *inipi*, the sweat ceremonies."

"Sure, be glad to."

Gavin had himself participated in the Sun Dance in his twenties, four years in a row. The scars on his chest, where he had been pierced and the chokecherry skewers were inserted, were not as prominent. But they were always a reminder of who he was and that he was a part of something old beyond remembering. Of course, in both his personal and professional life he did not reveal to anyone that he was a Sun Dancer. What was an act freely and unselfishly given was a status not achieved for bragging rights. Although there were invariably the few who broke the unspoken tradition, Sun Dancers generally never revealed their status. To do so diminished the sacrifice they had made on behalf of the people.

"Good Voice Eagle put people up on this butte," Andrew said, invoking the memory of a medicine man ancestor. "That was after 1877, after Crazy Horse was killed." He gestured toward the butte. "So, this is a powerful place. I think those boys up there are finding that out because Jimmy and I heard some sounds last night."

Jimmy Ashes was just at the end of the firelight, splitting wood with an axe. Gavin took the opportunity to tell his uncle about the conversation with Hightower in Edna's Restaurant. "He told me he earned his way to the U.S. by working on a container ship. Then he worked in a warehouse."

"Is that unusual?" Andrew wondered."

People do that, of course. But Caleb was a professor at Durham University and I'm sure his salary was fairly high. He should have been able to pay for an airline ticket, or passage on an ocean liner. Why would he pay for passage by working?"

"That bothers you?"

Gavin slowly shook his head and put another piece of wood into the fire. "It does. But there's something else. Joby Bone told me about an interesting incident."

"Oh, yeah?"

Gavin nodded slowly. "Yeah. Joby saw Caleb in the evening, near dark, in his university car at the cut-off road by the junction west of Kincaid. When he turned off, Joby said he looked sick or frightened when he opened the car door and leaned out for air. Caleb later got back on the highway headed west. What the hell was he doing, and where was he going?"

"Have you asked him?"

Gavin was staring into the fire. "No. But he was in a university car so maybe it was work related."

"Are you having doubts about your friend?"

"I think he's leaving," Gavin said. "He resigned as department chair and asked for the fall semester off."

The old man sighed deeply. "Well, there's one thing I know about people. We don't always show everything we are. Some people keep things back because of humility. Some keep things back because they're embarrassed, or ashamed, or because they want people to see them in a certain way. By what I saw in my dream, maybe your friend is hiding a part of himself."

Gavin couldn't disagree, and his uncle's dream was nothing to dismiss. He decided to change the subject after Jimmy Ashes brought an armload of wood to the fire and took a seat.

"So, *Leksi*, what year was it that you were a lookout for that last Sun Dance until you started one again?" Gavin knew that his uncle had chosen his current Sun Dance site where one had been conducted when Andrew was just a boy.

"It was 1949," the old man recalled. "A medicine man by the name of Chips came down from Cheyenne River. There were only six dancers. Your dad and me were lookouts on the butte here. Other boys were positioned all around, watching for the BIA police because it was illegal to do the Sun Dance. Luckily, they didn't come, but it was like holding our breath every day watching for their black cars. They would have arrested all of us and probably put Chips in jail if they had known about it."

Young Jimmy Ashes was shocked.

"Yeah," Andrew went on. "It wasn't legal for us to do our ceremonies until 1978, until the American Indian Religious Freedom Act was passed."

The evening passed too fast. Coyotes began to bark and howl all around them in the darkness, affirming the reason for the name of the butte. Jimmy Ashes listened in fascination to the stories and topics of conversation at the fire. He learned more about Lakota history and tradition in one evening by a fire than he ever had in one year of his high school Lakota Studies class.

Not once did either Lone Wolf or the medicine man glance at a wristwatch. Finally, after a prayer for protection for the young men on the hill, Gavin and Jimmy crawled into sleeping bags. The medicine man wrapped himself in his elk sleeping robes.

Everyone was awake and out of their beds at dawn. After another prayer to greet the day and a morning song, Andrew made coffee. Just after eight, Gavin left for the university, wondering what he might see and know by the time the sun went down.

## THIRTY-NINE

After a long day of immobility at his desk on campus, Gavin was glad for the familiar setting of his log house, even embracing the still-lingering memories of Soldier Woman. They were not the only thoughts and images lingering in his consciousness as he stepped down from the pickup and walked around to the barn.

Great-Grandpa's ledger was front and center. People from NMAI were on campus to open the ledger. There was of course no way to know exactly what was on those pages, but the logical assumption was drawings or sketches since Grandma Maud No Horse/Little Turtle had written "book Story many drawing pictures" of the Greasy Grass Fight. Furthermore, it was only natural to assume there would be sketches since Cheyenne and Lakota people from the late nineteenth century had used old accounting ledgers to draw their experiences. Such drawings were important historical records that depicted personal experiences such as imprisonment at Fort Marion in Florida. Some of those prisoners had sketched the life they had before imprisonment.

In any case, whatever was on those ledger book pages would be known, hopefully, in less than twenty-four hours.

Floating somewhere amid the anticipation regarding the ledger was the conversation he had with Caleb Hightower in Edna's Restaurant. Why had Hightower paid for his trans-Atlantic passage to the United States by working on a container ship? It didn't make sense, nor did it fit his personality. And why had he taken a job at a warehouse instead of going right into academia in the U.S.? It was a part of Caleb's life that seemed out of place.

Gavin shook off the thought as he reached the corral and leaned on the top rail, glad when Dancer and Red Wing walked over to sniff him thoroughly. For the next few minutes, he soaked up their unconditional affection and returned it by scratching their ears and rubbing their necks.

Gavin, and everyone else in the department had accepted Hightower without question. All academics were vetted prior to being hired and the man had arrived with his credentials in hand and fit in immediately at the university. Yet Uncle Andrew had never steered Gavin wrong on any issue or circumstance or question. So, for the time being, it was only a matter of waiting to find out what the dream about Hightower meant. Gavin had no doubt that the image revealed to his uncle was significant.

Back inside, Gavin made a cup of tea and sat down at the table, his gaze automatically drawn to the landscape out the east window, Uncle Andrew's words echoing in his mind: *If there was trouble coming, it would come from the east*

## FORTY

Hightower walked into his house, tossed his keys on the table, and took a seat. From his pocket he pulled out the flip phone and laid it on the table, then turned his attention to the bag of fast-food from the drive-in in Kincaid.

He glanced at the calendar on the wall as he unwrapped the burger. He knew he had to be patient waiting for Caruth, number 2, to contact him, but he was annoyed. What if Caruth couldn't pull it off? Hightower wondered if he should consider a back-up plan for finding that damn pistol. But where would he start?

In the meantime, he had to keep up appearances. Scrolling names and numbers on his phone he stopped at Gavin Lone Wolf and made the call.

"Gavin Lone Wolf," was the answer on the other end.

"That sounded very professor-like," Hightower quipped, trying to sound nonchalant.

"Oh, hey, Caleb. Didn't really check the number. What's up?"

"Just wondering what's happening with the ledger project."

"It's moving along. There's an unveiling of sorts, tomorrow."

Hightower detected a bit of hesitancy in Lone Wolf's tone. "Really? What time?"

"Ah, ten, in the admin building."

"Great, I'll see you then."

Hightower disconnected the call, a bit of nervousness fluttering in his stomach. He was bothered by Lone Wolf's tone. Maybe he'd had a hard day. One thing Hightower learned early on about Gavin Lone Wolf—the man was unflappable. No matter the situation his behavior had always been courteous. Not that he had been discourteous in the brief exchange they had just had. But there was something in his voice.

Hightower took a deep breath and exhaled slowly, glancing at his silent phone as he did. Even if Caruth called or texted and said he had the Little Bighorn pistol in hand, it would be wise to show up tomorrow to ward off any suspicion.

The next morning, Gavin saw Hightower's old SUV as soon as he pulled into the SRU Administration Building lot. Stepping out of the truck, he strode through the front doors of the building and down the hall to the office at the end. His gaze immediately fell on an object about the size of two phone booths that was on wheels. Gavin shook hands with Doug Eagle Shield and nodded at the capsule he had heard about. "I don't know whether to be impressed or afraid," he said, as Caleb Hightower came across the hall from the academic vice president's office and stepped into the room.

"Well," Eagle Shield said, grinning, "it is quite a contraption." He shook Hightower's hand and gestured toward a man near a table. "Gavin, you remember Dr. Theodore Wells, of course?"

Gavin stepped over to shake hands with the conservator. "Good to see you, Dr. Wells." He turned and indicated Hightower, forcing himself to sound cordial. "This is my colleague, Dr. Caleb Hightower. Caleb, this is Dr. Theodore Wells from the National Museum of the American Indian."

"A pleasure, Dr. Wells," Hightower said, reaching out a hand. "I've been keen to know what's in Gavin's ledger, since the moment I laid eyes on it."

"Ah, you obviously came from across the pond," Wells said, referring to Hightower's accent. "Well, hopefully we shall be able to satisfy all our curiosities. We're quite excited to get started." He pointed to two young men in the room. "Gentlemen, these are my co-workers, Haley Glanville and Toby Hanson."

"Pleased to meet you," Gavin said, and pointed at the capsule. "I'm very glad you know what to do with this."

Hightower stepped aside and out of the way, leaning against a wall.

Three of the four sides of the capsule had large windows. The lower half of the fourth side was essentially an instrument panel. It contained a console with rows of switches and gauges, but the apparatus that caught Gavin's attention was two round cutaways, about eighteen inches apart. On the other side, reaching into the interior compartment was a pair of rubber sleeves. A padded stool stood in front of the sleeves.

The environmental control capsule was humming slightly, and the interior was softly lit. A circular platform approximately eighteen inches in diameter stood on four sturdy legs. The side to the left of the console did not have a window. On one inside wall were mounted three six-inch-wide shelves and a lock box about eighteen inches square. Behind the shelves and box, inside the walls, the conservator explained, was the power unit for the capsule.

Dr. Wells pointed to the small, double wheels at each corner, not unlike those used on rolling luggage but larger. "We'll roll it inside the vault at night, or anytime it's not in use," he told Gavin. "Each time we take it into the field, we reassemble and test it. We assembled it two days ago and spent yesterday testing it. All systems are go."

"Great. So, the ledger will remain in there until you're finished doing whatever it is that you need to do?" Gavin asked.

"That's correct. Since air, moisture, and heat are the greatest threat to old artifacts, the interior of the capsule is like a vacuum, a constant forty-two degrees Fahrenheit and drier than a bone."

Gavin noticed that Wells had already glanced several times at the briefcase he was carrying with the ledger inside. "As I think I mentioned before," Gavin said, "I've kept the ledger wrapped in soft cloth inside my safe. I can guarantee it was a dry environment, though I don't know what the temperature was in my basement." He handed the case to Wells who, along with Glanville, put on latex gloves.

The curator took the ledger to a nearby table. After opening the case he lifted out the bundle and handed it to Glanville. The young man accepted the bundle and took a seat on the stool near the console. He pushed a button and a hidden bin popped out, just below the bottom of the glass.

Glanville carefully laid the bundle in the bin, closed the lid, and pushed the bin in so that the bundle appeared on the other side. Leaning forward, the technician slid his latex-gloved hands into and through the sleeves. Gavin stepped to one side to get a better view and watched the technician lift out the bundle and place it on the circular platform. Glanville glanced briefly at Toby Hanson and spoke one word: "Camera."

Hanson touched a button on a hand-held apparatus, not unlike a control for a video game and moved to the table with a video monitor. In less than three seconds an overhead view of the bundle appeared. "You're good to go," he said to Glanville.

Moving a small handle, Hanson zoomed in for a close-up as Glanville's gloved hands inside the capsule began to carefully unwrap the bundle. After several slow and deliberate movements, the ledger was visible.

Glanville lifted the ledger with one hand and discarded the cloth wrapping with the other. The conservator stepped behind Glanville to get a view of the ledger itself. President Eagle Shield and Gavin watched the monitor as the gloved hands turned the ledger over to show the front cover. Hightower stepped closer.

"There is writing and a faint image," Glanville described. "Toby."

Toby Hanson was already snapping photographs of the outside cover. On the monitor appeared the writing and image Glanville had mentioned.

Atchison Accountants.

Below the name was a faint image of a wolf's paw print.

"That is essentially my great-grandfather's signature," Gavin said.

The technician glanced up at Dr. Wells, who nodded and turned to Gavin.

"Dr. Lone Wolf, with your permission we will proceed to open the ledger."

Gavin glanced at Hightower, who winked encouragement, and nodded. "Of course."

Wells turned and leaned forward. The attention of Gavin, Doug Eagle Shield and Toby Hanson was riveted on the monitor.

"The first task is pull up the cover," Glanville said, "so here I go. Good, there doesn't seem to be any resistance."

"Resistance would indicate adhesion," Wells commented, for Gavin and President Eagle Shield's benefit.

"It's coming up nicely," Glanville went on. "And—and there we have it. The book is open to the inside cover."

Although everyone in the room could see everything on the monitor, Glanville continued with his verbal description. "There is, on the inside cover, the words 'Atchison Accountants' again, and an address, 'One, one, two Milk Road, Atchison, Ohio,' and nothing else. The cover page appears intact, no cracks, no discoloration, or distortion."

"That certainly bodes well for the entirety of the book," Wells commented again.

Glanville continued. "I will attempt to turn this page, starting at the top right. A gentle tug upward—. Again, good news, no resistance, ah, yes, it's coming up nicely, and—oh, my!"

Everyone inched forward for a closer look. The image on the monitor showed the cover page up and out of the way.

"Ah, yes, this is—," Wells said, leaning over behind Glanville, and trying to contain his excitement. "What we have here is a sketch—the colors have faded somewhat—of a figure, a man in profile, mounted on a horse and facing to my right. He is holding, I think, a spear in his right hand and an upraised rifle in the other. The man has a long braid; he wears yellow trousers and a blue shirt. The horse appears to be brown, a bay, rather. There is a single cord, a rope attached to the animal's lower jaw and—and this is strange—it's tied around the man's waist.

"As we can see, this sketch practically fills the entire page. Dr. Lone Wolf, I believe this is a self-portrait done by your great-grandfather," Wells concluded.

"It certainly is," Gavin agreed. A shiver went through him, as Hightower stepped to the capsule and gazed intently at the sketch.

"Man, oh, man," President Eagle Shield said reverently. "This is amazing, and that is one bad-ass warrior."

Gavin chuckled. "I couldn't agree with you more."

Nearby, Toby Hanson was busily snapping photographs.

Dr. Wells stepped back and turned to Gavin. "Here's the procedure I think we should follow. Since the first image is clear and unobstructed, we turn the page once Toby is done photographing it. I know we all want to see all the sketches right away; however, there is no guarantee that the subsequent pages will be in as good a condition as this one. So, we photograph, insert acid free paper between the pages, and move on. That means slow going. But we knew going in that we wouldn't be finishing in ten minutes."

"Of course," Gavin said, "I understand."

"This is exciting," President Eagle Shield said. "I mean, this is primarily what this university is about, preserving our Lakota history, our language, our culture. I think you should write a book, Gavin, I really do."

Gavin nodded, eyes still glued to the image on the monitor. "My brother had the same suggestion. Let's see how many sketches we have and what kind of story they tell."

"I'm done," Toby Hanson said to Glanville and Wells.

"Wonderful," Wells replied. "On to the next."

Gavin glanced at Caleb Hightower and immediately noticed the intensity in the man's gaze, locked on the ledger. "What do you think, Caleb?"

"Amazing, my friend," Hightower replied. "Simply amazing."

## FORTY-ONE

Hightower hurried across the Administration Building's parking lot to his car. He was smiling. Gavin Lone Wolf had told the NMAI conservator that the ledger had been in his safe. And he had mentioned a basement, a space that Hightower was not aware of and had not been in. He had spent the night once in the spare bedroom and had not noticed any entrance that might lead to a basement. Since Lone Wolf had mentioned it, that's where the "six-shooting gun" probably was.

There was, of course, a chance that Lone Wolf might have put the gun in a bank safe deposit box, if he knew what it was worth. As a historian he had to have some inkling.

A thought poked its way in and cast a pall over Hightower's mood: perhaps Lone Wolf had already sold the pistol or sent it somewhere for analysis. What were the odds that he had? Hightower had to admit that scenario was certainly possible. Obviously the pistol was a closely guarded secret, known only to the Lone Wolf family. He sighed and turned the ignition to start the engine, and slowly drove through the lot.

Something could have happened in Washington DC concerning the pistol. Thomas Hale had taken excellent photographs of the ledger, and the NMAI had obviously accepted those photos as proof of the ledger book's existence and, of course, the Lone Wolf family's connection to the Battle of the Little Bighorn were strong and credible factors. So, it was reasonable to assume that there were also photos of the pistol. Those same factors might have motivated a collector, or the NMAI itself, to make an offer for the pistol.

Hightower slammed his palm on the steering wheel. "Fuck! That bastard wouldn't do that, would he? That would be a royal cock-up!" Turning onto the road leading away from campus, he glanced in the rear view mirror and saw the Administration Building framed in it. He had to know if that damn pistol was still on the reservation. Dr. Wells, the conservator, might have an answer but asking questions about a pistol no one knew about would get back to Lone Wolf.

There were obviously two possibilities: Lone Wolf still had the pistol, or it was not here. If the pistol was gone, he was fucked. Not only a few million dollars gone, but he would have to call off Caruth, and he would have to take care of a pain-in-the-ass situation himself.

There was no choice. He had to learn where that damn pistol was and there was only one place to start—Lone Wolf's house. The list of reasons that he shouldn't go there was long and frightening. There was only one thing in his favor; Lone Wolf didn't have a dog.

Of course, he could assume the pistol was still in Lone Wolf's possession, and not say otherwise to Caruth. And if the pistol was nowhere to be found, he could take his chances with Caruth. Caruth would not be pleased and would more than likely assume that Hightower had lied to manipulate him into solving a problem.

There was only one way to avoid broken bones or worse. He had to break into Lone Wolf's house and find the pistol himself. And if he did find it or couldn't or if it wasn't there, he would still have time to get word to Caruth and call it off.

A bummer of a choice, as he saw it; broken bones if he pissed off Caruth or an arrow in the gullet if Lone Wolf caught him.

## FORTY-TWO

Patrolman Jason Singer knocked on the partially open door of Primault's office. "Lieutenant?" he called out.

"Yeah, Jason, come on in."

The weariness on the young officer's face was apparent. "I think we might have made a bit of progress," he reported.

"Lay it on me."

Singer looked at the paper in his hand. "We measured the tracks in the photos we took, and the distance between the tires and we came up with a probable axle width of seventy-two inches. And after going cross-eyed looking at websites, I've narrowed it down. The vehicles with that axle width are General Motors products, a Chevrolet mid-size sedan or a mid-size truck."

"Damn, that's good."

"Right. Although there has to be a boat load of mid-size Chevrolet vehicles in Kincaid County, and the surrounding counties. It's another damn haystack, sir."

Primault leaned back in his chair. "It sure the hell is, but it's also a specific starting point. Any thoughts on where to go from here?"

"Yeah, yeah, I have a thought. We can contact Kincaid and the surrounding counties to see how many of those vehicles are registered."

"Makes sense to me, Jason."

"Right. I'll get on it. Might be easier, sir, if the FBI could help."

The Lieutenant crossed his arms and gazed at the young officer. "Yeah, it might. But until they darken our doorway this is our case. And we're not doing anything differently than they would."

Singer nodded and stood. "Got it."

"What about those partial tread marks?"

Singer paused and shrugged. "That's a bit of a puzzle, a clear piece of tread in the middle of the tire. I used to help my dad rotate tires on our car because he always wanted to get the most out of each set. And sometimes there was uneven wear, you know? But I never saw that kind of a wear pattern. It was as though the outer edges were sliced off, leaving that middle strip. That's what puzzles me."

Primault nodded. "I'd call that a good clue. How can a tire get worn on the sides and not in the middle? I'll bet if we could figure out that riddle, we might be a step closer to finding that particular tire, and the car it's on."

Singer nodded and walked out the door with a glint in his eyes.

## FORTY-THREE

By nine o'clock, as dusk was yielding to night, Hightower was on the futon in his small living room, grinning up at the ceiling. He had reason to grin. He had just finished a long talk with his friend Del Conway.

"Hey, I got some great news for you," Del had said. "I checked with several people about that there pistol of yours. Damn, that must be a doozy of a gun. I tell you what, I got estimates from six to fifteen million. That's damn hard to believe, I mean, that any damn gun can be worth that much!"

After a deep sigh Hightower stood and hurried to the small desk with a deep drawer and pulled it open, pushing aside the few files inside, he yanked out a state highway map. Unfolding it atop the desk he clicked on the small gooseneck lamp and lowered it, focusing his attention on the south-central part of the state—the Smokey River Reservation. Reaching into the top drawer he found the magnifying glass and held it over the map, looking for one road in particular. He found it and traced it with the tip of a pen.

The farm-to-market road, also known as Ring Thunder Road, was gravel and meandered more or less fifteen miles southwest from the town of Cold River to State Highway 17. More importantly, it passed two miles north of Gavin Lone Wolf's place. Most importantly, someone could approach from the southwest through a remote portion of the reservation. Hightower knew for a fact that traffic on that stretch was normally light, practically nonexistent at night.

He sighed again. All he needed was the nerve to carry out a plan that had been forming in the back of his mind. It was simple enough. Drive northeast from the Highway 17/Ring Thunder Road junction and turn off at an abandoned rural school three miles south of Lone Wolf's land. There he could hide his SUV and walk to Lone Wolf's house.

Hightower shuffled to the refrigerator, took a can of beer from the door shelf and retreated to the couch. He knew what he had to do.

Hightower had never been assertive or aggressive, preferring to avoid confronting anything daunting or anyone bigger. Working with Caruth in New Jersey he had always been a follower, the lackey who cleaned up afterward, always the observer rather than the doer. Only in a couple of extreme situations had he struck the first blow and pulled the trigger when it was either that or being dead. But always there had been that fearful flutter in his gut, that hesitancy to take the risk.

He gulped from the can and stared across the room. If he hesitated now he would never know the unfettered power of millions of dollars, the heady sensation of having anything he wanted, the freedom to go anywhere he wanted.

"Oh, crikey, you duffer!" he exclaimed. "Get off your arse!"

It was now or never.

Three hours later he sat in the chair next to his bed, laced up his hiking boots, and grabbed a light jacket. Without turning on lights he stepped carefully through a short hallway into the living room and then the kitchen. Picking up the backpack from the kitchen table, he exited the side door into the semi-darkness.

Getting into the SUV he carefully laid the pack on the passenger seat. In it were bottles of water, binoculars, snack bars, a hunting knife, and a multi-tool. With a nod he started the engine.

Forty minutes later he turned off Highway 17 onto Ring Thunder Road. If memory served no one lived near this gravel road. He was in the Soldier Creek District, but the main housing area was to the south. All other home sites were rural and away from the road. He drove slowly because he was near the Little White River and its outlying shrub thickets and groves of cottonwood and oak trees were shelter for white-tail deer. Plus, he didn't want to attract undue attention. A few miles later he slowed for a left turn, relieved because he was the only vehicle on the road. Now he was heading into an even more remote area. Gaining a plateau, he could see only one outside security light in the distance. Still keeping his speed down, he came to the next turn after a few more miles, this time to the right. Now he was less than ten miles from the abandoned schoolhouse.

Though he watched for the turn-off on the section road, he nearly missed it, and even after he turned there was no assurance he had found the right road. He slowed after an eighth of a mile to do a U-turn, thinking he was on the wrong road, and saw the building at the far reach of his headlights. It had apparently been abandoned long enough for grass to reclaim the short driveway. Staying on it he followed it to the end and turned right to circle the building, parking his car behind three tall cedar trees, hoping it would be out of sight from all directions once daylight came.

Lifting his pack from the seat, he slipped out of the car and locked the door. From here the plan was simple. Walk to Ring Thunder Road and follow it north. Walking on the road would be faster. If there was any traffic, he could jump over or crawl under the fence and hide. He illuminated his watch—the digital face indicated 12:12 a.m. With any luck he should reach Lone Wolf's turn-off in an hour.

Owing to a life free of unnecessary exercise, his pace slowed considerably after an initial burst of energy. At 2:23 a.m. he reached the turn-off into Gavin's pasture. Half an hour later he found a thicket on a slope he knew was out of sight from Lone Wolf's long driveway. With the flashlight he probed the sparse thicket and was relieved to find nothing but grass and twigs. After downing an entire bottle of water, he laid down, using the backpack as a pillow.

Zipping up the jacket to his chin, he curled up and stuck his hands under his armpits. After he had stopped moving, the air felt chilly.

"Six to fifteen million dollars," he whispered. "Six to fifteen million dollars."

## FORTY-FOUR

When he awoke the fourth time it was finally light, and he immediately felt the sharp chill in the air. Awareness of his situation took longer to fall into place, followed by an immediate feeling of apprehension. All the bravado of the night before had evaporated. Sitting up slowly and somewhat stiffly, he rubbed his eyes and pushed up the sleeve of his jacket to check the time—7:18 a.m.

"Come on, you duffer," he rasped. "You came this far."

Muffled rattling of a vehicle pulling a stock trailer reached his ears. Looking north he saw the top of a plume of gray dust moving east. Relief coursed through him knowing he was out of sight from the road. In a moment the noise passed. After stretching out his arms and flexing his ankles, he slid farther into the shrubbery. Fortunately, his jacket was gray and blended in.

Behind him over the slight rise to the east was the pasture road leading to Gavin Lone Wolf's house. To the south, though he wasn't certain how far, was the Little White River. Peering through the leaves of the low thicket, he heard the muttering of an engine and saw the roof of Gavin's pickup moving north toward the highway. That meant Lone Wolf was heading for the SRU campus and would be gone for the day.

It was now or never.

Hightower looked south toward the river. There were deep as well as shallow swales and gullies he recalled. A couple of years ago he had taken a walk with Lone Wolf in his pasture. Following a gully to the river and then circling east would be best. That would eliminate the chance of anyone in a passing vehicle seeing him.

Pulling his pack around, he unzipped it and took out an energy bar and a bottle of water. Zipping the pack closed, he rose to a kneeling position, looked around, and listened intently. Standing, he turned toward the river.

From behind a small plum thicket Hightower watched the front of Lone Wolf's house through binoculars. Only the Jeep was parked in front. Behind the house he could see the stationary blades of the wind generator. Rising slowly, he made his move and began marching toward the house. At the east door to the kitchen, he paused to open the pack and find the rubber workshop gloves and put them on. Next he reached up and ran a hand over the top of the sill and found the door key held in place by a small clip. Hightower removed it, unlocked the door, and put it back in the clip. There were no alarms as he recalled, but he paused nonetheless, waiting for nearly a minute.

Stepping inside, he lowered the pack to the floor and looked immediately toward the doorway of the master bedroom. He decided to look there last. Walking to the desk in the living room he opened both drawers, and then each of the three drawers of the wooden file cabinet. From there he went to every room where a safe might be hidden. He found nothing and then looked for doors or access to the basement Lone Wolf had mentioned. He found nothing obvious.

Finally, he walked into the master bedroom closet and flipped on the light, surprised that it was fairly large. On the wooden floor was an area rug that covered most of it. Clothes hung on either side of the longer walls, with shelves above each, with a floor shelf at the far end for shoes and boots. But no doorway to a basement.

Lone Wolf had told the conservator that the ledger had been in his *safe*, and he had mentioned a basement. There was only one possibility—it was hidden. Hightower looked under the hanging clothes on each side for seams in the wall. There was nothing obvious. The wall to his left was the wall of the living room and the wall to the right was the shared wall with the bathroom. On the other side of the wall behind the floor shelves was the closet to the spare bedroom.

Only one other possibility came to mind; the room where the storage batteries for the solar panels and wind generator were housed. Hightower quickly exited the house and hurried to the ground level door next to the north foundation wall. It was padlocked. An image came to mind and he hurried back into the house, taking the flat key hanging on a nail next to the kitchen door. It opened the padlock, but that only led to further disappointment.

In the narrow partial basement were four green-colored batteries the size of large trunks, and nothing more.

Back inside the house he did one more walk around because he could think of nothing else to do. He even checked the narrow broom closet next to the kitchen sink. Dejectedly he walked back into the master bedroom closet, worrying that he had been in the house too long. He glanced around in desperation. On an impulse he reached down and pulled up the edge of the rug and saw a seam running perpendicular to the floorboards. His heart raced. Walking to the other end, he lifted it and saw another seam. Leaning down and looking closely at one end of the seam, he suddenly noticed that the space between the floorboards leading to the other seam was slightly wider. Excitedly, he turned and checked the opposite end of the seam and saw the same kind of space. His heart rate increased.

This had to be some kind of opening. He guessed it measured three feet by seven feet. And there had to be a way, a mechanism, a switch, or handle that opened it.

Though he pulled back the edges of the rug, he saw nothing that might be a handle. He pushed on the edges of both seams, but nothing happened. Standing next to the seam, he lifted a foot and stamped on the inner edge of the seam. Nothing. He tried the other end. Same result

Frustration mounted. Mere feet below him was likely the safe Lone Wolf had mentioned, with the Little Big Horn gun in it, and he couldn't get to it.

Frustration increased his desperation, pushed by the thought of something worth millions of dollars literally within reach. Surely there had to be heavy tools in Lone Wolf's barn, an axe or a heavy wedge of some kind.

Hightower shook his head. "No, no," he breathed. "We can't go there." He pulled himself back from the brink of desperation-fueled foolishness. Even if he did manage to open this obvious trap door and there was indeed a safe down there, it would be locked. And if the safe could be opened, that damn pistol might not be there.

He took a deep breath to clear his head.

"You've narrowed it down, old boy," he said to himself. "That's something."

Carefully he pulled the rug back into place. It was time to leave while his luck was still holding. Now, at least, he had credible information for Antonio Caruth.

Nonetheless, he allowed himself a final gesture, banging his fist on the floor, the grimace on his face matching his frustration.

After assuring himself that everything in the house was in place, he picked up his bag and exited through the kitchen door. Outside he practically sprinted to the cover of the shrubbery south of the house. After stopping to catch his breath, he looked at the terrain to the southeast, not looking forward to the three-mile hike to his car.

An hour later he rested on the bank of a dry creek as he finished off a bottle of water. There was a lot at stake, a lot he was putting on the line. Perhaps getting his hands on the Little Bighorn pistol was a foolish idea, nothing more than a fool's dream. And he had given into that foolish dream by hiring Caruth. He was dealing with people, situations, and circumstances that were unpredictable. He had little or no control over them. Perhaps it was time to ride off into the sunset.

Yet—six to fifteen million dollars. He sighed and exhaled sharply, blowing out his frustration. Maybe, just maybe, he didn't have to figure it out the way Caruth would. After all, he had survived to this point by his own wits and his own schemes. He had learned a lot from his time in the shadows and that was his strength.

One thing was in his favor. Lone Wolf didn't know that he knew about the pistol.

## FORTY-FIVE

Patrolman Singer rubbed his eyes and leaned back for a moment from the worktable in the conference room. A tiny spark of anticipation flared. After countless hours of looking at tire websites and printouts of tires and tread designs, he had found a possible match to the partial tread mark from Flat Butte Dam.

Lifting the magnifying glass again he compared the side-by-side images—the photo of the partial tread and the printout from a tire company website. It was a match. He would bet his next paycheck on it. A few moments later he knocked on Lieutenant Primault's door and entered when the CI answered.

"From the look on your face, you must have good news," Primault said.

"I'm hopeful, sir, because I found a match for that partial tread."

"Show me."

Singer placed the photo and the printout side by side on the CI's desk pad and pointed to the areas he had circled on each. "You tell me, sir," he said, handing over the magnifying glass.

Primault studied the images for nearly a minute, comparing the tread designs, and finally leaned back. "Hey, I'm with you, Jason. Looks like a match to me. I guess our next step is to find the real tire with that tread and the car it's on."

"Well, here's what I know, sir. We know the axle width of the car that made the tracks is a midsize General Motors vehicle. The tire brand is domestic and most of their customers are car makers, and they sell to General Motors. So that tire brand is on cars and light pickups as they roll off the assembly line."

"Then what happens?"

"Well, from what I've read a certain number of cars are designated for fleet sales."

"Okay, you mean to places or companies that buy cars in lots," Primault assumed.

"Right. You know, like car rental companies, federal and state governments, schools, and so on."

"And do we know specifically who bought such vehicles around here?"

"Well, I've identified all the organizations in our area that are fleet buyers. BIA and IHS get their vehicles through GSA—General Services Administration—which is a fleet buyer. Our department vehicles are GSA. The other fleet buyers here are the rural electric co-op, the Cold River and Kincaid County school districts, St. Ignatius Indian School, and Smokey River University."

"Really? What kind do they buy?"

"I'm not sure. That's my next step, to talk to people at the schools and the university."

Primault nodded slowly, his gaze shifting to the images on his desk. "Well, tell you what, the obvious connection here is SRU." He glanced at his watch. "Maybe it's reaching a bit, at this point, but I think you and I start there and go talk to their transportation department."

Fred White Horse, the Smokey River University Transportation Director looked up and asked the two men at his door, "Something I can help you with?"

Lieutenant Justin Primault showed his badge and handed White Horse a business card. "I hope so, Mr. White Horse. I'm Justin Primault and this is Patrolman Singer. We have a few questions if you don't mind."

White Horse pointed at the gray chairs against the wall. "Sure, come in and have a seat." He looked expectantly at the two officers.

"I'll get to the point," Primault said. "Does the university buy fleet vehicles?"

"Yeah, we do."

"Okay, what make?"

"Ford vans and trucks and Chevrolet sedans."

"Chevrolet sedans," Primault repeated "Are they midsize?"

"Yeah, Malibus."

"How many do you buy at a time? Of the Chevrolets, I mean."

"Not that many, only six the last time. That was last year, nothing this year. We won't replace those for another three years."

"Where are those vehicles now?"

"They're assigned to department heads so if they're not on campus they're probably being used. There is one in the shop, brought in for maintenance."

"What kind of maintenance?"

"Oil change, tire rotation if necessary. Just routine stuff."

"Who drives the car you're talking about?"

White Horse looked at the tag on the car's key and checked it with a number on a large bulletin board. "Dr. Roger Carter, math department."

Primault nodded. "I see. We're looking for a particular vehicle with a certain brand of tires on it. We have photos we want to compare to tires on the vehicles. Do you mind if we have a look at the one here?"

White Horse picked up the car's key. "No, not at all. It's in the shop." He rose and reached for the keys.

"No," Primault said. "We don't need the keys. At least not yet."

White Horse led them out through a door into the main garage, and past two vans to a dark gray car. Then he stood back as the officers measured the axle width with a tape measure, and then did a side-by-side comparison to photographs from the file to each of the tires.

When they finished, the CI approached White Horse. "Do all the Malibus have the same brand of tires?"

White Horse thought for a second. "I think so."

Primault stared at the car. "Mr. White Horse, we're investigating the murder of Arlo High Crane, and we'll need to check the tires on all the other cars, as soon as we can. We could get a search warrant."

"I don't think that will be necessary," White Horse said. "I'll ask my boss. We should be able to get the other five cars in here. I'm guessing you want to do that right away."

"We'd sure appreciate it. One last question: is Dr. Carter non-Native?"

"Yeah, he is."

# FORTY-SIX

Hightower stared at the text on his phone:

> *Turned south to Cold River.*
> *Will contact you later.*
> *Will see to your problem first.*
> *Delete this text.*

Caruth was here.

Hightower sat silently for several long moments staring at the opposite wall. He shook his head and went back to the text.

Rising from the chair at his table, he slowly surveyed what he could see of his house, trying at the same time to shake off the tightness in his chest. The situation had taken an unexpected turn. Suddenly Caruth was here, somewhere. That was slightly favorable.

Looking down at his phone he typed out a text:

> *Great. Solid indication item you seek is in a SAFE*
> *kept in basement room accessed through floor of*
> *master bedroom closet in Lone Wolf house. Location*
> *of latch to open floor entry unknown.*

Hightower knew Caruth would figure out the seams in the closet floor, and he wouldn't have the slightest qualm about using whatever means, whether force or finesse, to open whatever door or entryway was there.

With a sigh and a tiny spark of hope renewed, he pressed Send.

# FORTY-SEVEN

Primault turned into the narrow parking lot at the Kincaid County Sheriff's office at the east edge of Kincaid. Not surprisingly only a deputy was in the small office.

"Lieutenant Primault," the young man said, rising from a small desk to greet Primault and Singer. "What brings you to our little corner of the world?"

Primault shook hands with the young man. "A situation has come up and we need your help, Kenneth."

"What's up?" Kenneth Blaine asked.

"We would like to talk to a man by the name of Roger Carter in connection with our investigation into a homicide. He's *wasicu* and an SRU faculty member."

Blaine nodded. "Got it. Josh Lytle is off today," he said, referring to the other deputy. "The sheriff is checking into a possible horse theft. Let me check with him, but I don't think he would mind if I gave you a hand."

A couple of minutes later Deputy Blaine followed Primault and Singer back to the university campus. After presenting themselves to a rather confused secretary in the Math and Science Building, they followed her direction and found a small office at the end of a hallway. In it sat a small man with a thatch of white hair and glasses perched precariously at the end of his thin nose. Turning his intense gaze away from the computer screen, his expression turned to confusion at the sight of three strange men, one in uniform and all wearing side arms.

"Yes?" he said, obviously surprised and puzzled.

"Dr. Carter," Primault said courteously. "I'm Justin Primault with the tribal police. This is Patrolman Singer, and Deputy Blaine with the Kincaid County sheriff's office."

Carter turned in his swivel office chair, a flicker of recognition in his eyes as he glanced at Blaine. "What can I do for you, gentlemen?" he asked, rising slowly from his chair. "Ah, I'm afraid there's only two chairs."

"No worries, sir," Primault assured him. "Let me get to the point. Patrolman Singer and I are investigating the murder of Arlo High Crane."

"I see."

"And, sir, since you're not a tribal member, Deputy Blaine is here with us."

"Of course. How can I help?"

"A few questions, sir. One is a necessary formality, the others, not so much. Can you tell us where you were on May sixteenth?"

Carter glanced at a large calendar above his desk, marked profusely in red and blue. "Here, on campus. I had a class in the morning and one in the evening."

"Thank you," Primault said, writing in his notebook. "Second question, sir. Do you have a university vehicle assigned to you?"

"Yes, a Chevrolet Malibu."

"Do you use it often?"

Carter shook his head. "Once or twice a week usually. It's parked in the transportation garage, or in their yard, I think."

"Does anyone else ever use it?"

Carter shook his head again. "Not usually, but's it's possible, I guess."

Primault looked up from his notebook. "Thank you, Dr. Carter. Sorry to have disturbed you."

"Of course. How goes your investigation? I knew that young man. He was in one of my classes a few years ago."

"Ah, we're doing our best. No suspects, yet. Thank you, again."

Primault turned to Deputy Blaine after they reached the parking lot. "Hey, thanks, Ken."

Blaine nodded toward the Math and Science Building. "How did that old man figure in your investigation?"

"Someone might have used his car to transport the victim out to Flat Creek Dam."

"Oh, shit. But it wasn't Mr. Carter."

"Right, it wasn't him. But it does mean it was someone who had access to it."

"Maybe someone in the transportation department," suggested Singer.

Primault nodded. "So that's our next task. As long as we're here, we need to talk to Mr. White Horse and get a list of everyone who works there."

He glanced down at his phone's screen as an incoming call buzzed in and answered. "This is Primault."

"Hello, this is Fred White Horse. My boss just gave me the go ahead to get all those cars in today. They're all on campus so it shouldn't take long."

"Wonderful! Thank you, Mr. White Horse."

## FORTY-EIGHT

Gavin was filling the horse tank with water when Primault's call came. "Good evening," he answered, glancing at the position of the sun over the western horizon. The man was working late since the caller ID showed the police station number.

"Good evening, Gavin," the CI responded. "If you don't mind I have a question regarding our investigation."

"Sure."

"Thanks. I know what time Arlo sent you the email on the evening of May sixteenth, but my notes don't show where he might have sent it from. Just trying to nail it down."

"Right. At 5:30 he was still in the building, according to the time stamp on his email. And when Ramona talked to him before she left, he was in his study room."

"Study room?"

"Yeah, Since Arlo was a TA, a teaching assistant, he was assigned a study room, a small office on the first floor in the Lakota Studies Building. That's where he did his work, wrote reports, and so on. It's still locked, as far as I know. Ramona will know."

"Got it. We need to see what's on that computer. There's something else," he said. "I haven't had time to process everything that's gone down today. But the tire tracks do point to Dr. Carter's car. We need to confirm that and have a look at the tires on the five other Chevrolet Malibus."

"Well, I don't disagree with you," Gavin replied. "But what about the implication raised by the tire treads, since it wasn't Roger Carter?"

"Well, whoever put that young man in that trunk had to be physically capable, or crazy, or desperate enough to do that, and more than likely pointing a gun."

"Yeah," Gavin agreed, "there are over three hundred people who work for the university, not to mention about twelve hundred students, and most of us don't fit those criteria. But even that doesn't narrow it down enough. I think it has to be someone who knew Arlo."

"Right, I agree. If you have other thoughts I'd love to know them. Can you spare some time in the next day or two?"

Gavin was a bit surprised by the CI's question. "Sure. Sometimes I have lunch at the Bistro in Kincaid."

"Damn, I have a training session over the noon hour tomorrow. How about the day after?"

"Listen, I'm driving out to Coyote Butte this evening. My uncle Andrew No Horn is camped out there. He's a *wapiya wicasa* (medicine man) and he's got a couple young men on the hill. You're welcome to join me."

"Where's Coyote Butte?"

"Fifteen miles west of Cold River. We can meet at Edna's Restaurant, and you can ride with me from there."

"That works," Primault decided. "I'll let my wife know and I'll head out in about five minutes."

Gavin tossed a couple of armloads of firewood into the truck for his uncle's campfire. Less than two miles out on the way to Coyote Butte, Primault put on his investigator's cap.

"Patrolman Singer and I have eliminated most of Arlo's friends and relatives as suspects. They all have confirmed alibis for the evening and night of May sixteenth. We'll concentrate on his friends and acquaintances at SRU next."

Gavin nodded as he kept his eyes on the road. "Well, there are six staff members in Lakota Studies, and there are two classes that Arlo helped to teach—one for Denise Archambault and one for Caleb Hightower. I'm guessing that's nearly thirty students."

"Is Denise Archambault one of the staff members?"

"She is—an instructor. If you talk to Ramona, the department secretary, she'll have the class schedule. I mention that because a lot of our classes are in the evening."

Primault jotted in his notebook. "Thanks. So, anyone teaching an evening class on the sixteenth can probably be crossed off the list."

"Right. I know all those people, except for most of the students, and some better than others. All of them are good people," Gavin said.

"Is that a character reference?" Primault wondered.

"Not officially, just an observation for what it's worth," Gavin clarified. "Listen, I don't think any of us are given to assessing our friends or colleagues. Nevertheless, I've had some level or extent of interaction over several years with all of them, including a few of the students, and I'm having a hard time thinking there's a killer among us."

Primault nodded thoughtfully.

"But, having said that," Gavin went on, "I know there's a high probability that one of us is. I don't envy you your task."

"You're right. A high percentage of murders are done by someone known to the victim," Primault pointed out. "The difficultly lies in the fact that the reason for murder varies widely—jealousy, hate, greed, fear, anger, unrequited love, childhood trauma, self-preservation, and even accidents."

"And what are the odds that the murderer is the one least expected?"

"Probably high."

Gavin chuckled. "Yeah? But that probably describes the majority of us, doesn't it?"

"Unfortunately, yes."

A familiar curve appeared in the growing dusk. Gavin slowed for the turn to Coyote Butte and followed the pasture trail for two miles until the butte loomed above the prairie.

Even on a warm evening Andrew No Horn had a fire burning. The medicine man poured coffee after inviting his guests to sit. It was the first time Justin Primault had ever used a traditional Lakota chair. He was impressed.

He also realized that within seconds of meeting Andrew No Horn, he had been thoroughly assessed, beginning with the handshake. There was intensity in the old man's gaze, although it lasted for only a moment. White people used the phrase "old school" for anyone who was a throwback to an earlier time or thinking or behavior. Native people sometimes used the world "traditional." Primault sensed that the medicine man fit both those descriptions. He had no idea of the man's age in years, but he was still strong, evident in the strength of his grip and in the way he carried himself. He was tall, like his nephew Gavin, and wiry. That he was a medicine man, a traditional healer, wasn't readily discernible in his appearance. It never was, not with the genuine healers. Yet this old man had an essence that as yet Primault couldn't label.

"So, this is the young man that sees what the eagle sees," Andrew said, smiling, and pointing toward the sky.

Primault was taken aback, and even Gavin seemed a little puzzled. A second later the CI realized what Andrew No Horn was referring to—the drone. How the heck did he know that? No one but Jason Singer and Ben Avery knew about the drone flying above Flat Butte Dam. He nodded, smiling nervously.

"Yeah," he admitted. "That's me." He sheepishly glanced at Gavin. "I used a drone a couple of weeks back, checking tracks out at Flat Butte Dam. There's nothing like a bird's eye view."

Gavin nodded. "*Leksi*," he said, "Justin made a breakthrough in his investigation into Arlo's murder."

Andrew No Horn leveled an expectant gaze at the CI.

"Ah, yeah," Primault said. "We know that the young man was taken out to Flat Butte Dam. And now we might have identified the car that probably took him out there. It's a university car. Its tire treads match the photographs of tracks made out at the dam on the trail around the east side of the water."

Andrew No Horn sipped his coffee and nodded, fixing a narrow gaze at the fire. "That's good," he said, after a moment. "Now you're looking for the person who was driving it and took Arlo out there, in the dark."

Primault shot a quick glance at Gavin and then turned to the medicine man. "Well, according to the SRU transportation department, the car in question is assigned to a man named Dr. Roger Carter. But we know he isn't Arlo High Crane's murderer." He paused. "You knew it was dark when Arlo was taken out to Flat Butte Dam?"

Andrew No Horn nodded. "Bad things are done in the dark."

"Makes sense," Primault allowed. "Whoever used that car to transport that young man out to Flat Butte didn't want to be noticed. In any case, there's still a murderer on the loose, and maybe he, or she, has left the reservation by now."

Andrew No Horn shook his head. "I don't think so."

After a long moment of silence, Gavin leaned forward. "Why do you say that *Leksi?*"

"Why was that young man killed?"

Gavin glanced at Primault. "We don't know that, yet *Leksi.*"

Andrew No Horn nodded, keeping his gaze on the undulating flames in the fire pit. "When you know that, you will know who killed him."

The sound of an approaching vehicle ended the conversation as the old man looked south and stood from his chair. Primault and Gavin stood as well. Primault reached out his hand to Andrew. "Thank you, Grandfather," he said, using the title of respect.

"Good to meet you, Grandson," Andrew replied. "Tell me this. What is the one thing that is the hardest for us to see?"

Genuinely puzzled at the question, Primault glanced at Gavin before he shook his head. "I don't know."

"The nose on our face," Andrew said, a hint of a smile in his eyes.

## FORTY-NINE

Just after nine that evening Justin Primault walked into the department's conference room and took a seat. Seconds later Ben Avery strode in the room, outright curiosity etched on his face.

"Thanks for making some time for me, Chief," Primault said.

"No problem," Avery said, taking a seat. "I need to talk to Captain White Bear and a couple patrolmen on the second shift anyway. What's on your mind?"

"Just wanted to bring you up to speed about the High Crane investigation."

"Okay. Last I heard you spoke with people on the SRU campus."

"Right. Jason Singer matched tire treads to the partial tread mark we found at Flat Butte Dam. After further research he found out that the Chevrolet Malibus purchased by the university come off the assembly line with those particular tires on. At this point I don't know yet if all six cars have the same tires, but we verified that the one assigned to a Dr. Carter is a match."

"Damn. So, if that car went out to Flat Butte Dam on May sixteenth, who was driving it?"

"Can't verify that yet, sir. However, we've eliminated Dr. Carter. He had a class that evening."

Avery was surprised. "Damn! Well, then that sort of suggests someone at the university. Makes sense though, since young Arlo was there as an intern."

"And someone there might have had a reason to kill him."

"Sure, and if we figure that out, then we know who it was."

Primault chuckled. "That's what someone else suggested. And beyond that, after talking to Dr. Carter earlier today, I know the suspect could turn out to be non-Native, and thereby within federal jurisdiction."

"Of course. Well, it might be helpful if the feds would get involved."

Primault shook his head in disgust. "It would be so much easier if tribes could exercise sovereignty when it comes to major crimes and non-Native law breakers on the rez. That way we could investigate, charge, indict, and put non-Natives on trial."

"I'm afraid that's never going to happen," the Chief said. "You know the law. Felonies are handled on the federal level, ever since the Major Crimes Act of 1885. And white on Indian felonies are also handled by the feds. Another form of white privilege."

"Sure, sure, a double standard that is blatantly paternalistic. If a tribal member assaults or kills a non-Native person off reservation, he gets tried in state or county courts and gets sent to a state penitentiary. If it's the other way around, the federal government steps in and we're lucky if the white perpetrator even gets charged for a crime against one of us."

"It's a goddamn stacked deck," Avery agreed angrily.

"Well, let's say for the sake of argument that we do establish a white person as a suspect. How helpful would the FBI be then?"

"I see your point," Avery said. "Tell you what, here's a thought since they're not paying attention to this case. Let's just keep working it and wherever the evidence might lead, let's build a rock-solid case and then put it in front of the feds."

"Okay. I can live with that."

"So, let's kick this into high gear and see where any trail of evidence leads, or doesn't.

Primault nodded. "Right. We start with checking out those cars tomorrow."

"Sounds good. Anything else?"

"Yeah, I spent a couple hours with Dr. Lone Wolf and met his uncle, Andrew No Horn. The adjective that comes to mind regarding both is formidable. What do you know about them?"

Avery put his elbows on the table and folded his hands. "Well, Gavin Lone Wolf has a PhD, and has a twin brother, Gerard, also a PhD. Their sister, Loren Hale, is director of nursing at the hospital. Gavin is a professor and part-time big game hunting guide. He's into primitive bows and arrows, and he's skilled in martial arts. Judo. He holds a fifth-degree black belt."

"Damn. Not the kind of guy you'd want to piss off. What about his uncle?"

"Ah, other than being a medicine man, he was a government surveyor until he retired. He was in the Marine Corps, a sergeant in the infantry, I think. Went to Vietnam."

"More than meets the eye, both of them."

"Yeah, but here's what else you should know. They're not about what they are in the outside world. As far as I can see, they are about who and what they are as Lakota people. Both speak the language fluently. Lakota people respect them for that, and for the traditional values they live by: generosity, compassion, respect, and humility. We need more people like that in any tribe. Why do you ask?"

"Just wanted to know," Primault said. "Didn't want to ask them."

# FIFTY

Just after noon a green 2002 Ford Ranger pickup pulled up to the front of the Riverfront Motel in Pierre. Hightower looked over at the driver.

"Hey, Brady, thanks for the ride. You saved my ass, big time, my friend."

Brady Thomas, who looked much younger than twenty-six, waved off the money the older man offered. "No, no, you keep it. You'll need it to get a new ride."

Hightower reached over and stuffed the bills into Thomas's shirt pocket. "I've got enough for that," he said. "You drove sixty miles just to pick me up."

"Thanks! So, what are you going to do about your old Dodge? Seems a shame to leave it out in that pasture. If you want, I can borrow my boss's one-ton dually and pull it back to your place."

"No, no," Hightower insisted. "Not your worry. I'm thinking of getting a three-quarter-ton truck, so if it comes to that, I'll haul that worn out Dodge to the junkyard, blown transmission and all."

"Okay, okay. Say, when do you suppose we can do some shootin' at the black powder range again? We haven't done that in a while. Had a chance to practice with that black powder pistol, by the way?"

"Ah, hey, not too much, lately. I might take a trip, so that'll put a lot of things on hold. It won't be soon, but I'll let you know."

Thomas looked disappointed. "Oh, okay." He reached out a hand. "Hey, good on ya, if I don't see you for a while."

"Same to you, young man. Thanks again."

By nine o'clock, as dusk was yielding to night, Hightower was on the bed in the motel on his back, grinning up at the ceiling. The partially eaten pizza sat on the credenza near the flat-screen television. He had a reason to grin.

He had just finished a long talk with his friend Del Conway.

"Hey, I got some more news for you about that there pistol of yours," Conway had told him. "I talked to several brokers who specialize in old guns. They all say that a cavalry pistol from the Little Bighorn, if it's, ah, what's that word—oh, if it's authenticated—it damn well could start a bidding war. I mean, high double-digit millions!"

High double-digit millions, and he had probably been within mere feet of it. He doubled both fists in frustration. Now he had to put his faith in Antonio Caruth.

# FIFTY-ONE

A man pulled up to the gas pumps at the only convenience store in Cold River, three blocks north of Edna's Restaurant. He stepped out of the new Chevrolet midsize SUV and stretched while he did a quick visual assessment. Another car, an older sedan, was at the other set of pumps. A young Native man was pumping gas but paid no attention to the driver of the Chevy. Several vehicles were parked around the store, an assortment of old pickup trucks, a couple of newer sedans, and SUVs of various sizes and colors. A typical scene, the man concluded.

Hands in his pockets, he walked slowly toward the store, nodding affably to a couple of young Native men who emerged, engaged in an earnest conversation. At the door he stepped aside for an old Native woman and followed her inside, then glanced around at the interior before he went to the coolers for a bottle of water. After that he got in line for the cash register.

To a casual observer the man's age was hard to determine, probably in his early forties, if anyone were to hazard a guess. His face was pleasant, though not handsome, and he wore a friendly expression along with a five o-clock shadow. The clothes he wore were not gaudy, but neither were they nondescript—dark blue designer brand cargo pants, a gray shirt with a button-down collar, and expensive sneakers.

He made it to the counter and put down the bottle of water. "This and twenty-five on pump three," he said, pulling out cash from his pocket. The young cashier, a pretty young Native woman smiled at him and glanced out the window. After ringing up his purchase she returned his change and a receipt.

"Thank you," she said. "Have a good day."

"Thanks," the man replied, "you, too." He stopped in mid turn. "Oh, do you happen to know how to get out to Gavin Lone Wolf's residence? I know it's along the Little White River, but I don't know the exact location. I'm a friend of his."

The young woman shook her head. "I don't," she replied, and pointed toward another part of the store. "Harriet," she called out. "Do you know where Gavin Lone Wolf's place is?"

"Yeah, I do," a voice called out.

The man nodded toward the cashier and walked toward the voice. "I'm here for a short visit," he explained. "I've never been to his new place."

Harriet was the cook behind the food counter, a close-to-middle-age pale redhead with a smoker's voice. "Ah, take Highway 33 west, it's at the south end of town. After the bridge take a left on Ring Thunder Road. After about, oh, seven miles, and it's all gravel, look for a small stock dam on the right side. Just past that on the left is his mailbox. There's a road by that mailbox, a dirt road. It'll take you to his place."

"Hey," the man said, smiling. "Thanks, Harriet."

Harriet nodded politely and watched him leave the building. Walking to the large picture window near the counter, she saw him at the gas pump and got a look at his car. Judging from his accent, he wasn't from these parts. Hurrying to the small galley where she cooked, Harriet found her cell phone. "Eunice," she called to the girl at the till. "Can you find Gavin Lone Wolf's phone number? It should be in the book."

"Okay, just a second," the girl replied. Finding the regional phone book, she flipped through the pages and found it under Cold River.

At the pump, the man put in the nozzle and started the gas flowing. This was the middle of nowhere, as far as he was concerned. Miles and miles of grassy hills and flats south of the interstate highway, and then a small town pops up out of nowhere. And people actually lived here, mostly Natives or Indians as Hightower had said. He'd never seen a real Indian before. They looked nothing like the ones in the movies.

Harriet listened to the rings and watched out the front window for the man's car to turn onto the highway. Gavin's outgoing message came on.

"Gavin, it's Harriet Keyes, at Rabbit Run. Hey, listen, I just gave some guy directions to your house because he said he was a friend of yours, and now I'm—ah, sort of second-guessing myself. He's a white guy, forty-ish, maybe. Looks like he's in good shape, has dark hair, and eastern accent, like New York, I think. I didn't get his name. Ah, just a second—Eunice, what's that white guy driving, the one who was just in here? Okay, thanks. Eunice says he's driving a mid-size Chevy SUV, dark blue. So, I hope you have a friend like that. Bye."

Antonio Caruth finished gassing up his rental car and put back the nozzle. There was no highway heading west on the north end of town, where he had come in. According to that woman's directions Highway 33 was on the south end. Starting up the car he eased away to the highway, turned left, and immediately saw the sign for Highway 33.

He was glad he had opted to rent a four-wheel-drive vehicle, given the terrain in this interesting landscape. On the passenger seat were maps, one highway and one topographical. Antonio was thorough and many of his jobs required going into territory and areas new to him, so he had learned to research—and ask questions.

He had not rented a GPS unit because they could be traced. But thanks to Hightower's thorough directions and a question at the right time, he had zeroed in on Lone Wolf's residence. He had had to ask for directions. Normally he would not leave any type of trail behind because unobtrusiveness was a necessity in his line of work. But now he knew where he was going. And twenty percent of six to twelve million dollars was a good payoff for finding and taking a gun. He'd heard about that battle, or read about it somewhere, the Battle of the Little Bighorn. His research revealed the battle was important. General George Armstrong Custer had gotten himself bumped off by Indians like those around here. Funny thing though, these Indians looked more like beggars than General-killers. Except for the girl at the counter—she was a looker.

He found the sign for Highway 33 and glanced at it as he stayed on Highway 83 and drove south. It was rough country out here and desolate. He drove along, wondering what would bring people to actually live out here. He couldn't wait to finish his job and leave. This was no place to spend any amount of time.

And what the hell was *stock dam?*

# FIFTY-TWO

A gleaming white four-passenger pickup turned off of Sage Meadow Road four miles west of Agency Village, and onto a little used pasture trail that eventually led to an old barn surrounded by tall grass. Stopping in front of weathered and faded double doors, one hanging off its rusty top hinge, the engine shut off and a tall man stepped out of the vehicle. After carefully perusing the surroundings, nothing more than thickets of trees and shrubs, he turned and walked through the open door. It had been months since he had been here.

Pausing just inside for a moment, he waited until his eyes adjusted to the dim interior and moved away from the door. In another moment he saw the figure in a hoodie hidden in deep shadow and sitting on a box near an old stall.

"We haven't met here in a while," the tall man commented. The figure stood from the box and pushed the hoodie back revealing a pale narrow face with blue eyes. It wasn't the person the tall man was expecting to see. His initial confusion and surprise were swept away by shock when he saw the semi-automatic pistol with a sound suppressor in the hoodie man's hand as it came up and pointed at him. He gasped involuntarily.

The tall man's voice went up an octave, his eyes wide with shock and fear. "Wait a minute! What is this? Who are you?"

"I ask the questions," Hoodie replied tersely in a clipped accent. "You give the answers. First, put your hands on top of your head, now!"

The tall man complied.

"Where is the information hidden? Who has it?"

"I—I don't know what you're talking about!"

POP!

A round traveling at eleven hundred and fifty feet per second tore through the tall man's flexed bicep, slicing through fabric, skin, and muscle, sucking out blood in its wake, hardly slowing as it exited through the barn door. Pain erupted a second later, and a scream.

"AHH!!"

"Keep your hands on your head!"

The tall man's arm trembled in pain and shock as he struggled to keep his bleeding arm up.

"Now, I ask again. Where is the information? Who has it? You know what I'm talking about! You've been blackmailing a friend of mine to the tune of two thousand dollars a month. I want to know who else has the information you've been using to fleece him. No answer or a wrong answer will cost you a kneecap!" The pistol moved down, pointing at the tall man's knee.

"It's—no one has it. No one has it! Please, I was just bluffing!"

"Really?"

"Yeah, yeah!"

The pistol came up, this time aimed at the tall man's forehead. "All these years you've been playing a bluff?"

"Yeah, yeah! I swear!"

"If you're lying your wife and son will die. I know where you live. I know where your wife works. I know she drives a dark green sedan."

"What? No!"

"Who has the information? Who did you tell?"

"No one, I didn't tell anyone!"

The hoodie man held the gun unwaveringly, his cold gaze scouring the tall man's face as it visibly drained of color, his breathing ragged. Blood was rapidly staining his right shirt sleeve.

"Okay, I believe you."

The gun popped again, and a dark hole appeared instantaneously in the middle of the tall man's forehead at the same second the back of his head erupted with a spray of bone and brains. For a split second, the tall man was bizarrely frozen in place before his legs folded and his body crumpled to the dirt.

The man in the hoodie calmly removed the suppressor and slipped it into a sleeve on the black belt holster he wore. He holstered the semi-automatic and bent to find the two spent cartridges and put them in his right trouser pocket. Putting on rubber gloves, he searched the dead man's pockets until he found a cell phone and expertly disassembled it, taking out the SIM card and snapping into pieces and then smashing the battery.

Walking forward he opened the two weathered gray doors and looked cautiously around. Satisfied that other people were not in the area, he walked to the truck. Climbing into the cab, he started the engine and drove the vehicle into the barn, parking over the body on the floor. Climbing out of the cab, Hoodie closed the doors and walked away from the barn, disappearing into a thicket of chokecherry shrubs.

# FIFTY-THREE

Primault parked his cruiser in front of the office of the SRU maintenance garage at just after 1 p.m. and hurried around to the vehicle yard. The excitement in Patrolman Singer's voice had been unmistakable when he called. In the yard were six gray Chevrolet Malibus and several police officers assisting Singer.

"Over here, sir. I think you need to see this!" Singer called out.

The CI saw a Chevrolet Malibu with its trunk and doors open. Singer was leaning over into the trunk snapping photos with a flash attached to his camera. Primault waited for Singer to finish.

"Find something?" he asked.

"Did we ever," Singer said, pointing to the floor of the trunk.

Primault stepped over, leaned in, and saw two objects; one was a pen covered in a colorful sheath with Lakota designs and the other was a short, tubular object. "That's a pen," he said. "But what's that?" he asked, pointing to the other.

"Well, frankly, I don't know," Singer admitted. "It looks like a—a spool, of some sort. That's my guess."

"These were in the trunk?"

"Affirmative. The pen was jammed up under the weather stripping. The spool, or whatever it is, was in the corner behind the carpet. I couldn't see it at first because the carpet is black. When I pulled the carpet aside to look in the spare tire well, it rolled out. There was nothing in the compartment but a doughnut spare, a small jack, and tire wrench."

Primault leaned in for a close look at the pen. "I've seen those before. It's a pen covered with a porcupine quill sheath. Did you say it was under the weather stripping?"

"Yes, sir." Singer pointed with his pencil to the exact spot. "There, almost like it was placed there deliberately."

"Uh-huh," Primault said. He turned his attention to the short tube. "I've never seen anything like that," he said. "I think it's cardboard."

Singer rolled the short tube, using the eraser end of his pencil, and revealed marks on the surface. "There's a mark there," he pointed out. "I'd say it was made by the pen."

"A mark?"

"Yes, sir. Right there." Singer pointed to it, a mark about two inches long resembling a capital V with a line at the bottom. He stood back up.

"Okay," he said. "Bag them and let's get them to where there's better light and take photos. Anything else?"

"Yes, sir. That," Singer said, pointing to a circular hole in the carpet on the underside of the trunk lid. An obviously cut stub of a wire, barely visible. "That's what's left of the emergency trunk release, I think. To prevent anyone from accidentally being locked in. There should be a small handle of some kind. It's not anywhere in the trunk. We looked, Jake and I," the patrolman added, pointing to a mechanic working nearby.

Primault nodded slowly. "Okay. I want this car roped off and no one touches it. We're taking this vehicle back to our garage to go over inch-by-inch, inside and out. What about the others? Do the tire treads match our photo?"

"All of them have the same tires," Singer replied. "And all their emergency trunk latches are still intact."

"Okay. I want you to get all their mileage logs and the name of the person each car is assigned to."

Primault looked at the one with the broken trunk latch. "Is that Dr. Carter's car?"

Singer nodded. "It is."

"Damn," Primault intoned. "So, who drove it out to Flat Butte Dam?"

Primault stopped off at the transportation office and was not surprised to see the University's facilities director there. "Thanks for helping us out by bringing all those vehicles in," he said.

"Glad we can help," Marshall replied. "Is there anything else we can do?"

Primault shook his head. "I don't think so. We've narrowed it down to one car. I do want to have a look at the mileage logs of all the cars. I want to see the entries for May sixteenth, especially for Carter's. Then you can have them back."

"Carter's?" Marshall was perplexed.

"Dr. Carter is not a suspect," Primault declared. "Someone probably used his car to haul Arlo High Crane out to Flat Butte Dam."

Marshall nodded, somewhat taken aback.

Thirty minutes later Primault knocked on Chief Avery's door, and stepped in. Looking up from his computer screen, Avery immediately saw the mixture of excitement and disbelief in the criminal investigator's expression.

Sometime after six, Gavin Lone Wolf parked his truck next to the Jeep and stepped down, though he didn't immediately go into the house. He took a leisurely turn around his yard and then circled the barn, just to do a visual check. Both horses were in the two-acre paddock connected to the barn, grazing peacefully.

Entering the house through the kitchen door off the east deck, he stopped to put water on for tea. As he dropped his pickup keys in the bowl atop the credenza near the front door, he saw the message light on his landline phone blinking slowly. He walked over and pressed Play and heard the message from Harriet Keyes.

As he sat on the chair in his bedroom to slip off his loafers, he was trying to remember who he knew that matched the description Harriet had left—a forty-ish white guy with dark hair and an eastern accent. No one came to mind.

# FIFTY-FOUR

In stocking feet Gavin walked to the stove for the pot to make himself a cup of tea. A bright flash came through the east window of the kitchen as he walked past it and then was gone in a split second. There was nothing in that part of the pasture that should be reflecting the late afternoon sun. A slight shiver went up his back. Hesitating only a second, he walked back into his bedroom to look out the north window. Dancer and Red Wing were a hundred yards north of the barn, standing together and staring intently toward the south. Something had apparently caught their attention. He hurried to his bedroom closet and opened a narrow, hidden door behind the row of hanging shirts. From it he grabbed his Glock 9mm semi-automatic, its holster, and a clip of ammunition.

From the shoe shelf he took a pair of hiking boots and put them on.

He silenced his cell phone and stuck it in his trousers as he crossed the living room. From the peg near the south door, he took the small binoculars and stepped out the west door. He jogged west for nearly fifty yards, into a gully, and then south towards the river. As long as he stayed near the river, he was out of sight of the spot from where the flash had come. At the river he turned east.

Moving quickly through the brush along the river, he stopped for a brief rest, and loaded the pistol, returning it to the clip holster. That flash of light was probably something innocuous, like a piece of glass. But whatever it was, he would know soon.

There was good cover along the river, mostly brush and thickets of chokecherry shrubs and buffalo berry trees. Slowing his pace, he went east at least fifty yards beyond the spot he guessed the flash of light had come from. Squatting between two snake berry shrubs, he pulled up his binoculars and glassed the area to the north. It was all pasture, no trees, and only an occasional patch of low-standing shrubs.

The flash had been bright, for no more than a split second. That kind of intense reflection indicated a highly polished surface, such as aluminum or glass. Furthermore, the sun was low in the sky, suggesting to him that whatever had caught its angle of light was more or less perpendicular, vertical to the ground; thus sending the reflected light through the house window through which he had seen it.

It could have been the bottom of a glass jar or a bottle, or an aluminum can, he admitted to himself. If so, he would be immensely relieved and perhaps feel a bit foolish. But he couldn't dismiss the uneasy feeling in the small of his back, because of the voice message left by Harriet Keyes.

Behind him was the river, and all around him was tall grass and low thickets. If his guess was correct, the origin of the flash was beyond a rise at the ten o'clock position. He would be able to approach it unseen just in case whatever was there had eyes. He stood and moved forward, his feet making only the slightest swish of sound through the grass.

Staying low, he moved steadily, stealthily, eyes on the rise ahead and to his left. He headed to a slightly higher rise about fifty yards west of it. Thirty seconds later he was there and lying prone in a tall clump of grass.

He pulled up his binoculars and immediately saw the profiles of his house and barn. Scanning down in a straight line, he saw the dark outline of a man sitting in a clump of young chokecherry shrubs.

When the man's head turned left, Gavin saw binoculars against his eyes. The lenses had probably reflected the sunlight and caused the flash he saw. Solving that question, however, obviously led to another. Why was this man sitting in his pasture? And was it the man Harriet Keyes had described in her message?

There was only one way to answer those questions. He guessed it was about seventy yards to the sitting man. In the few seconds he had observed him through the glasses, the man had not looked behind him. His attention was focused on Gavin's house. That meant Gavin could walk slowly toward him, weapon ready, and approach within a few yards without the man hearing or seeing him—if he didn't turn around.

Gavin hung the binoculars around his neck and drew his pistol from its holster and slowly pushed back the breech to load a round into the chamber, muffling the click with his hand. Standing slowly, he took a few quick steps to gauge the noise from his movements. He moved forward again, walking at a normal pace, his heart pounding.

Twenty seconds later he was thirty yards closer. Another twenty seconds and he was just beyond ten yards from the man. Incredibly, the man had not once turned to look around. Gavin decided not to push his luck and took a stable shooter's stance, holding his pistol muzzle up and ready.

The man's shoulders were wide and his hips narrow, indicating he was trim and probably physically fit. He wore a dark blue hoodie, and his hair was not overly short or long. To the right of the man's butt was a dark object in the grass—probably a weapon, a firearm. It wasn't a rifle. *At least he's not a sniper,* Gavin thought. But he was also not someone who just happened to be in the neighborhood. Gavin would lay good odds it was the man who had told Harriet Keyes he was a friend.

"Don't move! Slowly put your hands on your head!" Gavin commanded.

Startled, the man's back arched, his head turned to the left, and his hands came up slowly.

Gavin lowered his weapon and pointed it at the man.

"Okay! Okay!" the man said. "I got lost out here, I'm just—."

"On your knees!"

"Okay! Okay!" The man got to his knees.

"Move to your left, now!"

The man complied. A warning bell was going off in Gavin's head. The man had quickly recovered his nerve and was doing nothing to further exacerbate the situation. He shuffled on his knees to the left.

"Stop! Don't move!"

Gavin slowly walked to the object in the grass, a semi-automatic pistol in a leather holster with a sound suppressor in a sleeve. He moved to the right and studied the youngish-looking man, not an ounce of fat on him and certainly not dressed for an outing on the prairie. He regarded Gavin with a hint of curiosity in his blue eyes, and a fair amount of wariness. But he was not panicked.

"Who the hell are you?" Gavin asked

The man did not respond, only stared deliberately at Gavin, an indication that he was not unused to difficult situations.

"Who are you and why are you in my pasture?" Gavin said.

"I'm lost."

"Really. You're well off the beaten path. The road is two miles away. Where were you going?"

"To get help. I ran out of gas."

Gavin recognized an eastern accent. He gazed at the man and considered his options. He had caught a strange white man in his pasture, looking at his house through binoculars. That fact alone was bothersome and had all the earmarks of a big legal headache, especially if he hurt the man in any way.

"South, I was going south."

"Where's your vehicle?"

The man tilted his head slightly toward the north. "Back there, off the road."

Thus far all the man's answers had been vague. Gavin's gaze flicked down to the pistol in the grass and back to the man. And he had a weapon—a third bothersome fact.

"Do you have any form of identification?"

The man nodded. "I do. In my right back pocket. I can get it if you want."

"No," Gavin said. "Don't move, not even a flinch." He moved slowly, circling the man until he was behind him, while keeping his Glock trained. "Face down and put your arms out."

The man complied.

Gavin stepped closer. He could see a square bulge in the man's right rear pocket. Reaching down, he extracted a small wallet, and stepped back a few feet. Opening it, he found a driver's license from New Jersey. The name on it was Antonio Caruth.

"Well, Mister Caruth, you're a long way from home. What the hell are you doing here?"

"Just passing through, my friend, and—as I said—I ran out of gas."

"And that's why you're sitting in my pasture looking at my house through binoculars, with an automatic pistol in your possession. The circumstances don't measure up to your answers." Gavin stepped forward and bent to do a cursory search, feeling for any hidden objects, especially another weapon. He finished by feeling around the man's ankles, the most likely places a weapon could be hidden.

Two facts were gnawing at him: this was the man in Harriet Keyes' voice message, and, according to her, he had asked for directions to his house and told her he was a friend. Why? If there was a legitimate reason, the man would have driven up to the front door and knocked. Gavin decided to err on the side of caution and considered the circumstances.

Ugly legal realities came to mind. A white man shooting an Indian anywhere in this state usually didn't make it to trial. An Indian shooting a white man, even on Indian land and even protecting life and property, was guaranteed life in prison, if not a death sentence. Not that he was planning to shoot the man, but any kind of a legal confrontation between Indians and whites in this state invariably was settled in favor of whites. Nevertheless, he wasn't about to let the man off.

"Turn over and slip off your shoes," he ordered.

"What?"

"Turn over, and slip off your shoes and socks, now!"

The man complied. Gavin kept his Glock pointed at him while he stepped over to pick up the man's holstered weapon.

"On your feet."

Slowly the man rose to his feet.

"Unbuckle your belt and slide your trousers down."

"What?"

"Unbuckle your belt and slide your trousers down, to your ankles."

The man obeyed, his eyes never leaving Gavin, then stood back up, a hint of uncertainty in his eyes.

"Now," he said, coldly. "Turn around and start walking toward my barn. You know where it is."

The man's first few steps were awkward, until he settled into a short, choppy gait to accommodate the restrictive trousers around his ankles. Because of his bare feet he was careful where he stepped.

## FIFTY-FIVE

Gavin bound the man's wrists together behind his back with three heavy-duty zip ties. He searched the trouser pockets and found fifty- and hundred-dollar bills in a silver clip, car keys, and a flip phone.

"Over there," he instructed, pushing him toward the stack of small square alfalfa bales at one end of the barn. After the man awkwardly complied, Gavin sat on a folding stool, facing his prisoner.

This was the man Harriet Keyes had described, down to the eastern accent. But that didn't answer the questions, *Who is he and why was he watching my house?* He holstered his Glock and stared at the man.

The accent indicated New York or New Jersey, and his initial demeanor suggested someone who had survived tough circumstances and probably caused them as well.

Gavin assumed that this man would not volunteer answers, or he would give misleading information. But he did see a bit of uncertainty in his eyes.

"What are you doing in my pasture?" Gavin asked.

The man shook his head, and softly cleared this throat. "I—I just got lost," he said.

"I see. Where were you going?"

"Just for a drive."

"Right. Just going for a drive in your dark blue SUV. Where is it?"

The man's eyes widened. Caruth was silently cussing. *How the fuck did he know the color and make of his car?* Hightower had been straight up with him when he said this guy was no pushover. But he wasn't cussing Hightower. He—Caruth—had clearly screwed up. And who would have guessed the son-of-a-bitch would sneak up on him? *Fuck, what am I gonna do? Cooperate, maybe, and wait for the right moment, an opening of some kind...*

"Just going for a drive, got lost, walked to the middle of a pasture and decided to turn peeping tom," Gavin said, mockingly. "With binoculars and a Sig Sauer semi-automatic, no less, with a sound suppressor. And if I find your vehicle and check the gas gauge, I'm betting it won't be on empty."

Caruth tilted his head and shrugged.

"Bullshit," Gavin said, calmly. "You're not lost. You were given directions to my place. But instead of knocking at my front door, I find you in my pasture looking at my house through binoculars."

Gavin saw the uncertainty intensify in the man's eyes. It was time to apply some pressure, because this man had no legitimate reason to be in his pasture.

"I figure you've been in tough situations, mean streets and all, right? And I'm betting you're a smart guy, too. So, here's what I think I'll do. I'll take all your clothes, bind your ankles and hang you upside down from that beam above your head. A human body can survive up to thirty days without food, but after a mere four days without water, it starts to die. Of course, the human body isn't designed to be upside down, suffocation is inevitable. It gets really painful toward the end, I hear. And there's nothing you can do about it. When you shit it'll run down your back. The only thing you can do is yell and scream, but we're two miles from the nearest road. No one's going to hear you."

Caruth stared at his feet. Fuck, this guy's gonna bury me if I look cross-eyed at him. He's a badass and he ain't taking no shit.

"Well," Gavin continued, "I can see you're not taking me seriously."

Caruth watched as Gavin stood, grabbed a long braided rope hanging from a peg, fashioned a loop at one end and tossed it over the aforementioned beam. Then, pulled out his Glock.

"On your belly, now!"

Caruth complied in a flash. He felt his trousers being pulled off over his feet, then a loop sliding over his ankles and tightening. Before he could protest, he was jerked upward until his head was about a foot above the dirt floor. It was a new experience for him.

Gavin ignored the awkwardly trussed up man, sat on the stool, and took out the flip phone and opened it.

Almost immediately the pressure of the rope around Caruth's ankles became excruciating. "Ah, sir, sir," he rasped, trying to twist his neck and shoulders around to see his captor.

The phone was a throw-away, but it did have Contacts and Call Log icons. There were no numbers in the Contacts and only one in the Call Log.

Gavin recognized the number immediately. He knew it as well as his own. He felt his cheeks growing hot. For a moment, he felt overwhelmed, almost nauseous.

"Well, well," he said, suppressing his shock and confusion. "I see we have a mutual friend. One Dr. Caleb Hightower. What are the odds? Small world, huh?"

Caruth felt the blood rushing to his head and his feet were tingling and starting to feel numb.

"Lo and behold," Gavin continued. "My friend's phone number is on your call log. What's that about?"

"I—I can explain," Caruth rasped.

"I sure hope so, because I'm inclined to just walk away and leave you hanging and come back in a few days to take your body down and give your carcass to the buzzards. You know, I'm betting you're the kind of guy that flies below the radar, on purpose, meaning not many people—with the exception of our mutual friend—know you're out here in the boondocks trying to be a boogeyman. In any case, I think the world would be better off without you."

"Okay, okay! What do you wanna know?"

Gavin took out his own cell phone, brought up the screen and tapped icons until he had the Video function ready. Standing, he pulled the slip knot tied around a pole. Caruth flopped heavily to the ground with a grunt. Grabbing him by the front of his shirt, Gavin yanked him none too gently to a sitting position.

"Get ready for your close-up," he growled. Positioning the stool, he took a seat and touched the screen to start the video recording.

"What's your name and where are you from?"

"Antonio Caruth, from Jersey City."

"Do you know Caleb Hightower?"

"He worked for my dad, years ago, in New Jersey."

"Why are you here?"

His father's voice whispered in Caruth's memory: *It's the cool cucumbers you gotta watch out for. They control their anger like a gun pointed at your head.*

"Caleb Hightower asked me to do a job for him."

"Really? What kind of job?"

"Ah, he—he wanted me to find something for him."

"Find what?"

This is not going to end well. "A—a gun, a pistol."

Gavin had been holding his phone and watching to keep the man centered in frame. He glanced past it, hitting the man with an icy glare.

"What kind of a pistol?" he demanded.

The man's gaze was down. "A six-shot revolver. He said you have one, uh, said it was really old, over a hundred years."

Gavin controlled his surprise. "Okay, let me get this straight. Hightower told you that I have an old, six-shot revolver?"

"Yeah, yeah, that's what he said."

"So, you're here to get that pistol?"

"Yeah."

"Define 'get.'"

"To—find it and take possession—whatever it took, even if it meant getting you out of the way."

"And he gave you directions to my house?"

"Yeah, he said the pistol was likely in your house, below your main closet."

Gavin felt his face growing flush. He stopped the video and gazed angrily at the trussed-up man naked from the waist down. But he wasn't angry at him. He was reacting to the man's words. How did Caleb Hightower know about the safe room? He had never mentioned it to him, much less shown him where it was.

"What was the plan after you acquired the pistol?"

"To meet Hightower, give him the pistol, and work out the arrangement for him to pay me."

"Where?"

"Wherever was convenient."

"And you contact him by phone?"

"Yeah, by text only."

Gavin glared at the man, but his growing anger was with Hightower. A shiver suddenly went up his back.

*It will bring him to you,* Uncle Andrew had said.

Was he looking at Arlo High Crane's killer? That was certainly an implication, but he had an immediate problem: what to do with this man.

"One last question. Where's your vehicle?"

"East, about a mile from here. I parked it in some bushes."

Half an hour later Caruth was sitting on the floor in the center horse stall, his back against the wall, totally naked. His hands were zip-tied behind him and his ankles were bound as well.

Gavin closed the stall door, sat on the stool, and pulled out his phone. It was answered on the second ring.

"This is Justin Primault."

"Good evening, this is Gavin Lone Wolf. I hope you have a couple minutes to talk."

"Sure."

"Good. I have a situation that happened in the past couple hours, and I need your help."

"Okay. I'm listening."

"I apprehended an intruder whose intentions are questionable and he's not Native, so that's part of the problem. I'm wondering if it's possible for you, and perhaps the Chief as well, to come out to my place. I'll call Sheriff Triplett, too."

"Damn. Let me find the Chief and I'll call you back. We'll need directions."

## FIFTY-SIX

It was dark outside. Only one light was on in the barn as Gavin paced up and down in front of the stalls. A question gnawed at him mercilessly, outright mocking him. How had Caleb Hightower learned about the Galand and Sommerville?

The situation seemed far-fetched. Almost as far-fetched as having a man trussed up in his barn. And the very presence of that man led to another question: had Caleb Hightower hired a man to kill him, if necessary, to obtain the Galand and Sommerville?

"Damn," he said out loud. "How's that for life on the rez?"

After another minute or so of pacing, Gavin stepped to the center stall and turned on the overhead light. Caruth closed his eyes against the sudden burst of brightness. After his eyes adjusted, he looked warily up at Gavin.

"I have a couple more questions," Gavin told him.

Caruth nodded, his eyes blinking rapidly.

"How did your friend Hightower know about my pistol?"

Caruth stared at the blanket. "I don't know."

Gavin nodded. "What kind of gun did he say it was? The brand, I mean."

"A Colt."

Gavin stepped away from the stall. Something about Caruth's answer rang true, but he wasn't ready to accept it as truth. Time would tell.

Gavin was waiting on the front porch when the officers arrived. He met them as they pulled up in an unmarked cruiser.

"I have to admit, Gavin," Avery said, "I'm a little puzzled."

"Come on in, I have coffee on. I'll tell you what happened."

For nearly thirty minutes both officers listened with rapt attention, taking notes along the way. Gavin left out no details, from Harriet Keyes' call to Caruth's capture. To cap it off he played the video of his captive's confession. He waited for Avery and Primault to finish their notes.

"I know I stepped over some lines and maybe broke a few laws," he said. "Abduction and imprisonment, not to mention coercing a witness."

"Not to be hypocritical," Avery said, "but as far as I'm concerned, the ends justify the means. I mean, a man you thought of as a friend hires someone to steal from you. That's not an everyday sort of life problem."

"It seems to me," Primault added, "finding Hightower's number on Caruth's phone was a kick in the head."

"For damn sure," Gavin affirmed. "I'm sure Caruth has a scary past. So, since I pulled you into this situation, what do I need to do legally?"

Avery nodded, contemplating for a moment. "Well, he was trespassing on your land so that would make it a federal case. We can show your video to a federal investigator, but it will likely be ruled inadmissible in court if the feds think Caruth was coerced. All your boy has to do is clam up. Let's not forget, he's white. In this state, that's two strikes against us."

Gavin nodded slowly. "Right. But there is the phone message from Harriet Keyes at Rabbit Run. She told me someone matching Caruth's description was asking for directions to my house. That eliminates the random 'I got lost' story. Caruth intended to come to my place."

"I have a question, Gavin," Avery said. "Do you actually have a pistol that your friend Hightower is interested in? Is it real?"

Gavin looked at each of the officers in turn. "I'm going to shorten a long story. We dug up a ledger book and a pistol that had been buried for over ninety years. Sketches in the ledger are of the Battle of the Little Bighorn and are being photographed. The gun is in my safe. My great-grandfather Lone Wolf drew the sketches, and he took the gun from Last Stand Hill after Custer's five companies were wiped out."

"Jesus, Gavin! No wonder Hightower wants it!" Avery blurted out, stunned.

"Exactly, he saw the ledger, so he knows it's real. I didn't tell him, but he somehow knows about the gun. He even knows it's in my safe."

Avery sighed. "Right. Okay, maybe it's time to meet this Caruth character. I think we should turn him over to Mel Triplett. He can do wants and warrants and maybe get him fingerprinted."

"I've got his pistol, a Sig Sauer," Gavin told him, "with a sound suppressor."

"Even better, we'll lift prints from that."

A few minutes later Gavin led Avery and Primault to his barn and unlocked the stall door. The prisoner glanced up for only a second. His face turned noticeably paler at the sight of two men with service pistols on their belts.

## FIFTY-SEVEN

By the time Sheriff Mel Triplett arrived, Antonio Caruth was sitting in the stall wearing one of Gavin's old gray coveralls, his wrists and ankles unbound. Avery had filled in Triplett over the phone as much as he could.

"Hey, Mel," Avery said, shaking Triplett's hand. "Good to see you. Thanks for coming out." He pointed to Primault "Do you know my CI, Justin Primault?"

The Sheriff reached out his hand. "I do now. Good to meet you, young man."

"Likewise, Sheriff."

The Sheriff turned to Gavin. "Seems like you been busy."

"Not by choice, Mel. Thanks for coming out."

Triplett gazed coldly at the prisoner as he walked into the stall. "So, what did you say his name is?" he asked.

"Antonio Caruth, from Jersey City," Gavin told him.

"Ah, we've got something to show you," Avery told Triplett. He nodded at Gavin, who brought up the video on his phone and pressed Play. Triplett put on his glasses and watched.

"I'll be damned," he muttered, after it was over. "I thought that there Hightower fella was a friend of yours, Gavin."

Gavin shrugged. "I did, too."

"So, what can I do?" the Sheriff asked.

"As I said, we'd like you to take Mr. Caruth off our hands, and hold him for a few days while we figure out a couple of things. Maybe take his fingerprints and we'll run his background."

Triplett nodded. "Be glad to, as long as you transport him into town for me. I came in my personal truck, not a cruiser."

With Primault's help, Gavin pulled the prisoner to his feet. Caruth moved stiffly, flexing his leg muscles, unsteady on his feet from the hours of sitting.

Triplett watched him flex his fingers and rub his wrists. "Out there," the Sheriff directed, a pair of handcuffs in his hand. "Get out of the stall, face against the wall."

Caruth staggered a bit as Triplett followed him out of the stall. Gavin was behind them and Primault was last. Avery was off to the side, watching. Gavin, meanwhile, turned and headed for his workshop. Two seconds later he heard a sharp grunt behind him.

He turned to see Triplett staggering back and Primault reaching out to catch him, and Caruth running for the open front door. Gavin reacted instinctively, bolting for the door to block him.

Caruth stopped for a split second before he launched his right fist doubled and aimed at Gavin's face.

Gavin leaned back to avoid the blow, pivoting on the ball of his left foot at the same time he moved his right foot back. Then his left arm and leg moved simultaneously. His left hand grabbed the fabric below Caruth's armpit and pulled him forward, while his leg impeded the man's forward movement. His right hand grabbed the man's right wrist—all of this in less than a second.

Gavin's right hand twisted Caruth's right wrist as his momentum propelled him toward the floor. As the man's chest slammed into the floor, Gavin dropped to his knees, straddling Caruth to avoid dislocating the man's shoulder. In the next instant, his left arm encircled the man's neck, his forearm and bicep relentlessly squeezing Caruth's windpipe.

"Extend your arm," Gavin told him.

Caruth straightened his left arm, sliding it on the floor.

"If you twitch I'll break your fucking arm."

Caruth nodded as much as he could as he gasped for air.

"Hey, Mel," Gavin called out. "Can you bring the cuffs over here?"

Triplett didn't waste a second putting the handcuffs on the prisoner. He looked at Gavin with a mixture of respect and puzzlement. "Those were some fancy moves, my friend. Remind me never to piss you off."

Gavin grinned sheepishly. "I learned just enough Judo to be dangerous," he said. "I knew it would come in handy one day."

---

His cell phone chirped forty minutes later as Gavin sat at the dining table slowly stirring the honey in his tea. It was Avery.

"Hey, we got Caruth tucked away in the Redoubt County jail. Justin took a mug shot and we'll put that on the wire, and we'll check his weapon for prints. If you don't mind, stop by tomorrow and give us an affidavit."

"Of course."

Gavin disconnected. A moment later he found the keys to his Jeep and headed out the door. Uncle Andrew was still out at Coyote Butte, and he couldn't think of a better place to be at the moment.

## FIFTY-EIGHT

A crackling fire cast reddish-orange hues of dancing light. Andrew No Horn listened quietly. His only movements were occasional sips of his coffee and careful glances to note his nephew's facial expressions and the shadows in his eyes.

From the tanned deer-hide bag hanging from his belt, the medicine man pulled out a small bundle of prairie sage and took a burning twig from the fire. He lit the end of the sage and watched as the breeze wafted the smoke around. Standing next to Gavin he softly sang a Spirit Gathering song as he pushed the smoke toward him.

Finishing the song, he sat back down.

"Thank you, *Leksi*."

The old man smiled and nodded. "There's an Old One here," he said. "She's here to take away your anger."

Gavin nodded.

"You have a right to be angry. We all do when something hard happens to us. But there comes a time to let it go. If we hang on to it, we will hurt ourselves. I'm reminding you because you know this."

Gavin nodded again.

"I'm also reminding you what the Spirits said about that gun, that it would bring you Arlo's killer."

Gavin glanced up at his uncle. "Are you saying that Caleb might have killed Arlo?"

The medicine man shook his head. "I don't know. I do know that the Spirits don't lie. And don't forget about my dream about that mask over your friend's face."

"Yeah," Gavin agreed. "So, what do I do now?"

"Hang on," said Andrew. "It's not over."

## FIFTY-NINE

Justin Primault sat back and rubbed his face. Late nights and early mornings sometimes took a toll, but it wasn't lack of sleep keeping him on edge. A lot had transpired in the past three days, most of it hard to believe. As if that weren't enough, he had just endured a conference call from BIA regional law enforcement. Despite all the catch phrases and verbal postulating, it was nothing more than a spin on the lack of progress on various investigations into Native women missing from all the northern reservations.

Primault and a CI from one of the other reservations had tirelessly pushed for an inter-agency raid on the man camps that had sprung up near the oil fields, especially in North Dakota. But there were too many jurisdictional issues with the tribes, the states, and the feds. Who knew that rules and borders would be more important than the lives of Native women?

An expletive popped out of his mouth as he stood.

"I hear frustration talking, my friend," Chief Avery said from the doorway.

"Oh, damn, sorry. It's just that, well, the goddamn state of North Dakota and the feds are quick to roll out APCs and water cannons against peaceful protestors up at Standing Rock, but they hide behind the laws when it comes to missing Indian women."

"It's because of brown skin, pure and simple," the Chief declared. "They put brown-skinned kids in cages because they're 'invading' this country. So far this year there's six hundred thousand white-skinned illegal immigrants from Europe, but they don't put them in cages. Most of the pipeline protestors—the water protectors—had brown skin, and the missing women have brown skin. Brown-skin pain and heartbreak doesn't matter to them."

"Yeah, but there's got to be a way."

"Well, I like your plan of unannounced, periodic inter-agency searches of all the man camps. We'll keep pushing for that."

Primault nodded. "Yeah, we'll keep at it. Anyway, you didn't come to listen to me rant."

"Still sounded righteous. Anyway, Dr. Lone Wolf is on his way."

---

On his way to Agency Village, Gavin stopped at Rabbit Run and went back to the food counter. Going behind the glass-covered warming shelves he walked up to Harriet Keyes and gave her a hug. She smiled in surprise.

"Wish every morning started out this way," she said. "What was that for?"

"For letting me know about that guy asking for directions," he said.

"Oh, was he a friend of yours?"

"Not exactly."

Harriet's grin turned to a frown. "Oh, dear. Everything okay?"

"Everything is okay," Gavin told her. "Just wanted to say 'thanks.'"

Harriet watched, slightly puzzled, as Gavin walked away. At the front door he turned and waved.

A few miles from Agency Village, Gavin answered his chirping cell phone. It was Loren.

"Hi Sis. Haven't heard from you in a while."

"Hi, yourself. Been to Portland and Minneapolis since the last time I saw you," she said. "That's my excuse, what's yours?"

"Don't have any. The acting-chair job at the University is keeping me busy."

"Oh, of course."

"What's up?"

"Oh, nothing, just checking on you."

"Hey, thank you, sis. Listen, I'm on the way to a meeting in Agency Village. How about I give you a call later?"

"Sure. Have a good one."

Gavin was immediately shown into the conference room at the police station. He accepted the receptionist's offer of coffee and took a seat at the table. The coffee came just ahead of Chief Avery and Lieutenant Primault. Primault had a file in his hand.

"We have some preliminary info on Caruth," Avery said. "He has a record. He is a bad man, a real bad man."

"Damn! How bad?"

Avery shook his head. "Well, here's what we turned up after we ran his fingerprints. He goes by Antonio Caruth but his father's name is Napoli, and they have connections with a couple of other organized crime families."

Gavin stared at Avery in disbelief. "Oh, crap! You mean I got the drop on a mobster?"

"Yeah, a mobster obviously out of his element. Didn't he tell you that your friend Hightower worked for him?"

"Yeah."

"Doing what?"

Gavin shook his head. "I don't know. Caleb did say he worked on the east coast in a warehouse, though he never said what he did exactly. What bothers me is that Caruth knows him well enough to do a favor."

Primault nodded. "A real big favor. I watched that video a few times. Caruth mentioned that he would do whatever it took to get that pistol. Considering who and what he is, I shudder to think what might have happened if you hadn't gotten the drop on him."

"And that leaves us—you particularly, Gavin—with a serious situation," Avery pointed out. "What do you want to do about your friend, Dr. Hightower? He hired a hit man to go after you."

"Well, I guess I can't bump him off, since you guys know about it."

Primault and Avery exchanged puzzled glances.

"Sorry, bad joke."

Avery leaned forward, elbows on the table. "It's attempted theft. From what you told us that pistol of yours is probably worth an eye-popping amount of money. Hightower would know that, given he's an archeologist." He paused for a few seconds. "How extensively does the university check into anyone applying for a job?"

"I was on the search committee for that position," Gavin said. "But all we did was identify the candidates with the required credentials. Once the list was narrowed, then Human Resources did background checks. As I recall, Henry Berkin was on the interview committee. But you'll have to ask the HR people how extensively they checked."

Primault shot a glance at Avery. "Chief," he said, "I think we should do our own checking, given what Dr. Hightower attempted to do."

"Go for it," Avery concurred. He turned to Gavin. "Where did he work before he came here?"

"Ah, three colleges in the south—Troy College, Newhurst Community College, and Burnhill College."

Primault wrote in his notebook. "Okay. We'll start there." He glanced over to Gavin. "The question remains; what do you want to do?"

"Well, if I wanted to press charges I would have to have solid evidence, and it would be a federal case, I'm guessing," Gavin surmised. "Maybe we wait until you finish checking his background."

"Okay," Avery agreed. "That will be our plan."

Gavin sighed and stood. "Life on the rez has suddenly taken a twist."

"I'd say so," Avery agreed. "First you capture a man—with mob connections, no less—spying on your house; then you learn he was sent by your friend Hightower. Cluster fuck would be a better description."

Gavin turned to leave and paused in the doorway. "Let me know what you dig up."

"Count on it," Avery assured.

Walking across the parking lot to his truck, Gavin remembered his uncle's dream: *I saw him with a mask he kept putting in front of his face, but the mask had no features, no eyes, nose, or mouth. Then it turned into his face—*

A shiver ran up his back. It was impossible to put the situation out of his mind as he drove to campus and the work waiting for him. In his office, Gavin called Uncle Andrew to fill him in. "The man I caught spying on me, believe it or not, has east coast mob connections. How's that for life on the rez?"

"*Itesniyan?* (Really?) You mean, *the* Mafia?"

"Yeah."

"*Ohan.* (I see.) Trouble always comes from the east. Makes me want to use the *wasicu* cuss words I know. What's going to happen now, to your friend, I mean? The tribal cops can't arrest him, can they?"

"Ah, well, I don't think he was ever really my friend. Tribal cops can apprehend him, but the FBI has overall jurisdiction—if I want to press charges."

"He shouldn't get away with that crap."

"I agree. We just have to figure out what to do."

"Okay, in the meantime sage your house when you get home," Andrew advised. "That man has been in your house several times. You need to get rid of whatever of him is lingering there."

Gavin picked up his phone again and called Loren.

"Hey, little brother," she answered. "Your timing is right on. I just finished a long staff meeting and I'm heading to the lounge for coffee."

"Good for you. I just wanted to check back since we had to cut short our conversation this morning. How's everyone at your house? I think I saw my nephew going into the Education Building a few days ago."

"We're good. You know, living the *wasicu* lifestyle and busy up to our eyeballs. How about you? I hear something in your voice."

Gavin chuckled. "You definitely inherited that from Mom. I could never get anything past her either. Well, there's something totally out of left field, as it were. Really would love to buy you lunch at the Bistro and tell you about it."

"We'll make it happen, bro. See you about twelve-thirty?"

"You got it. Thanks, sis."

Gavin clicked off the call and leaned back in his chair. If he couldn't get a hug from his mom, the next best thing was one from his big sister.

He sighed. "Damn you, Caleb! What the hell are you doing?"

At that moment the shift sergeant in the Smokey River Tribal Police station, Cicely Two Bears, pulled up the intake form on her computer and glanced up at the attractive, distraught woman sitting in a chair. "When was the last time you saw your husband?"

"Three days ago," Mavis Berkin replied. "He said he was coming here, to the tribal office, and that he might be going to Rapid City, too."

The Sergeant spoke as she typed. "Does he have a cell phone?"

"He does," Mavis said. "I called and kept calling. It just goes to voice mail, and now a message says it's out of service."

"Mrs. Berkin," the officer said gently, as she finished the putting preliminary information on the form. "I know who your husband is. Give me a minute and I'll try to get ahold of Lieutenant Primault." As she entered the commands and waited for the printer to kick out the form, Sergeant Two Bears dialed the CI's number.

"Sir," she said, when he answered, "I have a missing person situation. Mrs. Mavis Berkin is here; says her husband Henry has been gone for three days."

## SIXTY

As much as he kept checking for any text messages on his phone, Hightower knew that something had to have happened to Caruth. Anything could have happened, although he hadn't heard about any car crashes. More than likely, something more important than a possible payout for an antique gun had come along. Something like Antwon Napoli needing his son for a job no one else could do. Whatever the reason, unless he did something about that six-shooting gun himself, he could for damn sure kiss six to fifteen million dollars goodbye.

He sipped on a can of beer as he walked around in his house. It was furnished sparsely with old and second-hand items. One of the only redeeming lessons of the past twenty-some years was that getting by on next to nothing was necessary. Things could be replaced. And there was another hard-learned lesson. His penchant for keeping a clean house was not for the sake of cleanliness. If he had to leave at a moment's notice, there would be little if anything to provide a clue as to where he had been or where he was going.

For the moment, he was not leaving. He didn't want to leave. Six to fifteen million dollars was irresistible, even to the edge of throwing aside caution and good sense.

The question was whether or not he had the nerve. He sipped the last of the beer and crushed the can, tossing it into the wastebasket near the kitchen sink.

## SIXTY-ONE

As he finished his morning jog Gavin made the decision regarding the Galand and Sommerville. In terms of dollars, it was probably worth hundreds of thousands, if not millions. As a historic artifact it was probably a step or two down from the Holy Grail for collectors of Old West Americana. Given those realities, might Hightower have talked to anyone else?

An hour later he emerged from the safe room with the gun. After he wrapped it in plastic and then a piece of tanned deer hide, he placed a call to Gerard.

"Damn," Gerard intoned after Gavin finished. "A lot of crazy things happen on the rez, but hiring a hit man, that's a new one on me. I think you're wise to put that pistol in a safe deposit box. And maybe consider an alarm system for your house, or sleep with a gun under your pillow."

"Well, I'm thinking that Hightower is keeping things close to the vest because he wants the gun for himself. He's probably waiting for word from Caruth."

"I hope you're right."

"An alarm system I will consider," Gavin assured his brother. "There is a favor I do need to ask."

"Sure, what can I do?"

"I want an old Army Colt as a decoy, one that looks authentically old. Hightower found out about the pistol, but he told Caruth it was an Army Colt."

"Ah, so he doesn't know what it really is. Yeah, I'll get on it. Anything else?"

"No. Appreciate your help."

Gavin transported the Galand and Sommerville in a black leather briefcase. Renting a safe deposit box didn't take long, and Gavin walked out of the only bank in Kincaid with two keys in his pocket. One he planned on giving to Uncle Andrew.

As he stepped into his office on campus a chime announced a text. It was from Gerard.

> *May have found what you need.*
> *Will eyeball it later today. Stay tuned.*

Smiling, Gavin texted back his thanks as a stray thought floated into his mind. Opening the file drawer in his desk he pulled the SOLDIER WOMAN file and opened it. Katherine's photograph was there as he expected it would be, but something was different. Sitting for a moment he reconstructed the moment he had placed the manila envelope with the copies of the map and Great-Grandma Maude's note in it. He knew, without a doubt, he had put the envelope *behind* the photo.

Gavin shook his head, jaw clenched in anger. He knew how Caleb Hightower had learned about the pistol. How Caleb had gotten into this office, or why, he didn't know, but he was certain that that the man had gone through this file.

The sequence of events was easy to surmise. Caleb had looked in all the files, found the envelope in the SOLDIER WOMAN folder, opened it, and found the copies.

Gavin would bet anything on it. There was no doubt in his mind.

Picking up the desk phone he touched 1 to call Ramona on the intercom.

"Hello, this is Ramona."

"It's Gavin. I have a question."

"Okay."

"Do you have a master key to all the offices?"

"Yeah, I do. Do you need it?"

"No. Has anyone borrowed it?"

"Well, not recently but a couple months ago one of the janitors did because she forgot hers. And, I think it was last year, Caleb borrowed it because he forgot his office key. Why do you ask?"

"No reason. Just wondering. Thanks. I'll be down for coffee."

Gavin hung up the phone and slipped the SOLDIER WOMAN file and the yellow envelope into his briefcase. Now he knew how Hightower had learned about the pistol. But what was he looking for in this office in the first place? And he had to have made a copy of the key. Did he regularly break into the offices in the building?

Gavin sat trying to sort out the whirlwind of thoughts and emotions. He had brought the map and handwritten note the Monday after Grandma Annie's funeral and copied them. Hightower had to have found the envelope after May twentieth and didn't waste time contacting his old friend Caruth. Gavin had captured Caruth on June eleventh. As an archeologist Hightower had some idea of the market value of what he thought was a genuine 1873 Army Colt from the Battle of the Little Bighorn.

Gavin remembered Arlo High Crane showing the musket barrel found in the Big White, which turned out to be nothing but a worthless replica. Gavin also recalled that Hightower had shown keen interest in the stories of the 1728 *sieur de la Verendrye* expedition up the Missouri through Lakota territory, and the French fur traders that followed. The basis for that interest was not in any way scholarly, as Gavin had naively assumed. Hightower wanted artifacts to sell.

Perhaps that was the mask Uncle Andrew had seen in his dream. In any case, the question remained: What was to be done?

It was a decision not his alone. He picked up the phone and dialed a number.

## SIXTY-TWO

President Douglas Eagle Shield looked down at the blank legal pad on his desk and glanced up at Gavin Lone Wolf. "Well," he said incredulously, "now I know why you shut my office door and asked me not to take notes. I'm glad you brought this to my attention, I think. What do we do?"

"That's the question, Doug. As I said, Lieutenant Primault is doing an extensive background check. I think Hightower's personnel file would be helpful to him."

Eagle Shield nodded and reached for his phone. "Easy enough," he said. "I'll give HR a call for his file."

"Wait," Gavin cautioned. "It shouldn't raise any suspicions that might get back to Caleb."

Eagle Shield nodded. "Got it covered." He punched in numbers and waited. "Yeah, Carla, this is Doug. Listen, I've decided to do an informal review on all the department heads, past and present…yeah…can you send me all their personnel files…right away, if possible…thanks."

"Thanks, Doug. I thought you should know, although I feel a bit like a snitch."

"No, you shouldn't," Eagle Shield replied, holding up a cautionary hand. "We've worked hard to put this institution back on the map after the missteps of the previous administration. We cannot afford any stain on that hard-earned reputation. I would be highly interested in what Lieutenant Primault uncovers. Between you and me, I'm inclined to take some action to rectify. But I do have a question for you."

"Sure. Ask away."

"I'm just curious. Did you keep that pistol under wraps because you were worried that this very thing would happen?"

"Yeah, we were all worried. My family, that is. Personally, I'm of the opinion that the pistol doesn't measure up to the scholarly value of the ledger."

Eagle Shield nodded. "You're right to be cautious. I hope Dr. Hightower hasn't shared this information with anyone else."

"You and me both."

Twenty minutes later Gavin walked out the main entrance of the Administration Building with Hightower's personnel file hidden in an SRU Foundation canvas gift bag. He called Lieutenant Primault.

"I have something for you," he told the CI. "I have Caleb Hightower's complete personnel file, which includes previous places of employment, names, phone numbers, and email addresses."

"Great, that will save time. I'll send someone for it. Thanks."

"Glad to help. And you should also know that it comes directly from President Eagle Shield. I felt it was necessary that he knew what has transpired regarding Caleb. He wants to know what you uncover."

"Of course. No worries there," Primault concurred.

## SIXTY-THREE

The disappearance of Henry Berkin had hit the radio airwaves on the reservation as well as several social media platforms. Photographs of him and his nearly new Ford pickup went out state and region wide. Dozens of tips were phoned into the Smokey River police, enough to require two officers following up on leads, but all to no avail. The council representative from the Fast Creek District seemed to have vanished into the proverbial thin air. Oliver Bear King, Henry's brother, moved in temporarily to help his nephew Darrell run the ranch.

Berkin's two sisters-in-law took up temporary residence to keep Mavis Berkin company. Both were tough as nails scarred veterans of life. Adele, the eldest, was a widow and Rena, the youngest, had been divorced for five years. Neither of them had ever used make-up, a lasting influence of their German Lutheran mother. Yet they all were still attractive, inheriting dark skin and brown eyes from their mostly Lakota father. Over coffee on the fourth morning after Henry had disappeared Adele wasn't pulling any punches.

"Are you sure he doesn't have a girlfriend somewhere? I mean, a lot of men go through that mid-life thing. You know?"

"He doesn't have a girlfriend. He's not very good when it comes to women. I had to ask him out for our first date."

"What about his job?" Rena wondered.

"What do you mean?"

"Well, I think he's made a few enemies," Rena replied.

Mavis shook her head and raised her eyebrows. "So, you think he left, or something, because he had enemies? He used to be a cop. You know that he knows how to take care of himself."

"People take their politics seriously these days," Rena countered. "A couple of years ago, a man I worked with found out Henry was my brother-in-law. He said, 'Henry Berkin is like one of Custer's scouts.' There are people out there who don't like your husband."

"Bottom line is, sis," Adele said, "he's your husband and we're here for you. How's Darrell holding up?"

"Hard to say, he isn't saying much. He's holding a lot in," Mavis fretted.

"Did you talk to the police?" Adele asked.

"Yeah, we both did, Darrell and I."

"Are they helping?"

"Yeah, they're looking."

Adele refilled coffee cups for her sisters and took a long look at Mavis. "I know you hardly slept last night. Not sleeping isn't going to help you stay strong. Rena and me are here to take care of things for you. Your job is to take care of you. So, we're going to cook and you're going to eat, and later today you need to have a nap. We all got ears; we'll hear the phone."

Primault put aside his own developing opinion of Henry Berkin as he stared at the information on his computer screen. The list of phoned-in tips was long and there were many email tips. Berkin had been seen at the Agency Village convenience store, at the tribal building, driving east on Highway 17, west on Sage Meadow Road and at least a dozen other sightings. Most of the tips seemed to be genuine. There were, of course, those that ranged from tongue-in-cheek to outright cruel—*he went to DC to renew his white politician license; I heard he joined the Trump space force; I sent him to a Lakota language immersion school; check with his side-chick; he hung himself when he found out he was more Lakota than white...*

Berkin was far from being a popular member of the tribal council. His "progressive" stance about Lakota culture was not popular with the Lakota traditional community, which was at least half of the enrolled membership of the tribe. He, like many *iyeska* or "mixed-blood" tribal members, could care less that the Lakota language was slowly dying. He was a devout Episcopalian and frequently and openly criticized the practice of Lakota spiritual rituals and ceremonies, describing them as "Stone Age" and "useless."

None of that mattered to Justin Primault because the situation wasn't only about Henry Berkin. His wife Mavis and son Darrell were distraught and on the verge of fearing the worst. Primault reread the printed transcripts of the sessions he had with them.

Primault: "Did you have bad arguments?"

Mavis: "A few times."

Primault: "Did he ever threaten to leave?"

Mavis: "No."

Primault: "Did he ever stay away without telling you?"

Mavis: "No, he was good about telling me if he was going to be late or delayed."

Primault: "Do you think there was something he wasn't telling you about?"

Mavis: "I don't think so. He didn't say much about politics at home."

Primault: "How are things for your family financially?"

Mavis: "They're good now. We went through a rough time a few years ago. I think he worked things out with the bank though."

Primault: "How is your relationship, your marriage?"

Mavis: "We're good. There were problems. I had a miscarriage a couple years after Darrell was born. Henry wanted a daughter, but I couldn't get pregnant after that, but we got through it."

Primault: "How's Henry's health?"

Mavis: "It's good, he's good. He gets plenty of exercise around the ranch, he and Darrell. They both work hard."

Primault: "Darrell, when was the last time you talked to your dad?"

Darrell: "Uh, four days ago. We were going to move some cows to a different pasture after he came back."

Primault: "Where was he going?"

Darrell: "To the tribal office for some kind of meeting."

Primault: "Do you and your dad get along?"

Darrell: "Yeah, sure. He can get a little bossy sometimes, but I guess all dads are like that."

Primault: "Could there be anything going on with your dad, and he just might need time to solve it or straighten it out?"

Darrell: (after a few seconds of silence and a slight shrug) "I—I don't think so."

Primault: "I imagine your dad has guns."

Darrell: "Yeah, a couple of shotguns, a hunting rifle, and two handguns."

Primault: "Where are they, right now?"

Darrell: "All of them are in the gun safe."

Primault: "Do you have guns?"

Darrell: "Just a hunting rifle, a .270."

Primault was once again looking at the list of phone and email tips when he heard a knock on the door. Chief Avery waited a second before he stepped in and took a seat. "How goes it?" he asked.

"If you're referring to the Berkin situation, not much progress I'm afraid."

"Yeah, that's what I meant. I just got a call from President Lone Hawk. He's not pushing, and he wasn't asking for favors, he was just asking. I get where he's coming from. Berkin is, after all, a tribal councilman."

"Well, I have a plan, sort of," Primault replied. "We'll need at least two patrolmen to zero in on a couple of the more credible leads we have. One of them will need to be Jason Singer and that means we pull back from the High Crane investigation for a few days."

"Why Singer?"

"He's learned how to fly my drone. Quite good at it actually," Primault said. "Berkin was seen on Highway 17, a heavily used road and more than a few farms and residences along it, not to mention the Youth Detention Facility. If his pickup was in the ditch or near the highway, someone would have seen it by now. And I've had a couple of units check. So, my plan is to check all the roads from Agency Village to Berkin's ranch. There are four BIA roads and parts of each are fairly remote. We'll use the drone to get a bird's eye view and eyeball anything that looks promising."

Avery nodded. "Works for me. I won't speculate no matter how I may feel about Henry Berkin. His wife and son need our help, and maybe Henry does, too."

"Right. Singer's on his way in and we're going to map out how we're going to check those remote areas."

---

Sometime after four that afternoon, Patrolmen Jason Singer and Travis Left Hand finished scouting a large floodplain at a bend in the Little White River northwest of the village of St. Ignatius. There was not a single hint of a white Ford pickup, or any telltale vehicle tracks spotted from the drone's viewpoint. A system based on Singer and Primault's aerial reconnoiter of Flat Butte Dam was just as effective in this situation. Singer flew the drone and Left Hand remotely operated the camera and video recorder.

They took a break as they plugged a drone battery into an adaptor to recharge it using the cruiser's battery. "Where to next?" Left Hand asked.

Singer took a large plat map they had procured from BIA Range Management and unfolded it on the cruiser's hood. "Well," he said, "since we're checking the really remote areas, the next one close by is north of Sage Meadow Road, here." He pointed to an area nearly four miles to the northeast. "It's more bottomland next to the river and tribal land and part of the tribal buffalo pasture." He looked up at the sky and then his watch. "No clouds so if we hurry we should have plenty of daylight left."

Half an hour later the officers turned onto an approach on Sage Meadow Road and unwrapped the wire from the post of a gate that had obviously been closed for several years. From there they drove into an open meadow. Ten minutes after that the drone was in the air and slowly flying expanding circles. On the fourth round the camera picked up an abandoned barn and faint vehicle tracks leading to it. The old building, Singer estimated, was about five hundred yards from their location.

Nearly forty minutes later Lieutenant Primault answered his cell phone.

"Sir," Singer said, "I have news. Bad news, I'm afraid."

Primault detected an edge in the young officer's voice. "Let's have it."

"We found Henry Berkin in an old barn off Sage Meadow Road. He's dead, one shot to the head. Body is rather ripe. I'd say he's been here several days."

"Damn! Okay, ah, maybe you can wait for me on the road. And not a word to anyone."

"Right. If you turn left onto Sage Meadow Road after the bridge off BIA 14, we're not far from there."

Primault's next move was to call the Chief. "Oh, hell," Avery said, emitting a deep sigh after hearing the news. "Ah, let's keep this under wraps at least until we talk to Mrs. Berkin. What do you need, right now?"

"Just my gear. I'll try to get back to you as soon as I can."

"Take your time. I've got a call to make and then I'll take the news to Mavis Berkin."

Chief Avery dialed President Lone Hawk's private office number.

"Lone Hawk," he answered.

"Mr. President, this is Ben Avery. I have some sad news."

"I assume this is about what we discussed earlier."

"It is. Henry Berkin's body was found about five miles from here. He was shot."

President Lone Hawk uttered something in Lakota that Avery couldn't understand. He waited until Lone Hawk spoke again. "I don't know what the protocol is, exactly, in a situation like this," he said. "It's not a task I look forward to, but I think I should deliver the news to Mavis Berkin. And if you could accompany me in case she has questions, I'd appreciate it."

"We can go at your convenience, sir."

And so it was that at 6 p.m. Mavis Berkin answered the knock on her front door. She immediately began trembling at the sight of the President of the Smokey River Sioux Tribe and the Tribal Chief of Police standing shoulder to shoulder on the doorstep.

## SIXTY-FOUR

Just before eight in the morning Rhonda LaPlatt knocked on Lieutenant Primault's door, several sheets of paper in her hand. "I know this might not be the time, sir, but this email came in for you."

The CI looked up and reached for the pages. "Let's have a look," he said.

The young woman stepped in and handed the pages to Primault and took a seat to wait. "It's from the last college on the list," she said.

"Oh, damn, that was sooner than I expected," Primault said, turning his attention to the long email. His eyes skimmed over the first page and paused and smiled at the dispatcher. "Thanks, Rhonda."

For the moment he pushed aside the Berkin file and turned to his file on Hightower, which included his entire personnel file from SRU and emails from Burnhill, Troy, and Newhurst Colleges. He was leaning toward requesting Hightower's personnel files from those schools since the emails contained nothing particularly informative. Hightower appeared to be a valued but very ordinary employee, which somehow didn't mesh with his academic credentials from one of the most prestigious universities on the planet.

Primault composed a formal letter of request for personnel files on Dr. Caleb Hightower that he asked Rhonda to send to each college's HR department. She received replies almost immediately that the schools would be mailing hard copies of the information in the files and stuck her head in to tell Primault he should have them in a few days.

As the dispatcher exited the room, Primault answered his phone. It was the Chief.

"Where are we with the car, the Malibu?" he wanted to know.

Primault cleared his throat. "Well, a real mystery. All six of the university's Malibus have the same tire treads that match our evidence. We brought Dr. Carter's car back to our garage and we're going over it inch by inch."

"What about the Berkin situation?"

"We've done our due diligence as far as the crime scene is concerned. I made diagrams, took photographs, and collected all the evidence we could find. I know how he died, sir, I just don't know who killed him or why. Mavis and Darrell Berkin have agreed to talk to me again later today."

"Right," Avery replied. "Suddenly we have two homicides to solve."

"Does that mean the FBI won't get involved?"

"That's why I asked. They will get involved but later rather than sooner. It's just as well. At least they won't be jumping to the wrong conclusions so they can close the case. I don't know when they'll darken our doorway, but until then it's your case."

"Thank you, I think."

"If you'd like, I can request Regional BIA Law Enforcement to temporarily assign a CI to help you," the Chief offered.

"As helpful as that might be, I've got a bright young man already on the case. I think we're good."

"You've got it."

As Primault disconnected the call Jason Singer's number came up. "Jason, what's up? Sure, I'm on my way."

At Singer's direction, Primault leaned down into the trunk and scrutinized a six-inch square area in the middle of the carpeted trunk bed.

"Because the carpet is black, we almost missed it," Singer said. "They showed up in the flashlight beam. Words in Lakota, I think."

Primault studied what at first looked like mere scratches. "Have you taken a photograph?"

"I did. Here it is," Singer affirmed.

Primault straightened and looked at the marks on Singer's camera screen. His brows furrowed in concentration. "You're right, those are words," he muttered.

Singer nodded in agreement.

"Tell you what," the CI went on. "Check the rest of the trunk for any more marks, of any kind. When you're done, cut them out so we can have the ink—or whatever it is—analyzed. And can you print an enlargement of that photo for me as soon as you can?"

"Consider it done."

"Great. I want to show it to someone."

---

Gavin studied the marks in Primault's enlarged photo. The lettering was rough and uneven, resembling a small child's attempt at printing words:

Pehan miye.

Sitting in a chair against the wall of Gavin's office, the CI waited nervously.

"This was scrawled in the trunk of Dr. Carter's car?" Gavin asked.

"It was. What does it mean?"

"It's someone identifying himself."

"Himself?"

"Yeah. The words say, 'I am Crane.'"

Primault's eyes opened wide. "Damn! As in—."

"Arlo High Crane. I heard him introduce himself to some elders that way; *Pehan miye yelo*. 'I am Crane.'"

"Oh, damn! That likely means he was in the trunk of that car, and he was trying to leave a message. That would explain the pen wedged up under the weather stripping."

"Pen?"

Primault looked in his file folder and pulled out a photograph of a pen covered in a porcupine quill sheath and handed it to Gavin.

After a deep sigh, Gavin looked up at the CI. "That looks like a pen Arlo had."

Gavin's gaze lingered on the photos as he held them side-by-side before he handed them back to Primault. "Arlo is telling us he was in the trunk of that car. Find out who was driving it and you have his murderer."

"For damn sure. Whoever it was covered his tracks by using Dr. Carter's car. We've dusted that car for prints and we're waiting for the results. But I'm guessing the only prints will be Dr. Carter's. It's logical that anyone who goes to the trouble of throwing us off the trail would have wiped that car clean."

"That's not encouraging. What's your next step?"

"Well, we're checking every inch of that car, inside and out. I will instruct my people to carefully remove all the carpeting from the trunk and go over it with ultraviolet light. Maybe that poor boy left more clues."

"Right. Is there any way I can help?"

"Yeah, if you can give me a written translation of the name on the carpet, that would be helpful. We can copy the photograph here and attach your translation to it."

"Glad to. Anything else?"

"No. That's it for now."

"Right. Any news about Berkin?"

Primault paused in the doorway. He debated for a split second before he nodded. "Yeah, I'm afraid so. We found him yesterday in an abandoned barn a couple miles off Sage Meadow Road. He was shot."

"Damn! I sure didn't expect to hear that kind of news."

Primault nodded somberly. "I'm on my way to interview his wife and son."

"Do you have any idea what happened?"

"Well, from the evidence we pretty much know what happened. He probably went to see someone in that barn because he was inside, along with his truck, and his phone was smashed to pieces. One shot to the head, an efficient job. The question is who did it and why?"

Gavin stared at his bulletin board in mild shock for nearly a minute after Lieutenant Primault left. The Smokey River Reservation had its second murder in less than a month.

He could only shake his head. Henry Berkin was probably the most controversial person on the rez. But it was hard to believe he might have been killed for his attitudes or beliefs. Henry Berkin had met his murderer in an isolated location. He had driven his pickup possibly to meet someone. He was killed in an old barn in a remote area of the reservation. It was not random. Berkin couldn't have just stumbled into someone with a gun.

Gavin looked up at the clock on the wall. It was time to call it a day.

On the way home he answered a call from Uncle Andrew. "I just heard on the radio that Henry Berkin's body was found. There wasn't much else. Have you heard anything?"

"I did. Justin Primault said Berkin was shot once in the head."

"*Hosti.* (Oh, no.) We're living and dying like the *wasicus*," Andrew lamented.

Gavin couldn't argue with that.

## SIXTY-FIVE

Justin Primault returned the landline phone to its base on the desk and rubbed his eyes with both hands. Taking out his cell phone he called his wife.

"Hey, hon. I'm on my way home. See you in a bit."

"Good. I'll warm up your dinner," she said. "Be careful, there's deer along the road."

Before he turned out the light he glanced at the clock on the wall—9:17. He was feeling the effects of a long day in his neck and shoulders. Poking his head into the dispatch room he motioned to the young women on duty. "I'm on my way home," he told them.

"Roger that," one of them said.

"Good night, sir," said the other.

During the twenty-minute drive he couldn't ignore the images competing for attention in his head. The marks in the trunk of the Arlo High Crane "murder car," as the gray Malibu had been dubbed, and then the photos of Henry Berkin's body. The abandoned barn where Berkin died was nearly twelve miles from Flat Butte Dam, if that mattered. As soon as he turned into his driveway, Primault forced the stresses of the day out of his mind.

What was left of the evening and then the night passed too quickly, and a gray morning started his routine over again. The stress was waiting.

After they cleared the breakfast dishes and before they gathered themselves to go to work, Primault put his arms around his wife and pulled her close, enjoying the fresh scent of her shampooed and still damp hair.

"I envy those summer school kids of yours," he said softly.

"Oh? Why is that?"

"Because they have the blessing of your presence. And we only get to see other when we're tired—."

"Distracted, grumpy," Sandra said.

He pulled back and gave her a worried look. "Oh, damn. Was I distracted and grumpy? I'm sorry."

She tiptoed up and kissed him. "A bit, these last few days. I know some heavy stuff is on your mind. Just don't make distracted and grumpy a habit though. Okay?"

He smiled. "You got it. And I will do my best to be home early. You have a great day, hon."

"You, too. Above all, be safe."

Primault walked into his office and heard the knock on the door before he reached his desk. Patrolman Singer entered a second later. "Good morning," he said. "I have something for you." The officer held up a small plastic strip clamped in tweezers.

"Okay, what have you got?" Primault asked.

"A vehicle identification tag," Singer said. "It was separating from the door frame, so we pulled it, and it came off, and there was another VIN tag beneath it, a different number."

"Two different VIN numbers?"

"Correct. We checked the dashboard plate," Singer said, "you know, just under the windshield on the driver's side. There was a strip glued on top. We peeled it off and there was a number under it. Somebody covered the real number with another, sir."

"Looks that way. But who, and why?"

"I have an idea," Singer said, "The number that peeled off is probably from the vehicle assigned to Dr. Carter."

Primault contemplated for a few seconds. "So, you're saying that the vehicle we have was assigned to someone else?"

"I don't know. Maybe it's just, uh, misdirection. Someone hoping to throw us off," Singer asserted. "We know Carter isn't a suspect. The person who switched the number has to be our suspect."

"You're right. Well, in that case we need to talk to Fred White Horse," Primault concluded. "Give me both VIN numbers, so he can check them out for us." Primault called the SRU transportation director and gave him the two VIN numbers. Not five minutes later the transportation director called back and revealed an unexpected bit of information.

"The vehicle you have is the one assigned to Dr. Carter," Fast Horse said. "The second VIN you gave me is not on our property list."

"What do you mean?"

"It doesn't match any of our cars."

"Really. You're saying that the VIN number on top of the real one is fake?"

"I don't know about fake, but it is not on our list of the six cars."

"Thanks, Fred," Primault replied, a bit surprised.

"Someone was definitely wanting to cause some confusion," Avery concluded, after the CI reported the new development to him. "Maybe trying to make it look like Carter changed the VIN?"

Primault shook his head. "Maybe. But we know Carter isn't a suspect."

"And whoever it is had or has access to the cars," Avery agreed. "Maybe we should check into maintenance records for all six of the Malibus."

"I have a thought," Primault said. "Arlo was taken out to Flat Butte Dam on the sixteenth. I'll call Fred Fast Horse and ask if one or more cars were in for maintenance on the days up to and including the sixteenth."

Primault made the call, and posed the question after turning on the speaker function.

"Hey, Fred, its Justin Primault again. Now I'd like to know which, if any, of the Chevrolet Malibus were in your garage for service just before and up to the sixteenth of May."

"Sure," White Horse replied. Clicks on the computer keyboard could be heard over the speaker. "Ah, here's what my records show; only one Malibu was in for service, and that was on the fifteenth. It was finished and picked up on the seventeenth."

"I see. That vehicle was assigned to Dr. Carter?"

"Yes, it was his car."

"And it was the only vehicle in your garage from the fifteenth to the seventeenth?"

"Correct."

"Thank you, Mr. White Horse."

"Sure. Anything else?"

"No, that's it for now."

Primault hung up and glanced at the Chief. "My hunch was right. Carter's Malibu was in for service on the fifteenth of May. Someone took it because it was conveniently available."

Avery nodded slowly. "Sure looks that way. I have a thought," he said. "You said you didn't want me to request an investigator to help you."

"Yes, and that's because most of the CIs with Tribal or BIA police are not Native, and the process of getting someone assigned to us might take a while. What's your thought, sir?"

"I can assign some administrative functions to Captain White Bear to help you with some of the load you're facing. We can work together on both these murder cases or I can take the Berkin case."

Primault immediately saw the wisdom in Avery's offer. After all, Ben Avery had been a criminal investigator before he took the job as Chief of the Smokey River Tribal Police Department. "Chief, that would be outstanding," he said. "I think it would be sensible for you to take over the Berkin investigation. Especially since our FBI friends don't seem to be too interested in helping us."

"Right. I'll have a meeting with Jim White Bear today. In the meantime, you can send me everything you have in that case file."

"Thanks, Chief. And keep in mind that Patrolman Singer is doing a hell of job. I don't think he'd be opposed to lending you a hand if you need it."

"Sure. As long as he's willing." Avery paused and sighed deeply. "So, what does your gut tell you about the Berkin homicide?"

"Precision," Primault replied without hesitation. "One round into the musculature of the right arm, second round to the head not quite an inch above the bridge of the nose. No spent shell casings anywhere. Berkin's truck was in the barn and doors were closed. Nothing random, not a crime of passion."

"A professional hit," Avery concluded.

"Exactly."

"Strange as it seems, or maybe not, who do we know that fits that assessment?"

Primault looked at the three files in the organizer on his desk, pulled one and pointed to the name on the file label: Caruth.

"Damn straight," the Chief agreed.

"Okay. A professional hit man is good at covering his tracks. I think we should have a look at Caruth's rental car." As the Chief stood, Primault took the Berkin file and handed it to him.

"I'll have Rhonda copy my computer files onto a thumb drive for you," he said. "On it is a complete transcript of my last interview with Mavis and Darrell Berkin. They're waiting to hear when the autopsy will be finished, so they can plan a funeral."

"Okay. I'll check on it," the Chief said, lifting the file. "Time to go to work."

Primault's landline phone rang. He gestured for Avery to wait and put the call on speaker. "Hello, Fred. Got something else for me?"

"I sure do. We just found a logbook for one of the other cars that might have been tampered with."

"Really? What do you mean?"

"Yeah, it looks like someone swapped covers with another logbook The cover on this one is taped on."

"Taped on?"

"Yeah. There's a cut, like with an exacto knife, a straight cut, and taped on."

"That's interesting. Whose car is it?"

"It's the one assigned to the Lakota Studies Department, to Dr. Hightower."

## SIXTY-SIX

Hightower drove his newly purchased Buick sedan along an abandoned back trail on a segment of tribal land a couple of miles northeast of Hilltop. He slowed and turned toward a large brush pile a few yards off the trail. Beneath the pile was his old Dodge. An hour later he drove away in the SUV and the new used sedan was covered with brush. The last thing he needed was a couple of his nosy neighbors to see that he had a different car, at least not until the time was right. Lying to Brady Thomas about his SUV being out of commission was the last thing on his mind.

His nerves were on the ragged edge because he hadn't heard from Caruth. Hightower had expected some word about the Little Bighorn pistol, especially after the news of Henry Berkin was on the radio. Despite the overwhelming urge to run and hide, Hightower knew that going back to his house was the smart move. He wanted his neighbors to see him at home, to see that things were normal. Besides, there was a small chance Caruth might show up there if he had decided communication by phone or text was too dangerous.

Amid the uncertainty permeating the present circumstances there was one scary reality; the dye was cast. The purpose of his call to Caruth had been partially fulfilled. However, he would have preferred that Caruth had found and taken the pistol first.

Hightower turned left off the highway and drove slowly on Second Street before he turned into his driveway. Across the street Mrs. Litchfield was tending her backyard garden. With a wave in her direction, he nonchalantly climbed the steps to his front door. He knew damn well other eyes were watching him. Smiling despite his anxiety, he unlocked the door and stepped inside. Now he would wait and hope he could keep it together until word came from Caruth.

---

On the white board in the conference room, Justin Primault listed the information regarding the Arlo High Crane case:

- victim taken to Flat Butte Dam in trunk of 2017 Chevrolet Malibu
- car belongs to SRU
- logbook altered
- victim identified himself as person in trunk of car
- cause of death one shot to back of the head with large caliber firearm
- death occurred between 5:37 p.m. May 16 and 5:20 a.m. May 17

As he stepped back to read the list again, Patrolman Singer entered with a small booklet in his hand. He glanced at the list and then at the CI. "Sir," he said, "I think I might have found something in this logbook."

"What is it?"

Singer handed the open logbook to Primault. "The mileage entries do match the car's odometer readings. That is Dr. Carter's vehicle. Most of his trips are short, like into Kincaid. The longer trips are to outlying SRU classrooms, such as Black Pipe School and the Grass Creek Community Center. Those destinations are regular and entered in the log." Singer pointed at the logbook. "If you look on the open page, there's an entry that doesn't make sense. Between the last entry—end of a trip—on May eleventh and the beginning entry for a trip to Kincaid High School there's a gap of forty-four miles. I don't know if that means anything, but there it is."

"Forty-four miles unaccounted for?"

"Yes, sir. I called Mr. Fast Horse at the transportation garage, and he says Dr. Carter sometimes forgets to make log entries, but that he does catch up. Fred noticed the gap, too, but can't explain it."

Primault thought for a few seconds. "I'm guessing that from the SRU campus to the high school in Kincaid is just under three miles, that's not quite six miles round trip. Several trips could account for the missing miles."

"That's possible, but two of the days in between are the weekend. The car was parked," Singer pointed out. "And here's something else. Carter's trips to the high school are on Tuesdays and Thursdays. There's no way he would have made five round trips to the high school on Monday the tenth."

Primault had to agree. "Good point. So where is this leading?"

"Well, I have a thought. Maybe we should find out the round-trip miles from the campus to Flat Butte Dam, and back."

Primault nodded. "Let's do that, and since you know where the body was and the tire tracks ended, I think you should do it. Start at the transportation parking lot." The CI then took a close look at the book and his eyebrows rose. "You know, this cover looks like it's taped on, and I'll bet the VIN number on the inside won't match the real one on the car."

"It doesn't," Singer affirmed. "I think maybe we should have a look at all the other logbooks to see if they're taped like that one."

"Yeah, we'll do that."

Nearly an hour and a half later Patrolman Singer stopped his cruiser near the east shore of Flat Butte Dam and looked down at the trip odometer he had zeroed on the SRU campus. It showed 21.8 miles. Double that was 43.6. He called Lieutenant Primault.

"Good job, Jason."

Primault left his desk and walked down the hall into the conference room. To the list on the whiteboard he added:

- mileage from Lakota Studies Parking lot to Flat Butte Dam and return-43.6.

Who drove the car? That was now the burning question. There had been only one other set of footprints near Arlo High Crane's body. Those tracks belonged to whoever drove the car and killed Arlo. Primault stared at the white board as if willing an answer to appear.

Of course, there was the issue of Caruth. To Primault, Hightower was a sneaky son-of-a-bitch. Anyone who would hire a hit man to harm another human being, if necessary, to steal a valuable historic artifact obviously didn't care about right and wrong. But did that unethical behavior mean Hightower had anything to do with the murder of Arlo High Crane?

Primault knew he was reaching and needed some probing analysis. Other than Chief Ben Avery there was only one other person who could deliver that: Gavin Lone Wolf.

## SIXTY-SEVEN

Primault invited Gavin Lone Wolf to coffee at The Bistro in Kincaid. At midafternoon there were only three other patrons in the eclectic little café. The CI waited while Lone Wolf bought and delivered coffee and sandwiches to three homeless people standing on the sidewalk just outside. After chatting with them for a couple of minutes, he came back in and joined the officer at a corner table.

"I'm guessing our people didn't have a homeless problem in the old days," Primault said.

"Not even close," Gavin affirmed. "Our ancestors took care of each other. They were guided by values that stood for taking care of and defending the helpless ones first. 'You must help others before you think of yourself.'"

"That's powerful. A hell of lot has changed since then."

"Yeah, thanks to Christianity and capitalism. But I don't think you're here to talk about history."

"Unfortunately, no. I'd like to get your thoughts on a couple of conundrums. Especially since you're involved with some of what's happening."

Gavin nodded. "A lot going on. Damn shocking about Henry."

Primault slowly shook his head. "Yeah, for sure. Everything about that situation is shocking. The Chief is putting his investigator hat back on to handle it. I decided to stick with Arlo's case. That's why I wanted to visit with you. I need your help."

Gavin nodded slowly to hide his surprise. "Well, sure. I'm far from being an investigator, but I'll be glad to do what I can."

"Thanks, critical thinking is what I need help with most of all. We've uncovered some information that suggests we should take a close look at Dr. Hightower. The question is: how might he be involved?"

"Hightower hired Caruth, so he's capable of dirty tricks," Gavin said.

"Well, in that case, I have to ask; how well do you know Dr. Hightower?"

"Not very well," Gavin admitted. "I know about his academic background, and that he taught at three schools before he came here. He only generally shared personal information; his parents are dead, and he has a brother in the British Army. That's about it. He invited me to his house a few times and he's been to mine. Because he's an archeologist I involved him in the ledger book project."

Primault took notes. "Given all that, how would you characterize him?"

Gavin sighed. "Oh, well, from what he told me he came from a lower middle-class family and gained an education, culminating with a doctorate from a prestigious university; yet he isn't the most erudite person I've met. He comes across more like a backroom gambler than a highly trained academic. *Wasicus* describe that as provincial, or maybe 'down to earth.'"

"I'm assuming you haven't talked to him recently."

"No, not since he was on campus when we opened the ledger book."

Primault slipped the plastic cover off the paper cup and sipped his coffee. "Hightower aside for a moment, I'm impressed with what I've learned about Arlo High Crane. So far in this investigation, we can't put a finger on anyone who might even remotely be considered his detractor or enemy. What does that mean?"

"Either he has no enemies or detractors, or they, he, or she, is hidden. Maybe hidden in plain sight, as my uncle Andrew suggested."

"That doesn't narrow it down much."

"Have you eliminated the obvious people? You know, those that had regular contact with Arlo, including all of us in the Lakota Studies Department."

"For the most part, yeah."

"No one's asked me where I was on the night of May sixteenth," Gavin pointed out. "Was that an oversight?"

Primault shook his head. "No, it wasn't. We know you were with your grandmother, at her house."

"Okay. You said, 'for the most part.' Is there someone in Lakota Studies that doesn't have an alibi for the night of May sixteenth?"

"Funny you should ask. Only one not confirmed is Dr. Hightower. He told Agent Dempster he was at home that evening, and, of course, he lives alone."

"I know for a fact that Caleb Hightower had no evening classes last semester. I taught an afternoon class on May sixteenth. As I was leaving I met Arlo. He was with Darrell Berkin. I talked to Arlo for a few minutes, and he mentioned that Caleb was on his way back to campus from the Big White River. I did not see him at all that day."

"Right. Mrs. Red Star did tell us she saw and spoke to him and left the building before he and Arlo did. And Dr. Hightower told me he left around 6:30, and Arlo was still in the building."

Gavin gazed out the window. "You know," he said, "I don't think there was an evening class in the Lakota Studies Building that evening, but there were classes elsewhere on campus. I'm sure we can find a schedule."

"What are you getting at?"

"Next closest building is the Education Building, and then Math and Sciences. Hightower had to drive by both buildings on his way to the highway, and he's had that old SUV for years—people on campus know it. Maybe someone saw him leaving."

"Possibly," Primault agreed. "Who has that schedule of classes?"

"Dr. Carla Yellow Bull, the academic vice president. I can call her and let her know what you need."

Primault smiled and nodded. "Ironically, I think I know someone who had a class that night."

"Really?"

"Yeah. Dr. Carter. I talked to him because of his car. His alibi was his class."

"Tell you what, we can get the Math and Science number and see if he's there, if you want to talk to him."

Dr. Roger Carter immediately recognized both men who were standing outside his office door. "Gavin," he called out. "To what do I owe the pleasure of your visit?"

"I wish we could say nothing more than the pleasure of your company," Gavin replied. "Instead, I have to tell you that Lieutenant Primault has a few questions for you."

Carter nodded. "Regarding Arlo High Crane, I presume. Please, come in and have a seat."

After they were seated Gavin gave a nod to the CI who took out his notebook.

"Dr. Carter, the first time we talked you told me you had a class on the evening of May sixteenth. So, my first question is this: what time did you leave here?"

Carter narrowed his eyes in thought. "My usual routine was to leave no later than 9:30."

"I see," Primault said. "Which way do you leave the campus?"

"By the west exit from campus, so I drive by the Administration and Lakota Studies buildings."

"Did you see any vehicles in either parking lot on your way out that evening?"

Carter gazed alternately at the two men as he thought. "Well, sometimes there is someone working late at the Admin Building, but I think only the President's car that night."

"Personal vehicle or a school car?"

"His school car, I'm sure."

"I see. What about in the Lakota Studies parking lot?"

"As I recall, on my Wednesday class night there was no evening class there, at Lakota Studies. So, there was usually just the university car." Carter glanced at the extensively marked up calendar he used for a desk pad. "It seems to me that—either that evening or my next class night—there were two cars there, in that lot."

"Do you recall what they were?"

"I'm sure it was a light-colored sedan, an older one, I think, and Caleb Hightower's Dodge Durango."

"What about the university car?"

"I don't think so."

Primault glanced at Gavin, finished writing in his notebook, and turned to Carter. "So, it's very possible that on the night of May sixteenth, as you were driving away from here, you saw a light-colored sedan and a Dodge Durango in the Lakota Studies parking lot around 9:30."

"Yes, I did see the vehicles. I'm not exactly sure of the date, however. It was either May sixteenth or the following Wednesday, May twenty-third, which was my last class of the semester."

Primault finished writing and looked up. "Thank you, Dr. Carter. If I think of any follow-up questions, may I give you a call?"

"By all means. I hope I was of some help."

"Yes, I'd say so."

They drove out by the route Carter said he used so Primault could look at the placement of security light poles. "How bright are the streetlights," he asked.

"Fairly bright," Gavin told him. "A couple years ago after several serious break-ins into a few buildings, the facilities director upgraded the lighting."

"So that means Dr. Carter had a good look at any vehicle in either lot."

"Yes, and if it was on the sixteenth that means the two cars in the lot were Arlo High Crane's light brown sedan and Caleb's SUV."

"Yeah, and if so, Dr. Hightower might have lied to the FBI. If he wasn't in the building, where was he? Was he driving his university car somewhere?"

Gavin pulled over to the side of the road leading to the highway. "I think there is someone you should talk to."

"Who?"

"My cousin, Joby Bone. He lives in the Lower Horse Creek Housing, and he said he saw Hightower in his university car one evening, a few weeks ago."

## SIXTY-EIGHT

An hour later they were at Joby's house. He wasn't home, so they drove to Edna's Restaurant in Cold River, Primault's cruiser following Gavin's pickup. Inside, less than a minute after Gavin asked the bartender if Joby was working, a gaunt figure in faded jeans and a worn sweatshirt came out from the back. A slight frown appeared on Joby's face at the sight of the pistol on Primault's belt.

"Hey, *Tahansi*," Gavin said. "This is Justin Primault, a friend of mine with the tribal police, and he'd like to talk to you."

Joby cautiously reached out a hand to Primault. "Okay. Any friend of Gavin's is a friend of mine," he said. "Good to meet you."

"Likewise. Join us if you don't mind."

Joby sat next to Gavin in the booth where he and Primault had been seated. "Sure, what's up?"

Gavin took the initiative. "I thought maybe you could tell Justin about seeing that friend of mine, Hightower, at the cut-off road a few weeks ago."

"Ah, sure. I was coming back from the hospital in Agency Village, caught a ride to Kincaid, did some business and then started walking back out to the Cold River junction. I decided to rest a bit, so I sat down against the fence at the cut off road, at the corner. A car came from Kincaid, turned right, and went down the cut-off road, and then came back a few minutes later. It pulled up at the stop sign, the driver opened the door and spit on the ground, and then he turned right and went west."

"Who was the driver?"

Joby pointed a thumb at Gavin. "His friend, that bald-headed white guy."

"What kind of car was he driving?"

"I don't know, it was dark colored, but I saw the sign on the door."

"Sign?"

"The logo of the college, the medicine wheel with the letters SRU."

Primault was writing hurriedly. "Okay. So what day was that, and do you remember what time it was?"

Joby reached into his trouser pocket and pulled out a small spiral notebook and flipped through the pages. "It was the day of my appointment at the hospital clinic," he said. "I have to get my sugar checked regular. Ah, that was May sixteenth."

"What time?"

Joby shook his head. "I don't have a watch, but it was after the sun was down, not quite dark yet."

Primault checked his notes and reached a hand across to Joby. "Thanks, Joby, glad you could spare us the time."

"Sure. Did I get that guy in trouble?"

"No," Gavin said. "If he's in trouble it's of his own making. Hey, if you're not doing anything this weekend, I need some help putting in an alarm system at my house."

"Oh, sure."

After Joby went back to work, the bartender stopped by with menus in hand. "Can I get you anything?" he asked.

"Tell you what," Gavin said, "I'm going to live dangerously and have one of Edna's humungous cinnamon rolls, and a black coffee."

"Just a coffee for me," Primault said, consulting his notes. "What your cousin told us sent chills up my back because I remembered what your uncle said that the hardest thing to see is the nose on our face."

"Right. So maybe you should take a closer look at Hightower."

"I am. I've already requested personnel files from the places he taught before he came here. Those are coming by snail mail. I want to know everything about him. Of course, it might all be for nothing if he leaves."

Gavin shook his head. "I don't think he'll be leaving anytime soon. He wants the Little Bighorn pistol, so he'll stay. As long as word doesn't get out that Sheriff Triplett has Caruth locked up. Or," he said, after a momentary pause, "maybe that's our ace-in-a-hole."

"Caruth?"

"No, the pistol."

"What do you mean?"

"Okay, bear with me. I should have realized this before. Hightower's been keenly interested in the French fur traders who came to this area in the early 1700s. He's talked to people and researched possible trading camps along the Big White River. I don't think that interest is scholarly. I think it's purely financial. He wants to make money."

"And he knows about your pistol."

"Right. Maybe we dangle it in front of him.

"I'd hate to put your pistol at risk."

"Won't happen," Gavin assured him. "My brother found a replica of an 1873 Army Colt. I asked him to do that. He had someone age it, make it look old."

"And that's what you want to dangle?"

"Right. According to Caruth, Hightower thinks my pistol is an Army Colt, the kind issued to the 7th Cavalry. So, if I showed him a photograph of that replica, he would believe it."

"Okay, so what would be our reason for using that as bait?"

"Keep him around, at the very least, while you do your investigation."

They paused while the coffees and the cinnamon roll were brought to the table.

"You know," Primault said, "we can't ignore what your cousin told us. Tie that to Caruth and it's hard to comprehend. All we can do is see where it leads us."

"Indeed."

"Okay, so I have to ask, if your pistol isn't an Army Colt, what is it?"

"It's a British made revolver called a Galand and Sommerville. My brother Gerard's research indicated a strong possibility that a British lord gave a pair to Lieutenant Colonel George Custer and another pair to his brother, Captain Thomas Custer. Whether that's true or not, that's what my great-grandfather found on Last Stand Hill on June 25, 1876."

"Holy shit! What do you think it's worth?"

Gavin shrugged. "I don't know. A small fortune, probably."

"If your friend Hightower knew that, he'd go crazy."

"Right. Uncle Andrew said that greed is like the sun in your eyes. It blinds you to everything else."

## SIXTY-NINE

Primault wasted no time obtaining warrants to search Hightower's office and basement workshop. By early the next afternoon he was on campus. He watched the main printer in the Lakota Studies Building push out the last of twenty pages and turned to Ramona Red Star.

"Thank you," he said, "I appreciate your help."

She nodded, pensively. "You're welcome. I hope it helps you find whoever killed our Arlo." She stacked the printed pages and handed them to Primault, who nodded.

"This isn't everything from the computer Arlo used," she said.

"It's enough," Primault assured her. "I have the history of his activity, and the last email he sent to his professor at the University of Nebraska. Arlo was here when you left and still here at 7:12 p.m. on May sixteenth, according to the Sent file on that computer."

Ramona Red Star shook her head sadly.

Gavin had run interference with Ramona Red Star, mainly to explain what had lately transpired. She was not pleased.

"You're telling me that Caleb—Dr. Hightower—is being investigated," she had asked.

They were in her office. "Yes, we all are. Lieutenant Primault is doing his job."

Ramona was sitting with her arms crossed and mouth set in a hard line. Gavin knew it wasn't a refusal to believe him. She was defending someone she believed in.

"Is that why Lieutenant Primault wants to look at the files on Arlo's computer?"

"Yeah. Well—that..."

"And he said they found Arlo's pen—and, you know, I made that quill sheath for him. If that was in Caleb's, well, the school's car, what does that mean, Gavin?"

"It means they're following evidence. Arlo was killed, we know that, and the evidence points to that car."

Ramona sadly shook her head and wiped away a tear. "I just don't understand why anyone would want to hurt Arlo. Life is hard enough. I hope Lieutenant Primault finds the truth."

Gavin walked down to join Primault in Hightower's workshop. He had never been in this room. It was an add-on, built after the building was completed and taken over by Hightower after he had arrived. Four long tables stood against two walls. There was a table vise, digging tools, hand tools hanging on the walls, and several cardboard boxes beneath the tables. "I've never been in here," he admitted.

Primault pulled out what Gavin thought was a pen, then extended it like an antenna. He used it to move objects on the table and open boxes.

"I don't know what I'm looking for," he explained. "I'm just looking."

Primault's intensity was obvious. Gavin stayed out of the way as the CI moved objects around with his probe and looked into boxes. He paused over one box in particular.

"What's this?" Primault asked, pointing into the box.

Gavin stepped over, knelt, and saw a round wooden ball with a 4-inch long dowel protruding from it.

"It's called a short starter," he said. "It's used to push a round lead ball into the barrel of a black powder rifle, a muzzleloader, to seat it, or get it started. Once the ball is seated, then you push it down the length of the barrel with a ramrod. That," he went on, pointing at the short starter, "is used to fit the ball just inside the muzzle."

"Was Hightower into muzzleloaders?"

"I don't know, other than finding them in the river. I never heard him talking about them."

Primault stared at the short starter. "So why is this here?" he mused. Taking a plastic bag from his back trouser pocket, he pushed it into the bag with his pointer. "How does a person get a muzzle-loading rifle?"

"Some sporting goods stores have them, and gun shops, of course. You can walk in and buy one and walk out. No background check required. Same for cap-and-ball pistols."

"A cap-and-ball pistol?"

"Yeah. A cap-and-ball pistol uses black powder; they're usually replicas."

"Oh, yeah, I've seen them. Who uses black-powder rifles and pistols?"

"Some hunters use modern versions of black-powder rifles. Some people own historical replicas and are recreational shooters, or historical re-enactors."

Primault gazed at the short starter as if there were an answer on it. "So, if Hightower wasn't a gun person, recreationally or otherwise, what is this doing here in his workshop?"

"Good question," Gavin admitted.

Primault bent to look into the box where he had found the short starter. With his probe he pushed aside papers, paused, and then slowly reached in. Carefully he lifted out a business card, holding it between his fingertips as he read it.

"Ever heard of a man named Dennis Evans, or of a place called the Missouri Valley Black Powder Club in Chamberlain?"

Gavin shook his head. "No."

Primault slid the card into his evidence bag. "Maybe he sold the short starter to Hightower."

A few minutes later Gavin took him up to Hightower's small sparsely furnished corner office on the ground floor. Gavin had always thought of his former friend as "Spartan" in the sense that his house was nearly as sparsely furnished as his office. He had never been in a full professor's office where every inch of space wasn't overflowing with file cabinets, piles of papers, and cases of books. Hightower's space seemed to be an exception.

Primault only glanced at the framed art on the wall as he perused the office. The desk was bare, except for the university-issued desktop computer screen and keyboard and a small copy machine on the credenza. "This doesn't feel like a teacher's space," he noted.

A tapping at the door interrupted any further conversation. They both turned to see Ramona.

"Gavin," she said quietly, "there's a young man at the front desk. He's looking for Caleb. Says he's a friend. What do you want me to tell him?"

"Maybe I should talk to him," Primault said.

Gavin held up a hand. "No. If he is a friend and you ask him questions, he'll tell Caleb. I'll talk to him. What do you want me to ask him?"

"See if he knows where Hightower is."

Gavin approached the young white man standing in the lobby with a polite smile on his face and a straw hat in his hands.

"Can I help you?" Gavin asked.

"Ah, well, I don't know. I was looking for a friend of mine."

"Might that be Caleb Hightower?"

The boy nodded. "Yes, sir. Is he here?"

"No, he's on leave. May I ask who you are?"

"Brady Thomas, from Chamberlain."

"Well, nice to meet you, Mr. Thomas," Gavin replied affably. "Is there any particular reason you're stopping by today?"

"Well, sir, ah, Caleb's car broke down a few days ago, over by Hilltop way, in a pasture. I just drove down to help him drag it out, borrowed my boss's dually. I stopped by Caleb's house, but he wasn't home, and he isn't answering his phone. So, I just wanted to check if he was here."

"I see."

"This is my day off. I also brung down a gift for him. It's his birthday, tomorrow."

"A gift? I'm sure he'll want to see that."

"Yeah, it's a rifle. A muzzleloader. He and I shoot black powder. Do you know where he might be?"

"I'm sorry, I don't. I haven't seen him for over a week. But I'll let him know you stopped by if I see him before you do."

"Okay, thanks." Nodding toward Ramona the young man exited the building before he put on his hat. Gavin watched until he climbed into what was probably a one-ton pickup with dual rear wheels.

He rejoined Primault in Hightower's office. "I never heard Caleb mention him but the boy's name is Brady Thomas, from Chamberlain.

He didn't know where Hightower is but he did say he and Caleb shoot muzzleloaders together."

Primault's eyebrows rose. "Really?" He lifted the plastic bag containing the short starter and the business card, which he read again. "I'll bet they do that at the Missouri Valley Black Powder Club. I think I'll pay them a visit."

"Good idea. And before you do, what do you think of dangling our bait."

"Why now?" Primault asked.

"Just to see if he'll come out of the woodwork, and if he does we'll set the hook. If he's nervous about Caruth he might leave. He needs a reason to stay around. We need him to stay around until you prove or disprove his connection to Arlo's murder."

## SEVENTY

Gavin's plan was simple: make a call and talk to Hightower or leave a message on his phone. An email would be useless because Hightower had barely used the Internet when he was in his office, and he didn't have a computer in his house.

He scripted the call and rehearsed it, trying to sound nonchalant. At the last minute he decided to use his landline phone because Hightower would recognize it. After a cup of strong green tea, he took the phone handset to the recliner.

A small flutter of relief coursed through him when his call went directly to voice mail.

"Hey, Caleb. This is Gavin. If you're still in the area I'd like to talk to you. We haven't told anyone that there was another item in the same container with the ledger, and I'm at a loss as how to get it authenticated. Call me if you have time to hear the details."

He hung up, thinking he would give Caleb several hours to pick-up the message. But Hightower was already listening to it.

A shrill tone sounded just as Hightower was opening his door. He covered the eleven feet to the small desk in a few seconds to pick up the phone, thinking it might be Caruth. But when he saw the name and number in black letters and numbers against the green screen, he let the call go to voice mail.

After listening to the message, Hightower pulled out the chair from the desk and sat down, his heart pounding, his legs rubbery.

# SEVENTY-ONE

After leaving the message for Hightower, Gavin drove into town to fetch Joby after his shift ended so he could spend the night. Uncle Andrew came over and fixed his slow-fried potatoes while Gavin grilled three pheasants. Joby made coffee over the open fire in the backyard. When they finished eating, they convened to the fire pit to talk away the evening. Not a single word of English was spoken.

Uncle Andrew came back to Gavin's in the morning for coffee just as Ted Stilman arrived. Stilman was the owner of Kincaid's only computer and electronics store, and—as far as Gavin was concerned—a total techno nerd. He came in his van with all the supplies and equipment necessary to install motion sensor lights and interior alarms. While Gavin, Joby, and Stilman got to work, Andrew saddled up Red Wing for a long ride. They were nearly finished with the interior alarm—the sound of a large dog barking—by the time Andrew and Red Wing returned. Not surprisingly there was no response yet from Hightower.

Installing alarms was, for Gavin, a grudging nod to technology, and an unnecessary step if not for the Galand and Sommerville; and, more to the point, greed. On the other hand, if he hadn't left those copies in his file drawer, none of this would be necessary. There was enough blame to go around.

Gavin decided motion-activated cameras would be best for the exterior of the barn, with a monitor on the kitchen wall and another in his bedroom. In the back of his mind was the thought that it would all come down after the Galand and Sommerville was no longer an issue.

After all the cameras, sensors, and lights were installed and wired, Stilman would program the receivers and monitors. Half an hour later he had to drag the man away from his computer to grab a bite of lunch. After lunch they left Stilman to his techno-wizardry and other worldly mumblings while they talked about new barbless fencing for the horse pasture.

They stood at the corral and watched the horses rolling in the dirt.

"*Tahansi*," Joby said, "if you got a small notebook or something to write on, I'd like to walk the pasture and measure the fence lines, just to be sure."

A few minutes later with pencil and a small pad of paper in hand, Joby set about his task. Andrew, meanwhile, pointed to the cameras on the side of the barn.

"Something I've been thinking about for a long time now," he said. "When I was a boy our house was heated with a wood stove, and we used kerosene lamps at night. In the warm weather we had a shade north of the house. I think I want to go back to that, at least part way."

"Part way?"

"Yeah, get a generator and disconnect from the electric co-op. I got an old-fashioned phone that doesn't need electricity. I can use the generator when I need it. Couple of months ago I traded for a small heating stove. That can heat my bedroom in the winter."

"What about your water pipes?"

"If you remember, the main line from the pump is below the frost line. There's that styrofoam insulation in the crawl space below my kitchen sink and bathroom. I can double insulate all the pipes."

The horses had followed Joby out of the corral and were walking behind him as he headed toward the north fence line.

Smiling, Gavin nodded at his uncle. "You let me know when you're ready to do that, and I'll help you. You'll probably have to get a new junction box because the co-op will take theirs, and probably their highline poles, too."

Andrew grinned. "That's alright. They don't look natural anyway."

Gavin saw the horses look west for an instant before he heard a muffled rattle. A dark vehicle came over the rise—Hightower's SUV.

"It's time to set the hook," he said.

"Going fishing?" Andrew asked.

"Yeah, something like that. I'll tell you about it later."

Andrew's gaze turned dark after he recognized the approaching vehicle. "Just be careful. A man with two faces can never be trusted. You want me to hang around?"

"No, I don't think that's necessary."

"Well, maybe I'll catch up to my nephew out there," Andrew said, pointing toward Joby. "We'll see you later."

Gavin was on the front deck when Hightower pulled up and parked next to Stilman's van. Hightower didn't give it a second glance as he stepped down from his car. A flash of anxiety in his eyes was discernible. Gavin hoped his own was not as noticeable.

"Hey, Gavin," Hightower greeted him, stepping onto the deck.

"Caleb. I'm assuming you heard my message."

Hightower squinted in the bright afternoon sun and nodded.

Gavin couldn't remember the number of times Hightower had come to his house. This was the first time he had ever arrived without calling first.

"Just didn't want you to think I'm ignoring you." He nodded toward the van. "Something in disrepair?"

"No. Just had an alarm system installed."

Hightower's eyebrows went up a notch. "Oh?"

"Yeah. Come on in."

Inside Gavin pointed toward the couch and waved at Stilman who was set up at the dining table. "We won't be long," he assured him. Stilman nodded without looking away from his laptop screen.

Gavin went to his file cabinet and took the large envelope from the top. Taking a seat on the recliner he pulled out several photos and laid them on the coffee table. Hightower's eyes focused on them like lasers.

"Have you ever seen a weapon like that?" Gavin asked, as he finished spreading the pictures.

Hightower scanned them quickly. "Indeed, I have. I believe that is an 1873 Model Single Action Army Colt. Is that the 'item' you mentioned in your message?"

"It is."

"Since you are showing me photographs, may I assume that the artifact is not on the premises?"

"You may."

"It was cached with the ledger?"

"It was."

Hightower's gaze was riveted on the photographs. Each was a different perspective: a left profile, right profile and close-ups on the barrel, cylinder, and both sides of the handle. The metal surfaces were slightly pitted and tarnished and the wooden handle grips had apparently darkened with age.

Hightower's fascination with the photographs mattered only in the context of his and Primault's plan. With a strange sense of detachment, rather like looking through a veil, Gavin observed Hightower as one detail of Caruth's confession played over and over in his mind: *...to find it and take possession—whatever it took, to get you out of the way...*

Hightower sat back and shot a quick glance at Gavin. "What's your plan?" he asked.

"We're not sure. The broad choices we've talked about are bequeathing it or selling. But we want to assess its worth in order to make an informed decision."

"How can I help?"

"I'll give you these photos if you think you can find out what it's worth."

Gavin saw the vein on Hightower's temple pop out as he reached for the photos. "Yeah, I think I can do that. Is there a deadline?"

"You tell me."

Hightower carefully slid the photos into the envelope. "I need to make some initial contacts, and then I'll let you know."

Gavin stood and shook the hand of the man who regarded him as an obstacle to be removed. On a warm June day Hightower's hand felt cold.

With a nod and a side glance in Gavin's direction, Hightower turned and walked out of the house. Gavin took a deep breath and sat down. A month ago, Gavin would have been puzzled by Hightower's uncharacteristically brusque behavior and abrupt departure. But not today. Hightower had validated Caruth's words.

"I think we got all the bugs out," Stilman called out.

It took a second for Gavin to react. "What?"

"All the cameras are working," Stilman said. "You'll know tonight after dark if the floodlights work. But they should."

Gavin rose and stood for a moment. "Great. Thanks. You have an invoice for me?"

"Get it to you by email. Let me show you how it all works."

Gavin followed Stilman to the left of the east kitchen door. Attached to the wall was a three by five inch gray box with push button switches.

"The top is the master; it turns everything on." Beside each round button was a hand printed label:

Front deck

Barn

Interior alarm – 1

Interior alarm - 2

Dog.

"If you want to turn one off, push in the button," Stilman went on. "Interior Alarm 1 is a soft bird whistle to alert you to an intruder on your deck. Interior Alarm 2 is just a buzzer and that indicates an intruder at the barn. Motion turns on the cameras and starts recording and triggers the alarms, and you can see the intruder or intruders on your monitor. The Dog is mainly for when you're not here. There's a small speaker under your coffee table so it'll sound like the Hound of the Baskervilles barking inside."

Stilman tapped the gray box. "This is just a switch box. Come with me." He turned and stepped to the part of the cupboard on the east wall of the kitchen and pointed to a larger flat black box attached underneath it. "This is the brains of the outfit. It's connected to everything, wirelessly. It's powered by four D batteries so when you see this glow red," he said, pointing to a tiny plastic knob, "you replace them."

"D batteries?"

"Yeah. It's my protest against little Black kids forced to mine lithium in Africa.

After Stilman organized his gear and left, Gavin strung his war bow and went to his shooting range on the east side of the barn.

It felt like the thing to do.

## SEVENTY-TWO

South of Cold River Hightower turned left off Highway 83 onto Highway 33 and pulled onto the shoulder and stopped. On the passenger seat was the envelope with the photographs of the Little Bighorn pistol. The images of the gun were seared into his mind, next to Galbreath's email with the estimate of seven to twelve million dollars.

His hands had finally stopped trembling a few miles from Lone Wolf's place. Photographic proof would be good to hook a buyer's interest, but he was still light years away from holding the damn gun in his hands. That was the god-awful problem.

First, he had to learn where it was—if Lone Wolf was telling the truth. Hightower wasn't totally convinced it was not in Lone Wolf's house since Ted Stilman was installing an alarm system. Why else would Lone Wolf go to the trouble, and expense, if that had nothing to do with the pistol?

To complicate matters there was still no word from Caruth. Perhaps it was time to send him a message, especially since an idea was beginning to form. If he could figure out all the angles, it might not matter where that damn gun was. Maybe there was a way past alarms and into bank safe deposit boxes. Maybe he could leave this god-forsaken place once and for all.

If he could find the nerve to make his plan work, that could be in a matter of days. He opened his cell phone to look at the date on the screen: June nineteenth. That was six days away from the anniversary of the Battle of the Little Bighorn.

How ironic would it be to have that pistol delivered to him June twenty-fifth?

## SEVENTY-THREE

Primault turned off the interstate at the fist exit west of Chamberlain and onto the old highway into town. It took him past a few motels, convenience stores, various tourist traps, and a popular restaurant toward the old bridge across the Missouri River. Beyond a marker for County Road 32 he turned north, and almost immediately saw a faded sign:

Missouri Valley Black Powder Club

2 ½ miles north

Open Sundays

Five minutes later he found the turnoff. The paint on a life-sized plywood cutout of a mountain man leaning on his long musket was fading. It stood guard to the right of the entrance to a small, graveled parking lot. Two pickup trucks were parked at the end. As Primault stepped down from his unmarked car, dressed in his dark blues, he heard the BOOM of a rifle somewhere behind the green metal building with double front doors made of glass. Off to one side was a sliding metal door that obviously went over the glass doors.

Two rows of shelves stood in the small interior. Shelves were also mounted on the east wall. No weapons were on display and all the shelves held shooting accessories for black powder firearms. On the wall behind the counter were paper targets with bullet holes showing shot patterns. A tall, slender, bearded man stood behind the counter, eyeing the CI suspiciously. His gaze flicked to the Glock service pistol in its quick-draw holster clipped to Primault's belt.

"Something I can help you with?" the man asked, almost as a challenge.

Primault decided to get to the point. "Do you have a member list, or roster?"

"Yeah, we do, but what's it to you? Who the hell are you?"

Primault was always amazed at the stupid arrogance of some white men. Slowly approaching the counter, he showed his badge and identification. His gesture coinciding with another muffled *boom*.

"I'm looking for information on a man by the name of Caleb Hightower. Is he one of your members?"

"We don't give out that kind of information, mister. You're not even the local law."

Primault was undeterred "I know that a young man by the name of Brady Thomas is a member. He told me that Caleb Hightower is also a member here. Is that true?"

"Like I said, I can't give you that information." With a mixture of nervousness and false bravado, the bearded man kept a wary eye on Primault.

"I'm here because of a murder investigation," Primault went on. "I'm in the process of gathering relevant information. And my question to you is very simple: Is Caleb Hightower a member of your club?"

Another *boom* from outside. The man raised his hands, indicating either dismissal or helplessness. "Like I said before, I can't give you that information."

"Mr. Evans, you are the owner, is that correct?"

"Yeah, so what?"

"So I can tell the FBI the name that goes on the federal search warrant. If you won't talk to me, you'll have to talk to them."

"Shit, go for it."

Primault pulled out his cell phone, gazing coldly at the man. He'd seen many like him. White men who assumed that bluster and bad attitude were the ways to deal with Indians. He opened his phone and dialed his home phone number and waited until he heard Sandy's voice on the outgoing message was done, and then spoke.

"Hello," he said, "this is Lieutenant Justin Primault with the Smokey River Tribal Police Department. May I speak with Special Agent Johnson, please?" He waited for several seconds, his gaze still leveled at the bearded man. "Yes," he said, "I'm here at the Missouri Valley Black Powder Club, west of Chamberlain across the river. I'm requesting assistance and a federal warrant for the place of business I mentioned, at 646 County Road 32, owner's name is Dennis Evans."

The expression on the bearded man's face changed from haughty disbelief to a cloud of apprehension. "Ah," he rasped, and then cleared his throat. "Just—just hold up a bit. I—ah, there's no need for that. I think I can help you."

Primault lowered the phone. "You think?"

"I—I can help. Yeah."

Primault lifted the phone. "Sir," he said, "we may not need a warrant."

Relief washed across the bearded man's face as he watched Primault put away his phone. Of course, there was no "Special Agent Johnson" that Primault knew of, and he would have to delete the sham call from his home phone later.

"Mr. Evans," he said, "is one of your members Caleb Hightower?"

"Yeah, he is."

Primault slipped his notebook from his shirt pocket and clicked his pen. "Did he ever come here with Brady Thomas?"

Another *boom*.

"Sure, he did. They came together a few times."

"They used your range?"

"Yeah, they did. Hightower mostly shot a cap and ball pistol. He was a decent shot, but he always had trouble loading. You know, measuring the powder load."

Primault nodded as he wrote. "Do you sell black powder rifles and pistols?"

"Yeah, I do."

"Did you sell anything to Hightower?"

"Well, no, not exactly. I helped him place a couple orders—one for a black powder pistol, a .45 caliber Army Colt, and one for a French musket. The musket was a few years ago."

"Did he order them at the same time?"

Evans shook his head. "No, the long gun first, and the handgun a few months later."

"Thank you, Mr. Evans."

"Yeah. So, ah, what about the FBI?"

"Primault shook his head. "I think we're good. But if I have any more questions, I'll be back."

Evans nodded nervously.

Primault turned and walked out the front door, smiling.

## SEVENTY-FOUR

Antonio Caruth's mid-size GMC rental SUV was in the gravel parking lot next to the small jail behind the courthouse in Cold River. It had no GPS, but there was the latest edition of a South Dakota highway map in the glove box. Patrolman Singer found it and was surprised to see it reveal south central South Dakota when unfolded. He also noticed the vehicle's starting mileage written on the rental contract, he assumed from Joe Foss Field in Sioux Falls. He copied it in his notebook and wrote in the accumulated mileage on the odometer. Using the calculator on his phone he did the subtraction and looked at the answer—341 miles. Something didn't jive.

Singer knew that from the I-90 and I-29 interstate junction on the northwest edge of Sioux Falls west to the Highway 83 exit to Cold River was 204 miles, and from there to Cold River was 23 miles. After adding in 7 miles to Gavin Lone Wolf's place, the total was 234. He double checked his math and concluded that Caruth had apparently driven 107 miles beyond the distance from Sioux Falls to Lone Wolf's place. Even after accounting for the ten miles or less from the airport to the edge of Sioux Falls, a hundred or so miles was a lot of miles to be lost or wander off the main roads.

Singer wrote a notation—*Show Lieutenant Primault*—in his notebook and closed it. Getting out of the car he handed the keys to Sheriff Mel Triplett.

"Find anything interesting?" the Sheriff asked.

"Maybe," Singer told him. "Has your prisoner talked to you at all?"

Triplett shook his head. "Just the usual stuff. 'Good morning' and so forth. He's polite but he's not a friendly type."

"What do you mean?"

"Well, sometimes there's a look in his eyes, ah, you know, sort of calculating," the Sheriff said. "When I was a kid I cornered a young coyote, a pup, in our chicken coop. I saw that same look in that pup's eyes that was in that city boy's eyes. That pup knew he was cornered and the survivor part of him kicked in, something between desperation and courage. He was going to do whatever it took to get past me. Only with that Caruth fella it's desperation and downright meanness. That man has a hole inside instead of a soul."

"What's his situation, legally?"

"The states attorney filed weapons charges against him, illegal possession, public endangerment. He's gonna be arraigned in a few days."

"Then what?" Singer wondered.

"Ah, we can try him in in circuit court here or turn him over to the feds. Since he was on Gavin's land, that technically makes it a federal case."

"Right, so you're basically trying to keep him in your custody as long as possible?"

"Yeah, at your chief's request. But, you know, the funny thing is he hasn't asked for his phone call. He hasn't asked for a lawyer. I don't trust that."

"That is strange. Anyway, thanks for letting me check out the rental car." Singer called Lieutenant Primault as he walked to his cruiser. "Sir," he said, "there was no GPS unit in Caruth's rental, just a road map. I've got it and I'm heading back."

Primault put down the phone after the call and turned his attention back to the two rows of photographs on his desk, all the marks and words left in the trunk by Arlo High Crane. Something about the V mark on the cardboard spool was familiar. A slight shock went through him when he remembered where he had seen it first—alongside the numbers on Arlo's palm. He sifted through the photographs until he found the one with the numbers. Above the numbers, at the base of his left thumb, was the mark on its side relative to the numbers: >|   0011497CR

It was the same as the mark on the spool and it was important enough to Arlo High Crane to draw it twice in the last moments of his life. But what was it? Primault grabbed the two photos and hurried to the dispatch room. There was someone who might know.

"Rhonda," he said, holding out the photos. "If you're not too busy can you scan these onto a file and then email them to Dr. Gavin Lone Wolf? I think his email is in the system."

Eyes twinkling, Rhonda took the photos. "Sure. Should take about five minutes."

"Thanks!" Primault hurried back to his office and called Lone Wolf's cell phone number.

"Gavin Lone Wolf."

"Gavin, this is Justin Primault. In a few minutes two photographs are going out to your email, and I was just wondering if you could take a look at them and give me a call."

"Certainly. Photographs of what?"

"Marks that Arlo High Crane scribbled in the trunk of the car he was in."

"Damn. Okay. I'll call you."

Primault tried not to look at his watch or the clock on the wall as he anxiously waited. Rhonda knocked and entered, handing him the photographs.

"He should have the email," she said.

Seven minutes had elapsed since he took the photos to her. "Thank you, again," he said. As Rhonda waved and stepped out his cell phone buzzed. "Hello?" he answered "I'm looking at the photos now," Gavin said. "One mark is on his hand and the other on some flat surface. I think I know what they are, so here's what I'm going to do. I'm going to photograph some framed art in Hightower's office and then text them to you, and then we'll talk."

"Okay, thanks."

Primault nearly resorted to pacing as he waited, not sure why he was so anxious. Finally, his phone chirped to indicate a text. When he opened the photo he nearly gasped. His phone rang as he was staring at it.

"Is that what Arlo sketched?" he asked. "And what are they?"

"One is a print of a painting and the other is a print of a sketch. The painting is a medieval European watchtower, and the black and white sketch is a symbol that represents the word *watchtower*. Caleb used that symbol, the one in the sketch, to represent his name—Hightower. They're hanging on his office wall, and you saw them a few days ago."

Primault stared at the photographs Rhonda had returned. Strangely his throat felt dry. "Damn, Gavin. Do you realize what this might mean?"

"I do. Arlo is identifying the person who put him in the trunk and killed him."

## SEVENTY-FIVE

Lieutenant Primault walked into the Lakota Studies Building twenty minutes after he left the police station at Agency Village, a large plastic evidence bag in his hand. Ramona Red Star had already unlocked Hightower's office. Before he took down the sketch and the print, Primault photographed every inch of the office. Gavin arrived just as he finished.

"Something was nagging at me the first time I was in here," the CI admitted. "I just couldn't put a finger on it."

"Now you know."

"Right." He pointed at the symbol in the framed sketch. "I saw that first on Arlo's palm, then it was scrawled on a cardboard spool found in the Malibu's trunk, and also on the carpet. I thought it was a V. I happened to look at the photos just about an hour ago and that's when I called you."

"I think you would have made the connection sooner or later."

Primault took down the pieces and put them into the plastic bag. "I never met Arlo, but it hit me on the way over here how much we lost when he was killed. Not many people would have thought to do what he did, sketch those clues, I mean. That young man's intelligence and courage were off the scale. The world is less without him."

"I couldn't have said it better myself. So, given what you know now, what's the next step?"

Primault talked as he carefully sealed the evidence bag. "The Chief and I would like to talk to you about that. He's on his way now to the Kincaid County sheriff's office. We would appreciate it if you would meet us there."

Gavin nodded. "I can do that."

Twenty minutes later Gavin accepted a cup of coffee from Sheriff Weston. Then joined Chief Avery, Lieutenant Primault, and the Sheriff around a narrow folding table in a back office.

"Thanks for coming," Avery said to Gavin. "I wanted to have this meeting here so Sheriff Weston knows what's happening. In the next few hours, I will have conversations with Sheriff Triplett and Sheriff Carter. We want our bases covered, just in case."

Gavin nodded and waited, curious as to why he was included in this meeting.

"Justin, you're lead on this case," the Chief said. "The floor is yours."

"Thank you, sir. Here's where we are. We've just uncovered evidence that strongly indicates that Dr. Caleb Hightower may be a suspect in the murder of Arlo High Crane," Primault stated somberly. "We're still collecting evidence and assessing information. In a perfect world we would be able to act on that evidence as a tribal police department. But, as we all know, criminal jurisdiction is a bitch around here, and we don't want that unfortunate reality to allow Hightower to slip through the net." The CI paused and turned to Gavin. "So that's where you come in, Dr. Lone Wolf."

"What can I do?"

Primault smiled sardonically. "As much as it might turn your stomach, we want you to play nice with Dr. Hightower."

"I see. Because you need time."

"Yes," Primault replied. "Today or tomorrow, we will have Dr. Hightower's personnel files from the three schools where he taught previous to SRU."

"What about Durham University?" Gavin asked. "Shouldn't you contact them as well?"

Chief Avery and Lieutenant Primault exchanged glances. Avery shook his head. "Frankly, I didn't think of them," he said,

"Just a thought," Gavin added.

"A good one," Avery said. "As soon as we're done here I'll go back to the office and send off a request, by email."

"I have a question, Ben," Sheriff Tim Weston said. "If your suspect comes in to our jurisdiction, do you want us to apprehend?"

"No, but we damn sure want to know if you lay eyes on him. Justin, you want to explain why?"

"Glad to. Tim, our plan is to apprehend him once we organize and verify the evidence we have, and that should just be a matter of days. We're doing this because Hightower is outside our jurisdiction and the tribe cannot prosecute him. While the crime occurred within the exterior boundaries of Kincaid County, it happened on tribal land."

"And that makes it federal," Weston said. "So, you're putting together a case that the feds have to take seriously."

"You got it," Primault asserted. "And dance on the razor's edge of jurisdiction."

"We're here to help," the Sheriff assured him.

"Thanks, Tim. If you can bring your deputies up to speed, we'd appreciate it."

"Will do. I'll get it done today. What's your next step?"

"Review the evidence and see what we find in the personnel files when they get here," Primault said.

"Right. What can you tell me about the Berkin situation?"

"Homicide, all the earmarks of a professional job," Avery said.

The Sheriff was astounded. "Here?"

"Yeah," the Chief said. "One shot to the head, isolated site."

Weston could only shake his head. "What's this world coming to, gentlemen?"

After a moment, Gavin turned to Lieutenant Primault. "So, basically what you want me to do is keep Hightower on a string?"

"Right. We want to make sure he doesn't leave the area."

"I think I can practically guarantee that he won't leave," Gavin said. "I dangled the carrot, as it were. I'm sure he's planning how to get his hands on the bait."

"I have a question," Sheriff Weston said. "If you decide to apprehend, do you have any idea *where* that might happen?"

"Given that this is a federal situation," Avery replied, "ideally on federal or tribal land. But we should be ready for anything. We'll keep you apprised, along with Sheriff Triplett and Sheriff Carter."

"Right. Like I said, we're here to help."

In the parking lot Gavin stood with Avery and Primault for a few seconds. "I didn't want to elaborate on your bait," the CI said.

"Thanks," Gavin said. "Caleb came to my place and saw the photos of the pistol my brother found, a replica 1873 Army Colt. He had it aged so it looks properly old. He seemed convinced, probably because that's what he was expecting to see."

Avery grinned. "You're right. I don't think he's going anywhere. More importantly, he'll come to the bait."

## SEVENTY-SIX

Hightower hated waiting. Hours had passed since he faxed the photographs, first to Del Conway and then to Jacob Galbreath. Any fantasies about instantaneous responses with dollar signs and endless zeros were dashed on the cruel edges of reality. Yet other layers of reality offered a glimmer of hope—there were plenty of dealers and collectors when it came to historic memorabilia, legitimate and otherwise. He would sell the pistol; of that he was certain. It was just a matter of time.

First, he needed to have that pistol in hand, and he had a plan for that.

Hightower locked the south door of the house after he stepped out. Everything he needed was in his small backpack or already in the Buick. He waved at Mrs. Litchfield as he unlocked the door to the Durango. He would be back sometime after midnight when he was certain Elsa Litchfield was asleep.

## SEVENTY-SEVEN

Primault watched Avery drive away and gestured toward Gavin. "Got time for a cup of coffee?"

They watched out the front window of The Bistro as the barista brought their coffees. "As I was saying, the FBI will step in sooner or later. So, the best thing we can do is gather evidence."

"Let's go in another direction for a bit. There's something I've been wondering about," Gavin admitted.

"And that is?"

"You learned at that gun range that Hightower shot a cap-and-ball pistol."

"Yeah. What about it?"

"Where is it? That pistol. Where is it?"

Primault glanced at Gavin and then turned a puzzled gaze out the window. "Are you thinking that might be the murder weapon?"

"It's possible. It might be a replica, but it's still deadly. Here's the thing, we know that the coroner took a misshapen piece of lead out of Arlo's skull."

"Yeah, that's right."

"Okay. Cap-and-ball pistols shoot two kinds of rounds, both lead. One is shaped like a modern bullet without a casing and the other is a round ball."

Primault glanced at Gavin, thoughts careening behind his eyes. "That is a very interesting fact."

"Right, and I'll bet that if you weighed that misshapen piece of lead, which the coroner determined was the cause of death, and weigh a round lead ball used in a replica musket, and in a modern black-powder rifle, and in a cap-and-ball pistol, you might narrow down the list of probable murder weapons to firearms that shoot lead balls that weigh the same as the piece of lead taken from Arlo's skull."

"Well, the misshapen piece of metal in Arlo's skull was lead. It's indisputable."

"There is one way you can turn speculation and supposition into fact."

Primault nodded. "Yeah, we can test it to verify what it is."

"Right but weigh it first. I have a box of round lead balls. My brother Gerard gave me a cap-and-ball pistol as a birthday gift. It's a .45 caliber. I'll give you one of those rounds and you can weigh it."

"Okay, we'll do that," Primault nodded.

"It's possible that the murder weapon is a black-powder firearm. And, as that man told you, Hightower owns a cap-and-ball, black-powder pistol. That's a broad scope, I know, but we can narrow it down by the process of elimination and the new facts we might uncover in that process."

Primault looked at Gavin with renewed respect. "I think you missed your calling, Gavin. You should be a criminologist, or a detective."

Gavin shook his head. "No. My first love is history, or I should say my second love."

Primault looked around for their server. "Really, if history is your second love, what's your first?"

Gavin smiled and turned a long gaze out the window. "An incredibly smart, drop-dead gorgeous raven-haired woman who broke my heart," he said. "Therein is a tale, but not today."

Primault looked down at his coffee. "I know one thing," he said, "in my mind, at least, anyone who hires a hit man to steal a valuable historic artifact is probably capable of murder. Statistics prove that once a person has done it, he will do it again."

"I agree with you. So, I have to ask again: where is Hightower's cap-and-ball pistol? If we're reasonably certain he fired the fatal shot and then ditched the weapon, where is it?"

Primault kept staring at his coffee. "Well, that depends on the circumstance. Was killing Arlo a premeditated act? If so, then the shooter very likely made a plan, such as switching vehicles to avoid suspicion, and that plan would also have to involve getting rid of the murder weapon. If, on the other hand, it wasn't premeditated—meaning an immediate reaction to a compelling event or situation—then there is not so much planning. We don't know which it was."

"Well, okay. But here's something to consider. I never observed or heard of any kind of friction between Arlo and Hightower."

"So, you're saying that Arlo's death was not premeditated," Primault concluded.

"Maybe. Ramona told me they were talking about that musket. She spoke to Arlo before she left, and he was working in the study room. If there had been anything—anger, anxiety, moodiness—she would have picked up on it."

"That would mean that whatever triggered Hightower might have happened after Mrs. Red Star left the building," Primault surmised. "Or before, and he just waited for her to leave."

"It would seem so," Gavin agreed. "At some point Hightower reacted to something that put him over the edge. So, he grabbed whatever weapon was on hand, and I'm guessing the black-powder pistol was in his workshop or office, or car. He took Arlo out to Flat Butte Dam. Then, after he shot Arlo, he disposed of the weapon."

Primault's eyes darted back and forth. "In that case, the first place he might have ditched it would be the dam. Maybe he tossed it into the water," he speculated.

Gavin nodded slowly.

"Well, damn. I have a friend who's a diver. In fact, he helped find the body of a drowning victim in the spillway below Fort Randall Dam. I'll give him a call."

"That replica pistol weighs almost three pounds. Find something that is similar in weight, a rock, maybe, and toss it in from where the shooter's tracks were."

"Great idea. That'll give us our search grid. An arc, really."

"Good. Get your friend to that dam as soon as you can. Like tomorrow."

## SEVENTY-EIGHT

Gavin arrived on campus the next morning and parked, pausing for a moment to think about the conversation with Primault before he walked into the Lakota Studies Building. Ramona Red Star's breathless excitement was almost a shock.

"Gavin," she called out as soon as she saw him. "They want you over at the Admin building. Something about your great-grandfather's book."

"Something wrong?"

"I don't think so. Dr. Wells sounded really excited. You know, happy excited. He said to tell you as soon as you got here."

Dr. Wells had always been fairly matter-of-fact when he described the project to anyone, so Gavin was curious. Doug Eagle Shield was just going into the temporary research office when Gavin arrived.

"Hey!" he said. "Ted has exciting news."

Wells and Hanson were standing behind Glanville, staring intently through the glass at the ledger book. Gavin glanced at the monitor, which was black. Wells turned to greet the two men.

"Gentlemen," he said, "Lady Luck is with us today."

"Thank goodness for that," Gavin said. "What happened?"

"As you know, we were at the twentieth page and the seventeenth sketch. Some pages have sketches on both sides, some don't. In any case, we've been gently separating the pages due to some very slight adhesion. As of this morning, however, the remaining pages have separated of their own accord. No more adhesion."

Wells stepped aside to let Gavin and President Eagle Shield look. Glanville had the book standing on end with all the pages fanned out in a circle, like points on a compass.

"I think maybe your great-grandfather decided to lend a hand," Doug Eagle Shield said.

They watched as the technician inserted sheets of paper, one at a time, between the open pages.

"That is acid free paper made from hemp," Wells informed them. "To protect the sketches and prevent adhesion."

"This is obviously a good thing," Gavin ventured.

"Oh, indeed," Wells said, beaming. "This means we'll be able to speed up the photography. I estimate we'll be finished in four days. And when the photography is done, then we begin selecting which shot of each page to print. That's where we'll need your help, Gavin."

"No need to ask me twice," Gavin said. "I can't wait to see all the sketches in order."

Justin Primault's news was good as well and affirmed Gavin's theory about the lead round. "We did the tests you suggested with the lead shot you gave me. Your bullet and the one that was in Arlo's skull weigh the same."

"Great. Then you'll establish possibilities, and as you gather more facts you'll—."

"Turn them into probability," Primault concluded.

"Exactly. We know how he probably took Arlo out to Flat Butte Dam," Gavin noted. "Assuming he used a cap-and-ball pistol, what did he do with it? And why that particular weapon? The answer to the first—as we agreed before—is he got rid of the gun as quickly and conveniently as possible—he buried it, threw it away, or whatever came to mind after he fired the fatal shot. The answer to the second is he used whatever weapon was on hand and available. I'm thinking the gun just happened to be in his workshop, office, or car."

"Right. My friend Cliff will arrive in a couple hours, I twisted his arm. I'm going out to Flat Butte Dam with him when he dives."

---

Gavin finished a three-mile jog just before sunset and walked four times around the corrals to cool down. Running helped to clear his mind and get back into a routine he had neglected. Routine was easily interrupted. But it wasn't that he had suddenly gotten lazy. There was some distraction. More to the point, he had allowed himself to be distracted.

Another reason he ran was to take the edge off his anger. Physical activity wasn't the answer to every situation in life, but it had always been a way for him to think and analyze. Movement of any kind propelled him toward some type of conclusion.

As he finished his cool down, a thought popped into his head. He had learned to load the replica handgun that Gerard had given him. It wasn't as simple as putting bullets into the cylinder. With a black-powder pistol, each load of powder had to be measured precisely into each of the six chambers of the cylinder. He hurried into the house, found his cell phone, and called Primault.

"You said the coroner is convinced that the probable cause of death was that misshapen piece of lead," he told Primault. "And there was an entry wound but no exit wound, which was puzzling because we think it was practically at point blank range."

"That's true," Primault agreed.

"Right. I should have thought about it earlier. If the murder weapon was the black-powder pistol, then it might have had light loads, not as much powder. Gun still fires but bullet velocity is not as high, therefore it shatters the back of the skull but does not exit."

Primault considered the possibility for a second. "If you're right, it seals the deal."

"Right, and how about the manager of that gun range? He might know something. Maybe he taught Hightower how to load his pistol."

"Good point. I'll give him a call."

Gavin went out onto the deck to finish his workout, doing push-ups, leg lifts, and jumping jacks. He did five sets of twenty repetitions and was feeling the effort. After walking around in the grass while his heart rate slowed, he went back inside for a shower.

Over a cup of tea, he called Uncle Andrew. "I'll bring over something to cook for breakfast in the morning," he offered. "Early, by seven."

"Sounds good," Andrew said. "I'll have coffee ready. Don't forget to bring everything that's on your mind."

"In that case it'll be a damn big bag of stuff," Gavin said.

"Okay. In that case I'll use the big coffee pot."

He was surprised to find an email from Katherine and even more surprised to read what she had to say.

I think you should write a book, Dr. Lone Wolf, about your great-grandfather's ledger sketches. You know there'll be white historians who will give their own interpretations, once they're made public, mainly to enhance their own reputations. Someone has to diffuse all that. I nominate you. Not only is Native history and culture your specialty, but also this is your great-grandfather's story. Do it for him, give him his voice. Whites have appropriated that event and made it their own. They've made heroes out of invaders and child killers. Most people who have heard of the Battle of the Little Bighorn think the 7th Cavalry was doing God's work to open up the west to civilization. That's not history, that's putting spin on genocide.

Her logic was damn hard to argue with.

Gavin retreated to the recliner, uncertain whether he should answer her note. He decided to wait until tomorrow to write at least a note of thanks. He stood and put the phone back on its cradle and began turning off lights. With the house cloaked in darkness and silence, he nearly jumped when the landline phone rang. It was Gerard.

"Hey, bro," Gavin answered. "You're keeping late hours in your old age."

"Yeah, right," Gerard chuckled. "Goes with the territory. I just got home from a long day, and thought I'd give you a call. I've been feeling a disturbance in the force, as they say, actually, for a couple of hours. Are you okay?"

"Yeah, for the most part. Just feeling a bit of frustration over the Arlo High Crane case."

"What's going on?"

Gavin filled his brother in on the events of the week past relative to Hightower.

"So now it seems as though your friend—former friend—is a suspect."

"Yeah."

"Here's a thought. Why doesn't Chief Avery send an FYI to the British authorities? You know, Scotland Yard."

Gavin nodded. "He did send a request for information to the University of Durham."

"That's all well and good. But here's my point. You don't know everything about Hightower before he came to the states."

"Good point. I'll suggest it to Chief Avery. Thanks."

"Hey, it's what older brothers are for," teased Gerard, who was two minutes older. "Mainly, I just wanted to check on you."

"Appreciate that. And, in that vein, you should hit the rack. You older folks need your beauty rest."

Gerard chuckled. "Will do, bro. Will do."

## SEVENTY-NINE

A breakfast of small buffalo steaks, boiled red potatoes, and poached eggs washed down with Uncle Andrew's good campfire coffee was the only way to start the day, as far as Gavin was concerned. And true to his word, the old man had brought out his big blue coffee pot, its sides perpetually blackened by smoke from the open fire. All the food had been prepared over the outside fire behind Andrew's house. When Gavin had finished cooking, he gave a Spirit Plate to his uncle, which contained tiny portions of the morning's fare, even a bit of coffee. The medicine man prayed and put the plate out for all the ancestors in the Spirit World.

"So, what else is on your mind, *Tunska?*"

Gavin smiled and poured more coffee into their cups. "Well," he said, "It all seems unreal, but Hightower has become a suspect and Justin Primault is scrambling to find evidence against him for Arlo's murder. What he does have sure points in Caleb's direction."

The old man was silent for another few seconds. "Sounds like a race of some kind."

"In a way it is, because we don't know when the FBI will choose to step in, especially because of the Berkin shooting. Justin Primault and Chief

Avery aren't convinced that they will be thorough, if they investigate at all, and that, *Leksi*, will be justice delayed or none at all for Arlo."

"You know," Andrew said, "I like that young man, Primault. He's smart."

"He is, but he's going to some need lucky breaks."

"How about those people in England, where your friend worked?"

"It's funny you should say that. Gerard had the same idea. You didn't talk to him, did you?"

The old man smiled. "No." He added a couple of sticks to the fire.

Gavin glanced at his watch. "I've got a meeting at ten, *Leksi*, with Doug Eagle Shield and the people from NMAI. I think they're going to give us photos of the sketches in Grandpa's ledger. Maybe you can come along."

"I wish I could. I got a couple things to do. Are they going to give you your own copies?"

"I think so, but I'll ask if they don't. Maybe you can come to my house this evening."

## EIGHTY

Gavin got down from his pickup and walked into the Administration Building. Four folding tables were set up in the conference room, and on top were forty-eight separate stacks of photographs. Each stack was of one of the forty-eight individual sketches in the ledger. The task was to pick the best photo in each stack. After that, the selected photographs would be printed and bound into twelve books: four for the Lone Wolf family, two for the university's permanent collection, and six for the National Museum of the American Indian. The photographs would also be enlarged to poster size and larger for the NMAI exhibit and for the Smokey River University's permanent exhibit.

Doctor Wells was beaming as he greeted Gavin. President Eagle Shield was already looking at photographs. Gavin was immediately struck by the clarity and detail of the photos. He said as much to Toby Hanson, the chief photographer on the project.

"We have cameras that are specially designed for this kind of work," he told Gavin. "And because they're mounted and stationary, that helps enhance the clarity. But the best camera in the world can't improve on the impact of your great-grandfather's sketches."

Gavin couldn't agree more. Although some of the original color from the sketches had faded to varying degrees, the sketches were still bold and captivating.

"I must point out something that, in my opinion, sets your great-grandfather's sketches apart from hundreds of others I've seen," Wells said. "He was very obviously cognizant of perspective. So, the size of the man on the horse is proportionately correct, for example. You'll see figures next to conical lodges, and the perspective is correct. The object in a person's hands, a weapon, tool, or shield, is drawn to the proper proportion. That means he has a realist's eye for details. Simply amazing."

Wells was correct as Gavin discovered. He decided to look at only the photograph on top of each stack, because he wanted to see them all in sequence. Very quickly it became apparent to him that his great-grandfather was telling a sequential story, from beginning to end. The first sketch was a self-portrait because he was the storyteller. After that came village scenes and depictions of his wife, Red Shawl, his mother-in-law, Blue Corn Woman, and his daughter, Little Shawl. He also depicted his brothers Black Wolf and White Tail Feather. The sketches depicting the attack from the south by Major Reno and Custer's attempted incursion at Medicine Tail crossing, and the subsequent pursuit of his column, fit hand-in-glove with the first-hand narrative accounts Gavin had studied.

The focus of his curiosity was satisfied when Lone Wolf depicted himself picking up a pistol from among the blue-clad bodies of soldiers on a hillside. Those sketches were obviously what the world had come to know, erroneously, as the heroic "Last Stand." One of the last sketches was another self-portrait. In it, Lone Wolf stood with his brothers, each holding a rifle, with indications of the wounds White Tail Feather and Black Wolf had suffered. In that sketch the captured pistol was tucked into Lone Wolf's belt. Never had he felt such a powerful connection to *ehankehan*—the past.

Gavin gazed at the last sketch. It was visual confirmation that the Galand and Sommerville was taken from Last Stand Hill. What to do about that was an issue for another day.

President Eagle Shield walked over and put a hand on Gavin's shoulder. "This is totally amazing," he said. "I just can't find the words to describe it."

"In the art world people sometimes use the terms 'seminal' or 'watershed' to describe a painting or a sculpture," Wells pointed out. He gestured to the piles of photographs. "This is both art and history, and those words certainly do apply. It's not an adequate comparison, but it's as if your great-grandfather wrote a graphic novel because he told a chronological story of one of the most well-known events in Western American history. He was an eye-witness and a combatant. That's hard to beat."

"And very honest," Wells added. "I've read letters written by some of the surviving soldiers and later interviews. Their accounts were colored by their bias, their unflattering opinions of Natives, and their tendency to misrepresent reality. Whereas Lone Wolf sketched what he saw—real and raw."

They didn't need much time to pick the lead photo of each sketch, finishing just before noon. On his way to his office Gavin put in a call to Gerard.

"Hey, little brother," Gerard answered. "How's life on the rez?"

"Damn exciting at the moment. We finished looking at photographs of Great-Grandpa Lone Wolf's sketches. I got goose bumps just looking at them."

"That's fantastic. Is there any chance of emailing them to me?"

"Yeah, I gave Dr. Wells your email, so he'll be sending you to a website where you can download some software to receive and download the file. He's going to send you a video file of all forty-eight sketches. Prepare to be amazed, bro."

"That's a given."

"Right. Uncle Andrew's coming to my house this evening to look at the hard copies I have. We'll give you a call."

## EIGHTY-ONE

Justin Primault called as Gavin was walking into the Lakota Studies Building.

"Hello, Justin. Let me guess. You found Hightower's pistol," Gavin teased.

"Don't I wish. My friend, Cliff, did three dives but came up empty. He had to leave because of other commitments. I really thought he would find it."

"Well, it was worth a shot. If you have time for a cup of coffee later, I would like to run something by you."

"Sure, meet you at the coffee bistro in, say, two hours?"

Primault was clearly disappointed as he joined Gavin. "We know he had that gun," he said, dejectedly. "Did you ever see it anywhere, in Hightower's office, his workshop?" he asked Gavin.

"No, but Dennis Evans has. He's seen Hightower using it on the firing range, probably helped him load it. He might be willing to sign a statement."

"All we can do is ask," Primault said. "But I think he will. The flattened round the pathologist took out of Arlo's skull was made of lead. That's pretty compelling evidence, but it falls short without the weapon itself."

Gavin couldn't refute that. "How much of an area did your friend search?" he asked.

"Well, we took a three-pound brick, spray painted it orange, and threw it from the spot where the shooter's footprints stopped. From where it entered the water we plotted out an arc. Cliff searched within that arc and beyond. He retrieved the brick and a couple of glass beer bottles, but that was about it."

They continued their conversation over coffee, in a corner of the bistro.

"My brother and my uncle suggested something," Gavin said. "That you should inform the British authorities at Scotland Yard that Hightower is the only suspect in the murder of Arlo High Crane."

"What would we hope to gain by doing that?"

"I don't know, exactly. Maybe getting to them before the FBI steps in."

Primault mulled the suggestion for a moment. "They probably won't care that Hightower murdered one of *our* people. I mean, they're all the same, right, the white English and white Americans. White privilege is white privilege."

"Yeah, maybe. We've been putting up with their attitudes, their rules, and their laws. That's part of our reality. In any case, what have we got to lose? Tell them."

"Yeah, you're probably right."

"But whether you do that or not, Gavin said, "the evidence leaves little doubt that Hightower did it. He murdered Arlo High Crane. We have a damn good idea how he carried it out. Having that weapon would seal it. If it isn't in the dam, where the hell is it?"

Justin Primault turned his gaze toward the large front window of the coffee bistro "Maybe down some damn prairie dog hole."

Gavin shook his head and sighed. "Well, there's got to be some clue, somewhere."

## EIGHTY-TWO

Despite the dramatic photographs of Lone Wolf's sketches, the missing murder weapon still lingered annoyingly in Gavin's head. Supper grew cold as he and Uncle Andrew studied the sketches one by one. Andrew ran his fingers over each sketch gently and reverently. They were laid out in two lines on the floor.

"These pictures pretty much show what my father heard from your Great-Grandpa Black Wolf, and my dad told the story in the same words," Andrew said. "Those words put pictures in my mind. These pictures are the same as the words."

"That is a good way to describe it, *Leksi*."

When they called Gerard, he was, at that very moment, watching the video file of the sketches for the third time.

Gavin hung up from the call and poured himself another cup of coffee, moving to the recliner. Andrew came to the couch and took a seat. "Big day, huh?"

Gavin nodded. "It sure the heck was."

"You know, I think I would like to take Grandpa Lone Wolf's drawings to the Greasy Grass, and walk the story as he told it," Andrew said, reverently.

"I think that would be a special connection for all of us, as a family. We should talk about it with everyone."

Andrew turned his gaze from the photographs and cleared his throat. "What's going to happen next, with Arlo's case? I mean, a lot points at your one-time friend."

"I don't know. The evidence is saying that Hightower murdered Arlo, as far as I'm concerned. The only thing missing is the murder weapon. Finding that would prove it beyond any doubt. On the other hand, even if Primault does find the pistol, where do we go to get justice for Arlo?"

Andrew No Horn turned his gaze out the window, out at the darkness. "Maybe it will come from the place you least expect."

# EIGHTY-THREE

Sandy Primault glanced at her husband with a suspicious glint in her dark eyes, a hint of worry on her attractive features. He was reading an email from the dispatcher on duty at the police station. She resented any kind of communication from the police department during her husband's off hours. In most instances it meant he had to respond to some situation somewhere on the far-flung reservation. While the overtime pay came in handy, she much preferred for him to be safe at home with her.

"Just information," he assured her. He closed the laptop and stood up from the couch, then went into the kitchen to make himself another cup of tea. "Do you need anything while I'm here?" he asked.

"Sure, push Start on the dishwasher," she replied. "I forgot to do that."

The dishwasher began to swish and swirl as he waited for his tea to steep, with his mind swirling as well. Primault poured honey into his tea, then walked back to the couch.

Sandy pointed to the paused image frozen on the television screen. "Tom Hanks might be able to hold that grimace forever, but I want to see how it all ends."

"Sorry," he said, picking up the remote and pushing the Play button.

Sandra gazed at her husband for a moment. His eyes were on the television, but he was seeing images other than those on the screen.

"Was that about the High Crane situation?"

He nodded.

"Was it about Hightower?"

He nodded again.

"Can you prove he did it?"

"I think so. There's still one piece missing."

"And that is?"

Primault shook his head. "The murder weapon." He pointed to the image on the screen. "I'm sorry. Let's finishing watching."

## EIGHTY-FOUR

Antonio Caruth stopped pacing in his tiny cell. Through the bars of the cell, he saw the clock on the wall in the holding area, which was another cramped room. It was nearly time for a deputy to show up with tomato soup, crackers, and a bottle of water. The only positive thing about his incarceration was the variety of soups—chicken noodle, cream of mushroom, vegetable beef, clam chowder, and tomato. There was no radio or television, and the jail was apparently neither heated nor cooled. It was warm in the day and cold at night.

It was exactly five steps from one end of the narrow cell to the other, and except for the occasional sound of a vehicle passing by somewhere outside, it was unnervingly quiet. There were no other prisoners. He had never been so utterly alone.

"Young man," the Sheriff had said. "We're not in too much of a hurry out here. It might take us awhile to put your mug shot out on the wire. We'll get around to it one of these days, I s'pose. Meanwhile, we'll make sure you're fed and watered."

It was all part of their plan, and he knew it.

## EIGHTY-FIVE

Justin Primault closed the last of three files and leaned back, glancing at his watch. Nearly three hours had passed, and he had no substantive new information about Caleb Hightower. It was as though Hightower expressly intended to live a mundane existence. In the sixteen years before he came to Smokey River University, his longest term of employment was six years at Newhurst Community College in Alabama. After that it had been four years at Burnhill College in Tennessee and five at Troy College in Kentucky. Despite his impressive credentials from the University of Durham he never rose higher than an associate professorship. The only exception was SRU, where he was a full professor and an acting chair of the Lakota Studies Department. He picked up his phone and found Gavin Lone Wolf's number on his Contacts list.

"I don't know what I was expecting," Primault admitted. "For someone with such stellar academic credentials, he's been nothing but ordinary. I mean, his kind of credentials would get him into places like Harvard or Yale, wouldn't they?"

"Usually," Gavin agreed.

"Then I have to ask—why is SRU the largest institution on his resume. The others are small, no more than seven hundred students, and one is a two-year community college. It just seems strange to me."

"As if he's keeping a low profile?"

"Exactly."

"I recall that Doug—President Eagle Shield—had to talk him into taking the job as department chair of Lakota Studies," Gavin said. "He took it on an interim basis."

"There's a reason for it and I'd like to know what it is. But maybe it won't make a difference to our case. I'm confident that we're building a solid case that makes him a definite suspect."

"That's the main thing, right?"

"It is, Gavin. And I'm sorry."

"For what?"

"He was your friend."

"Don't be sorry. The operative word is *was*."

"Alright. Our intrepid dispatcher is knocking on my door. I'll talk to you later."

Primault looked up at Rhonda. "Chief Avery would like you to see something in the dispatch room," she said. "An email. A reply to the inquiry he sent yesterday."

"From the University of Durham?"

"I think so. We're printing it on the main printer."

Janice, the second dispatcher, stapled two piles of collated material and handed them to Avery and Primault.

"The email is the first page," Avery said. "The rest of it, eight pages, is the attachment that came with it. I think you better have a seat before you read it. I'll be in my office, and I think we need to call Dr. Lone Wolf," the Chief said.

Primault nodded without looking up, his eyes focused on the pages.

> Chief Avery:
> Please find attached material pursuant to your inquiry about Dr. Caleb M. Hightower, who was a student and later a faculty member in the Division of Applied Science.
> Unfortunately, Professor Hightower was presumed dead in 1988 after he and his diving partner failed to return from a cave dive in Yugoslavia during an archaeological research project.
> The attached materials are provided for your information.
> Cordially,
> Henry Stedham-Jones, PhD
> Vice Chancellor
> The University of Durham

Primault blinked, reading the note twice before he turned to the attached pages, which included a 1989 newspaper article from the *London Herald* reporting the recovery and identification of one the bodies of two divers that had drowned in a cave dive in 1988. There were photographs of the two divers and obituaries as well. Primault stared at the black and white head shot of a man identified as Dr. C. M. Hightower. It strongly resembled the man he had talked to several weeks ago. Hightower's obituary listed his parents, Charles and Michaela Burmeister Hightower, and a brother, Carey M. Hightower.

If he was a betting man, Primault would lay odds that Carey Hightower was impersonating his brother. He joined Chief Avery a minute later.

"How do you like them apples?" Avery said.

"An 'oh, shit' moment if there ever was one," replied Primault. "A conundrum wrapped up in a mystery labeled 'What the Hell?'" He took a sticky note from the Chief's desk and wrote out Gavin's email address. Avery nodded and went to work as Primault pulled out his cell to text Gavin.

> *Hey, Gavin. If you have a moment,*
> *Chief Avery is forwarding an email*
> *we received less than twenty minutes ago.*
> **Take a look and give us a call.**

Gavin read the text but wanted to finish his conversation with Denise Archambault before responding.

"Your proposal is what we should have done years ago," he said to her. "If anyone should be offering a total immersion course in the Lakota language, it's us—SRU. So, if you would, give me a structured proposal. I'll sign off and give it to Dr. Yellow Bull. I know Doug will approve. You have time. The faculty review committee doesn't meet until September. We should be able to offer the course next fall."

"*Wopila* (Thank you)," Denise said, smiling broadly. "President Eagle Shield's predecessor probably wouldn't have approved. In fact, he circumvented the faculty review committee several times. For some reason he didn't like our department."

"I remember," Gavin said. "Now we have a president who is forward thinking and innovative. He's not in it for personal glory."

Gavin found a pen and briefly summarized the meeting with Denise Archambault in his notebook before he brought up his email account and clicked on Chief Avery's name. When the email opened a heading in bold letters immediately caught his attention: The University of Durham.

After the second time through the brief note, Gavin realized he was clenching his jaw. Opening the attached file was an additional shock. He stared at the news photo of Dr. C.M. Hightower. The resemblance to the man whose office was on the first floor was astonishing and the implications scary.

After he read Dr. Caleb Hightower's obituary he dialed Primault's number.

"Hey, Gavin," the CI answered. "I'm in the Chief's office and I'm putting you on speaker."

"No problem. While it's on my mind, I would like to share this new development with President Eagle Shield," he said.

"By all means," Avery replied.

"Quite a kick in the nuts, wouldn't you say?" Primault commented wryly.

"Yeah. Explains a lot, answers some questions. But it does raise another one. Why would Carey Hightower cross an ocean to impersonate his dead older brother? Was he just a crass opportunist, or is there something else behind it all?"

"We haven't thought that far ahead," admitted the Chief. "We're still in shock, but you're right."

"I think the more important issue is what should be done," Gavin ventured.

"That's what we're talking about here," the Chief agreed. "Mr. Hightower should be in custody."

"Whose custody?"

"Ours," the Chief said. "Obviously, there's an issue of tribal sovereignty that we can't ignore. At the same time, we can't ignore the feds. Caruth committed his offense on your land, so we thought of prosecuting in Redoubt County. Arlo High Crane was murdered on tribal land, so we thought of

Kincaid County. But either way is pretty thin ice and would only erode tribal sovereignty. Having said that, Gavin, we know there's definitely thin ice in turning Hightower over to the feds—because he's white. Our best hope is to pile up so much evidence that the damn feds will have to do what's right."

"Knowing the racial attitudes of federal and state law enforcement here, white privilege will rear its ugly head, especially in a case like this," Gavin agreed. "So, what's the plan?"

"Well, here's the thing," Primault said. "The minute we make a public arrest of a white guy, the feds are going to know. So, it has to be covert, downright sneaky, as a matter of fact. That's the problem we have to solve."

"You need a diversion or a smoke screen," Gavin suggested. "It may be a stretch, but we laid the groundwork by dangling my pistol in front of Hightower. That is something he won't ignore. I think I may have an idea, but, as I said, Dr. Eagle Shield needs to know about this latest shocker. I want to talk to him, because he and SRU could be part of what I have in mind. And, for this to work, we need to keep it close to the vest. Can you two drop by my place this evening?"

## EIGHTY-SIX

Two unrelated factors were about to meet at the intersection of chance and necessity: the ledger book project and the murder of Arlo High Crane. Or perhaps entwine more than meet.

Doug Eagle Shield walked over to the small refrigerator in the corner of his office and brought back two bottles of water, handing one to Gavin. "If I had something stronger, this is the moment I would pour us a stiff drink," he said.

Gavin took the water. "It is that kind of moment," he agreed.

"Damn, Gavin, I hired that—that person!"

"He fooled us all, Doug."

Eagle Shield was on the verge of livid. "He damn sure did. Now some things make sense; he didn't want to go to conferences, he turned down invitations to write articles for some prestigious publications, like on that Kennewick Man debate. Most scholars live for those sorts of things. And now he's the only suspect in young Arlo's murder. So, what's to be done?"

"I have an idea," Gavin said. "It will need your okay, and then I'm getting together later with Chief Avery and Lieutenant Primault."

Four men sat around the glow of orange flames from the fire pit in Gavin's backyard; they were, essentially, planning an attack by a war party.

"Doug Eagle Shield and I composed the email together before I left his office," Gavin told Chief Avery and Lieutenant Primault. "If the two of you agree with the plan, I'll give him an okay to send it."

"And that email is inviting the university staff to attend a private opening of an exhibit of your ledger book?" Avery asked.

"Right. Since Dr. Wells and the two techs have been here, the rumors have been hot and heavy. People have been stopping in to watch them work. So, the university community will show up in force," Gavin said. "Hightower will get an invitation from Doug himself, a phone call since he doesn't have a computer in his house. I will also call Hightower and tell him that I'm going to make an announcement regarding the Little Bighorn pistol and bring it to show."

"Damn," Primault said, "he isn't going to ignore that."

"We hope," Gavin said. "The other part of the plan is for me to show it privately to Hightower, and that's where you make the arrest."

"After that we take him to our shop and hide him in our old drunk tank, and only the jailer will know he's there," Avery said. "From that moment we'll be going into uncharted territory. If it all works out, we'll gather all the evidence and haul his ass up to Pierre and turn him over to the feds. If it doesn't work out, the feds will come down hard on us."

"Why would Carey Hightower impersonate his brother? That's what bothers me," Gavin said. "The obituary mentions he was in the army. So, he gets out and decides to become his brother. Why?"

Avery nodded thoughtfully. "I think we've gotten all the information we can from Durham University. I'll send an email to Scotland Yard, inform them of the situation here, and inquire about Carey Hightower. In fact, I'll stop by the station and do that tonight."

"Is that their FBI?" Andrew asked.

"It is," Avery affirmed.

"What do you think about all of this, *Tunkasila* (Grandfather)?" Primault said to Andrew.

"Well," Andrew replied, "there's always more than meets the eye. Maybe this is like an onion. Maybe there's more than one layer."

## EIGHTY-SEVEN

Hightower had no intention of accepting President Eagle Shield's invitation until Gavin Lone Wolf called and left a message. After debating for all of two minutes, Hightower returned the call.

"Top of the morning, old boy," he said, affecting cheerfulness. "So, what's this shindig at the university all about?"

"Dr. Wells is putting up an exhibit for the university faculty and staff," Gavin told him. "A photographic display of all the ledger sketches. It's happening tomorrow evening in the Student Union."

"I see. Your message said something about the Little Bighorn pistol," Hightower reminded him.

"Of course. After talking about it, my family and I decided this is the time to bring it out in the open. We also decided to bequeath it to NMAI."

"Blimey! That's rather generous."

"Be that as it may, it means we can stop worrying about it. I thought you'd like to see it first." Gavin thought he heard a gasp.

"I hope you're not jerking my chain."

"Not at all. If you do, meet me in my office before the ledger exhibit starts. I'll be there at six-thirty. It'll be my pleasure to show it to you."

"I appreciate that. When will you turn it over to Dr. Wells?"

In any other circumstance Hightower's question would be inconsequential. In this case Gavin assumed he might be looking for an opportunity to make a play for the pistol. That would be a harmless maneuver, since it wasn't the real pistol, but would offer an opportunity to apprehend Hightower.

"Well, that's the thing," he said, hurriedly concocting a tale. "Two armed security people from NMAI will be at the exhibit to guard the pistol. After that it will be placed in the university vault. If you want to see it before all of that happens—well, it's up to you. The offer is there."

"Right. In that case, I'll see you in your office."

Heart pounding, Hightower returned the phone to its cradle.

There it was—the opportunity of a lifetime.

Taking deep breaths, he paced slowly around the house. The plan he had only generally formed began to take more precise shape. Two important steps had to be taken, and both today.

Stopping for a moment he tried to sort out the details churning in his mind. He began pacing again, thinking. Tonight would be the last night he would sleep in this house. Tomorrow he would be on his way to being a rich man. He glanced at the calendar hanging next to the refrigerator. Tomorrow's date was June twenty-fifth, the one hundred forty-second anniversary of the Battle of the Little Bighorn.

# EIGHTY-EIGHT

At Gavin's suggestion Doug Eagle Shield asked Ramona Red Star to supervise meal preparation for the evening so that she would not be in the Lakota Studies Building when Hightower arrived. Early in the day Primault had returned the framed prints to Hightower's office, just in case.

Just before six Gavin arrived at the Student Union, which was already bustling with activity and buzzing with conversations. Photographs of Gavin's great-grandfather's ledger sketches had been enlarged into poster sized prints and arranged in a large circle in the main dining area. Ramona approached and took him by the arm.

"This is spectacular," she said. "A story for the ages."

"That's a good way to describe it," he said. He looked around, noticing that the place was filling up. "I'll be back. Something I have to check on in the office."

Stopping off at his pickup he unlocked a door and took his brief case with Gerard's replica in it from the back. Gavin glanced at his watch again as he walked toward the front doors of the Lakota Studies Building. He didn't notice Hightower's vehicle anywhere among the vehicles in the lots.

Patrolman Singer, in plain clothes, had taken up station in Arlo High Crane's study room and Lieutenant Primault was in the first-floor janitorial closet, where with a door open a crack he had a view of the front door.

Except for the hidden officers and himself, the building was empty of people. Gavin unlocked his office and quickly took the blue Styrofoam container out of the briefcase and placed it prominently on his desk. Next he opened the Messaging program on his phone and typed in a text to Singer and Primault's cell phones—CH in the room—and placed it on the desk pad. After Hightower arrived, he would access Messaging and press Send. At the precise moment he glanced at his watch he heard the front glass door click open.

Hightower never used the elevator, always the stairwell. The door to the stairwell opened and closed. Several seconds later the access door to the second floor opened. Gavin sat back in his chair and picked up his phone.

"All the excitement seems to be at the Student Union," Hightower declared as he stepped through the open door without knocking.

"It is," Gavin said, pointing to a chair. He saw Hightower's gaze land on the blue Styrofoam box. "Have a seat."

Hightower was not dressed in his usual summer T-shirt and board shorts. Cargo pants with side pockets, a long sleeve safari shirt, and hiking boots were his choice. After the man sat, Gavin pulled up Messaging and pressed Send.

"I know the food will be good," Gavin said, making small talk even as he noticed a flash of nervousness in Hightower's blue eyes. "You should think about stopping by over there."

Hightower cleared his throat. "Yeah, maybe I will." He pointed at the blue case. "Is that the gun?"

Gavin nodded and grabbed the case, carefully pulling up on the top half. Hightower leaned forward, anticipation twisting his face into an almost comical grimace. Gavin lifted the top half of the case, revealing the pistol wrapped in plastic and fitted snugly in a custom cutout. Oblivious to everything else, Hightower scooted forward for a closer look as Lieutenant Primault stepped through the door, a hand on his holstered weapon.

"Mr. Hightower," he said firmly, "keep your hands where I can see them. Down on your knees, now!"

Hightower hunched his shoulders as if expecting to be hit. Gavin pushed his office chair backward until it rolled up against the east wall of the office.

"What?" Hightower seemed to be genuinely shocked. "Gavin! What's this about?"

Primault drew his weapon. "On your knees, now!"

With a look of panicked resignation, Hightower complied.

"Mr. Hightower, you are under arrest for the murder of Arlo High Crane. Hands on your head!"

Patrolman Singer stepped in as Primault placed the cuffs on Hightower's wrists. His expression of shock turned to wary anticipation.

"You can't arrest me! I'm not subject to your jurisdiction," Hightower protested.

"We just did. On your feet," ordered Primault. The officers pulled him to his feet and did a quick but thorough body search, pulling out a car key attached to a door remote and a flip phone.

"Wait. Wait! I have something to say to my friend Gavin!"

Gavin stood from his chair and stepped forward. "You have nothing to say that would interest me, Mr. Carey Hightower. I know now why you had to work your way to the United States on that container ship. Did you come over as Carey or as Caleb? Did you turn imposter after you got here, or on the way over?"

Hightower blinked in surprise as realization fell into place. "What—what—whatever you think you know, I have three words," he rasped.

With cold detachment Gavin stared at the handcuffed man.

"Esther Red Thunder," Hightower said.

"What did you say?"

"You heard me, Dr. Lone Wolf."

"What about Esther?"

"I suggest you take a look at my phone, in the photo gallery."

Gavin glanced at Primault who pulled the phone from his pocket. "Who's Esther Red Thunder," he asked, handing the phone over.

"An elderly relative," Gavin said. "She lives in Lower Horse Creek housing." Gavin opened the phone and tapped icons until he brought up the Photo Gallery. There appeared to be only one photo. After another tap it filled the phone's screen, sending a cold flutter up his back. Looking pensively into the camera were three people; Esther Red Thunder and her two grandkids, Chris and Nora Janis.

Gavin lifted a cold gaze. "Where are they?"

"Well," Hightower sniffed, "that answer comes with a price." He glanced at the pistol and then at Gavin. "Your pistol. I leave here with that, and you will hear from me in one hour with a location. But you should know they don't have water or food."

"You could be bluffing."

"One way to find out. Call their phones. You know, the cell phones you bought those kids and the landline in their house. I'm sure you have their numbers."

Passing Hightower's phone to Lieutenant Primault, who immediately looked at the photograph, Gavin found Esther's landline number on his phone, and dialed. There was no answer. He tried Chris and Nora's numbers as well. Same result.

"Those kids' phones are still in their house," Hightower said.

"You just admitted to abduction," Primault hissed.

Hightower glanced sideways. "So what?"

Primault nodded at Gavin. "Your call."

"Is there an officer in or around Cold River?" Gavin asked.

Primault immediately called the dispatcher. "Janice, this is Primault. I need a welfare check in Lower Horse Creek Housing…yes, south of Cold River…immediately." He looked at Gavin. "House number?"

"Thirty-seven."

"Thirty-seven," Primault told the dispatcher. "I want to know five minutes ago…right. Thanks." Grabbing Hightower by the arm, the CI pushed him toward a corner. "Stand there, and don't move!"

Hightower backed against the wall, warily glancing at each of the other men in the room. Gavin saw something else in Hightower's demeanor, an undercurrent that he was in control of the moment.

Patrolman Singer stationed himself in the doorway and stood with wrists crossed over his belt.

Primault stepped over to stand with Gavin. "Tell me about Esther," he said.

"She's in her seventies, a widow, guardian and caretaker of her two grandkids. Her daughter and son-in-law died two years ago, ran out of gas coming back from Chase Creek during that brutally cold weather we had. They tried to walk and froze."

Primault's gaze at Hightower was outright disgust. "And that son-of-a-bitch added to her already hard life."

Gavin's office turned coldly silent as they waited for a call from Dispatch. Hightower was smart enough to keep his eyes down.

It might as well have been a siren blaring when Primault's phone rang.

"Primault," he answered.

"Sir," Janice said, "the officer reports that the front door at that address was open, and no one is in the residence. He searched in the yard as well."

"Thanks, Janice. Tell him to secure the house and remain on site until further notice."

"Will do, sir."

Primault spoke to Gavin. "Esther's house is empty. This is your call."

Gavin stepped to the desk and put the lid on the Styrofoam case. Primault nodded at Singer who walked over and removed Hightower's cuffs as Primault placed the car key and phone he had confiscated on top of the case.

Gavin moved back and pointed at the case. "There it is," he said. His voice turned into a low growl. "If I don't hear from you in one hour I will move heaven and earth to find you."

Hightower nodded nervously. "No cops," he rasped. "If I see one damn tribal cop, you won't hear from me."

"Get out of my office."

Hightower moved hesitantly, grabbing the case, key, and phone and a few seconds later they heard his descending steps in the stairwell. Gavin held up a hand and stepped to the doorway. Below them in the lobby Hightower pushed the front door and turned left after he exited.

Gavin turned to the officers. "..." At each end of the hallway are windows, one faces east. The officers hurried to the hallway.

Running into his office and to the east window he quickly spotted Hightower getting into a silver sedan. After he backed out of the parking slot, it headed for the east exit from campus.

Primault was already on his shoulder mike as he returned to the balcony. "This is Primault for all Smokey River units in and around Kincaid. Primault for all units in and around Kincaid. Clear all your units from Highway 17 east and west. Repeat! Immediately clear all your units from Highway 17 east and west!"

He met Gavin on the balcony. "Which way do you think he's going?" he asked.

"I'm guessing after he gets on Highway 17 he'll get onto some back road to stay out of sight."

"I'm so sorry, my friend, about your relative."

"I think I know where they are."

"Really? Where?"

"Hightower's basement. I recognized a partial brick wall in that photo. If I'm right, that means he's not going to his house. He's planned this out down to using a different car."

"Right. Hilltop is thirty miles from here. We'll wait a few minutes and take my unit." Primault turned to Singer. "Let's cover all the main roads, just in case. We know Hightower is driving a silver, four-door Buick Sedan. Without being obvious I want someone on Highway 83 south, at the casino, 83 north at Cold River at the junction with Highway 33. Someone at the youth detention center on Highway 17 west. Provide a physical description of the subject and instruct to observe and report if he's spotted anywhere."

Singer wrote hurriedly in his notebook.

"Call Dispatch, those ladies will know which unit is where."

Primault noticed Gavin glancing at his watch.

"Let's go," he said. "I've got an unmarked car."

At the highway they turned east and immediately Primault floored the Dodge with the interceptor engine. "No lights or sirens," he said to Gavin, "just in case our friend is heading this way. How far to the Hilltop turn-off?"

"Twenty miles."

"You really think that son-of-a-bitch will call?"

"Probably not, so I hope I'm right."

"Most criminals are not innovative," Primault commented. "They tend to stay with the familiar. If a convict escapes, the first move for cops is to look in the escapee's home turf. They almost always go back to the familiar. It stands to reason Hightower would use his own basement. Besides, that way he doesn't have to involve anyone else who might talk."

"Well, he was innovative enough to take hostages," Gavin observed.

Primault's phone rang, a call from Chief Avery.

"Rhonda just filled me in. What happened?"

Primault gave a quick and concise report. "He was one step ahead of us. Gavin and I are heading to Hilltop to look in Hightower's basement for Esther Red Thunder."

"Right. Keep me posted."

"The one thing I didn't think of is an ambulance."

"We'll handle that. What's the exact location?"

Primault glanced at Gavin for a second. "What's Hightower's address in Hilltop?"

"Second Street. His house is the last one in the southwest corner of town."

Primault passed on the information and disconnected the call.

"Thanks for doing that," Gavin said. "What are the odds we'll ever see Hightower again? He's got a lot to answer for."

"We'll get him."

Fortunately, there was little traffic on Highway 17 east. Gavin didn't ask how fast they were going, but it was fast enough for high line poles to flash past like one long picket fence. They finally slowed for the left turn toward Hilltop and eight minutes later they skidded to a stop in Hightower's driveway.

Both men jumped out of the vehicle and ran up to the front door, which was locked. Primault stepped back and launched a powerful kick, nearly separating the doorknob housing from the door itself. Gavin led the way to the basement. A small crowbar through a hasp was barring the door. Primault yanked the bar away and pulled the door open.

A small form was curled on a thin mattress on the concrete floor, in the dark, damp room. Two other forms were sitting against the wall, huddled under a blanket.

"Auntie!" Gavin said, kneeling beside the woman. She was looking up, her eyes wide with dread. In the next instant came disbelief, and then relief.

"Uncle Gavin!" Nora yelled as she and her brother threw off the blanket and jumped to their feet.

"*Tunska!*" Esther said, in a small plaintive voice. "Is it you?"

"It's me, Auntie. It's me. Can you sit up?"

"Yeah, I can, if you help me."

Gavin grabbed her thin shoulders gently and pulled her to a sitting position, with help from Christopher, and immediately noticed the dried blood on the knuckles of both her hands.

"Let's go upstairs," Gavin told them. "There's an ambulance coming. I want the EMTs to check you all out."

"Oh, we're okay now, *Tunska*."

They made Esther comfortable on the futon as they waited for the ambulance. "Auntie," Gavin said. "I'm sorry for all this. What happened to your hands?"

The old woman smiled sheepishly. "I was trying to slide my hands behind that little window in the basement. We tried to open it," she admitted. "My hands got stuck. The window was too small, anyways." She waved a hand toward her grandkids. "I'm just glad those ones are okay. We were all scared." She pointed at Primault. "I didn't know angels carried guns."

Primault smiled.

"Do you hurt anywhere, Auntie?" Gavin asked. "Did he hurt you?"

"No. I bumped my elbow, but I'm okay," Esther said.

Nearly twenty minutes later the ambulance arrived. The EMTs quickly and efficiently examined Esther and the children. Gavin had a thought and called Loren. He quickly explained the situation.

"Can you meet me at Auntie's house in Lower Horse Creek? I'm going to ask Lieutenant Primault to take us there."

"I'm on my way."

An officer was still parked in Esther's driveway when they arrived. In the house, Gavin put on coffee and joined Esther at the table. "Lieutenant Primault, your angel, wants to talk to you about what happened. He has some questions. Is that okay?"

"Yeah, sure."

Loren arrived as Primault was taking Esther's statement. Gavin took a few moments to fill her in on what had transpired, and then called Uncle Andrew. After Primault finished with Esther he spoke with Christopher and Nora.

A call came in for Primault from Dispatch. He pulled Gavin aside to tell him the news. "One of our officers saw a silver Buick sedan heading north on Highway 83 through Cold River. The only one in the vehicle was a male driver. That was just after seven o'clock."

"So, it's possible he's heading north. Damn! He's on the interstate by now."

"Probably," Primault agreed. "I'll talk to the Chief about putting the word out to the counties and state highway patrol."

"He didn't call to tell us where he had hidden Auntie Esther," Gavin said angrily.

"I'm not surprised. Lucky you recognized the room."

Loren and Gavin stayed after the officers had gone, waiting for Uncle Andrew, and Loren fixed a meal. When Andrew arrived, they ate with Esther and the children. Loren announced she was staying the night, and Andrew drove Gavin to the campus to retrieve his pickup.

"I don't know how we screwed it up, but we did," Gavin told his uncle.

"You didn't," Andrew replied. "That man knows how to be sneaky. That's his life."

"Well, by now he's well on his way east or west on the interstate."

"Maybe not," Andrew said. "He's smart enough to know that the tribal cops will put out the word. Maybe he's laying low somewhere, or maybe he'll use nothing but back roads. From what you told me he wanted that gun awful bad, so he probably made some plans."

"You could be right. He thinks he got something worth millions, so maybe he's thought it through."

"Yeah," Andrew said. "So maybe he's not going down the road with his hair on fire. Maybe he's hiding. Maybe he's hunkered down somewhere."

"You think so?"

"Yeah. A hunter who is hunted will eventually turn and fight. Your friend is not a hunter, he never was. A person like that is more likely to hide."

"A person like that," Gavin repeated. "A few weeks ago, I bought that person a steak in Edna's. Now he's a murder suspect on the run. And, if you're right, he could be hiding anywhere."

"He can't hide where he doesn't know the layout, or the land," Andrew said. "He's probably going to stick with the things he knows."

## EIGHTY-NINE

When Gavin finally arrived home, he tried not to think of the disconcerting circumstances and how the day had played out. He had known disappointments, large and small. But Hightower slipping from their grasp was a sharp blow. Yet Uncle Andrew's suggestion made sense. Maybe Hightower was hiding in some place he knew.

Taking the landline phone from his desk, he called Gerard.

"Hey, bro," Gerard answered. "What's up?"

After Gavin finished relating the day's events, Gerard responded, "Damn, bro. He didn't just disappear. Uncle Andrew may be right. He's out there somewhere. He's not that good. Damn lucky maybe, but not that good."

"I agree. The issue is what to do."

"Hey, bro, if there's anyone with scary instincts, it's you. Remember how we tracked that Whitetail buck we wounded when we were thirteen? I would've sworn you were in that buck's head. Use those instincts, bro."

"Well, at this point it'll take some stroke of luck to find him."

"Sometimes that happens; sometimes you make the luck, you know?" Gerard insisted.

The intense regret and disappointment Gavin was feeling prompted thoughts of Arlo High Crane and the last moments and words he had shared with him.

*May I ask you a question, Dr. Lone Wolf?*

*Sure, what's on your mind?*

*Ah, well, how long have you known Dr. Hightower?*

*Well, no longer than anyone else here, I would guess. I was on the screening committee…*

*So, he was vetted thoroughly?*

*I assume so. I'm sure Human Resources did.…By the way, where is Caleb?*

*He's coming. He had to break camp.*

*He camped?*

*Oh, yeah, just west of the Little White, and south from the Big White where he found the musket barrel…*

He had camped in that area, several times, Gavin recalled, and suddenly he was examining a plat map of Redoubt County he pulled out of his wooden file cabinet. He found the page that showed the flood plain south of the confluence of the two rivers—the Little White and White Rivers. A circle in red pencil caught his eye—south of the confluence. Odds were it was nothing, especially since he knew he didn't make that mark. Then he remembered who could have. Hightower had borrowed the book for a class.

*Why was that circle there? Perhaps to mark a campsite?*

*Use those instincts, bro.*

There was a fine line between good instincts and wild-ass guesses, but he was willing to take a chance. His grandfather had been born near the location of the red circle and the bottomland west of the Little White was still tribal land. There was an area where people camped although it was not a public campground. What were the odds that Hightower had camped there—and was there now?

There was only one way to determine that.

He reached for the phone and scrolled the contacts until he found the number he wanted and placed the call.

"Hello," a low raspy voice answered.

"Hey, Andy, this is Gavin Lone Wolf. How are you?"

"Gavin! I'm good, mostly, just aches and pains that come with being seventy-three. How are you?"

"No complaints, Andy. Say, listen, is that Skyhawk still flying?"

"Sure is, need to do some flying?"

"Well, there's a situation up here, on the reservation, and we might need your help."

"Oh? What kind of a situation?"

"A guy who is the only suspect in a murder case got away from the tribal police."

"Hell, that doesn't sound good. How do you need my help?"

Gavin sighed. "Well, Andy, I think I know where that guy is right now. And if the tribal police chief agrees, I'd like to, ah, sort of drop in on the fugitive."

"Drop in? You mean literally?"

Gavin chuckled. "You got it, Andy. But I just wanted to see if you might be available to fly up here and pick me up this evening."

"Sure, I don't see why not."

"Okay, thanks, Andy. I'm going to call the police chief and run it by him. I'll call you right back."

Gavin disconnected the call and glanced out the window. Night had fallen. That wasn't the issue. Andy Gardner was an experienced, instrument-rated pilot. The issue was parachuting in the dark. Walking to his bedroom closet, he turned on the light and grabbed the parachute pack he had bought two years ago.

He did fifty-six jumps over the past ten years from varying altitudes. Four with military-style canopy chutes. Most were with glide chutes, which is what he had. Out of fifty-six jumps only one had been at night, but that was about to change.

Back in the living room he picked up his phone and called Avery.

"Ben Avery," the Chief answered, sounding tired.

"Ben, it's Gavin. Just wondering if you have a minute."

"What's on your mind?"

"I'm assuming Justin filled you in."

"He did. Disappointing the way it turned out," Avery sighed. "I guess we'll regroup."

"I think I know where Hightower is."

"Really?"

"An educated guess. A few weeks ago, when Arlo helped him dig that musket out of the Big White, he camped near there. As a matter of fact, he's camped there several times. He was obsessed with that area, because he thought there were historic artifacts all over the place."

Avery was intrigued. "Well, that might explain why he disappeared so quickly. He went to familiar ground. Do you know where he camped?"

"I know the area. It's south of the confluence of the two rivers. I think it's worth checking out, and I might have a way to do that."

"Okay. What do you have in mind?"

Gavin looked out his front window. There was no moon tonight. "It's actually very simple," he said cautiously. "Driving in would alert him if he's there. There's a better way."

"Hiking in?"

"Even better. I'm a skydiver, and I have a glide chute. I'll jump."

Avery was silent for a few seconds, "Sounds a bit dangerous, my friend. Besides, you don't have an airplane, do you?"

"No, but I have a friend who does, and he's ready to fly me over the area. He's standing by."

Avery was silent again. "Damn, you are serious, aren't you."

"As I can be. My friend Andy Gardner from Valentine is an experienced pilot and has a Cessna Skyhawk, a four-place. He can fly me over the area."

"Okay, and you jump out, in the dark, and look for Hightower."

"I know the area—my brother and I played there when we were boys. I've been there countless times over the years."

Gavin could hear Avery's deep sigh. "I sort of get the sense that, even if I don't go along with this idea, you're doing it anyway."

"I hate the thought of Hightower getting away with murder."

## NINETY

Gavin drove to the airstrip just outside of Cold River. He made one more equipment check as Andy Gardner was turning from the base leg onto his final approach. By the time the Cessna landed and taxied up, he was ready to go.

Opening the passenger side door, he pushed the front seat ahead and maneuvered himself into the back. It was a tight squeeze since he was wearing his chute pack and carrying other equipment.

"Hey, Andy," he said, after closing the door. "I sure appreciate you doing this on such short notice."

"Hey, my friend. All I'm doing is taking off, flying, and landing. You got the tough job. Where we going?"

"As the crow flies, about ten miles north northeast of here. But I want us to approach from the northeast." He handed Andy a piece of paper. "Those are the coordinates, but we can probably do it visually. We head east, then north to the interstate, and then southwest."

Gardner began taxiing to the end of the strip. "Okay. How high?"

"Oh, about five thousand, I should think. There's a slight breeze here, hopefully it's about the same at the drop. I don't want to hang up there too long."

"Gotcha. Are you armed?"

"Yeah. Keeping it light, though. Got a .45 caliber 1911 with extra clips and a K-Bar my brother gave me. Hopefully I won't need those."

"Who is this guy you're going after?"

Gavin chuckled wryly as he checked over his equipment yet again. "Used to be a friend of mine," he said. "There's strong evidence he killed a young man a few weeks ago, shot him in the back of the head."

Gardner turned the Cessna into the wind and did a quick run-up and check. "My friend, you stay safe. Sounds like a bad man." Setting the flaps for take-off he pushed the throttle forward, and the plane lurched ahead.

After climbing steadily Gardner leveled off at five thousand feet and soon after turned to heading zero, or north. "It's clear enough for VFR," he told Gavin. "I figure we'll do our turnaround at the interstate."

Gavin looked out the window. "In that case, bring it to two-two-zero after your turn."

"Roger." Gardner pointed to a small screen attached to the top of the instrument panel above all the lighted gauges. "As a backup, I have this new-fangled gadget. It's a GPS thing, based on sectional maps."

Gavin leaned forward, feeling clumsy in the tight chute pack, focusing on the screen, as Gardner pushed an arrow button until the south-central portion of the state appeared. "There," he said, "there's the Big White River, and from the south is the Little White River."

Gavin pointed. "About a mile south of the confluence is where that man is camped, I think."

"Alright, so what's your plan?"

"That area, the flood plain just west of the Little White, has thickets of oak and big cottonwood trees. So, I'm thinking east side of the river. It's hilly, but no big cottonwoods to get hung up."

"Okay. No moon so it might be tricky, especially if it's hilly like you say."

"Yeah. I have this glide chute, Andy. I can fly it down, guide it."

"Okay. We're coming up on the interstate. Listen, I wrapped the footrest out there with non-stick tape, and the lower part of the strut as well. When we get over your spot, I'll go to twenty percent flaps and slow this puppy down as much as I can."

"Thanks, Andy. I'm ready." He slipped on leather gloves with non-slip grips on the fingers, then strapped on his helmet and goggles.

After a slow left turn, Andy Gardner leveled the aircraft and dialed in the flaps, dropping his airspeed. "Altimeter is five thousand. Want to go lower?"

"Yeah, if you got time, maybe four, that'll give me about thirteen hundred to the deck."

"Roger." Gardner checked the GPS screen. "About five minutes, I'd say. Push the seat up as far as it'll go. It'll get windy and loud when you open that door. Airspeed is falling, get ready."

"Roger, that." Gavin pushed the seat forward and reached for the door handle.

"Good luck, my friend. Give me a shout, let me know you're okay."

"Will do, as soon as I power up my satellite phone."

Gardner's eyes swept over the gauges, his hands steady on the yoke. He pulled back slightly on the throttle and checked the GPS screen. "Go, my friend. Go," he said.

"Talk to you in a bit," Gavin said. Crouching forward he opened the door. Cold wind and noise filled the cabin instantaneously. Pushing hard on the door to force it open, and leaning out, he found the footrest with his right foot and grabbed the wing strut with his left hand. Making sure he was not hung up on the door or the seat, he leaned forward—then pushed off.

In his peripheral vision the plane's right horizontal stabilizer flashed past above him. A second later he opened the chute and braced for the jolt. He wasn't near terminal velocity, so the jolt was not hard. The wing-like chute opened with a pop above him. Less than a minute was his time window to orient himself to the ground. The drone of the departing Cessna's engine grew fainter in the distance. Grabbing the steering lines, he peered down, trying to acclimate his vision to the dark. Slowly he began to discern subtle variations in the darkness below him. Keeping his eyes fixed on that darkness, he began to count down in his head.

Twenty, nineteen, eighteen, seventeen, sixteen…

The best he could do was to guess when to flare the chute to slow it down.

Fifteen, fourteen, thirteen, twelve, ten…

Variations in shadows and shapes began to form, touchdown was any second. He flared the chute, and then leveled off. He wanted to avoid a face full of sharp soap weeds with rapier-like bristles. Suddenly, he made out the gentle slope of a hillside and put his feet together and bent his knees. Three seconds later his boots made contact. After a short slide, his butt hit the ground, and he felt tall grass all around as the chute started to collapse. Only then could he feel his heart pounding.

Gavin unbuckled from the harness and took a deep breath. Undoing the chin strap, he slipped off the helmet. He knew he was on a slope east of the Little White River. In between him and the river lay a little used road and two barbed wire fences. The most immediate task was to roll up his chute. But first things first, he pulled out the satellite phone from his inside jacket pocket and powered it up, then held up the illuminated face of the compass strapped to his wrist. Finding north, he turned himself around to face west. Below him was the river.

He dialed Andy Gardner's cell number.

"Hey, are you in one piece?" Gardner asked. Gavin heard the cockpit noise in the background.

"As near as I can tell."

"Great! You be careful. Let me know how it goes."

"You got it. Thanks, Andy. Couldn't have done this without you. Buffalo steaks are on me."

"Sounds good!"

"Bill me for your time and fuel."

"No, no, just the fuel, my friend. Just the fuel."

Touching a button on his watch he checked the time—11:14. First objective, after rolling up his chute, was to get his bearings. Knowing how far he was from Hightower's probable camp was critical. Crossing the road and the river would provide some clues. Fifteen minutes later he finished stuffing the chute, harness, and goggles in the carry bag. Feeling around with his feet and looking closely, he found a narrow gully to hide the bag. Luckily, the bag was a drab, flat green in color and would blend in for recovery later.

Pausing on a slope, he could see the landscape around him. Adjusting his web belt and harness, he checked to make sure his knife, pistol, and canteen were in place. He loaded the 1911 and holstered it. In his left leg pocket was a bag of *wasna*, called "pemmican" by white people. It was the food carried by Lakota hunter/warriors in the old days, a mixture of dried elk meat—sometimes deer or buffalo—dried chokecherries, and a bit of buffalo tallow. He was ready. First, he had to make another call.

Justin Primault answered at the first ring.

"Hey, Gavin. It's good to hear from you. Where are you?"

"On a hillside east of the Little White River. I'm about to move down to the river. Once I'm across I'll start looking for Hightower's camp, where he might have camped before, I mean."

"Okay, Mel Triplett's deputy, Tyler Huffman, will help us," Primault said. "He's going to take a position on County Road 14, about two miles east of the Little White, up on a flat, he said. Jason Singer and I will be west of the river. If Hightower is where you think he is, he has to get back on CR 14 to go anywhere. If he's there we've got him boxed in, and we're ready to roll as soon as we hear from you."

"Right. I'm moving to the river now. I'm guessing I'm generally south of the campsite he used, but how far I don't know." He illuminated his watch to check the time. "I'll call in about thirty minutes, or before if I find anything."

"Okay. How was it, jumping at night?"

"Dark and scary. I won't do it again."

Feeling energized and exhilarated, he wove through the clusters of soap weeds on the slope, but suddenly the two-strand barbed wire fence materialized in the dark. Crossing it, he tied his helmet to the lower strand, as a marker to find his chute later. He stopped on the gravel road and happily realized the surface was smooth. Having driven the road many times over the years, he knew he was close to CR 14. Farther south the road was rough.

The river was 40 yards west of the road. Whispers of flowing water touched his ears, and he could smell it when he came to the shoreline. At this time of the year, it was still running high. Dry feet and socks were a must, so he found a spot to sit and took off his hiking boots and socks and rolled up his trouser legs as high as he could. Then he stepped into the cool water.

# NINETY-ONE

A bull was bellowing in the distance, and coyotes were barking and yelping all around. Miles overhead Gavin heard the muted roar of a passing jetliner. These things he perceived peripherally as he negotiated the river bottom, which was mostly sandy, some slippery shale, and a few rocks. Vague and shadowy, rectangular shapes of long-abandoned concrete pilings appeared in the darkness, remnants of a 1920s bridge.

With a thought toward rattlesnakes, he found a low sand bank and sat to put his socks and boots on. After a drink of water from the canteen, he walked east. The floodplain was filled with thickets of oak, ash, and cottonwood trees. Not to mention various types of small trees and shrubs, such as the ever-present buffalo berry trees and chokecherry bushes.

The abandoned pilings in the river affirmed that he was south of Hightower's probable campsite, at least the area that had become a favorite unofficial camping area. It was tribal land and a rancher pastured cattle here. Gavin recalled that Hightower mentioned obtaining permission from that rancher to camp on the land.

Fifty yards from the river he turned north. The brush was easier to walk through. There was occasional flat cactus, Gavin recalled, and a lot of deadfall and the ubiquitous soap weed. All the events, information, and images connected to Hightower roiled in his mind as he walked, carefully picking his way. The coyotes were singing, and he suddenly recalled something about mountain lion sightings near a ranch in the White River valley.

Gavin estimated he was half a mile south of County Road 14, which was less than a hundred yards south of the White River before it bent to the north. The nearest residence of any kind was half a mile east and the nearest ranches were miles in any direction. This was an isolated area, a good place to camp if one wanted to hide.

He considered the odds that Hightower was here somewhere, at this moment. A car was not easy to hide. It could be parked in a thicket, but it would not blend in, even in the dark.

Moving slowly, parallel to the river, he explored every thicket he came to. All the campsites he knew of were close to or next to the river, but the brush and undergrowth near the water made it difficult for any vehicle to move through. Pausing next to an ash tree, he illuminated his watch and checked the time. He needed to call Primault soon. He started again.

Sensations, impressions, perceptions, and thoughts moved with him. This was the land of his ancestors. His great-grandfathers—the warriors of Greasy Grass—had lived here with their families, in camouflaged dwellings to hide from whites. They had survived on deer, rabbits, and squirrels and catfish from the river. They dug wild turnips, gathered chokecherries, buffalo berries, and wild potatoes in season. As his dad, Gabriel, had told many times, they were all lean and healthy—and free.

Gavin could sense other things in the dark—ghosts. There were spirits that wandered the land day and night. People ignored the fact, or perhaps had not learned, that the Earth was old and countless beings had lived on it before now. Their flesh and bones, no matter who and what they were, were now dust, and no one alive remembered them. But some essence of them was still here; so were their old trails, their homes, and their favorite places.

Even as a primal part of his psyche reveled in being home and feeling connected to the land beneath his feet, something caught his eye. A hint of something other than shadow was there, something that did not belong in the natural contours of darkness.

Gavin stopped and probed the darkness with his eyes, sweeping back and forth and slowly up and then down. Ahead of him was a thicket and beyond it was an anomaly. His ears strained to the sounds. Somewhere there was a cricket chirping softly, and closer to the water he heard a bullfrog. Those were all sounds that belonged.

He moved forward, walking slowly, easily, his feet perceiving the ground and the brush of their own accord. After several steps, he stopped. Something was there, beyond the thicket.

Keeping his gaze on the anomaly in the brush, he moved slowly and silently to the left. A shiver went up his back, and he stopped, and then moved forward again.

It was a vehicle of some sort. Ten feet or so from it, he knew he had been right. It was Hightower's car. Beyond it was a small dome tent.

For a few moments he stood, not moving, with his mind racing. He should have been prepared for this moment. As he took a cautious step forward, he almost didn't hear the sound of a motor. It was the light through the trees that caught his attention. Headlights of a car bounced, slicing through the tree branches and thickets. The lights were approaching, and he finally heard the motor. As quietly as he could manage, he stepped behind the thicket and found another several yards farther. There he flattened down into the grass, hoping that no rattlesnakes were around.

The sound of the motor grew louder. Gavin guessed it was following the trail from CR 14. Where did it come from and how had it gotten past Primault? What were the odds, he wondered, that this would happen. As yet, there was nothing from inside the tent, now about thirty yards away, to indicate that Hightower was reacting to the sudden intrusion.

Gavin decided that if Hightower tried to run, there would be no other choice but to move in and apprehend him, disable him, if necessary.

As the vehicle came closer, Gavin recognized the whine of a four-cylinder Jeep engine and could hear faint rattles. To his surprise and dismay, it turned left in the direction of Hightower's camp. Skirting the thicket, he crawled toward low shrubs behind the tent. There was no way Hightower was getting away again.

A few seconds before the vehicle stopped next to Hightower's car, Gavin heard the tent door being unzipped. In the headlight beams, he saw the man emerge, fully dressed, and obviously not alarmed by the arrival of the Jeep. Abruptly the headlights were turned off and then the motor, and then he heard voices.

"Hey, Caleb. How are you?"

"I'm good, Wes. I'm good. Thanks for coming out."

"Yup, yup. I would have come sooner, but my daughter got home late from work, and I couldn't leave her kids by themselves."

"No problem. So, you ready to make a trade?"

"Yup, yup. Though I think you might be on the short end of the stick. How's that for honesty from an old horse trader, huh?"

Hightower laughed, as Gavin was trying to remember anyone named Wes. His accent indicated he was Lakota and maybe an older man.

"Not a big deal. I know you took good care of that Jeep, that's the main thing."

"Okay, as long as you know what you're getting. How shall we do this?"

"I tell you what, let's get in your car and we'll trade titles. And then we're good."

Gavin was surprised, and relieved. At the very least, Hightower was probably not driving away, not in the next few minutes in any case. The dome light of the sedan came on, and a muffled conversation between the two men could be heard. Gavin's mind raced through the possibilities. Hightower might leave soon, perhaps in minutes, but the fact that he had pitched a tent could mean he would stay the night. If Hightower did show signs of leaving, decisive intervention would be necessary. But Gavin did have the element of surprise.

Hightower and Wes stepped out of the car. The dome light stayed on. "Here are the keys," he heard Hightower say. "The tank is full."

"Yup, I filled the tank on that thing, like you asked," Wes replied. "Got good tread on the tires. It's good to go. Key is in it."

Gavin heard movement and saw the dome light go off as soon as the door shut and the engine started. The sedan backed away as its headlights came on. Hightower was briefly silhouetted. Gavin came up to a crouch, waiting. He heard the car moving off, its headlight beams bouncing through the trees. After a few seconds, Hightower could be heard entering the tent, and then some slight rustling noises from inside. And then quiet.

Gavin waited, quietly settling against a tree. He illuminated his watch, thinking it was time to call Primault. No more noises came from inside the tent, indicating that Hightower was settling down for the night. On the chance that he was still awake, Gavin moved, making a wide circle around the thickets near the tent. He stopped behind a large, wide cottonwood and opened his phone.

"What's the word?" Primault answered.

"He's here, in a tent about forty yards from me." Gavin said, speaking in a low voice.

"Damn, your hunch was right. Do you want us to move in?"

"Yeah, but I just saw him trade vehicles with someone named Wes. So, you might see the silver Buick, but Hightower's not in it. He now has a Jeep Wrangler. You can move in anytime. In the meantime, I'm going to let the air out of one of his tires."

"Good idea. Okay, I'll call the deputy and we'll move in."

Gavin put away his phone and moved closer until he found a young oak about twenty yards from the tent. From there he walked slowly until he was at the back of the Jeep. A faint smell of hot oil came from the vehicle and even in the dark Gavin could see it was old, a ragtop. In it, Hightower would have eluded detection even in broad daylight.

Pulling out his knife, he knelt and jabbed the sidewall of the right rear tire, making a small hole. All he wanted was a slow leak. From the sound of the low hiss of escaping air he guessed the tire would be flat in minutes.

As he stood slowly he heard light snoring from the tent.

## NINETY-TWO

Back at the young oak tree, he sat and considered his options. A surprise move on Hightower was not out of the question. The man was probably asleep. His only means of transport was disabled, meaning his only means of escape—if it came to that—was on foot.

Gavin pulled out his phone and called Primault. "His transport is disabled," he said, "and he's down for the night probably thinking he's got the world by the tail."

"Jason and I are on CR 14," Primault said. "Deputy Huffman is coming down the hill. I say we move in and take him."

"My thoughts exactly. On 14, half a mile east of the main highway, is an approach on the south side, has blue reflectors and it goes into a pasture. It immediately turns into a pasture trail. About a hundred yards in it separates into two trails though the thickets, then comes back together. Farther south past that is Hightower's camp, to the east near the river. He's got a dome tent and his new ride parked next to it. It's a dark colored Jeep Wrangler."

"Okay. Where will you be?"

"A few yards east of his tent, in a thicket. Your lights will probably wake him, and he'll go for the Jeep. I'll be close enough to put the collar on him."

"Okay, sounds good. Just be careful and assume he's armed. We're just now turning off CR 14 and will be there in a few minutes."

As he had anticipated, after they entered the clearing the headlights from the lead cruiser illuminated the tent. Though the vehicles were quiet, much quieter than the Jeep, Gavin saw Hightower's shadow. The man sat up, his movements jerky, and unzipped the door, looking out. Two sets of headlights approached and turned toward the tent and stopped. A second later the strobes flared, turning the night into garish, rotating swatches of red and blue.

"CAREY HIGHTOWER!" Gavin recognized Primault's amplified voice. "WALK INTO THE LIGHT WITH YOUR HANDS UP. WE KNOW YOU'RE THERE. COME OUT NOW WITH YOUR HANDS RAISED!"

Gavin moved through the brush, careful to stay behind the tent. He saw Hightower's silhouette moving, staying low. At one point it resembled a crouching rabbit. Instead of standing, Hightower crawled through the door, jumped to his feet with the Styrofoam case under his arm. He took two steps toward the brush before he saw a tall form changing colors from red to blue.

"Like the man said, get your hands up!" Gavin said.

Hightower was mostly in shadow, but Gavin saw no weapon anywhere, only the case under his arm. Hightower, on the other hand, could see Gavin's semi-automatic pistol in the light, pointed at his chest. He raised his arms and the case fell to the ground with a thud.

"Gavin! Don't shoot! Don't shoot!"

Gavin placed the muzzle of his Colt between Hightower's eyebrows. The man closed his eyes, expecting the worst.

"What happened the night you took Arlo out to Flat Butte Dam?" Gavin demanded. "Did you make him drive?"

Hightower opened his eyes. "No," he said, his voice thinned by fear. "Only—only part of the way, through town."

"Then you made him get in the trunk?"

"Yeah, yeah."

Gavin inched closer as he saw the officers silhouetted in the headlights and flashing strobes. "Why? Why did you kill him? Tell me!"

Hightower's jaw trembled. "He—he found out. He found out who I really was."

Gavin cocked the hammer back.

*...good people and bad are pushed to doing the deed, often during one moment of madness or weakness...*

In the next second Gavin stifled the urge to pull the trigger. Releasing the hammer, he lowered the gun and pointed with his right hand.

"Turn around. Walk toward the officers."

Hightower obeyed. Gavin stooped to pick up the case and followed.

Primault, Singer, and Deputy Huffman surrounded Hightower. Singer cuffed the prisoner and pushed him toward the tribal cruiser. Primault turned to the deputy. "Hey, Tyler, thanks for your help."

Deputy Huffman watched Singer putting Hightower into the back seat of the cruiser. "Glad I could help," he said. He turned toward Gavin and extended a hand. "Don't believe I've ever met you, sir."

"I'm Gavin Lone Wolf. As Lieutenant Primault said, thanks for your help."

"Yeah, yeah. So, you're the guy that jumped out of an airplane to catch that guy?"

"Well, I did use a chute," Gavin replied.

The deputy chuckled. "Man, that takes some balls, if you don't mind my saying."

"And a touch of stupid," Gavin said.

Singer joined them and pointed to the Jeep and the tent. "What about that?"

"It's evidence, technically," Primault said. "I'll send someone out for it tomorrow," He turned to Gavin. "Guess you'll need a ride."

"Yeah, my truck's at the airstrip in town."

"Hey, I'll be glad to give you a ride, sir," Huffman offered.

"Thanks," Gavin replied, and glanced toward Primault. "Give me a call in the morning and let me know what's going to happen."

"Will do. And, as Tyler said, it takes some balls to do what you did."

"Well, like I said, it won't happen again."

Forty-five minutes later he stepped into his house. He was tired and for the first time he felt a dull pain in his left knee. It was a small price to pay.

*Nicau kte lo*, the Spirits had told Andrew. It will bring him to you.

It certainly had.

# NINETY-THREE

Shortly after nine the next morning Gavin stopped and picked up Uncle Andrew on the way to recover his parachute.

"I stopped and checked with *Tunjan*," Andrew said, referring to Loren. "She said Esther is okay. A couple of neighbors came over while I was there. I'll check on her and the kids again."

"Yeah. I'll stop by, too."

"So, the Two Face is sitting in jail?"

"Yeah, in tribal jail."

"What's going to happen now?" Andrew wondered. "He's a white man in a tribal jail."

Gavin shook his head slowly. "I'm not sure. He's the only suspect in Arlo's murder, and he abducted an elderly woman. All that is the ironclad truth. The unknown factor is what the feds will do. They're likely to screw it all up."

"Their culture is like an unpredictable teenager, the whites, I mean."

Gavin's phone chirped. It was Chief Avery. He slowed and pulled onto the shoulder of the highway.

"Good morning, Ben."

"Good morning, Gavin. Justin finished filling me in on everything that went down last night. We owe you big time. And I just want to let you know that we sent another email to Scotland Yard asking for any information on Carey Hightower. We informed them that he's been impersonating his brother for twenty years and is the chief suspect in a murder. I'm sure we'll get a reply, just not sure when. Meanwhile, I have a meeting with our chief tribal judge. We're going to figure out how to proceed with this because we've got the feds hanging over our heads."

"Right. Let me know what happens."

"For sure. And we're wondering if we can have a conversation—you, Justin, and me—whenever it's convenient for you."

"Sure. Ah, right now my uncle and I are on the way to recover my chute; then I have some things to do at the university. Is tomorrow okay?"

"Tomorrow's fine."

Gavin disconnected the call and pulled back onto the highway. They drove in silence for a few miles.

"You know," Andrew finally said. "This is a long way from over. This thing with the Two Face."

"You're right. It's hard for me to accept that Hightower killed Arlo, but it's bigger than how I feel. Even if Justin puts together an unshakable case, the FBI will crash the party."

Andrew smiled thoughtfully. "Yeah, yeah," he intoned. "Maybe, but it's a long way from being over. It's not what the fat takers like to say 'cut and dried.'"

"Well, there's nothing about this situation that is simple, legally or emotionally."

"Yeah, but you know, with the colonizers on that side and the fat takers over here, something's going to happen."

Gavin chuckled, glad for his uncle's humor.

"It's all serious stuff, I know," Andrew went on. "But in the end, when all the smoke clears away, there'll be justice for Arlo."

"I hope you're right. But I think I screwed up big time."

Andrew shot a puzzled glance at his nephew. "What do you mean."

Gavin sighed. "Well, I had a moment with Hightower. I asked him why he killed Arlo, and he told me Arlo found out who he really was—is."

"What's wrong with that?"

Gavin shook his head in disgust. "I should have asked about the murder weapon," he admitted. "I should have asked what it was and what he did with it."

"So? Can't the police do that?"

"Yeah, if he'll talk. He might not."

"Hah, it's all crazy every time we get mixed up with the *wasicus*. The bad thing is, we can't get away from them. Anyway, so you jumped out of the airplane and snuck up on that son-of-a-bitch?"

"Yeah."

"That's the last thing he probably expected. It's what the old-time warrior would do. I don't mean the parachute thing. I mean facing the enemy."

Gavin had never thought of himself as a warrior, not by any stretch. His image and idea of *warrior* was his great-grandfathers, and all the Lakota males through the ages who had been trained to protect the helpless ones and meet the enemy in battle. To him *warrior* was his uncle Andrew, a Vietnam combat veteran, and his brother, with combat tours in Iraq and Afghanistan.

"Well, I don't know if what I did last night measures up to that standard," he replied. "In retrospect, I could have parked on the gravel road and walked in, instead of taking such a radical approach."

"Don't sell yourself short, *Tunska*. Not many can do what you did, including some cops. And I know you don't think you measure up to something because you haven't faced enemies in battle, but here's the thing." Andrew paused and gazed at the landscape as Gavin slowed to make the turn onto Country Road 14. "Here's the thing," he continued. "You went after Hightower because of Arlo High Crane. You didn't do it because it was your job, or for praise or attention."

"I joined the Marines because it seemed like the thing to do, and I went to Vietnam," Andrew continued. "I got shot at and I probably killed people, and I suppose something about being a Lakota man—that warrior lineage—came into play. Still, I didn't go into battle as a Lakota war fighter. I went into battle as a U.S. Marine, wearing the uniform of the colonizer, not the trappings of a Lakota warrior. Nothing I went through there was to defend people back here. It wasn't that kind of a war. No matter what kind of spin they put on it then, or now, the Viet Cong or North Vietnamese weren't about to invade the United States. The only thing I fought for were my buddies. Old mercenary white men sent us to bleed and die so they could profit. The war protestors should have spit on them. The only good meaning to come out of it was all the young people who faced all that shit with courage and sacrifice."

"Yeah? I've wondered about that now and then," Gavin admitted. "But not having served in the military, like you and my brother have, I didn't feel entitled to state an opinion."

"Yeah, well, what is your opinion?"

"The same as yours. With World Wars One and Two, there were barbarians on the world's doorstep. History has shown, I think," Gavin went on, "that Germany and Japan really did threaten freedom for millions of people. If either war had turned out differently, we'd have had to learn to speak German or Japanese. Whereas every military conflict this country has been involved in since then has not been defense against aggression like the world wars. This country has jumped into wars or started them to benefit us politically or economically, based on lies. Then the military becomes enforcers, not defenders of freedom as is always loudly touted."

"Yeah, you're right. But it's damn dangerous to speak that truth, even to most Natives," Andrew said. "Anyway, I'm afraid we Lakota today forgot what it meant to be a warrior the way our ancestors defined it and did it. And all I'm saying is that what you did last night was for that reason—to do what an old-time Lakota warrior would have done."

Gavin slowed the pickup for the turnoff onto the old road he had crossed. "I appreciate that, *Leksi*," he said. "I just hope it leads to justice for Arlo."

"Strange things do happen, *Tunska*."

Gavin grinned to himself as he kept an eye out for his helmet tied to the barbed wire on the east fence. He spotted it about a thousand yards from the turnoff. "There," he said, pointing. "Up that slope is where my chute is." He stopped and turned the pickup around to the north.

Stepping down from the cab he hiked up the slope and found the bag. Andrew was standing on the road gazing across the river when Gavin returned.

"So, he was down there?" Andrew asked.

"Yeah. I'll take you there."

A flatbed truck and a tribal police cruiser were already at the campsite. The truck driver had winched the old Jeep onto the truck and was tying it down. A uniformed officer was helping. The tent was still standing.

Gavin and Andrew stepped down and approached. Gavin knew the flatbed driver, Dennis Spotted Calf. "Hey, Dennis," he said. "Good to see you."

"You, too, Gavin," the big man said, a bit shyly. He shook hands with Andrew as well.

The officer stepped forward. "Dr. Lone Wolf," he said. "I'm Myron Turning Bear. I think we're related. The whole station's talking about what you did last night."

"Oh? Which part? When I snagged myself on the barb wire, or when I climbed a tree to avoid snakes?"

The officer chuckled good-naturedly.

"This is my uncle, Andrew No Horn," Gavin said. After a handshake, Andrew pointed at the tent. "Can I have a look," he asked.

The officer nodded. "Sure."

Andrew walked to the tent, which was still open. At the door he leaned in for a look and saw the buttons on the tail of a rattlesnake disappear under the red sleeping bag bunched up in the middle. Except for a bare pillow, there was nothing else inside. He turned toward the officer.

"If you're taking down this tent, there's a rattlesnake under that sleeping bag," he cautioned.

Turning Bear nodded and looked around for a long stick. Meanwhile, Andrew stood for a moment before he walked around the pop-up tent. For nearly a minute he stood motionless, staring at the ground, as if in a trance. After a shallow sigh, he lifted his head and walked away from the tent and stopped near Gavin.

"*Tunska*," he said, pointing at the tent. "That snake in there was drawn to this spot, where Hightower was sleeping. He—the man—left something there, nothing physical, but a part of himself. When the tent is gone I want to cleanse the ground."

After they caught the snake with a long branch, Gavin and Andrew helped the officer take down the tent. Gavin watched his uncle take the snake past a huge thicket and turn him loose.

Andrew waited until the truck and the cruiser were gone. Then he dropped a short twig on one particular spot where the floor of the tent had been. Gathering grass and other light kindling, he piled it on the spot and set it on fire. When the small fire burned down, he dropped a small bundle of sage into the glowing embers. He wafted the smoke with his hands to smudge over the area. When he was finished he had Gavin help him bury the remnants of the small fire.

"Fire is the cleanser," he said. "It purges and helps things to renew themselves."

"Is that why the snake crawled in?"

"Yeah, He was drawn to something here, something not good, so hopefully it won't cling to him. There's nothing quite as scary as a mean rattlesnake."

"That's for sure."

From the bag hanging perpetually from his belt, Andrew took out loose tobacco. "I'm going to pray," he said. Gavin stepped back and watched his uncle offer tobacco to Grandmother Earth, Father Sky, and each of the four directions beginning in the West, then North, East, and South, turning to each direction as he did. Finally, he made an offering to *Taku Skanskan Wakan*, the powerful life force and sacred mystery. Then he prayed in Lakota:

*Great and Powerful Mystery. I send my pitiful voice to you in humility. Take from this place the evil that came and send it where it will hurt no one or no thing. Protect all who were touched by it. I ask this for all my relatives.*

He stood for a moment before he turned to Gavin. "Now," he said. "I know you have things to do today. After you take me home, I will ask some of our relatives to help me get ready to do *inipi*—the sweat—tonight, for you. We have to do a cleansing for you, too."

# NINETY-FOUR

Chief Avery and Lieutenant Primault stood up from the conference table to meet Gavin as he entered the room. Their facial expressions were a mixture of deference and respect.

"Good morning," they both said.

"Good morning," Gavin said, taking a seat. A tray of cups and a carafe of coffee were already on the table. "Thanks for pushing back the meeting."

"No worries," Avery said. "How are you feeling today?"

"Relieved," Gavin admitted. "I was damn lucky."

Avery nodded. "Well, as the white eyes say, 'all's well that ends well.' Sometimes they actually make sense."

The good-natured chuckling was interrupted by a soft knock on the door. The dispatcher walked in, two printed pages in her hands. "This came in about five minutes ago," she told the Chief. "I just finished printing it."

Avery took the pages. "Thanks, Rhonda."

"Oh," the Chief said, as he began reading. "This is from Scotland Yard." His voice trailed off as he read, then his expression turned from surprise to incredulous. "You're not going to believe this," he said. "This is definitely unexpected."

"What is it?" Primault asked.

"Ah, this is in response to the FYI I sent about Hightower. He is a fugitive. He's wanted by the British Army."

"For what?"

"He was court martialed and found guilty of murder. There's an encrypted file coming." Avery handed the printout to Primault, who read it quickly.

Gavin was floored. "Murder? Well, he was in the army. That explains a lot. You think this message was sent to the feds here?"

"I don't think so, but I don't know."

"If so, you think they'll come after Hightower?"

"I'm sure they will." He pointed at the email. "That means our man is an international fugitive. He came here to hide and used his brother's identity."

"What will you do?"

"Wait," Avery said. "We wait for the file, and then decide what to do, if it hasn't been already decided for us."

"What about this last question, sir," Primault asked. "They want to know if he is in our custody."

"Yeah, I saw that. Well, we've got to tell them."

"And what does that mean for your investigation of Arlo High Crane's murder?" Gavin asked.

"Until the feds step in, I'm keeping it going," Primault insisted. "In fact, I'm going to get a search warrant and go over Hightower's office with a fine-tooth comb. I think I can talk Sheriff Casey into searching Hightower's house and inviting me along."

Gavin nodded. "It's getting real now, isn't it?"

"It sure the hell is," Avery affirmed.

Gavin glanced at the officers. "There is something, however," he said. "Two nights ago, under duress, Hightower admitted that he shot Arlo because he found out his—Hightower's—real identity."

"Damn," Primault said. "He did have some heavy crap to hide, didn't he? Anything else?"

"There should have been," Gavin admitted. "I should have asked him about the murder weapon. I didn't. I blew it."

"No, you didn't," Avery argued. "Interrogation isn't your job, it's ours. We'll get it out of him or figure it out. This is Justin's number one priority, right up until the feds come stomping up to our doorstep."

"The murder weapon is the clincher," Gavin pointed out.

"Right," Avery agreed. "As I said, we'll figure it out."

"What about the connection between Hightower and Caruth?"

"We know there is one and your video proves it, but it's unrelated to the High Crane case. All we can do is add it to his troubles."

## NINETY-FIVE

Gavin was sitting on the edge of the fire pit when he heard Uncle Andrew's old Ford pickup pull into the yard.

"*Tunska*," Andrew called out. "How are you? I thought the fire would be going by now to heat up all those rocks for the sweat."

Gavin reached out to shake his uncle's hand. "I was just about to," he said, "but I have something to ask you first."

Andrew nodded and sat down on the edge of the pit. "Is it about revenge?" he asked.

Gavin nodded. "Yeah, in a way," he said. "Justin Primault has strong evidence against Hightower, and the man practically confessed, but it won't do any good."

"Because the colonizers are coming to take him?"

Gavin nodded slowly. "Mainly, but also because we can't find the murder weapon, although we know what it is. What's more, we can't put him on trial ourselves. And that means, in a real sense, Hightower will get away with murdering Arlo. That's what it will amount to in the end."

"What's that got to do with revenge?" the old man said.

Gavin nodded again. "Well, there's got to be a way for us to make Hightower pay; but I shouldn't feel that way—this is the twenty-first century after all."

"Oh? What does the measurement of time have to do with it? Years, centuries, and ages go by, our clothes change, our houses change, but how much do we change as human beings? Are we better than our ancestors? Are we the same? Are we worse? Some things don't change, we still hurt each other, and we sure still kill each other. We don't evolve because of what some people call 'time,' we evolve because of what happens to us, because of what we do, because of what we've learned."

"I can't argue with you there, *Leksi*."

"In the old days, before the Long Knives herded us back up here into our own country and told us to live by their rules, there was revenge, and sometimes that involved, ah, restitution. You know our word for murder—*tiwicakte*—it means 'killing the family,' or the entire household. One person was killed, but it affected the whole family, the whole community. If it was outright murder, carried out with bad intentions, then the *tiyospaye*, the community, decided the punishment. In those instances, it was harsh."

"Banishment?"

"Yeah. The murderer was marked on the face, a deep cut or a brand, then he was thrown out, sometimes with only the clothes he wore. And no weapons, not even a knife. That mark identified him, or her, to other people, so no one helped him. Since that person had "killed a whole family," the privilege of family was taken away."

"And if the killing was not intentional, the punishment was different."

Andrew nodded. "Yeah, the offending person and his family were directed to make restitution to the grieving family. That could mean payment in horses, or the offending family had to provide food for a whole year, for instance."

Gavin nodded. "So, a life for a life wasn't always the way to rectify it. In a real way that makes sense."

"Yeah, yeah. But, you know what? Killing each other or murder among us, in the old days, didn't happen all that often, hardly at all. Things have changed. Our population is larger and many of us don't know the old ways."

After a long, heavy pause, the old man spoke again. "So, let me ask you this, are you wanting to avenge Arlo, or yourself?"

Gavin stared at the carefully arranged stack of wood around the rocks in the bottom of the fire pit. "Arlo," he said. "And I haven't forgotten what Hightower did to Auntie Esther."

"Okay, I expect that of you," Andrew said. "But he hired a guy to kill you. You have every right to avenge yourself."

"Yeah, but the fact is that Arlo High Crane," replied Gavin, "at twenty-four, was better than Carey Hightower will ever be. That probably doesn't matter to the people at Scotland Yard. And they may not care about Hightower killing Arlo. No justice for Arlo."

"That's a lot to think about. What did you say about the murder weapon?"

"Primault and I know that Hightower very likely used a replica black powder pistol. He bought one, and he practiced with it on a shooting range. The round ball they took out of Arlo's skull proves what kind of a gun it was. We just don't know where it is. I mean, I thought it might be in the dam. I think, or I thought, that Hightower threw it in the water after he shot Arlo."

"You know for sure it isn't there?"

"Well, Primault had a diver search in the water, but he found nothing."

"Okay. Well, maybe he was looking in the wrong place. It sounds like you are not totally sure about it."

"The diver only had so much time before he had to go. On the other hand, he was experienced in recovery of lost objects as well as bodies."

"Well, why don't you make sure? Why don't you satisfy yourself that the gun isn't in that water?"

Gavin gazed again at the pile of stacked firewood around the rocks.

"Well, I tell you what," the old man said, resolutely. "Let's get that fire going and heat those rocks. Charlie Lone Hill and the others will be here at sundown. I think we do a sweat and pray for answers. We pray for justice for Arlo."

## NINETY-SIX

Sergeant Gabby West, a blue-eyed combination of her Lakota father and Norwegian mother and the department's public information officer, knocked once on the Chief's door and entered. He looked up from a pile of reports.

"What's up?"

"London is about seven or eight hours ahead of us, right?"

"Yeah."

"We sent that email to Scotland Yard about two hours ago," she said, glancing up at the wall clock. "They replied already."

"Damn. Really?"

She handed him the printed reply. "It's very formal," she commented, with amusement in her blue eyes.

Avery took the page eagerly and looked.

> Sir: I am in receipt of a communiqué at 1420 hours this date from Scotland Yard regarding the subject of Carey Hightower. We understand said subject is in your custody. My office is requesting your department to maintain custody of said prisoner until further

notice. You may expect communication directly from our Office of Legal Services.

Might you be personally available for a telephone call today?
Sincerely,
Colonel Charles Binghamton
Office of Judge Advocate General
Headquarters Command
London, England

Avery read it a second time and looked up at Sgt. West. "They sure didn't waste time, did they?"

"No, they sure didn't. Are you going to talk to him?"

"Of course, are you kidding? Maybe he has one of those thick accents you hear in the movies."

"No doubt. You want me to reply?"

"Yeah, would you?" He tapped the pile of papers in front of him. "I want to get as much of this out of the way as possible."

## NINETY-SEVEN

Gavin drove into the parking lot of the Lakota Studies Building and walked to the two-story log building housing the SRU administrative offices. Doug Eagle Shield and the people from NMAI were in the conference room. The president's secretary brought him coffee as her boss slid a sheet of paper across the table to him.

"Doctor Wells and I are talking about a public exhibition of your great-grandfather's ledger sketches. Here are media outlets, print and broadcast," Eagle Shield told him. "Any other suggestions are welcome."

Gavin quickly scanned the list. "Looks good to me," he said.

"This ledger project has all the earmarks of longevity," the president said, happily.

"It certainly has," Wells continued. "Even if there is no initial flurry of excitement, it will, as Doug said, take off, especially when certain segments of the historical community realize the enormity of this discovery. You best hang on tight then."

"Well, just as long as it's manageable," Gavin said. "What about our announcement? What are the details?"

"We believe it would be best for you to take the lead," Eagle Shield indicated. "Then Dr. Wells and I will explain how our institutions are involved."

"That's fairly simple and straightforward. When are we doing this?"

"I think as soon as we have the materials we need for the actual display of the photos," Wells said. "Also, my concern is putting a public relations package together."

"And we also need time to get everything in place for a buffalo feed. We want as many of our people here as possible," Eagle Shield added. "We're thinking the second week of July."

Gavin nodded. "Works for me."

"This discovery is big news, no matter when it's revealed," Wells pointed out. "It's a hell of a story."

After the meeting concluded, Gavin took Wells aside. "There's something I would like to talk with you about," he said. "I know you're busy, but would you have some time, in the next few days?"

"Yes, of course. I'm at your disposal. Let me know when."

Gavin stepped into the president's office a minute later. "There's been some interesting developments with the murder investigation," he said. "I wonder if I could take about five minutes of your time."

Eagle Shield pointed to a chair. "I'm all ears," he said.

After Gavin finished, Douglas Eagle Shield stared in complete astonishment at the interim department chair of Lakota Studies. "I'm glad he's in custody."

"Yeah. He said and did all the right things, provided the right verifications and documents, endeared himself just enough, made sure he stayed under the radar. He fooled everybody. If this tragic situation hadn't happened with Arlo, he would have moved on. That was his pattern. In fact, I wish that had been the case. Then Arlo would still be alive."

Eagle Shield drummed his fingers on the desk. "Thanks for the update."

Gavin walked across the road to the Lakota Studies Building.

"Anything new?" he asked Ramona.

"Sure is. We're getting applicants for your job, though I wish you would take it on a permanent basis."

"Sorry about that," he said. "How many?"

She grabbed a folder from her desk. "The president's office sent these names over, four of them." She pointed to the second name. "I know this young woman's family. She has roots here."

"Doctor Caitlin Marshall. Sounds familiar. What's her background?"

"The facilities director's younger sister, you know, Michael Marshall. She has an undergraduate degree from the University of Washington, graduate degrees from Denver University, and Dartmouth. I don't know her personally, but something about her intrigues me. According to her resume, she has a black belt in Karate."

"What about the others?"

She waved a hand dismissively. "Nothing close to her, believe me."

Gavin laughed. "Okay, I'll go over all of them later."

"Oh, I almost forgot, one more thing." She unpinned an envelope from her bulletin board and held it out to Gavin.

"What is this?" he asked.

"It's a letter, for Arlo, from—from the University of Durham, in England."

He stared at her in mild shock and then took the envelope.

"I don't know who else to give it to, except maybe his folks," Ramona said.

He pointed at her letter opener and opened the envelope. "It is for Arlo," he said, barely above a whisper.

"What is it? What does it say?"

"As follow-up to your previous inquiry regarding Dr. Caleb Hightower, I have attached the article from the London Times, from November of

1988. It was published two weeks after he was reported missing and presumed dead. It was the one document I did not include in my letter of 6 May of this year. I trust you followed my suggestion to access the In Memoriam link on our website. As is stated there, his body was never recovered. Therefore, the individual you indicated is a professor at Smokey River University may be someone else entirely, but certainly not he who attended, graduated from, and taught at this institution. Our records indicate that the only Caleb Montrose Hightower to graduate from Durham University was reported missing and presumed dead. Thank you for your inquiry. Cordially, Alistair Maynard, Assistant to the Vice Chancellor."

They stared at each other in puzzled astonishment. "What does that mean?" Ramona finally asked.

Gavin shook his head. "It seems that Arlo got another letter back in early May. Do you remember that?"

"Yeah, I do. Arlo didn't get that much mail here."

"I think that letter was basically the same as this; so that means he knew Caleb Hightower was—was not really him, weeks ago, maybe even before."

"Oh, my!"

"I, ah, don't think it's necessary to give this to his folks. I do want to show it to the criminal investigator though."

Ramona nodded.

Justin Primault called as Gavin stepped into the copy room to use the fax machine.

"Hey, Justin. How's everything?" he answered.

"I have some interesting news," Primault said, chuckling dryly. "You'll be pleased to hear that the Chief spoke to a lawyer with the British Army's Legal Service."

"The British, when?"

"A couple of hours ago but keep it to yourself. They want us to keep Hightower in custody, and we're to expect an encrypted file about Hightower."

"Damn! That qualifies as interesting. I'd sure like to see that file."

"I'll let you know when it comes in."

"Well, I have a bit of news for you," Gavin asserted. "We have verification of Hightower's motive for killing Arlo, a letter from the University of Durham."

"Really?"

"Yeah. I have in my hand a letter from the University of Durham to Arlo High Crane. And he likely got one in early May as well."

"A letter? Why would Arlo be getting letters from there?"

"I think because he might have made an inquiry about Caleb Hightower, and the university responded. This letter came with a newspaper article about Caleb Hightower reported missing and presumed dead."

"Oh, shit! So, it's likely that Arlo brought it up to Hightower."

"Or Hightower found out that Arlo knew, somehow. In any case, I'm in the copy room right now and I'll fax you the letter."

Gavin finished the call and faxed the letter to Primault. His tasks finished, he took refuge in his office.

A minute later he got a call from Uncle Andrew.

"I talked this morning with Raymond and Agnes High Crane. They want to talk to you."

"Yeah, sure. I'll be glad to."

"Good. I'll come over to your place after you get home, and we can go over to Gray Grass together. They want to feed you. I told them what you did."

# NINETY-EIGHT

They arrived in Gray Grass before six. The sun was still high when they turned onto a trail that wound through trees on the bottomland east of a curve in the Little White River. A small, white frame house stood at the end of it, surrounded by a two-rail wood fence. At the end of the parking area was Arlo's old four-door sedan. A part-Husky dog came around the house to greet them. He and Andrew were apparently old friends. As they opened the gate, Raymond High Crane, an older version of Arlo, stepped out the front door. Gavin felt a lump in his throat.

"*Hau, Tunska. Tanyan yahi yelo* (Hello, Nephew. It's good of you to come)," he said and grabbed Gavin's hand.

"*Hau, Leksi. Yupiyakel miyecopelo* (Hello, Uncle. It's good of you to invite me)."

The old man gestured toward the house. "*Tima uwo* (Come in)."

Agnes High Crane came from the kitchen to greet Gavin and Andrew. She was thin and petite, her hair nearly white and in two long braids. Her face was lined and narrow with more than a strong hint of beauty in her youth. She smiled, showing the innate inner strength possessed by older Lakota women. She reminded Gavin of Grandma Little Turtle. She chose to greet Gavin in English.

"Nephew," she said, in a soft, warm voice. "We're glad you could come."

"I'm happy to be here, Auntie," he said, taking her small hand in both of his.

"The soup is done," she said, gesturing toward the kitchen. "But it needs to cool. We can sit and talk for a while."

The living room was small and tastefully furnished. Family pictures covered the walls. Gavin saw Arlo's photos immediately. He stepped toward the wall for a closer look. Next to one was his diploma from Smokey River University. It, and all his photos, were draped with black ribbons. A new framed Master of Arts in History diploma hung next to the SRU diploma. It was from the University of Nebraska, thanks to Dr. Eagle Shield who had petitioned for it to be awarded posthumously.

"He admired you," Raymond said. "He said you know how to be a true Lakota in this crazy world."

The lump in his throat grew. "Oh, I admired *him*," Gavin replied.

Supper, as the evening meal was called in this part of the country, among whites and Natives alike, was elk soup with potatoes, onions, carrots, celery, and cabbage, served with freshly baked bread, and plenty of coffee. Dessert was chokecherry *wojapi*, otherwise known as fruit soup, made from dried chokecherry patties.

Conversation centered on family and how their son had been something of a throwback to the old ways. Neither Agnes nor Raymond once mentioned the tragic event that had taken their son's life. What was not mentioned was akin to someone standing just outside the door, always there but only occasionally invited inside. After the meal was done and the table cleared, Agnes invited their guests into the living room while she went into one of the bedrooms. She re-emerged seconds later with a folded star quilt and a large, symmetrical eagle tail feather with its end quill wrapped in beads.

"These are for you, from my husband, our daughter, and me," she said.

Gavin stood, genuinely astonished at the gift. Among the Lakota it was never an "Oh, you shouldn't have" reaction when it came to gift giving. Gifts were accepted with humility and graciousness to match the generosity with which they were given.

"Thank you, Auntie. *Lila pilamayapelo* (Thank you very much)." He shook her hand then stepped over to Raymond and shook his hand. "*Pilamayapelo, Leksi.*"

"*Toh, hecel hoksila unkitawapi ohinniyan yeksuyin ktelo* (Yes, so you will always remember our son)."

"*Ohan, ese toheni ewaktujin kte sni yelo* (Yes, I will never forget him)," Gavin replied, the lump in his throat growing.

"The quilt is to keep you warm, like our memories of our son are warm," the old woman said, ever so gently. "The eagle feather is for what you did, for capturing that man. Your uncle told us. We know you did it for our boy."

Most of the drive home was in silence. Nearly six weeks or so had passed since Arlo High Crane had been killed, and there were still unyielding realities to be endured on the tough side of life. People do not "move on" after the death of a loved one, and grief does not diminish with the passage of days, weeks, months, and years, or a lifetime, especially when a mother and father bury a child. Not a day went by that Gavin did not think of his mother and father, and now Grandma Little Turtle. Lakota culture had taught him that death was part of the earthly journey, and though that lesson did not diminish grief, it did help to cope with that unavoidable reality of death. It was exactly that knowledge that was sustaining Agnes and Raymond High Crane.

Gavin sat for a few seconds after he pulled into his yard and shut off the engine. After a deep sigh he glanced over at his uncle.

"Now I'm sorry I didn't kill that son-of-a-bitch," he said.

"If you did Arlo's folks would not respect you the way they do. They respect you because you're the opposite of the man who tore their life apart. If you had killed him, you would have killed part of their faith in goodness. That's what you are to them, goodness, like their son was and still is to them. And there has to be goodness in the world, and that means in each of us."

"Well, thanks for putting me straight. I didn't look at it that way."

"Yeah. Can you cook me some coffee, real quick?"

"I can do that faster than it took Custer to realize he should have stayed at Fort Abraham Lincoln."

They laughed all the way into the house.

After the first sip, the old man gazed studiously at his nephew. "A lot going on, huh?"

Gavin raised his eyebrows and sighed. "That's for damn sure."

"Yeah, and before it all hits the fan—as the *wasicus* like to say—there's something you should know. Maybe you know it already."

"What do you mean?"

"That gun, your great-grandfather's gun, it woke up," Andrew said, somberly. "It's got blood on it, starting from the battle. Then that boss farmer wanted it bad enough to kill for it, forcing your great-grandfather to kill him. It will kill Hightower, too, because he wanted it so bad. Look what he was willing to do to get it."

"So, you're saying we should be careful."

Andrew nodded. "We need to get rid of it."

"Yeah, okay, how? Melt it, throw it into the bottom of the Missouri River?"

"Give it back, but not without making someone pay for it. Turn it into something good. It was made to take life. We need to make it give life."

Gavin leaned back in his chair, staring at the dark liquid in his white cup. "Maybe I was sensing this necessity the past couple of days. But I think there's a way. I was going to talk to someone, the man from the National Museum of the American Indian. He might be able to help."

The old man nodded. "Yeah. I think he will."

## NINETY-NINE

Of the four photographs of Arlo High Crane on the coffee table in the sitting area of the Lakota Studies Building lobby, Gavin pointed to the second from the right. "That's my choice," he said. He and Ramona Red Star were seated on the couch.

Ramona nodded, a soft, pensive smile on her face. "I like that one, too," she said. "So do Denise and Jesse, so that's a majority vote. We'll go with that. The Art Department is going to do a poster for us and mount it on canvas." She pointed to a bare area high on the wall of the lobby. "That's the place for it, I think."

"And there it shall be," Gavin agreed.

The front door clicked open, and a uniformed tribal police officer entered and looked around, a thick manila envelope in his left hand.

"I think you're looking for me," Gavin said, rising from the couch, "if you're Laurence Blacksmith."

The stocky officer nodded, affecting a noncommittal smile. "Yes, sir," he said, and came forward with the envelope, holding it out to Gavin. "Lieutenant Primault asks that you call him after you've read it."

"Thank you," Gavin said, taking the envelope. "I will."

Gavin took the heavy envelope and turned to Ramona after he glanced at the clock above the reception counter. "I'm calling it a day," he said. "I got something to do, but it's personal, so I'm heading home."

"Okay, boss."

The yellow manila envelope lay on the passenger's seat. Primault had told him the file was thirty-seven pages when he called and said he was sending it to him with an officer. A "page turner" he said.

Gavin pulled into the parking area at the front of his house, went inside and sliced open the top of the envelope with his pocket knife. The first page was a letter to Chief Ben Avery from Col. Jerome Tilden, British Army Office of Legal Services.

> Chief Avery:
>
> We are herewith transmitting to you the case file in reference to the investigation, court martial, and conviction of Corporal Carey M. Hightower for the capital offence of murder in the first degree in 1996. We appreciate that your department apprehended our fugitive and that you are complying with our request to keep him in your custody.
>
> Our Office has begun the legal proceedings to extradite said prisoner from the United States. This process may take several weeks and for the duration we respectfully request that your department continue to keep him in your custody.

Hazy images of "Caleb Hightower" and the day he was introduced to the faculty and staff in Lakota Studies slid into Gavin's memory. As a newcomer he was polite, even deferential, and well dressed. That, along with his accent, ingratiated him to everyone. He was the first Englishman ever on the faculty at SRU. He came with impressive academic credentials but as time went on he hardly talked about Durham University. What Gavin initially saw as humility was simply caution. Over the following months and years Hightower adjusted and fit in but always kept a low profile.

Gavin shook off the thoughts and concentrated on the file, which was pages of documents regarding Carey Hightower's military tour, the incident resulting in the killing of a fellow soldier, his court martial trial, and the sentence handed down after the guilty verdict: death by hanging. There were photographs of the soldier in his late twenties in dress and battle dress uniform. He had been in an infantry unit that had served in the 1990 Gulf War.

After sentencing, Carey Hightower's defense lawyers had filed the obligatory appeal. While that was pending Hightower had escaped and seemed to have fallen off the face of the earth.

Primault had attached a photograph of the real Dr. Caleb Hightower provided by Durham University in their communication. The resemblance was amazingly strong; the brothers could have been twins, although Caleb was four years older. No wonder Carey had flown under the radar for so long. Gavin assumed that it was Carey's plan to keep moving and leave as faint a trail as possible. He had chosen the three academic institutions because they were small.

Now that path had come to an end, probably in a place where Carey Hightower had least expected that to happen. A question that had been lingering in Gavin's margin of awareness now slid into focus: why had Arlo High Crane written to Durham University and inquired about Dr. Caleb Hightower? The consequence of that inquiry had been fatal.

With a deep sigh Gavin closed the file. It should have been different for Arlo.

He called Lieutenant Primault.

"Gavin," the CI answered. "I assume you read the file.

"I did, it's like a crime novel, and it provides a lot of answers, but I still have two questions."

"And they are?"

"One, why did Arlo write to Durham University to inquire about Dr. Caleb Hightower? And two, where is that damn black powder pistol? The first question is not as critical as the second. But the big issue for me is that we all did the British Army a giant favor and they've started the legal proceedings to extradite him back to England. Maybe I'm splitting hairs but that means Hightower's off the hook for killing Arlo High Crane."

"Right. I couldn't agree with you more. And there's something else," Primault pointed out. "Sooner or later, the feds are going to get wind of this because of the extradition process. Then they damn sure will take custody of our prisoner, and once they do all that will matter is that Hightower is an international fugitive. No one but us will care that he killed a young Lakota man, and there will be no justice for Arlo."

"So, what are we going to do?"

"Well, we have a strong case against Hightower and I'm going to make sure it will stand up in a court of law. That's my job. I owe it to Arlo High Crane and his family."

"Glad to hear it. And here's a thought," Gavin said. "Why don't you and the Chief call a press conference and announce that you've apprehended Arlo High Crane's murderer? It's been in the news and our people have a right to know. The feds may come and claim Hightower, but the fact is they did nothing help with this case. You did it, you and your department. Make the announcement because it may be the only justice for Arlo."

"I'll take your suggestion to the Chief."

Gavin reopened the file and flipped pages until he came to the photograph of Corporal Carey Hightower standing with a fellow solder. Hightower had been a sergeant, but because he had been involved in a money kick-back scheme at an NCO club, he had been demoted.

In the next moment, something struck him like a splash of cold water to the face. The way in which Carey Hightower was holding his rifle meant he was very likely left-handed.

Gavin sat back. As "Caleb," Hightower used his right hand predominantly and that led to another overlooked fact. Hightower's handwriting was terrible. His signature, written right-handed, was an illegible scrawl. Gavin stared at the photograph of Carey Hightower, his left pointer finger near the trigger guard of the L85 assault rifle, his right hand grasping the barrel housing.

He stepped to his desk and opened the file drawer, pulling out the photographs of the crime scene at Flat Butte Dam, sifting through them until he found the pictures of the footprints near the tire tracks. Finding the close-ups of those indicated as Hightower's tracks, he scrutinized them. From all indications, it seemed, they stopped approximately ten feet behind Arlo's body. One distinct print was off to the right, perhaps eighteen inches and at about a forty-five-degree angle from the other. It was the right foot.

As a left-handed throwing center fielder on the Horse Creek community softball team in high school, Gavin instinctively stepped into a throw, especially a long throw, with his right foot. Gerard, who played first base, did the same, since he was also left-handed.

Gavin stared at the photograph. Perhaps, just perhaps, that footprint angled to the right was because Hightower resorted to his natural throwing hand to toss the gun.

After a moment, Gavin picked up his phone and dialed Primault.

"Good evening again," he said, after Primault answered. "I have a question about where your friend searched for the gun at Flat Butte Damn."

"Okay, what about it?"

"Ah, in what direction did you throw the rock you used to simulate the gun?"

"Interesting question. Ah, let's see. We threw it in line with Arlo's body, lying mainly to the west. Why do you ask?"

Gavin stared at the photograph of the footprints "Is Hightower right-handed or left-handed?"

"Right-handed, isn't he?"

"I think the real Caleb was right-handed because Carey used his right hand predominantly, he had to. But I think Carey was left-handed. In the photograph of him in battle dress uniform, he's holding his weapon the way a left-hander would do naturally. I know because I'm left-handed."

"What does that mean?"

"It means in certain circumstances, people resort to type," Gavin pointed out.

"I still don't understand," Primault admitted.

"Carey Hightower had to function right-handed because Caleb was. Carey's handwriting was atrocious. But I recall him cutting his meat left-handed, quite skillfully."

"Okay, but what does that have to do with the gun?"

"I think he threw it into Flat Butte Dam, but not where we assumed he did, because—."

"He threw it left-handed," Primault concluded.

"He sure the hell did. Want to meet me in the morning out at Flat Butte Dam for another search?"

"Say when, and I'll be there."

## ONE HUNDRED

Gavin's first dive was nearly half an hour after sunrise, when sunlight slid over the water. Without oxygen tanks and a respirator, it was a free dive, though he did have a cold weather wetsuit, a facemask, swim fins, and a weight belt. Though Gavin's SCUBA rating as a rescue diver was valid, he hadn't dived since Alaska three years ago. A free-dive was the only option primarily because the closest place to refill his empty cylinders was Pierre, and he didn't want to wait.

The water was cold for late June. He made the first dive to acclimate to the water's depth and visibility and the contour of the bottom. Coming up and treading water some thirty yards from shore, he noted Primault's thumbs-up signal, telling him he was in line with the direction they had thrown the rock representing the pistol. On shore with Primault were Patrolman Jason Singer and Uncle Andrew.

Gavin estimated he was well within the range that Hightower could have comfortably thrown the pistol. Distance was likely not Hightower's priority; simply getting the gun into the water was. He was counting on the probability that no one would think to look here.

"It's over ten feet deep here," Gavin shouted to Primault. "And I won't stay down more than thirty seconds at a time." After the CI waved acknowledgment, Gavin took several deep breaths and submerged headfirst. His plan was to work out and away from the shore and stay off the bottom silt in order not to disturb it. Any amount of stirred-up silt would obscure the bottom, making his task harder.

A logical assumption was that the gun had settled on top of the silt among the bottom vegetation. If the gun was there, it had been nearly six weeks in the water. Hovering a few feet above the bottom, maneuvering with his hands and fins, his gaze swept slowly back and forth until he felt the need for air.

Surfacing for a few quick breaths, he dove again, repeating the process until he lost count. His instincts told him the cap-and-ball pistol was somewhere on the bottom, or perhaps that was only wishful thinking. If today's dive was unsuccessful, Primault would bring back the diver.

After yet another fruitless dive, Gavin treaded water slowly to rest a bit and bring down his heart rate. He felt a strange sense of encouragement when his uncle waved, and after a few deep breaths he submerged again, this time to the west side of the marker.

Leveling off at three feet above the bottom, he spotted a short, dark line perpendicular to the riffles in the silt. The water here was still no more than ten to twelve feet deep, apparently not deep enough for the silt on the bottom to escape the effects of high wind on the surface. Hence, the riffles, like tiny sand dunes. Reaching down slowly, he curled a finger under the dark line, no more than two inches long, and pulled up slowly. His finger curled around the barrel of a gun—*the* gun—his heart pounding against the wetsuit.

He tucked it into his belt, surfaced slowly, and swam for the shore. When he could stand in nearly hip-deep water, he pulled off his fins, then yanked the gun out of his belt, and held it up for them to see.

"Damn!" Primault yelled. "You found it!"

Opening the cargo area of his police SUV, Primault blotted the gun dry and used a magnifying glass to find the serial numbers. He read them to Singer, who verified it number by number with the documents obtained from the gun range manager.

Gavin was toweling his hair dry as he listened to the officers. The CI reached out his hand. "Great work, my friend! So glad you figured out that Carey Hightower was left-handed."

Gavin shook his head sheepishly. "So, here's what I think happened. Hightower pulls Arlo out of the trunk, unties him and makes him turn his back, maybe even walk away. He shoots him, makes sure he's down, and—realizing he had the perfect place to hide it—he throws the gun into the water."

Primault nodded. "That's probably how it went down." After a moment he put on rubber gloves and inspected the chambers in the cylinder with the magnifying glass. "The chamber under the hammer is empty, indicating it's been fired, and the other five appear to be still loaded. The percussion caps are still attached as well. I'll bet a month's pay that any of the remaining five lead rounds are the same weight as the one taken from Arlo High Crane's skull."

He slid the pistol into a plastic bag and placed it in a box. "As far as I'm concerned, this seals the deal," he said. "We have all the classic factors—motive, opportunity, method, and weapon. In a perfect world that would stand up in a court of law."

"Great job, my friend. You did it," Gavin said.

"No, no," Primault countered quickly. "*We* did it, all of us. Jason helped with hours and hours of research. But the two of you," he said, turning to Andrew and Gavin, "well, this result wouldn't have happened without you.

Grandpa Andrew, you helped in no small way," he asserted. "And you, most of all," he said to Gavin.

Primault paused and glanced out at the water where a breeze was creating small waves. "But you know, what I wish most of all is that young Arlo was still alive and that none of this would have been necessary."

"True," Andrew agreed. "But it is what it is. Justice doesn't raise the dead, but it should burden the guilty; it should scare the hell out of them. So, I think you should put all this evidence in front of that man, Hightower. He should know that we know."

## ONE HUNDRED ONE

Gavin stood in the middle of forty-eight posters on four-foot high stanchions arranged in a perfect circle in the SRU Multi-Purpose Center gymnasium. Each poster was one of his great-grandfather Lone Wolf's ledger sketches. Dr. Wells was doing a dry run, as it were. The display was breathtaking and arranged in the same order as the sketches were in the ledger. Gavin turned to Dr. Wells.

"This is outstanding," he told the conservator. "You've done a great job. Thank you."

"We're just finishing what he started," Wells replied. "He told an important story that adds an undeniable dose of reality. At the private exhibition we placed the framed posters on chairs. Stanchions are a popular way to display photographs. It was Dr. Eagle Shield's idea to arrange them in a circle, which is culturally appropriate."

Images of the display stayed with him as he walked back to the Lakota Studies Building. They and the upcoming exhibition were a welcome diversion from the darker reality of recent events. Ramona handed him a bundle of mail as he stopped off at the reception counter.

"There's a young man waiting for you in your office," she told him, somberly. "He just got here."

It turned out to be Darrell Berkin, looking utterly lost as he stood from a chair when Gavin walked in.

"Darrell. It's good to see you. Sit down." He hadn't seen the young man since Arlo High Crane's funeral. "What can I do for you?"

Darrell took a deep breath. "I—ah, my mom and I want to talk to you, if you have time."

"Yes, of course. Where is she?"

"She's outside in the car. We, uh, we're wondering if there's some place we could go, away from here."

They followed Gavin by car to a picnic area a quarter of a mile from the campus. As they walked to one of the picnic tables, he sensed a whirlwind of emotions from the young man and his mother.

"What can I do for you?" he asked gently, after they sat down facing him across a table.

Mavis removed her sunglasses and dabbed at her eyes with facial tissue. "First, please understand, this isn't easy for us," she said in a hoarse voice. "We don't know exactly what to do. Darrell thought of you, of talking to you."

Mavis was petite, an attractive woman with shoulder length black hair. Gavin knew her from high school. She had been a cheerleader at Kincaid County High School. Her maiden name was Bellineaux. She reached into her jacket pocket and pulled out a business size envelope folded in half.

"I was going through my husband's things," she said, "looking for his discharge papers from the Navy. His American Legion Post wants to do a military funeral." She held up the envelope. "I found this."

"What is it?"

Mavis stifled a sob. "It's a letter to me, and it sort of ties in with something that Darrell told me. Darrell can tell you his story, then I'll show you this letter." She turned to her son. "It's up to you, son. And just remember, I'm on your side."

Darrell had been staring at the top of the picnic table. Glancing briefly up at Gavin, he looked back down at his hands. "This has to do with Arlo and my dad."

Gavin nodded. "Okay."

The boy cleared his throat and licked his lips. "In the first part of May, Arlo asked for my advice about something. He got a letter from a place over in England, a letter about Caleb Hightower. He showed it to me."

Durham University flashed through Gavin's mind. "Okay. What was in the letter if I may ask?"

Darrell nodded slowly. "Yeah, it was information. It said that Caleb Hightower died somewhere over in Europe. There was even that, that thing about people when they die." He paused, obviously struggling for the word.

"An obituary," Mavis said.

"Yeah, obituary. It was with that letter."

"Okay. So, Arlo showed you the letter and the obituary?"

"Yeah, he did, and he didn't know what to do, so he asked me what I thought. I mean, I couldn't help, so I told him I could ask my dad, 'cause he used to be a cop, and he used to teach at the university."

"So, you asked your dad?"

"Yeah."

"What did he say?"

"He said it was none of my business."

Mavis had her hand on her son's back.

Gavin glanced at her briefly. "Really? So, then you told Arlo?"

"Not right away. When I did, I told him to talk to you. We talked about it on our way back from the river, that day." The boy leaned over, covering his face with his hands, doing his best to stifle a sob.

Gavin reached across and touched his arm. "It's okay, Darrell."

The boy nodded and wiped his eyes.

Mavis sighed and looked directly at Gavin. "Here's what we're struggling with." She opened the envelope, took out a folded sheet of paper and handed it to Gavin.

He took it and opened it and saw a handwritten note.

> Dear Mavis,
>
> This is a hard letter for me to write, so I will say this straight. If anything unusual happens to me, including physical harm or worse, it will probably be because of the man known as Dr. Caleb Hightower who is a professor at SRU. The REAL Caleb Hightower died in 1988. I found that out after I did a background check because I was on the interview committee. I was surprised when he was hired, I voted against it. At the time the bank turned down my request to restructure my business loan for our ranch. So, I used the information I knew about Hightower and blackmailed him. He paid me $2000 a month and that helped me meet the loan payments. Hightower was angry and I'm sure his real name is Carey, younger brother to Caleb. I told him I protected myself by giving the information to a lawyer and if anything happened to me that lawyer would tell the authorities. It was only a bluff, but he believed me and kept making the payments. I'm ashamed of what

I did and like I said if anything happens to me it probably is Carey Hightower getting even.

I hope you never have to read this letter.

Henry

Gavin could feel his face getting warm. A glance at Mavis revealed her pain and anguish as his heart went out to her and Darrell. The implications falling into place were simply overwhelming.

"What would you like to do?" he asked.

Mavis took a deep breath and exhaled. "Well, there's more, Gavin. I know this may seem crazy and disconnected to you but hear me out. Here's the thing. The evening of the day that Darrell came back from the Big White with Arlo, my husband saddled a horse and went for a ride. He was gone for at least three hours. I've never known him to do that, take a horse out after dark. It may be nothing, Gavin, but we live six miles from Flat Butte Dam. Our north pasture that we lease for our cows is next to the dam."

Darrell Berkin's head dropped lower as Gavin felt the heaviness of the implication.

"We don't know what to do. Like I said, maybe it's nothing, but we really didn't know who to talk to," she said, imploringly. The expression of dread and disbelief in her eyes broke his heart.

"Mavis, Darrell," he said. "I know it took a lot for you to tell me. The next step is totally up to you, whatever it may be. It can go no further than this—and your story is safe with me—or you can talk to someone else."

She dabbed at her eyes. "Who?"

"A lawyer, if you have one, or the police."

She nodded.

"I happen to know two tribal cops who are really good people, and they're good at their jobs," Gavin said gently.

"Yeah, I know who you mean." She smiled, a brave expression against the unknown. "Things have not been good for us at home," she admitted, glancing toward her son. "Not for a few years, because of politics, the ranch, money. And now this."

Darrell raised his head and looked directly at Gavin. "What do you think we should do, Dr. Lone Wolf?"

Gavin gazed thoughtfully at the young man. The boy was utterly conflicted, mired in confusion. "What I think doesn't matter. What you want to do, what the two of you want to do for yourselves, that's what's important. It's not easy to live with a burden of any kind, especially if you have the power to change that situation."

Mavis reached for her son's hand, grasping it firmly in hers. "For my part," she said to him, "I think we talk to the police. Lieutenant Primault is a very nice man."

Darrell nodded, and Gavin reached for his cell phone.

## ONE HUNDRED TWO

After he read it Hightower handed Berkin's letter back to Lieutenant Primault. They were sitting in a small room in the tribal jail, Hightower across the table from the CI. A uniformed officer stood behind Hightower.

"You keep it," Primault said, "as a souvenir of your exploits. I have several copies."

"I didn't kill Berkin," Hightower said.

"Oh, we know that. Because we have the man who did."

Hightower glanced across at Primault, a combination of shock and apprehension in his blue eyes.

"Yeah, your friend Antonio Caruth, from New Jersey. He's sitting in a jail cell in Cold River. Gavin Lone Wolf found him sitting in his pasture and took him prisoner."

"I don't know anyone by that name."

Primault smiled and took a voice-activated recorder from his briefcase, pressed Play and stood it in the middle of the table.

> What's your name and where are you from?
> Antonio Caruth, from Jersey City.
> Do you know Caleb Hightower?

Yeah, yeah. He worked for my dad, years ago, in New Jersey.

Why are you here?

Caleb Hightower asked me to do a job for him.

Primault stopped the playback and stared icily at Hightower. "I'd think twice before you tell any more lies," he cautioned. "So, it sounds like you lied to Antonio Caruth about your real identity as well. But we told him who you really are."

Hightower stared at Primault's chest.

"By the way, there's more on that recorder," Primault said. "Your friend Caruth talked a lot. In any case, Mr. Hightower, we've got you coming and going. We can prove you took Arlo High Crane out to Flat Butte Dam and shot him with your cap and ball pistol. We know you did that because he found out who you really are. Now, thanks to Henry Berkin's letter, we know you were in it together. But you got tired of the financial drain, so you hired Caruth."

Primault paused and allowed several seconds of silence to pass.

"Your silence speaks volumes, Mr. Hightower. Not a single peep of protest or denial."

Hightower cleared his throat. "What do you want me to say?"

"The truth and nothing but. I'm just curious. Did you tell Caruth to kill Berkin before Caruth arrived here or after?"

Another several seconds slid by as Hightower locked his gaze on the top of the table. "Before."

## ONE HUNDRED THREE

Antonio Caruth recognized the two officers who walked in behind the Sheriff. They were the Indian cops who had been at Lone Wolf's barn.

"My friends here have some questions for you," Sheriff Triplett said, as he slid two folding chairs up to the bars of the cell. He straddled a third chair and gazed with bemused interest at his prisoner.

Caruth was dressed in surplus prison garb given to small town police departments by the state penitentiary. The blue shirt didn't match the orange trousers. Always a fastidious dresser and attentive to grooming, Caruth was irritated by the mismatched clothes and the fact that he hadn't shaved in two weeks. His only grooming aid was an old hairbrush, part of the cell's décor, like the shower above the sink that came out of the wall and commode in one corner. There was no curtain, but at least there was soap and hot water, and threadbare towels.

The only redeeming factor of his situation was that he had been fed and watered regularly, as Sheriff Triplett had promised. There were two metal bunk beds in the cell. He remained seated on one of the lower bunks.

The two officers sat, the tall one opened a file in his hand, and looked up at Caruth. "We found the body of a man in an old barn, situated in a remote pasture five miles from Agency Village," he began. "The man was shot twice, once through his right bicep and once in the head. The headshot was the cause of death. We found a spent round thirty-five yards from the barn, lodged in the bark of a young oak tree. After a ballistics test in an FBI lab, that round matched those in the ten-round box of your Sig Sauer semi-automatic. That makes you the only suspect in the murder of Henry Berkin."

The facts in Avery's statement were that there was a dead man, an old barn in a remote pasture, two gunshot wounds to the body, and, of course, the dead man's name. The ballistics report was pure fabrication.

Avery continued. "We know that you know Caleb Hightower, whose real name is Carey Hightower. Mr. Hightower is a British national who's been hiding out for over twenty years in the United States. But you know that. Carey Hightower is the only suspect in the murder of a young man here on the reservation. Perhaps he didn't tell you that when he enlisted your help in the matter of acquiring a priceless historic artifact and eliminating Henry Berkin. You will be charged as an accessory in the murder committed by Mr. Hightower. Therefore, Mr. Caruth, you are facing two murder charges."

Caruth finally spoke, though he stared at the floor as he did. "I only knew Hightower by the name of Caleb. I don't know nothing about the other name. Why would he use a different name, if he did?"

"Carey Hightower was in the British Army. He murdered a fellow soldier. He escaped somehow and came to the United States. It doesn't matter whether you knew his real name or not, you and your father were harboring an escaped murderer who had been sentenced to death. The list of charges against you is growing, Mr. Caruth."

Caruth's expression didn't change, nor did he shift his gaze away from the floor. "So what? You could just be blowing smoke up my ass."

Avery pulled two sheets of paper from his file and slid them under the bars of the cell door. After a few seconds Caruth moved to pick up the pages. Sitting back on the bunk, he read them. One was the email from Durham University and the other was from Scotland Yard.

"You may not have heard about Durham University," Avery said, "but you have heard of Scotland Yard. Those emails are my whole cards, and my down cards will kick you in the nuts, Mr. Caruth."

"So, what's going to happen? What do you want?"

"Well, here's the thing. You were apprehended on Indian land, which makes it a federal case—FBI, U.S. Marshals, you know. Furthermore, Henry Berkin was killed on tribal land, therefore more federal jurisdiction. I'm sure you and your family have had dealings with the feds. Maybe you have a few of them in your pocket. In any case, I'm giving you one chance—and that chance expires in ten minutes—to tell us everything about your connection to Hightower. If—if, mind you—it corroborates what he's told us, we'll drop the accessory to murder charge."

A professional hit man, as far as Avery knew, had never come to the Smokey River Reservation until Antonio Caruth came to take Gavin Lone Wolf's gun, and kill him if necessary to acquire the pistol, pursuant to Hightower's instructions. And now Henry Berkin was part of that tangled web.

Avery had "down cards" as he put it. Caruth was a mobster and part of an east coast crime family, and Patrolman Jason Singer had proven that Caruth's rental car had traveled a hundred miles beyond the two hundred thirty-two miles from the Sioux Falls airport to Cold River. And that hundred miles was a few miles more than the distance from Cold River to the barn where Berkin had been found, and back. Finally, Gavin Lone Wolf had captured Caruth a day after Caruth had stopped for gas at Rabbit

Run in Cold River. If Caruth was Berkin's killer, he could only have done it before he was captured, somewhere within those hundred extra miles.

It was the fourth "down card" that was the winner.

Meanwhile the wheels were turning in Caruth's head. The man had said the feds would be brought in. If that happened, and once it did, he might have a chance. Feds were feds, or at least he hoped.

"What if I got nothing to say?" Caruth asked, sullenly.

"Well, look at it this way. Unless you have a GPS microchip implanted in your little white body somewhere, no one knows where you are. We'll return the rental car and tell the rental company it was abandoned. Then you'll just sit here and rot."

"I'll make sure you're fed and watered," Sheriff Triplett chimed in. "But what you see is what you get. Just three 'hots and a cot.' No radio, no television—no women. We may not be at the end of the world, but you can see it from here."

Avery took another page out of his file and slid it under the bars again. "Another of my down cards," he said. "I think you better read it."

Caruth hesitated for a few seconds before he picked up and read Henry Berkin's letter to his wife. His expression turned from bored contempt to wariness. "So," he said, with a hint of forced impudence. "This doesn't say anything about me."

Primault had opened his lap tap, waiting for the right moment.

"Yeah?" Avery said. "But this does." He nodded at Primault.

The CI stood and approached the bars of the cell as he tapped a button.

"The first voice is mine," Primault said. "I'm sure you recognize the other."

Your silence speaks volumes, Mr. Hightower. Not a single peep of protest or denial.

What do you want me to say?

The truth, and nothing but. I'm just curious. Did you tell Caruth to kill Berkin before he—Caruth—arrived here, or after?

Before.

Primault stopped the audio and stood at the cell door. Chief Avery rose from his chair and stood beside him.

"So, Mr. Caruth, is Mr. Hightower telling the truth?"

Caruth shrugged ever so slightly. He was screwed. He couldn't deny he knew Hightower. That was a provable fact.

"I got nothing to say." Caruth's stony expression was riveted on the cement floor.

"As much as Sheriff Triplett has enjoyed your company, we will be turning you over to the FBI," Avery went on. "I daresay, your cushy stay in the Redoubt County jail is coming to an end. But I think you're someone who knows about jails."

Outside the jail Triplett huddled with Avery and Primault at their car. "Well, maybe you softened him up a bit," the Sheriff suggested.

"Yeah, well, I didn't think he would spill his guts," Avery admitted. "Still, he's the only logical suspect I have. I'm going to give Agent Dempster a call. I'm sure he'll come get him off your hands sooner or later."

Avery's cell phone buzzed. A quick glance showed the station number. "Avery," he answered. "Okay, we're still in Cold River. We'll be back within the hour. Thanks, Rhonda."

Avery looked at Primault. "An interesting development. Another email came in from the British. The gist of it is their Department of State will petition our Interior Department to authorize us, our department, to be sole custodian of Hightower. Rhonda's sending the email to my phone."

"Sole custodian? Could that mean we won't have to turn him over to the FBI?"

"I don't know. We need to get a legal opinion." He waited for several seconds and then brought up the email on his phone.

> We have this date petitioned for the Extradition of Corporal Carey M. Hightower, to be returned to our jurisdiction for execution of his sentence. We have expressed our preference that this action be undertaken through your Department of Interior, and subsequently your Bureau of Indian Affairs. We have also requested that the prisoner—said Corporal Carey M. Hightower—remain in your custody throughout this process.
>
> At this point this would be a courtesy on your part until such time as we obtain a legally binding directive.

"Damn," Sheriff Triplett said. "That is about as high up the food chain you can get. You guys are playing with the big boys."

"Doesn't sound good when you put it that way," Avery said. "But since this process seems to be bypassing the DOJ, maybe the boys up in Pierre will leave us alone."

"Why do you want those folks off your back, Ben?" the Sheriff asked.

"Well, I guess it really doesn't matter now given that it's just a matter of time until the extradition is granted, then it's damn sure out of our hands," Avery said acidly. "Justin has put together an airtight case but it's looking more and more like we'll never take it to trial."

"Justice comes hard or not at all for us ordinary folks," Triplett declared angrily. He jerked his thumb in the direction of the jail. "That man in there is going to lawyer up, paid for by his filthy rich Mafia dad. They prob'ly got a few feds in their pocket. I'm guessin' they'll make some kind of deal and he'll get maybe three years and early parole. That's not justice, that's goddamn privilege."

## ONE HUNDRED FOUR

Chief Ben Avery and Lieutenant Primault had scheduled their press conference for 10 a.m. As soon as he arrived for work Gavin checked in with the president's office regarding the planning for the ledger exhibit.

"It's all good," Eagle Shield told him. "I assigned some assistants to Dr. Wells and his people. The plan is to do it the same as the private exhibition. The feed is at seven, then Dr. Wells and I will open the program. Then you're on. Will your family be there?"

"In force," Gavin said. "By the way, thanks for sending some of our media people to cover the press conference at the police station."

"Considering the circumstances, it's the least we can do. I'll call if we need you."

Gavin walked down from his office a few minutes before ten to join Ramona and several of the other staff in the lobby of the Lakota Studies Building. She had switched the television to SRU's channel for the live broadcast from the Smokey River Sioux Tribal Police Headquarters. The initial wide-shot showed at least a dozen people in the room, and as the camera panned it revealed one other television camera.

Chief Ben Avery stood with Lieutenant Primault and Sergeant West off to one side of the room. The Chief listened to the low murmur of voices as he looked at the eight other people in the room. The county's only weekly newspaper was represented, as were each of the three FM stations on the reservation, plus the tribe's own public information channel, and the media people from the university. With a slight tinge of apprehension, he recognized the white woman standing next to the second camera in the room. She was an investigative reporter from Sioux Falls.

At precisely ten o'clock, the police department's public information officer, Sergeant Gabby West, and Tribal Police Chief Ben Avery, walked to the front of the room.

Sergeant West stepped to the podium.

"Good morning ladies and gentlemen," she began. "Thank you for coming, and we welcome you to the Smokey River Tribal Police Headquarters and to this important briefing this morning. I am Sergeant West, the public information officer, and it is my honor to introduce our Chief, Benjamin Avery."

Ben Avery moved forward, with two sheets of paper in his hand, nodded at the sergeant as she stepped away, and adjusted the microphone at the podium.

"Good morning, and thank you for coming," he said, pausing to look out at the room. "This announcement will be brief, and when it is concluded, I and our Criminal Investigator Lieutenant Justin Primault, will take questions."

"Over six weeks ago," said Avery, "a young Lakota man, a member of this tribe, Arlo High Crane, was found dead at Flat Butte Dam. Cause of death was a gunshot to the back of his head. Arlo was a graduate student at the University of Nebraska and had been assigned as an intern to the Lakota Studies Department at Smokey River University. He was twenty-four years old."

The camera zoomed in for a close-up of the Chief.

"Several days ago, the only suspect in the murder of Arlo High Crane was apprehended," he continued. "That suspect is now in our jail."

"However, this is far from an open-and-shut case for at least two reasons: first, the suspect has a prior felony conviction, which is not unusual in some circumstances, but in this case, he is an international fugitive because he escaped before sentencing could be carried out."

Audible gasps could be heard throughout the room. The SRU media camera zoomed in even closer on Chief Avery.

"Second," the Chief continued, "the suspect is not a member of this tribe, nor is he a member of any tribe."

More gasps and a few low murmurs.

"Several days ago," the Chief went on, "our department notified the appropriate authorities in the suspect's country of citizenship. Those authorities have asked our department to retain custody of the suspect. That is the extent of this announcement, ladies and gentlemen. We will be happy to answer any questions at this time."

Avery motioned to Justin Primault, who had been standing well off camera, to join him at the podium. As questions began to fly, Avery pointed to a woman in the front.

"Sir," she said, "where is the suspect from?"

"The United Kingdom."

"Can you give us his name?" she followed up.

"Carey Hightower."

Avery pointed to another reporter, a young man from one of the Native newspapers.

"Chief Avery, ah, you left out some details. What was Mr. Hightower doing here and how long was he here?"

Avery smiled patiently. "I think Lieutenant Primault can fill you in."

Primault stepped to the microphone, looking a bit nervous. "Mr. Hightower came here, to the Smokey River Reservation, approximately four years ago. He was hired to teach at the university."

More murmurs erupted.

Primault held up a hand. "However, he obtained that job under false pretenses. He posed as his older brother, Caleb Hightower, who had a doctorate in archeology, and used his credentials. He has been here, locally, for four years, but our investigation revealed that he has probably been in the United States for over twenty years."

Hands went up and voices blurted out questions. Primault calmly pointed to another reporter.

"Lieutenant," she said, "what was his crime, back in England?"

"Carey Hightower was a soldier in the British Army. He killed a fellow soldier, apparently during a dispute."

The only sound in the lobby of the Lakota Studies Building came from the television, and no one moved, not so much as an inch. Everyone had heard rumors of the possible connection of Caleb Hightower to the High Crane case. The facts of the case were a definite shock.

Gavin was impressed with the way Avery and Primault were answering the questions. The question that he was wondering about finally came, spoken by the familiar voice of an investigative reporter well known in the state.

On screen, he could see Primault point to someone.

"Sir," the woman said, "this is obviously a white-on-Indian crime. I'm not as well versed in your laws as you are, but am I correct in assuming that tribes in the state cannot prosecute whites who have committed felonies on the reservation?"

Primault glanced at Avery and stepped aside. The Chief cleared his throat.

"Yes, ma'am, you are correct in your assumption."

"Should you not have involved the county, or the state, in the investigation of this crime? Or for that matter, the Federal Bureau of Investigation?"

Avery nodded, maintaining his poise. "The answer to your question is not a simple 'yes' or 'no,' unfortunately. The murder of Arlo High Crane took place on tribal land and, as such, falls under the Smokey River Sioux Tribe's jurisdiction. Because of the nature of this offense, a capital crime, we—as tribal law enforcement and judiciary—have the duty to assist federal authorities in their investigation. Though we notified the proper federal authorities, they did not respond. I will point out, however, that we did get strong cooperation from the Redoubt and Carter County sheriffs' departments."

The reporter followed up again, sensing a bigger story than what was being revealed to this point.

"But, Chief Avery, I'm wondering why you did not mention the FBI in your opening statement, and why they are not here for this briefing."

Avery nodded slowly and gazed thoughtfully at the reporter. "Well, I can say without a doubt that we are here today with this announcement because our department—the Smokey River Sioux Tribal Police Department—conducted the majority of the investigation that established Carey Hightower as the only suspect. At any time, the FBI could have taken it over, and they chose not to do that. Finally, with a fortunate turn of luck we were able to apprehend the suspect."

The woman reporter had one final question.

"Chief, you mentioned that 'authorities' have requested that you maintain custody of the suspect. Can you tell us who they are?"

"Yes, the Legal Office of the Judge Advocate General of the British Army."

Another reporter chimed in. "Wouldn't it be better to turn him over to the FBI?"

Avery smiled patiently. "The request is for us to hold the prisoner for the British Army. It is our intent to honor that request. Ladies and gentlemen, once again, thank you for coming. This concludes this morning's briefing."

As the camera lights switched off and the room dimmed a bit, Avery stepped over to the investigative reporter from the station in Sioux Falls. Her presence and questions might prove problematic, so getting on her good side would be a smart tactic. "I have a logistical question," he said.

She smiled. "Of course. How can I help you?"

"When will you air this, do you think?"

She looked at her watch and frowned. "Well, it's a four-hour drive back to Sioux Falls, which might be enough time to edit for the early evening news, but I don't know. We will, for sure, air it on the ten o'clock broadcast."

"Thank you," he said, extending his hand. "Thank you for coming."

She shook his hand. "You realize," she said, "the FBI will come down heavy on you once this hits the airwaves."

He nodded. "That was the reason for my question."

"Okay," she said. "I tell you what. It's my story and it will not be aired until the ten o'clock broadcast."

"I appreciate that," he told the reporter. "Thanks for being here."

He turned and followed Primault and Sergeant West back to the main station area with an apprehension settling in his back. He knew damn well the FBI would have a reaction.

## ONE HUNDRED FIVE

With the black briefcase hanging from his shoulder, Gavin crossed the parking lot to the SRU Administration Building and into the conference room where Dr. Theodore Wells was waiting.

"Thank you for taking the time to talk," Gavin said to the man, shaking his hand. He put the briefcase on the table.

"My pleasure, Dr. Lone Wolf," he said, as they both took a seat at the table. "What's on your mind?"

Gavin gazed at the man for second before he responded. "What's on my mind is a historic artifact."

"I see. Am I to assume it has to do with Lakota history or culture?"

"Lakota history, certainly. I'll get to the point. In the same stone jar from which my uncle, my nephew, and I extracted the ledger was another object. That object is a pistol taken after the battle, likely from Last Stand Hill, by my great-grandfather."

The man's jaw dropped slightly, his gaze shot to the briefcase, and he blinked rapidly, in time with the thoughts in his head. "Ah, yes, of course! Two of the sketches show a pistol. One depicts him reaching for one on the ground. Is that the pistol you're referring to?"

"It is, and as you've probably deduced, it is in this briefcase," Gavin touched the case.

"Oh, my! There are so many implications here."

"Exactly, which is why I really need your help. Would you like to see the pistol?"

The man's eyes widened to saucers. "Yes! May I?"

With a few deft motions Gavin pulled out a Styrofoam case, opened it, lifted out the pistol, and held it out to Wells. If any moment or circumstance manifested the words *awe* and *worship*, this was it. Dr. Theodore Wells turned into a veritable statue. After several long seconds, he blinked and reached out his hands.

"My, oh, my, oh, my," he said as he held the pistol in his open palms. "It's—it's a bit heavy. It is not an Army Colt."

"According to my brother," Gavin said, "it is a Galand and Sommerville."

Wells's reaction hinted that he knew the story of the Galand and Sommerville connection to George Custer. "Yes, of course. That makes absolute sense, especially since your ancestor found it at Last Stand Hill."

Wells finally looked up at Gavin after nearly a minute of worshipful inspection of the pistol. "Since you've brought this to my attention, how can I help?"

Gavin inhaled and exhaled slowly. "Well, this will be a family decision; in general, we would like to relinquish it—but not without fair compensation—to someone or some entity that would appreciate it for its place in history."

"Of course."

"I think you—the National Museum of the American Indian—would be such a place, or at least be in the best position to broker an arrangement, given the circumstances under which this came into my great-grandfather's possession."

Wells nodded. It was his turn to sigh deeply. "I do thank you for bringing this to my attention, to our attention. As you know, we have protocols in place to facilitate the procurement of objects such as this. First, we need to authenticate it, but I can practically guarantee that would be a mere formality."

"Well, that leaves us with some logistics," Gavin said. "When, for example, do we officially turn it over to you, to NMAI?"

"There are hoops," Wells said, "legal hoops. I'll get on the phone and apprise my superiors of this new development. There are forms, *i*'s to dot and *t*'s to cross, and signatures to be had, from you and us. It is a process, as you well know. Until then, you must retain possession."

"Understood. I will gather my family together this evening and we will discuss this and likely write you a letter bequeathing it to you, with some conditions, of course."

"That will do nicely," Wells concurred. Then reluctantly, it appeared to Gavin, the man handed the pistol back. "There is a question I must ask."

"Certainly."

"A lot of questions, actually, but why now? Wouldn't it have been better to reveal this along with the ledger, especially since it is part of your great-grandfather's story?"

"Frankly, Dr. Wells, we were afraid of what might happen once word got out," Gavin answered. "It is entirely possible, as you also suspect, that this pistol might have belonged to one of the Custer brothers. Just the suggestion that it did belong to one of them makes this a priceless artifact in certain circles, one that some people would do anything to possess. And that, we were afraid, could be dangerous for our family."

"That is a valid concern. We will handle this issue with the utmost discretion and secrecy. Only when it is in a theft-proof exhibit will it be revealed. In the meantime, please do us both a favor, as far as our personal well-being is concerned, and put it out of sight."

Gavin left the conference room with the bag over his shoulder, much too casually, as far as Wells was concerned. But then, he reminded himself, no one else here knew what was in the briefcase, and Gavin Lone Wolf was a very imposing figure of a man.

From his office Gavin called Loren, who was at the hospital.

"Hey, little brother," she answered. "How are you?"

"I'm good. Sis. Ah, listen, is there any chance Uncle Andrew and I can crash the party at your house this evening? There's something we all need to talk about, having to do with the pistol."

"Come on over. We'll all be home by six."

## ONE HUNDRED SIX

Ben Avery was wading through the paperwork on his desk when the call came from Acting Supervisory Special Agent Bryan Dempster. Which was more of a nuisance—the paperwork or Dempster—was a toss-up. He looked up at the clock on the opposite wall: 1:47 p.m. Word got around fast.

"Good afternoon," he said, trying not to sound annoyed.

"Chief Avery. This is Bryan Dempster. Can we talk?"

"What's on your mind?"

"A non-Indian sitting in your jail."

"I see. What about him?"

"You're holding him illegally."

Avery decided in a flash to put it all on the line. "Be that as it may, what is your interest in this person?"

"He's an international fugitive convicted of murder."

"He's the only suspect in the murder of Arlo High Crane. I'm sure you remember that situation," Avery pointed out. "You were here initially, and we requested your assistance since then on more than one occasion. You apparently had other priorities."

Avery could only label the chuckle he heard as condescending. "Well, now we can cover both bases. Let's look at it that way, Ben."

"Except for one thing, Bryan," Avery replied, matching Dempster's tone. "An extradition is in the works. The last communication we received from the British Army Judge Advocate General included a request for us to maintain custody of the prisoner. We are honoring that request. Meanwhile, maybe you should check with your people in the DOJ. The extradition will be handled through the Department of Interior, and then through the Bureau of Indian Affairs."

"You're joking."

"Okay, well, if you want to piss off your superiors because you think I'm joking, be my guest."

A few seconds of heavy silence passed before Dempster spoke again, his tone somewhere between disbelief and simmering anger. "I will get to the bottom of this, Chief Avery, and I'll call you back."

"I'll be here."

## ONE HUNDRED SEVEN

Thomas greeted Gavin at the front door. "Come on in," he said, his broad grin turning to concern when he saw the serious look on his uncle's face. "Everything okay, Uncle?"

"Oh, yeah, yeah. Just an interesting day."

Gavin informed everyone about his meeting with Dr. Wells, and that it was highly likely that NMAI would broker a satisfactory offer for the Galand and Sommerville. "It will probably mean some level of financial compensation."

Loren gazed at him. "You're saying sell that pistol?"

Gavin nodded. "Yeah, and Gerard feels the same way."

"What's the alternative?" Morgan wondered. "For that gun to sit in a safe deposit box for who knows how many years?"

"No, that's not what I meant," Loren countered, "I want us to get rid of it; I guess I just didn't think there was actually a chance it was worth anything."

"It's worth a considerable amount of money," Gavin confirmed. "The NMAI will help assess its worth after they've authenticated it."

Loren looked at Uncle Andrew. "What do you think, Uncle?"

"I think there are people out there, in the world," he warned, "who will do anything to have things like that gun. If they knew about it, if they knew that we have it, they would come after it and get it however they can. Those are scary and dangerous people. So, I think we let those museum people find a place for it. I don't care where, just as long as it's away from here. That way it might do some good."

"I vote for that, Uncle," Loren said. "So, okay, once we get an offer, a dollar amount—and I know this sounds totally materialistic—what do we do? Do we divide it up?"

"Yeah," Gavin said. "It's the simplest and fairest way. Gerard's suggestion is by primary descendants, and that is Uncle Andrew, you, Gerard, and me. And I have a further suggestion."

"And that is?"

"A scholarship fund at the university in Arlo High Crane's name. We take an amount off the top, whatever we decide, and then divide the rest."

Loren nodded. "Oh, that's a wonderful idea, little brother. I vote for that."

Andrew nodded his agreement.

"Great. I'll talk to Gerard," Gavin said. "I'm sure he'll go along with it."

"Good," Loren said, glancing toward the kitchen. The enticing aroma of broiled salmon beckoned. "Let's eat."

Gavin's phone chirped with an incoming call from a now familiar number. "Ben, how is everything?"

The Chief chuckled wryly. "There is a development relative to our prisoner."

"Really?"

"Yeah, earlier today I got a call from our friend, Agent Dempster. He wants custody of Hightower."

"Of course," Gavin said. "Now Hightower is worth paying some attention to. Is he coming down to get him?"

"I don't think so, not immediately anyway. He didn't know about the British Army's extradition request. And until we get a firm decision, we don't have much of a legal leg to stand on. I wouldn't be surprised if he shows up in force."

"So, he's sort of thrown down the gauntlet."

"Right, so I need your help."

"Sure, what can I do?"

"I think we need to get the tribal president and council involved. Do you think that's a wise tactic?"

"It couldn't hurt, but maybe speed is of the essence."

"Right, do you have any ideas?"

"Well, I know the president, and my Uncle Andrew has connections with many of the council members. If we have permission to talk about the details in this situation, I think we can help out a bit."

"Great, that's great! And, of course, fill them in. There are no secrets here. In fact, the more they know, the better. Lieutenant Primault and I will be available to talk to anyone."

"Okay, I'll talk to my uncle and President Lone Hawk." Gavin glanced at his watch. "Let's just plan on keeping in touch as this moves along."

"Right. It may be a bit of an overreaction, but I'm camping out here at the department. I don't trust the feds. I wouldn't be surprised if they try to surprise us."

Gavin disconnected the call and immediately realized that everyone had been listening in to his side of the conversation. There was a healthy dose of curiosity, but also somber looks of concern.

"Gavin," Loren said, suspiciously, "what is going on?"

"Well, I'll tell you, if you don't mind some really serious dinner conversation." He glanced at his uncle. "The Police Chief needs our help."

Andrew nodded.

Gavin turned to his sister. "Chief Avery thinks there's a good chance that the FBI might try to take custody of Hightower." He looked at Uncle Andrew. "He wants us—you and me—to talk to the president and council, to get them involved."

Andrew nodded, his expression a mixture of curiosity and anticipation. Then he turned to look out the window, at a whirlwind that had suddenly sprung up beyond the trees west of the house. It formed a gray twister, scattering leaves, twigs, and debris as it spun angrily.

## ONE HUNDRED EIGHT

Gavin glanced at the sun hanging low above the horizon as he pulled into the Lone Hawks' driveway. Clayton emerged from the front door to meet him and, at the behest of his wife Veronica, issued an invitation for coffee and dessert.

"Thank you," Gavin said to Veronica.

He had known Clayton Lone Hawk since he was a boy attending Uncle Andrew's *inipi* ceremonies where Clayton was a frequent participant. In junior high Gavin had learned of his friend's exploits on the track field where he excelled as a long-distance runner in high school and college. Only a freak injury had kept him off the U.S. Olympic team.

"I'm sorry only difficult circumstances seem to bring us together," Clayton said as they sat at table in the large kitchen. "Especially since we're neighbors."

"Me, too," Gavin admitted.

Gavin, of course, knew how tragic circumstances had brought Clayton Lone Hawk and Veronica Streeter together. Nevertheless, the sixty-seven-year-old retired school administrator and his wife, a foundation executive fifteen years his junior, could not and did not ignore the deep feelings they had for one another. They had married after a brief courtship.

"So," Gavin said to Veronica, "I'm sure you've observed the tenuous relationship the tribes have with the state and the federal government."

"I have," she said. "It seems to range from laughable to frustrating."

"Indeed. In any case, the reason I'm here is because of a situation with the FBI. I know Clayton's been keeping abreast of it. It has to do with the man arrested for the murder of a young man a few weeks ago. And my apologies that it has to be our coffee conversation."

"Not to worry," she assured him.

Gavin summed up the situation as succinctly as he could in five minutes.

"The feds are unpredictable," Lone Hawk pointed out. "Friends in one situation, adversaries in another. I'll start making calls. We'll convene an emergency Tribal Council meeting tomorrow morning."

Later they walked him to his pickup. "I heard about the project involving your great-grandfather's ledger art," Veronica said. "Sounds fascinating."

"It certainly is, and it's nearly finished," he said. "There are plans for a formal reveal, so to speak, in a few weeks at the university. My family and I would like you both to be there. The university will send out invitations."

"I'll make sure we are," she assured him.

Andrew was waiting in his driveway when he arrived home.

"I talked to seven council reps," the old man said, as they sat on the front porch with coffee. "The most influential ones. They'll get on the horn and make sure a full council shows up tomorrow. Anything else from the police chief?"

"No, and that's good. I'm going to call him in a bit. Clayton wants me to be there, and I know you'll be there."

"Yeah," the old man said, grinning. "Sounds like we're forming a war party."

Gavin watered the horses and stood listening to the coyotes yelping and calling under the early evening sky. There was no moon. The only thing missing was a tipi with a fire in front of it. He heard the grunts of nighthawks as they dived after insects. As far as he was concerned, the Lakota were the hawks and the FBI were the insects.

---

Forty miles away Chief Avery heard Gabby West's soft knock on his door. "Hey," he said, "I thought I sent you home."

"I'll be going in a bit. There's someone here to see you from the television station."

"Sure, send them in."

Marilee Rothen, dressed in casual running sweats, came in, clearly nervous.

"What can I do for you?" Avery asked politely.

"Well, my cameraman and I were about to pack up and head back to Sioux Falls, but I wanted to ask some further questions about the Hightower case."

Avery smiled. "Sure. What's on your mind?"

"First, can we talk off the record? And then maybe on camera?"

"Works for me, as long as you assure me you'll be here for the Tribal Council meeting tomorrow morning."

## ONE HUNDRED NINE

President Clayton Lone Hawk called the meeting of the Smokey River Sioux Tribal Council to order. Nineteen of the twenty chairs at the horseshoe-shaped council table were filled. In addition to the camera crew broadcasting the council meetings for the public channel, another cameraman was set up and ready to go. Lone Hawk had been informed he was from a Sioux Falls station.

After the opening prayer and a roll call, President Lone Hawk explained the reason for the emergency meeting.

"My relatives and friends, and members of the Tribal Council," he began. "We have an interesting situation developing, a legal situation. It pertains to the murder of a tribal member, a young man by the name of Arlo High Crane."

In a few short minutes he explained the situation succinctly, in Lakota and English.

"I am asking that you, the Tribal Council, enact a resolution directing our police department to hold the prisoner for the British authorities, as they have requested," he concluded. "I have invited Chief of Police Ben Avery to be here, and he is standing back there with my good friend Gavin Lone Wolf, who has been extremely involved with this case."

In less than twenty minutes, in a rare show of solidarity, the Smokey River Sioux Tribal Council unanimously passed a resolution directing the police department to retain custody of the suspect in the murder of Arlo High Crane until such time as he could be remanded over to the duly authorized representatives of the British Army's Judge Advocate General, and only to those representatives. Upon Gavin's request, a proviso was included in the resolution that the British Army's Judge Advocate General be fully advised as to the Smokey River Sioux Tribe's case against the suspect.

President Lone Hawk signed two copies of the resolution in his office in the presence of the Secretary of the Smokey River Sioux Tribal Council, James Bear, Chief of Police Ben Avery, and Gavin Lone Wolf. The first copy he handed to the Chief of the Tribal Police and the second he gave to the Tribal Secretary.

"This will not stop the feds from trying to stomp on us," Lone Hawk said to Avery, "but it does give you full authority to retain custody of the prisoner. You are now holding the prisoner at our behest."

"Thank you, sir," Avery said, "and if you will excuse me, I will return to my post."

Lone Hawk stood to shake his hand. "By all means."

Gavin walked with Avery out to the parking lot, wending their way through the crowds still standing around.

"Thanks to you and your uncle as well," the Chief said.

"Glad we could help. I wish I could say that the issue is settled, but you and I both know it's not. I think there's trouble just over the horizon. Uncle Andrew said trouble always come from the east."

"Yeah, you're right," Avery agreed. "We may no longer have to meet the *wasicus* on horseback with bows and arrows, but we still have to meet them. The problem is, they so often have outnumbered us."

"That didn't stop our ancestors from getting on their horses and stringing their bows. We can't stop now."

Avery extended his hand. "Spoken like a true warrior. Thanks again."

As Gavin walked a few yards to where his uncle was standing with a group of men, young and old, a conversation was happening on the other side of the Tribal Building.

Marilee Rothen was talking on the phone to her managing editor.

"Stan, listen to me. This is an important story. The FBI wasn't that interested in investigating the murder of a tribal member. Now that they know the suspect, a white guy, is an international fugitive, they're interested. And another issue is that this tribe—and any tribe in the state for that matter—cannot prosecute a white person for a capital crime committed on a reservation against a tribal member. That's how it's been since there have been reservations. So how is that not an important story?"

The voice on the other end was impatient. "Marilee, do you think the majority of people in this state really give a shit about that? Don't forget who the majority of our viewers are. Don't forget who spends the advertising dollars to be on our air. It certainly isn't the Indians."

Rothen was exasperated. "Oh, for heaven's sake, Stan. This story is about justice and fairness. These people are our neighbors, they were here before we were, for god's sake!"

"They're a conquered people. They should know their place."

"You know what, Stan? I certainly didn't know that's how you really feel! If Gary wants to leave, I'm staying here with the camera. You can fire me if you want."

# ONE HUNDRED TEN

At 3:17 a.m. the graveyard shift dispatcher knocked on Chief Avery's office door and waited. After a faint scuffling and the sound of a chair sliding, he opened the door, clad in his running sweats. The dispatcher gave him two pages.

"These just came through, sir," he said.

"Okay, thanks Jim," the Chief said. He turned on the office lights and circled to his desk chair, switching on the desk lamp. Sitting, he rubbed his eyes and read.

The first page was simple and direct and at the top of the page was the logo of the Bureau of Indian Affairs.

> SUBJECT: Attached communication from General Counsel U.S. Department of the Interior
> Chief Avery:
> Please find attached a letter to you from the General Counsel of the Department of the Interior. Your department and the Smokey River Sioux Tribe are authorized to comply with the directive in the letter.
> Dr. Harold Lansing
> Director North Central Region Bureau of Indian Affairs

The second page from Lansing, which was a communication to Lansing, bore the Great Seal of the U.S. Department of the Interior:

> RE: Corporal Carey M. Hightower
>
> Dear Dr. Lansing:
>
> We have been duly notified that the U.S. Department of Justice will grant Extradition of the above referenced individual, a citizen of the United Kingdom, from the United States to Great Britain. Upon approval and certification of said Extradition, personnel from the British Army will travel to the Smokey River Reservation to take custody. Until their arrival the Smokey River Sioux Tribal Police are directed to maintain custody of Corporal Carey M. Hightower and remand him only to British Military Police. Said police will present proper authorization in writing, including a copy of this directive.
>
> Michael Tremmerling
>
> Assistant Counsel Office of the Counselor General
>
> Department of the Interior

Avery read the letter twice before he leaned back in his chair, a smile spreading across his face. "Special Agent Bryan Dempster," he said, "I believe I have you by the shorthairs."

Standing, he walked to a fireproof filing cabinet against a wall, worked the combination on the dial, and pulled it open and carefully slid the two pages into a file marked Pending. Then he closed the drawer, spun the dial to lock the cabinet, and returned to the cot behind his desk.

Back under his sleeping bag, he was asleep in two minutes.

## ONE HUNDRED ELEVEN

Acting Supervisory Special Agent Bryan Dempster gazed in exasperation at the two other FBI agents in his office, Merrick Slattery and Timothy Young.

"Which part of the situation with the Smokey River Sioux Tribal Police do you not understand?" he asked.

Slattery, a blond high school quarterback type, pointed to his copy of the thick file in front of him on the table. "I've gone over this a few times," he said. "I understand all of it. The British are sending their people to take custody of Carey Hightower. At every level there is attestation to that statement, the State Department, Interior, and the Bureau of Indian Affairs. The Department of Justice isn't included. It's out of our hands, so I don't understand why you want to go down there and take the prisoner; or try to take him."

"Try? What do you mean try?"

"You're biting off more than you can chew, Bryan."

"I feel the same," said Young, a Texan with a ruddy complexion and a worried frown. "Maybe you should talk to Jim Atkinson, get his take on it."

"What? Are you serious?" Dempster shook his head in disbelief. "Jim Atkinson is detailed to DC and we all know why. He's up for a review because of that fiasco last year. That usually means a harmless desk job or early forced retirement, and that's why I'm acting supervisory agent. You think I should talk to him? And keep in mind, I will in all likelihood be the next Supervisory Special Agent."

"That's a threat if I ever heard one, Bryan," Slattery said.

"Well, here's what's going to happen, gentlemen. No matter what the British say or want, that damn Indian police department down there is wrong. They have no jurisdiction over Hightower, they should not have apprehended—."

"We sat on the sidelines regarding this case," Young insisted. "That was your decision."

"Don't interrupt me again," Dempster warned. "The Casper and Omaha offices have assigned agents to me on a temporary basis. They will arrive this evening. Tomorrow morning, we will travel to the Smokey River Reservation and take custody of their prisoner, a white male who is outside their legal jurisdiction. Is there anything about what I have just said that is not clear to you?"

Both agents shook their heads without speaking. Slattery raised a hand. "Service pistols only, I take it? Unless you want to requisition an armored personnel carrier."

"Your sarcasm is duly noted, Merrick. We will not need anything but hand weapons. We are the Federal Bureau of Investigation, and they are Indians. Any resolve on their part will wilt at the sight of FBI agents, believe me."

Timothy Young stared at the file in front of him and slowly shook his head.

# ONE HUNDRED TWELVE

Ninety miles away the reason for Agent Dempster's planned invasion of the Smokey River Sioux reservation stood up from the bunk in the cell rigged up just for him and walked slowly to the door. He was dressed in an orange jumpsuit, with only ankle-high socks on his feet.

Bars comprised all four sides of the cell. Inside a shatter-proof Plexiglas bubble in the ceiling at the front, a camera watched and recorded the prisoner's every movement: in this case, hours and hours of sitting motionlessly.

"Hello?" he called out hoarsely. He hadn't spoken a word in days. He cleared his throat. "Hello!"

The jailer watching the monitor kept his eye on the screen as he picked up the phone and punched a single number.

"What is it?" said a deep voice.

"The prisoner is up and at the door," the jailer reported. "He's calling out."

"Okay, be right there."

Correctional Officer Arnold Fielding left the small office at the front of the jail wing and turned down a short hallway. He waved at the jailer as he passed the monitor room and unlocked the heavy metal door to the holding cells.

Stepping inside he followed strict protocol and waited until the jailer remotely locked the door behind him, even though he was reasonably sure the prisoner couldn't get out. He had seen *Silence of the Lambs* once too often. A few steps took him to Hightower's cell, a converted drunk tank.

"Mr. Hightower," he said. "What can we do for you?"

Hightower cleared his throat again. "I want to talk to Gavin Lone Wolf," he said.

"Who?"

"Gavin Lone Wolf. He's a professor at the university."

"You are not allowed visitors, Mr. Hightower."

Hightower gazed blankly at the officer. "Please, it's all I'm going to ask for."

Fielding stared at the man. There was no light in the prisoner's eyes. "Okay, I'll ask my boss and see what he says."

Without another word Fielding turned and left the cellblock. Back in the office he dialed a number.

"Chief Avery," said a voice on the other end.

"Sir, you asked me to notify you if anything occurred with the prisoner," he said.

"What happened?"

"Nothing, sir. He's asking to talk to Gavin Lone Wolf.

"I see. Anything else? Has he been behaving himself?"

"Yes, sir. He's hardly moved for days."

"Good. Ah, tell Hightower that Dr. Lone Wolf is not available. Ah, wait a minute, I'll go over and talk to him. Be there in a minute."

Hightower sat on the edge of the cement bunk, staring down at the floor. The jail-wing door clicked open with a heavy metallic sound, and then closed. Footsteps approached the cell. He didn't look up.

"Mr. Hightower." The voice was vaguely familiar.

Hightower slowly turned his head. It was the Police Chief.

"Dr. Lone Wolf is not available," the man said. "What do you want to talk with him about?"

Hightower shrugged, keeping his eyes on the bare cement floor. "I just want to say some things to him. If he'll talk to me."

Avery shook his head. "No," he said.

Avery called Gavin as he was finishing a long horse-back ride. "Got a call from my man in Pierre. He said that two shiny black tops were in the employee parking lot at the federal building. They came in at different intervals, which means they came from different locations. Reinforcements, maybe, or it could be totally unrelated to Hightower."

"Well, why should we wait for them to make a move?" Gavin queried

"What do you mean?"

"I have an idea."

# ONE HUNDRED THIRTEEN

Two large black SUVs drove into the Pierre Federal Building parking lot just before eight in the morning. The people inside failed to notice a dark sedan and a black police cruiser parked at the curb in front of the building. The cruiser bore the logo of the Smokey River Sioux Tribe, and inside were two uniformed officers and a prisoner in the back seat. The sedan had three men in it with an unobstructed view of the federal building. Chief Ben Avery turned to the two passengers in his car.

"According to the officer I sent up here," he said, "those were the vehicles that arrived yesterday. But the good news is there were only two."

President Clayton Lone Hawk leaned forward from the back seat. "I think we should make our entrance," he suggested.

Avery glanced at Gavin Lone Wolf in the passenger seat, and then at Lone Hawk. "My thoughts exactly. We have surprise on our side."

Avery was in uniform. From the trunk of his car he took his utility belt and sidearm and buckled them on. He made sure his lapel camera was working properly. President Lone Hawk was dressed in a dark business suit while Gavin Lone Wolf was more casually attired in dark-blue cargo pants and a gray hunting shirt.

Avery, a large envelope in hand, walked to the cruiser as the driver side window rolled down. "Gentlemen," he said. "Time to make our move. Bring your prisoner."

Less than thirty seconds later the two Smokey River Tribal police officers had the handcuffed and shackled prisoner out of the back seat and on the pavement. The prisoner stood with his head down.

The Federal Building was familiar to Avery. He knew that FBI agents used the main rear entrance and entered there. As the entourage of six men reached the entrance, four agents carrying backpacks emerged, soon followed by others. Most of them cast somewhat puzzled glances at the Native policemen, a prisoner in handcuffs, and two longhaired Native men in civilian clothes. It was clear to Avery that the agents had orders to carry out.

Special Agent Bryan Dempster was the last to exit the building. He did an almost comical double-take as he walked past the five Native men and one white man in a jail jumpsuit, then stopped and turned around.

"Chief Avery?" he asked, obviously surprised, not to mention confused. "What are you doing here?" At 8:00 in the morning, Dempster was wearing mirrored sunglasses.

"Good morning, Bryan," Avery replied. "I thought we'd drop by and clear up a little misunderstanding."

Dempster hesitantly approached Avery, Gavin, and Lone Hawk, casting puzzled glances at each of them. "Ah, what do you mean, exactly?" He stared for a few seconds at the man in handcuffs and shackles. "Have you come to your senses and decided to deliver your prisoner to us?"

"No," Avery said. "We'll get to our prisoner in a bit."

Dempster was clearly confused. "This isn't Hightower?"

"No."

"Is this a joke?"

Avery's expression was inscrutable. Unlike Dempster, he wore no sunglasses. He handed the large envelope to the still confused agent. "Agent Dempster, in that envelope are official requests and orders. My department has been ordered to retain custody of Carey Hightower and remand him only to the proper authorities. These orders were issued by the Chief Counsel of the U.S. Department of the Interior and then by the Bureau of Indian Affairs, as requested by the British Foreign Office. Nowhere in this chain of authority was the Department of Justice—you folks, in other words—ever mentioned."

The other agents were gathering, equally as confused regarding the five Native men with a white prisoner. Dempster looked hard at the envelope in his hand but made no move to open it. He glanced at the other agents as he gathered his thoughts.

"So, Chief Avery," he said, "you drove up here just to tell me that? Where is your prisoner, Carey Hightower?"

"In our jail, as per those orders and directives," Avery replied calmly, pointing at the envelope.

"Then you must understand that I am one of those 'proper authorities,'" Dempster said, recovering some of his nerve. "Therefore, the wise move on your part would have been to deliver him to me."

"I am afraid not."

"And why not, Chief?"

"Because the 'proper authorities' in this instance are specifically named as personnel of the British Army's military police, and none other."

"I see, but until such time as they are on scene, we have jurisdiction over this case. You, sir, are illegally holding Mr. Hightower."

Avery did not relent. "The orders and directives I alluded to earlier give me full authority to hold Mr. Hightower. Furthermore, we have a directive from our Tribal Council to honor those directives."

Dempster slowly shook his head, on the edge of exasperation. "I see. Then I think you need to exercise some common sense, Chief Avery. Those proper authorities will not arrive any time soon; there is time for you to resolve this sensibly."

"Or else what?" Avery's gaze at the mirrored sunglasses was an outright challenge.

"I beg your pardon." Dempster's tone indicated he was on the verge of losing his cool.

One of the other agents stepped forward, clearly confused. "Bryan, what's this all about?"

Dempster flicked a glance at the man. "I'll handle this, Gallagher!"

Gallagher bristled at Dempster's dismissive tone.

President Lone Hawk cleared his throat and stepped forward and stopped directly in front of Dempster. "May I ask a favor, sir?"

"And who are you, sir?" Dempster asked, with a tone of irritation.

"Clayton Lone Hawk. I'm the President of the Smokey River Sioux Tribe."

"Yes, sir. What can I do for you?"

"Remove your sunglasses to start with, if you wouldn't mind."

Dempster glanced nervously sideways at the agents standing closest and slowly reached up and removed his sunglasses.

"Thank you," Lone Hawk said. "I think people should at least have the courtesy to communicate eye-to-eye. Agent Dempster, is that who you are?"

"Yes, sir. Acting Supervisory Special Agent."

"Of course. Well, Acting Supervisory Special Agent Dempster, I had a long telephone conversation last evening with a gentleman by the name of Terrence Ashley. Do you know that name?"

Dempster turned pale. "Yes, sir. Mr. Ashley is the Director of the FBI."

"Indeed he is. I apprised Director Ashley of your communication with our Tribal Police Department, and he does know of the situation regarding our prisoner and of all the letters and orders Chief Avery mentioned. He's fully aware of everything, as someone in his position should be. And, I must say, he was not too thrilled to learn that you, meaning all of you apparently," Lone Hawk gestured at the group of agents, "might be going to our reservation to try to take custody of our prisoner. Are you with me, so far, Acting Supervisory Special Agent Dempster?"

Lone Hawk's comments were not lost on the other agents standing nearby, exchanging nervous side-glances.

Dempster cleared his throat and nodded. "Yes, sir."

"Good. Well, it does seem to me that you've stepped outside your authority a bit. And to what end? You thought, perhaps, to go down there and bully us into giving you our prisoner, and why, just because you can? Just because you're the FBI?"

Dempster took a deep breath but said nothing. The agents to the right and left of him were standing with their heads down.

"That was not a rhetorical question, Agent Dempster. I would really like an answer," Lone Hawk insisted.

"Ah, my apologies—."

"That's not an answer; and apologies are nice, but I have a hard time believing you're sincere. Bottom line is this, Agent Dempster, it wouldn't have mattered if you had gone down there with a hundred agents. Do you know why? Well, of course you don't. It wouldn't have mattered because we've seen this sort of attitude and action on your part before, and many others with the power of your government and the impetus of society-wide complacency behind you. Yes, we're used to it, sadly. But, your bullying will not work this morning, not at this moment. Am I clear, Agent Dempster?"

Dempster nodded. "Yes, sir."

"One last thing, Agent Dempster. My tribe is officially lodging a complaint against you, for whatever good it will do." Lone Hawk looked at each agent in turn. "I'm sure the slap on your wrists won't be too painful," he concluded, sarcastically. He turned to Chief Avery. "Well, I believe I've taken a bit too much time. I'm done."

Gavin had been unobtrusively observing the other ten agents. Most of them were standing back on their heels, a few of them with backpacks over a shoulder. To Gavin, their posture and facial expressions were subtle indications that Dempster did not have their full support.

Avery kept his gaze on Dempster, who seemed to be struggling to give a response. "Special Agent Dempster," he said, "we have been apprised that military policemen from the British Army will come here once the extradition is granted. At that time, we will remand our prisoner to their custody. So, Bryan, I appeal to your common sense to interfere no further, or, if you choose, you're welcome to lock horns with Director Ashley, the General Counsels of the Department of the Interior, and the Bureau of Indian Affairs, not to mention the British Army."

Agent Gallagher stepped forward. He was a competent-looking man, the kind that favored a no-nonsense approach. "Bryan, for the record," he said, "I was under the impression you had authority from the top to do this. That was not the case, was it?"

"It—this was a judgment call on my part," Dempster said.

"Right," Gallagher said. "In that case, my two agents and I are standing down from this operation." He stepped forward and reached out a hand to Avery. "Chief, thank you for clearing this up. I'm Gallagher, from the Omaha Field Office."

"Thank you, Special Agent Gallagher," Avery replied.

Another agent stepped forward and Gallagher and two agents walked away. "Chief, I'm Bertram, from the Casper Field Office. Good luck with your prisoner."

"Thank you," Avery said.

Bertram turned and walked to an SUV, followed by two other agents.

Dempster, meanwhile, seemed rooted to the ground by confusion or indecision. An agent whom Avery recognized stepped forward, glancing sideways at Dempster as he reached out a hand to Avery. "Chief," he said, "if Special Agent Dempster insists on going down after your prisoner, he will be doing so by himself."

"Thank you, Special Agent Young. Thanks for understanding the situation."

"No worries. You all seem to have done a good job apprehending this fugitive."

"Right," Avery replied. "With a bit of luck."

Young nodded toward the man in handcuffs. "So, who is this?"

"This," Avery said, taking an envelope from one of the tribal officers, "is Mr. Antonio Caruth. Mr. Caruth is the only suspect in the murder of a tribal member by the name of Henry Berkin."

"A member of our tribal council," Lone Hawk interjected.

Avery handed the envelope to Special Agent Young. "This is the complete file," he said. "Be advised that Mr. Caruth is a member of the Napoli family of New Jersey. If you don't know about them, I'm sure Google has all kinds of information. In any case, Mr. Caruth is outside of our jurisdiction since he committed a capital offense, and we would like to turn him over to you."

"Of course." The agent took a key to the cuffs and shackles from one of the tribal officers. He turned to another agent. "Merrick, I could use a hand with Mr. Caruth." In a few seconds the two agents and Caruth were through the glass doors.

In another moment, the only agent left standing near the entrance was Dempster. He nodded toward Avery, though not quite looking at him. "Good luck," he muttered ambiguously, almost inaudibly, then turned and entered the building.

"Well," Clayton Lone Hawk said, "I think a fly on the wall in their various shops is going to hear some interesting conversations."

Avery nodded, as he loosed a long sigh, and turned to the two patrolmen. "Gentlemen, thank you. If you'd like, grab some breakfast before you head back."

"Thank you, sir," they said in unison.

Turning to Gavin and Lone Hawk, Avery allowed himself a grin. "Gentlemen, coffee's on me."

"Thank you," Gavin said. "I can't wait to see the footage from your lapel camera." He turned to Clayton Lone Hawk. "I like what you said. I sure hope the Chief's camera picked all that up. I think you should seriously think about teaching a course in race relations."

Lone Hawk chuckled. "Well, thanks, but I'm sure it went in one ear and out the other. That's the problem with communication. It takes two to make it work."

Avery turned and walked slowly toward their cars, as Gavin and Lone Hawk fell in step beside him. "I know one thing," the Chief said, nodding toward the federal building. "Most of those agents are smart guys, and hopefully a few of them will think about what you had to say."

"I hope so," Lone Hawk said. "Maybe there's hope for all of us." He turned to Gavin. "Really good idea you had, my friend. This was the way to diffuse what could have been an ugly confrontation."

"Well, my brother is a Lakota and a Marine—a hell of a combination. He would always say that a good tactician hits the enemy when and where he least expects it. It worked for us."

# ONE HUNDRED FOURTEEN

Sounds of drums and Sun Dance songs echoed in his head as Gavin carried a glass of iced tea up to his office. He was burned a deep brown after days in the sun, helping at his Uncle Andrew's ceremony. With a tiny bit of reluctance, he was back to the pile of work waiting on his desk.

The second SRU summer session was nearly half over and a lazy, laid-back feeling had settled over the campus. Henry Berkin's funeral had been during the Sun Dance, so Gavin was unable to attend. By all accounts it was the largest funeral in years. His body had been brought to the tribal council hall for one night of wake, and after the funeral service in Christ Episcopal Church he had been transported to the national cemetery near Sturgis.

Two weeks had passed since the showdown with the FBI in Pierre, and Hightower was still cooling his heels in the tribal jail, pending the granting of his extradition back to England. FBI agents had been in the area following up on Chief Avery's evidence regarding the murder of Henry Berkin. Antonio Caruth had been denied bail and had been transferred to a secure facility in Colorado. These had been the kind of times for which the only antidote was long horseback rides.

After remembering how Uncle Andrew cleansed Hightower's camp near the Little White River, Gavin suggested to the SRU facilities director that Hightower's office should be completely remodeled. That work was underway.

If there was anything constant in his mind it was memories of Soldier Woman, prompted by an occasional text or email from her. Each note brought her soaring into his awareness, a bittersweet frustration he shared in great detail with both Red Wing and Dancer on their long rides.

At nearly six he decided to call it a day after Ramona told him she was doing the same. Just outside the building his phone buzzed. It was Chief Avery.

"Good afternoon, Ben."

"Gavin. Hope you're doing well. I just received an official communication from the regional office."

"Ah, let me guess, regarding Hightower."

"You got it. The feds granted the extradition, and I was just told that it's only a matter of days before the British Army Military Police will be here."

"Well, we knew that day was coming."

"Yeah, and here's what Justin and I were discussing. The tribal council resolution that authorized us to hold Hightower also directed us to inform the British authorities of Hightower's crime here. The chief tribal judge is encouraging us to give the case file to them."

"Great idea. That certainly falls within the scope of 'informing.' You think the British will accept the file?"

"I think they'll accept anything relevant to Hightower," Avery asserted, "and we can argue that his crime led to us learning his real identity."

"I think you may be right," Gavin agreed.

"In any case, we're going to take your uncle's suggestion and present our evidence to Hightower. We'd like you to be part of it."

"Of course. Say when."

## ONE HUNDRED FIFTEEN

A bare room at the back of the cellblock was furnished with a table and chairs. Carey Hightower sat on one side facing Chief Avery, Lieutenant Primault, and Dr. Lone Wolf. A uniformed officer stood behind Hightower.

It was just past eight in the morning.

Hightower's eyes were on the edge of the table in front of him.

Primault spoke first. "Carey Mickelson Hightower," he began. "We know you are originally from Liverpool, England; you were a soldier in the British Army and came to this country about twenty-three years ago. You were employed, under false pretenses, at Troy College, Burnhill College, Newhurst Community College, and Smokey River University.

"We also know you abducted an elderly Lakota woman and her grandchildren on June twenty-fourth of this year, and before that—on or about May sixteenth—you killed Arlo High Crane with one shot from a .45 caliber pistol after you transported him out to Flat Butte Dam in your university-assigned car.

"Now, Mr. Hightower, if you would, look at the files we have on this table. Starting on your left is a request from the British Army's Judge Advocate General for us, the Smokey River Tribal Police, to hold you in custody until such time as they arrive—which will be tomorrow."

Hightower's face turned pale. It was the first time he had heard that information.

"Next to that letter," Primault continued, "is a directive from the Chief Counsel of the Department of the Interior, also to us, to comply with the previous letter. In short, Mr. Hightower, your pale butt has been sitting in our jail pending arrival of the British Military Police to take you back to England. And once back in England, the Judge Advocate General's Tribunal will probably order the original sentence from your 1996 court martial to be carried out—to be hung by the neck until dead. I'd say your days on this earth are on the short end.

"Now, you know who this man is, to my right. I have asked him to summarize the evidence we have collected against you for the murder of Arlo High Crane."

Primault turned to Gavin. "The floor is yours, sir."

"Mr. Hightower," Gavin began. "Let's begin with the third set of papers on your left. There are two letters from the University of Durham, signed by a vice chancellor, to Arlo High Crane. The first is a faxed copy dated May sixth of this year. It reveals that Dr. Caleb Hightower was reported missing in November of 1988, after diving into a cave in Yugoslavia. He was presumed dead, and his body was never recovered. The second letter, dated June tenth, is a follow-up to the first, again to Arlo High Crane, reaffirming the information in the first letter.

"We know that Arlo High Crane knew of your true identity, and you knew that he knew. There is your motive for killing him."

"The third letter is a copy of Arlo High Crane's letter to the University of Durham," Gavin continued, "the one that started a tragic chain of events. He was requesting biographical information because it was required by his program, and because he listed Caleb Hightower as a mentor who was—and I quote—'inspiring and caring.'"

Hightower's mouth was set in a hard line, his gaze vague.

"Next is the coroner's report identifying the compressed lead round taken from Arlo High Crane's skull, which was the cause of death. It was fired from a .45 caliber replica cap and ball revolver. The compressed ball was virtually the same weight as two of the lead balls extracted from the pistol recovered from Flat Butte Dam. Furthermore, one round had been fired from said pistol. The serial number of that pistol was matched to a sales receipt. The buyer was Caleb Hightower, your alias."

Hightower sat unmoving, his eyes barely blinking.

"Next is an affidavit signed by one Dennis Evans, owner and manager of the Missouri Valley Black Powder Club. It states that he helped you to place an order for a replica model of an Army Colt pistol, 1873 model. He attests that he has seen that pistol in your possession on numerous occasions, the same pistol recovered from Flat Butte Dam and is encased in plastic here on this table."

Hightower's eyes flicked toward the pistol.

"The next piece of evidence is a photograph, actually several, of the same symbol. It was sketched on the carpet of the luggage compartment, or trunk, of a 2017 Chevrolet Malibu sedan. It is the symbol for a watchtower, one you used to represent your name, and it resembles a pen and ink sketch of that very same symbol that hung in your university office. Arlo High Crane scrawled it in the luggage compartment and on his own hand to identify you as the person who put him there.

"The next photos are of a Lakota phrase—*Pehan Miye*—translated to English it is 'I Am Crane,'" Gavin said, with a hint of mist in his eyes.

"It was written by Arlo High Crane after you forced him into the trunk of that car, written on the carpet inside the luggage compartment."

Gavin pushed a plastic bag containing a pen with a porcupine quill cover toward Hightower.

"The only fingerprints on this pen match those on Arlo High Crane's laptop computer and the desktop computer in his study room. The pen was found in the trunk of the aforementioned 2017 Chevrolet Malibu."

"In other words, Mr. Hightower," Gavin said forcefully, "Arlo High Crane identified himself as being in the trunk of that car. And tribal police searching the Malibu noted that the emergency release handle inside the trunk had been removed, thereby making it impossible for Arlo High Crane to escape forced confinement in that trunk."

Gavin shifted some papers, "The next piece of evidence is the logbook of the 2017 Malibu which indicates an ending trip odometer reading of 8,243 miles, as of May sixteenth. The next entered odometer reading, the starting mileage, after the vehicle was turned in for maintenance is 8,287 miles, essentially a gap of 44 miles. Forty-four miles is the distance from the campus of the University to the east shore of Flat Butte Dam, and back to the campus. Additionally, the logbook from another 2017 Chevrolet Malibu, seen here, shows that the cover was taped back on after being cut off. That happened because you switched cars—your car for one assigned to Dr. Roger Carter. The logbook cover from your car was also switched."

Next Gavin held up a printout of the email Arlo High Crane sent to his supervisory professor at the University of Nebraska, which was from 7:12 p.m., Central Daylight Time, on May sixteenth. "This was found on the computer he used in the study room in the Lakota Studies Building, and it contradicts and disproves your statement that he left the building at or about 6:30 p.m. on that same day."

"The totality of this evidence leaves no doubt that you forced Arlo High Crane, at gun point, into the trunk of a 2017 Chevrolet Malibu, then transported him from the SRU campus to Flat Butte Dam on the evening of May sixteenth of this year," Gavin summed up. "Once you arrived at the dam, you forced him out of the trunk and shot him in the back of the head with a .45 caliber replica black powder cap and ball pistol."

"Mr. Hightower, this evidence will be given to the Judge Advocate General of the British Army," Primault announced somberly. "Tomorrow morning, at or about ten o'clock, British Army military police will arrive here. At that time, we will remand you to their custody."

Chief Avery looked toward the uniformed officer. "Please escort the prisoner back to his cell."

## ONE HUNDRED SIXTEEN

Gavin entered the isolation area in the tribal jail just before ten the next morning and paused as the barred door clicked shut behind him. He immediately noticed three uniformed men.

"Hello," he said, "I'm here to see the prisoner."

"Of course, I'm Captain Armbrister," one of them said in a clipped British accent. "This is Sergeant Leland, and that is Sergeant McMaster. We're here to escort the prisoner back to our transport aircraft waiting at Ellsworth Air Force Base in Rapid City."

"Honored to meet you all. I'm Gavin Lone Wolf." He noticed they were not armed.

"Splendid," the captain said. "Please, feel free. We cannot open the door just yet."

"Understood." Gavin walked to the holding cell. Hightower stood. He looked pale and thin and was dressed in an orange jump suit. His wrists were cuffed and attached to a wide leather belt around his waist. Leg irons were around his ankles. He took a hesitant step toward the bars of the cell."

"Chief Avery said you wanted to talk to me," Gavin said flatly. "You have two minutes."

Hightower took a deep breath and exhaled. "I'm—I just wanted to ask a question." He didn't look up to meet Gavin's gaze.

"About what?"

After a slight shrug, Hightower glanced up at Gavin but immediately dropped his gaze back to the floor. "Ah, about your, ah, Little Bighorn pistol."

"What about it?"

Hightower stared blankly at the floor. "Are you going to sell it?"

"Probably."

"Then—then I have a bit of advice."

"And that is?"

"Be careful of Jacob Galbreath."

"Who the hell is Jacob Galbreath? In any case, you're in no position to give advice about anything," Gavin said, his voice dripping with contempt.

Hightower did not shift his gaze.

"I thought, possibly, you would express remorse about Arlo or admit to your role in the murder of Henry Berkin," Gavin said, his voice choking with anger. "But that's not what you're about, is it? We took you in as a friend and gave you a place among us. But you came to take advantage of our hospitality and to use our kindness. And when your sins caught up with you, your real character came out and you tore the hearts out of two families."

Gavin glanced at the soldiers. They were listening, staring angrily at Hightower. Gavin took a step toward the bars. Hightower took a step back.

"You go to hell," Gavin whispered.

Hightower kept his eyes down.

Gavin turned away slowly and paused in front of the British MPs. "Thank you for coming to get him," he told them.

Armbrister nodded affably. "Glad to do it, sir," he said. "Chief Avery informed us that you engaged our fugitive and captured him. A night op as it were."

Gavin nodded.

"Good show, sir," Armbrister said. "Well done."

"You're not armed?" Gavin asked.

"Our weapons are aboard the helo with the fourth member of our detail, Corporal Hatcher," the captain explained. "We use stringent restraints to manage our prisoners. A transport awaits us at Ellsworth. It has a cage."

Gavin nodded as he shook hands with each of the solders. "Again, thank you," he said.

"Our pleasure, sir," they all said.

Gavin rode with Justin Primault and Ben Avery as they followed the large police SUV carrying the British soldiers and their prisoner to the Agency Village airstrip a mile from the hospital where an Air Force Blackhawk helicopter waited on the tarmac. The SUV stopped near the chopper and pulled away after the three MPs and their prisoner got out. Gavin, Avery, and Primault stepped out of their vehicle; then Primault, with a small briefcase in hand, approached Captain Armbrister.

"Captain, this is the file on Mr. Hightower, in two formats; there are paper documents and one computer thumb drive. And we will also transmit an encrypted electronic file by email as backup." He handed the case to the captain.

"Thank you," the captain said. "I will deliver this to the Judge Advocate General's office."

Fifteen minutes later the three men watched the helicopter lift off. Primault turned to Gavin. "I'm glad your uncle volunteered to explain this to

Arlo's parents," he said. "I don't know if I could tell them that we let their son's murderer get away."

Gavin shook his head. "Don't be too hard on yourself. You solved this case and Hightower will never walk free again."

"I think Mr. and Mrs. High Crane will understand," Avery affirmed.

"Yeah, well, I appreciate that from both of you," Primault returned.

They watched the Blackhawk getting smaller in the distance.

"Speaking of being there," Primault said, as they walked to their vehicle. "Sure wish I could see Hightower dangle from the end of a rope."

"You know what they say," Gavin warned. "Be careful what you wish for."

## ONE HUNDRED SEVENTEEN

Dozens of vehicles were already in the student union parking lot when Gavin arrived back on campus seven hours later. Anticipating more people than would fit into the lobby of the Lakota Studies Building, President Eagle Shield had decided on having the event in the student union, especially since food had to be prepared. There was, of course, no way to know how many people would attend. But a meal, especially buffalo stew, was always a draw.

Whatever reason people came to the SRU student union, they were greeted by a compelling display of Lone Wolf's ledger sketches. Forty-eight 24- by 36-inch posters were mounted on frames. The series of posters, with poster number one to the left of the main door of the huge dining room, progressed around the room, with number forty-eight ending the series to the right of the door. Gavin was greeted with the sight of dozens of adults, small children, and young people moving slowly along the line of posters, apparently drawn to the story as it unfolded before their eyes.

The actual ledger was displayed inside a tall Plexiglas case in front of a small stage at one end of the room. Also on display was Black Wolf's map. A small crowd encircled the display.

Uncle Andrew, Loren, Morgan, and Thomas were already in the room, standing near the case engaged in casual conversation with a small group of people.

To Gavin's surprise the reporter from Sioux Falls arrived with her cameraman. The SRU media people were already set up and filming. Marilee Rothen wasted no time approaching Gavin and Dr. Wells.

Dr. Wells had returned from Washington DC after going back there to make preparations for the NMAI exhibition opening.

"We appreciate the invitation," Rothen said to Gavin. "May I ask you both a couple of questions here before the evening really gets going?"

"Of course," Gavin said. "This sort of event is routine for Dr. Wells. This is a first for me."

Rothen smiled and nodded to her cameraman, who turned on his camera and moved into place, the camera on his right shoulder.

"Dr. Wells," she began, "I understand that the focus of this evening is a man who was a participant in the Battle of the Little Bighorn. Can you give us a brief overview?"

"Of course, it would be my pleasure. Lone Wolf, the great-grandfather of the Lone Wolf family, and his two younger brothers fought in all three engagements of the Battle of the Little Bighorn on June twenty-fifth and twenty-sixth, 1876. We are here this evening because he did something else extraordinary: he sketched pictures and used images to tell a story. That's what we see here, all around us. Many Lakota who were there did exactly that; they told the story verbally and in pictures. However, no one, as far as we know, produced this many drawings of one event—forty-eight in total."

Rothen turned to Gavin. "Dr. Lone Wolf, the caption with the ledger book indicates that it was only recently discovered. Your family knew your great-grandfather was at the Little Bighorn. Did you know about the ledger?"

"No, we didn't."

"How did it come to light?"

Gavin glanced at Uncle Andrew who nodded. "Our grandmother had in her possession a map drawn in 1924 by her uncle, Black Wolf. That map indicated where the ledger had been buried. So, to make a long story short, my uncle and nephew and I managed to find the location of the buried ledger and dug it up. And here we are."

"That's an amazing story; actually, several stories sort of intersect. What is your ultimate goal regarding the ledger and your great-grandfather's story?"

"To make prints of the ledger sketches available for serious study and to add yet another Lakota voice to the story of the Battle of the Little Bighorn."

"And why is that important?"

"Well, there have been thousands of articles, scholarly papers, books, and documentaries about that one event, and a very, very small percentage is directly from an actual Native perspective. Little Bighorn Battlefield National Monument was originally called the *Custer* Battlefield and was established in 1946 as a monument to the loser; the loser's version of the battle was the only one being told and was regarded as a true account. For some that version is still the 'mainstream opinion,' as it were. We need to make certain that the winner's version is given equal time."

At the scheduled hour, President Eagle Shield opened the formal presentation with a welcome. After a prayer by a medicine man, Eagle Shield introduced Dr. Wells from NMAI, tribal President Lone Hawk, and finally Gavin to talk about Lone Wolf's ledger book.

Half of the dining tables in the room had been moved aside to make room for rows of chairs arranged in a half circle facing the podium on the stage. Gavin was surprised to see that the chairs were filled and most of the tables as well.

He kept his remarks short, though he included a concise story of Lone Wolf's ledger. He finished by telling how Uncle Andrew No Horn, Thomas, and he had located the marking stones left by Uncle Andrew and had dug up the pot.

Dr. Wells concluded the program by outlining how NMAI and SRU would work together to create lesson plans based entirely on Lone Wolf's sketches for elementary and school history curricula.

During the meal of buffalo stew, Gavin and Andrew walked among the tables chatting with people, thanking them for attending. Among the crowd of nearly three hundred, many were acquaintances, colleagues, and friends of the Lone Wolf family.

The evening's program concluded with closing remarks by President Lone Hawk and then a popular local drum group sang a warrior's honoring song for Lone Wolf and his brothers Black Wolf and White Tail Feather. Gavin decided to stay until everyone had left and was joined by Uncle Andrew, Loren, Morgan, Thomas, Dr. Wells, President Eagle Shield, and the Lone Hawks.

Dr. Wells stepped over and encouraged Gavin to consider writing a book to interpret Lone Wolf's sketches. Gavin knew that he, at the very least, owed his great-grandfather his and the family's interpretation of the ledger drawings, given that they knew his story in great detail.

"Perhaps when you're in DC next week for the kick-off of our Lone Wolf exhibit," Wells suggested, "we can talk about possible publishers."

When the student union staff began turning off lights, everyone headed slowly for the main exit, glancing a last time at the sketches. Dr. Wells, assisted by security, carefully placed the ledger in a special case. It would rest in the university vault until Wells took it by special air charter to the NMAI in Washington DC on Monday.

At nine o'clock Monday morning, Dr. Wells accepted delivery of the Galand and Sommerville from Gavin. President Eagle Shield met them at the university's guesthouse to see the conservator off to the Sioux Falls airport courtesy of an SRU University driver and car. The technicians Glanville and Hanson had already left two days ago.

Wells had two special containers, though both looked like nothing more than black business briefcases. Inside one was Lone Wolf's ledger book and map and in the other was the pistol. The NMAI had insured the items based on preliminary estimates of their worth and had chartered an airplane to avoid the hassle of airport security. The items were that valuable.

They watched the university van leave the guesthouse driveway until it was out of sight. Two objects that had been five feet underground for nearly a hundred years would be flying over thirty thousand feet above the earth in a matter of hours.

## ONE HUNDRED EIGHTEEN

Gavin watched Washington DC traffic out the cab window while Gerard was on a cellphone talking to his office. Three days had gone by in a blur, starting with the call from Dr. Wells. Now they were on the way to the National Museum of the American Indian to meet with the man Hightower had warned him about.

"A collector has made an offer for your Galand and Sommerville, sight unseen," Wells had told him, almost breathlessly.

"That's amazing. Who is it?"

"One of the largest donors at NMAI. His name is Jacob Galbreath."

Gavin was speechless for several seconds. "Dr. Wells—Ted—did you say Jacob Galbreath?"

"Yes. He would like to meet you and your brother and discuss the offer."

*Be careful of Jacob Galbreath.*

"What can you tell us about Galbreath?"

"Well, he's quite wealthy, a billionaire and a collector of historic artifacts, especially Western Americana. His offer for your pistol is substantial."

"Really? How substantial?"

"Twenty million dollars."

Gerard, who was keen to meet with Galbreath because of Hightower's warning to Gavin, could hardly believe the amount of the offer. "There's a story there," he said to Gavin. "And I want to know what it is before I agree to any offer."

They arrived at Wells's office for a preliminary meeting and informed Wells about Galbreath's possible connection to Hightower, a convicted murderer. Wells was aghast at hearing the news. "Gentlemen, that is rather troubling. I hope there is a rational explanation. I think it would be sensible to ask Mr. Galbreath about Hightower."

"That's our plan," Gerard assured him. "Can you fill us in more on Mr. Galbreath?"

"Of course. He has been a widower for many years. His only child, a son and a Navy jet pilot, was killed in a training accident. His primary residence is here in DC, but he also lives in London because his ancestry is English. Mr. Galbreath made his money primarily through investments. He has fallen ill within the last year, ALS, I think. He funds a homeless shelter for veterans here and has put many of them through school. And, as I mentioned earlier, he has made generous contributions to us here at NMAI and to the Smithsonian."

"How can someone like that be connected to Hightower, and how long has he been a collector of historic artifacts?" asked Gavin.

"I can't give an answer to the first part, but I believe he's gotten into collecting only within the last twenty years."

"Well, he certainly didn't waste time regarding our pistol," Gerard pointed out.

"You know," Wells recalled, "before I went to your reservation, he did ask me if I had heard anything about a Little Bighorn pistol. Apparently he had gotten an inquiry, but he didn't say from whom."

"I'm sure a collector has a network of people he works with," surmised Gerard.

"Yes," Wells said. "And once a collector's name and tastes get out there, people with artifacts to sell or broker—real or otherwise—come out of the woodwork."

"That might explain how Hightower knew of him," Gavin said. He looked at Gerard. "I say we keep the meeting with him."

They watched as a silver-haired, blue-eyed impeccably dressed man in a wheelchair was brought into the conference room near Wells's office. The man smiled up at his helper. "Thank you, Hector. I'll call when I'm ready to leave."

As a young assistant brought in water and juices, Wells made introductions. A moment later a security guard entered and unlocked a small safe sitting in the middle of the long table, then took a position near the door.

Hard-charging Marine that he was, Gerard threw out the first question after everyone was seated. "Mr. Galbreath, why are you interested in our pistol?"

An amused twinkle appeared in the blue eyes. "Because it turns out your pistol is more than just another old relic. At my age I have realized the value of brevity, so allow me to briefly explain my interest."

"By all means," Gavin said.

"Thank you. Gentlemen, my ancestry is English. Before the War of 1812 some of my family immigrated here, others stayed in England. Genealogical research revealed an ancestor who was a gunsmith at the Galand and Sommerville Company in Liverpool. His name was Samuel, and he was employed there at the time your Galand and Sommerville was produced. I can't unequivocally say he had anything to do with that pistol, but there is a connection to it for me."

Gavin and Gerard exchanged glances. "Indeed," said Gerard. "Anyone else interested in the pistol would be hard pressed to make that claim."

"You are probably right," Galbreath agreed.

"Mr. Galbreath," Gavin said, "do you know a man by the name of Caleb Hightower?"

Galbreath shook his head. "I can't say I know him. I've communicated with him on a few occasions. In fact, it was he who told me of the existence of a pistol from the Little Bighorn. I was skeptical at first, until he provided proof."

"Proof? What sort of proof, sir?" Gavin asked.

Galbreath reached down to the slim leather briefcase in his lap and pulled out three sheets of paper. "Mr. Hightower faxed these to me in late May, I believe." He slid the papers across the table. "I believe they are copies of copies and redacted to some extent."

A split second after the first glance, both Gavin and Gerard knew what they were: copies of their Grandfather Black Wolf's statement dictated to their Great-Grandmother Maud Little Turtle. Gavin glanced at Gerard. "Hightower found copies in my desk at the university and copied them."

"Mr. Hightower assured me he could and would acquire the pistol," Galbreath told them, "and even arranged a time and place for him to meet my representatives, pistol in hand. Of course, he did not keep that appointment. So, there is a side to that story I don't know about."

"Sadly, that is true," Gavin said. "Suffice to say, Mr. Hightower is out of the picture. Our next question is: Do you want the pistol for your personal collection?"

"Gentlemen, my plan is to put it on permanent loan to the Smithsonian and the National Museum of the American Indian. I want it to be on permanent exhibit under the auspices of both, and its provenance and history from its manufacture, its capture at the Little Bighorn, and its recovery, to be accurately told."

"Thank you for that," Gavin said, glancing at Gerard and receiving a nod. "Mr. Galbreath, since we have powers of attorney from our older sister and uncle, we are ready to act on your generous offer."

Gerard nodded. "Yes," he said. "We will accept it."

"Wonderful! You've made an old man very happy. My plan for the pistol is spelled out in the purchase agreement that Dr. Wells has drafted for us to sign," Galbreath said. "If you would please review it at your leisure, and sign. Once I have the original copies, I will see to it that funds are dispersed. Now, may I ask a small favor?"

"Of course," Gavin replied.

"I should like to hold it."

"Be our guest, please," Gerard said.

Taking cotton gloves from Wells, Galbreath slipped them on and waited for the guard to take the gun out of the safe. "Incredible!" he said reverently as he cradled the Galand and Sommerville in his hands.

Both Gavin and Gerard would later comment that it was as though the man were seeing a long-lost relative. Nowhere in his expression was there any hint of avarice or ownership.

## ONE HUNDRED NINETEEN

Images, voices, and words played on a continuous loop in Gavin's head until the taxi rolled up and stopped in front of a familiar entrance: The Gemini Restaurant.

Gerard disconnected his call and looked out the cab window. "We're here," he announced cheerfully.

After being seated in the restaurant, Gerard chuckled and threw up his hands.

"Hey, bro," he said, watching a server approach. "I'm a bit numb."

They recognized the young woman who had waited on them in May. Gavin nodded and looked up at the server. "Alixandra, right?"

Her smile was genuine. "You remembered! Would you like anything to drink?"

"A glass of water and a shot of Jack Daniels, straight up, no ice," Gavin said.

"Times two," Gerard repeated.

Gavin waited until the server was out of earshot. "Twenty million dollars?"

"It's good we talked about this before, about what to do with the money," said Gerard. "Let's just go with that."

"Right, but I think we should all get together, face to face," Gavin suggested. "Can you find some time to go home? We can probably meet in Sioux Falls or Minneapolis."

"Sure, no problem, but the sooner the better. Hell of a lot of stuff happening for us, for our family, I mean."

Gavin stared down at the top of the table. "This—what happened today—was the furthest thing from my mind when Uncle Andrew, Thomas, and I dug that clay pot out the ground."

The server returned with their drinks and set them down. Stepping back, she said, "What may I get for you, gentlemen?"

"Ah, a generous dose of common sense to start with," Gerard said, "and then a large chef's salad with Italian dressing."

"I'll have what he's having," Gavin said, smiling up at the young woman with the hazel eyes, "but with French dressing."

"Thank you. I'll check with the chef about the common sense, sir," she said, looking at Gerard. "But we might be fresh out."

"No worries," he said. "As long as the salad is good."

As she walked away with a smile, Gerard lifted his glass of whiskey. "I don't know if Uncle Andrew would consider this appropriate," he said. "Nevertheless, here's to Great-Grandfather Lone Wolf."

Gavin lifted his glass. "To Great-Grandfather Lone Wolf."

"By the way," Gerard said. "I invited Katherine to join us because I think we need a lawyer to read the agreement. Pretty serious stuff, twenty million dollars." He glanced at his watch. "She should be here any minute."

Gavin nodded, his heart pounding, as Katherine walked toward the table.

She read the purchase agreement twice in less than fifteen minutes. "This is as simple as it can be," she said. "It is solid and fair. He accepts the artifact as is, there are provisions for exhibiting it at the Smithsonian and NMAI, with your input I might add, and the funds are to be paid in one lump sum. No red flags at all."

Gerard nodded, a satisfied smile in his eyes. "Great," he said.

"So," Gavin said, "we sign, then he signs, and that's it?"

Katherine nodded. Gavin caught the hint of her perfume. "That's all there is," she affirmed. "Congratulations."

Gerard grabbed the dinner tab. "This is on me," he said, as he scooped up all five signed copies of the agreement and slid them into his briefcase. "I know you have a plane to catch in the morning," he said to Gavin. "So, I'll drop by NMAI and give these to Dr. Wells." He looked at Katherine. "Did my brother tell you how he captured Hightower and found the murder weapon? Interesting stories. See you all later."

With a nod and a grin, Gerard slid out of the booth, waving as he walked away.

*That was a really sly move, brother,* Gavin thought. "Ah," he said, "there's a bar in this place, on the other side. Feel like finding a quiet corner for a bit?"

"I'd love to," she said, smiling. "And I'd love to know how you did capture Hightower."

# ONE HUNDRED TWENTY

After lunch with Uncle Andrew, Loren, and Morgan at the coffee bistro in Kincaid, Gavin drove back to the campus. Sometime after four, he and President Eagle Shield, and Carla Yellow Bull finished interviewing the last of the three candidates for the Chair of Lakota Studies.

"Is tomorrow too soon to let me know your recommendation?" the president asked them.

"No. As a matter of fact, I'll tell you right now." Gavin put three file folders on Eagle Shield's desk. "The one on top is my choice," he said.

"She's my choice as well," Dr. Yellow Bull affirmed.

Eagle Shield looked at the name on the tab. "Wonderful," he said. "She's my choice, too. I'll give her a call later."

"Great.

"Now, my question to you, Gavin, is can you stay at the helm until she and I agree on a start date for her?"

"Sure. I don't have any other plans."

Eagle Shield waved him off with a grin.

Ramona ambushed him with a cup of coffee as he walked into the lobby of the Lakota Studies Building. "Who's my new boss going to be?" she asked.

"Well," he said, "I'm not going to steal Doug's thunder. He'll probably make the announcement tomorrow. But let me put it this way. I think you'll like *her* a lot."

Ramona smiled and clasped her hands together. "Wonderful! Oh, ah, there's a friend of yours waiting in your office."

Ben Avery stood and offered his hand as Gavin walked in. "Word is you're giving up academia," he said.

"Well, at least as Department Chair. I'm not cut out to be a boss. What can I do for you?"

Avery waited for Gavin to take his seat before he sat down. "Well, I received a telephone call from the Judge Advocate General's office in London."

"Regarding Hightower, I assume. You're not going to tell me he's escaped again."

Avery chuckled. "Wouldn't that be a kick in the head? But no. They issued an invitation."

Gavin was intrigued and puzzled. "An invitation?"

Avery nodded, gazing studiously at Gavin. "Yes, an invitation. They've asked us to send a representative to England to present a brief at a summary hearing."

"I see. A hearing about Hightower?"

"Right."

"I'm not a lawyer, Ben, if you're asking me to present a brief."

"No, oh, no. I'm not asking you to do that. But I am asking if you would consider going. Here's the thing. The Chief Judge of the Tribal Court recommended that we send Justin Primault, since he essentially did all the investigative work, with your help."

Gavin nodded, still a bit suspicious. "Okay, go on."

"Right. Justin is willing and he is going; and by the way, the Judge Advocate General's office is paying for it all, everything."

"I think Justin is the one to do that."

"Yeah, but he wants you to go along," Avery cleared his throat. "Next week. We've been exchanging emails to plan the travel. This is an opportunity to ensure justice for Arlo High Crane. The evidence that Justin and you compiled will be placed on the record by their military tribunal. Justin will formally turn over our evidence to that court and make a summary statement. I think you should witness it."

## ONE HUNDRED TWENTY-ONE

Gavin and Justin Primault spoke very little on the taxi ride from Heathrow Airport to Hotel Kensington on Cromwell Avenue in London. By the time they arrived at the hotel it was nearly six. After checking in they walked down the street for dinner at a small, cozy restaurant.

Diners at the nearby tables immediately noticed the American accents of the two brown-skinned men at a corner table. A precocious young man called out to them.

"Are you from America?"

"No," replied Gavin, "we are from the Lakota Nation on Turtle Island. It's a mite older than America."

The reply apparently confused the young man and his three companions who resumed their own conversation.

It was nearly eight by the time they were back at the hotel. A car was scheduled to pick them up at nine the next morning. The proceedings, they were told, would start at precisely ten o'clock.

Primault and Gavin met in the lobby to go over last-minute details. An agenda for the hearing had been provided. It was not a retrial, simply a summary hearing for the Judge Advocate General to attest to the original sentence and set a date and time for Hightower's execution by hanging.

The third action in the process was labeled as a Friend of the Court Brief: Primault's summation of the evidence against Hightower for the murder of Arlo High Crane.

The next morning the car arrived precisely on time to take them to a facility called Cantwell Barracks. Primault was clearly nervous. He was dressed in his dark blue service uniform and cap.

"Nothing to worry about," Gavin reassured him. "We're here at their invitation."

Cantwell Barracks was a three-story brick building with an unpretentious front door. Once inside they presented themselves to a sergeant standing behind a high wooden counter. She entered their names in a computer and escorted them to the hearing room. It was small, no larger than an elementary school classroom, in Gavin's estimation; but the ceiling was about fifteen feet high. At the front was a long, elevated judge's bench, with three high-backed chairs behind it. Behind the bench were double doors. Against the wall to the left of the bench was what appeared to be an enclosed podium with vertical bars. Gavin realized it was the prisoner dock. Next to it was a door. Below and in front of the bench was a long table, with two wooden chairs at each end. In the middle atop the table was a podium facing the judge's bench. Behind the table were two rows of wooden benches, not unlike church pews, with an aisle down the middle. At the back of the room on either side were wooden chairs against the wall.

The sergeant pointed to the wooden chairs. "Have a seat if you would, please, gentlemen. The hearing will convene in a few minutes."

After they sat, with Primault on the aisle, Gavin noticed there were no paintings or photographs on the walls, or flags for that matter. A tall, thin soldier with the chevrons of a staff sergeant entered the room through the door by the prisoner dock, and immediately approached them, his shoes clicking on the polished wooden floor. They rose as he stopped in front of them.

"Lieutenant Primault, I presume?" he said to Primault. He pronounced the rank as "Leff-tenant."

"I am," Primault replied.

The staff sergeant nodded and reached out his hand to Primault. "That would mean you are Dr. Gavin Lone Wolf," he said, looking at Gavin.

"Indeed I am," Gavin said, shaking the sergeant's hand.

"A pleasure, gentlemen," the staff sergeant said. "The hearing will commence momentarily. The bailiff will call us to order and the judge will enter. After the judge enters and opens the session, the prisoner will be brought in. Lieutenant, when you are called, walk to the podium. From that moment the floor is yours and you will have five minutes. Do you have any questions, sir?"

Primault shook his head. "No. Thank you."

Only seven other people entered the room. Four took seats at the long tables, two at each end, another, whom Gavin assumed was the clerk, set up her recording equipment at the far end of the judge's bench, and another sergeant took a position below her. The staff sergeant who had spoken to them entered, took a position by the door on the far right, and nodded at the sergeant who apparently was the bailiff.

"Hear ye, hear ye!" the bailiff called out in a loud voice. "This special summary hearing of the headquarters district of Her Majesty's Office of the Judge Advocate General is now in session. All rise!"

Gavin and Primault stood in unison with everyone else.

"This special hearing is conducted under the command of Brigadier General Leslie Herrold."

One of the double doors behind the bench opened and a stocky brigadier general in uniform entered and took a seat at the bench in the middle high-backed chair.

"Please be seated," he said affably in a strong voice, though his expression was somber. "This summary hearing is for the purpose of presenting final statements in the case of Corporal Carey Hightower, who was tried and convicted of a capital offense, specifically murder in the first degree, by a duly convened military tribunal in 1996. Before execution of sentence, Corporal Hightower escaped and remained at large for twenty-three years. He was only recently apprehended in the Unites States of America. Corporal Hightower's appeal for reduction of sentence to life in prison at his original trial was then denied. As a consequence of his escape, the corporal has no further legal recourse. However, this court did issue instructions for defense and prosecutorial statements and is ready to hear those statements at this time."

The judge paused and looked at the barristers at the table. "Are you ready to present?"

Receiving their affirmations, he looked to the staff sergeant standing near the door. "You may bring in the prisoner."

## ONE HUNDRED TWENTY-TWO

Primault and Gavin watched as two military policemen escorted Hightower into the room. He was dressed in a white jumpsuit with handcuffs on his wrists. His beard had been shaved and his face looked white as paper. The sergeant opened the door to the prisoner's dock and shut it after Hightower entered. He stood facing the room, with his head down.

Gavin looked at Primault and saw the anger in the younger man's eyes. Gavin leaned close. "Calm and cool, my friend," he whispered.

Primault nodded and fixed his gaze on the judge.

Gavin, however, kept his gaze on Hightower. If he had ever truly come close to hating another human being, it was that man in the prisoner's dock. He tore his gaze away and looked toward the front of the room.

The judge pointed at the barristers to his right. One stood and stepped to the podium. "Sir," he began, "the defendant does not contest the evidence presented in this matter as it relates to his escape and capture. He does, however, humbly and respectfully pray for clemency regarding the execution ordered by the 1996 sentencing and for reduction of sentence from death to life in prison. Thank you, sir."

After a nod from the judge, the barrister returned to his seat. A barrister from the other end of the table rose and stepped to the podium.

"Sir," he began, "in late 1996, seven months after Corporal Hightower's conviction of murder in the first degree, his appeal was denied. No further evidence came to light to warrant further appeals, and the corporal's escape must and can only be construed as further affirmation of guilt." The prosecutor then went on to establish precedence by citing similar cases, some going back to World War I, where military tribunals had carried out sentences immediately after escaped convicted prisoners had been recaptured. "Therefore," he concluded, "we recommend execution of the 1996 sentencing without further delay. Thank you, sir."

At the Judge's nod the barrister returned to his seat. The Judge finished writing on a pad and then looked up. "Thank you, gentlemen, for your statements. At this time the court invites a Friend of the Court Brief from…" the Judge paused to consult typed notes in front of him, "Lieutenant Justin Primault, an investigator with the Smokey River Sioux Tribal Police from the Smokey River Sioux Tribe, a sovereign nation located in the state of South Dakota, the United States of America. Lieutenant Primault, if you would please."

Acknowledging Gavin's nod with his own, Primault left his hat on the chair, tightened his grip around the thick file containing evidence against Hightower, and walked ramrod straight to the podium. All eyes in the room were on him. He placed the file on the table and carefully arranged his written statement on the podium.

"Thank you, Your Honor," he began, "for the opportunity to present to this hearing and enter evidence on the record. May it please the court, Sir, I offer our complete file and the full written transcript of our testimony at this time."

At a nod from the Judge, the bailiff approached the podium and accepted the file from Primault, then carried it to the bench and handed it to the clerk.

"Thank you," the Judge said, with a nod. "Please proceed."

Primault flawlessly delivered a concise narrative that summarized the investigation and the trail of evidence that led to and established Carey Hightower as the primary suspect in the murder of Arlo High Crane. For an added touch, he spoke briefly and glowingly of Arlo High Crane.

"In closing, my department, and the people of the Sicangu Lakota Oyate, also known as the Burnt Thigh Nation, on the Smokey River Reservation thank you for this unprecedented opportunity. Your Honor, this concludes my statement."

The Judge nodded. "Thank you, Lieutenant Primault. Was any further information added to the file after it was submitted electronically to us?"

"No, Your Honor."

"In that case, unless there are objections forthcoming," the Judge said, looking at the barristers in front of him, "I shall order said file to be a permanent part of this hearing record."

No one objected. "Very well, so ordered," the Judge said.

Primault turned and walked back to his seat and received a firm handshake from Gavin.

The judge paused to consult his notes and the papers in front of him. "This hearing is conducted under the authority of the Judge Advocate General, under the further auspices of the Military Court Service. The prisoner, Corporal Carey Hightower service number 86-39129, was listed as inactive until such time as sentence is executed. At this time, he is reduced in rank to private." The judge paused to look at his notes again and then lifted his gaze toward Justin Primault.

He spoke solemnly. "This court is—no, I, as an officer of this court—was shocked to learn of the heinous offense committed by the prisoner while in the United States." The Brigadier General turned a cold stare at Hightower for several long moments, then back to face the room, which was waiting in absolute silence. "Now he has the impudence to pray for clemency. That request is denied, based in no small measure on the testimony herein given by the people of the Burnt Thigh Nation.

"This case, given the designation HMA-92-17, and since adjudicated, is now concluded with the following order. The prisoner shall be immediately remanded to the authority and control of the military police at Basilton Prison for execution of the sentence that he should be hung by the neck until dead, which shall be carried out within the next forty-eight hours. This hearing is adjourned."

"All rise!" the bailiff called out as the Judge stood and left the bench.

Gavin had been watching Hightower during the brief hearing. The man had not once lifted his head. He had nothing left, except to die. Strangely, however, Gavin didn't feel a sense of victory, as he thought he might. He wondered what Primault was feeling. That would be a conversation for later.

The room emptied as quickly as it had been filled, barely less than half an hour ago. But the two of them remained standing at the back of the room and watched two military police enter through the side door and take Hightower away. The man would soon be dead.

As they were leaving the room, the staff sergeant who had initially instructed them as the court supervisor caught up to them. "Brigadier General Herrold asked me to pass on his appreciation," he said to Primault. "And if you would be so kind as to verify your contact information, we shall provide you with a copy of the complete transcript of today's hearing."

"Of course," Primault replied. Taking out a business card, he handed it to the staff sergeant.

"As you heard, the evidence you provided effectively blocked any chance for clemency. The defense was obligated to make a request for clemency, and they did so only on that basis, without stating justification, because there was none."

The staff sergeant took them to the counter in the front room. "Bring up a car for our guests," he instructed.

The first few minutes during the ride back to the hotel were strangely silent. Gavin spoke first.

"You did better than most lawyers would have, Justin," he said.

Primault nodded, his expression on the verge of sadness. "Thanks, I don't know why, but I don't feel like celebrating."

"That's the difference between good people and bad," Gavin said. "Good people feel compassion, even at a time like this. And maybe even a little nausea."

Primault continued to stare out the window. "Hightower will be dead soon. Arlo High Crane will still be dead. Is this what justice feels like?"

"I'd say so," Gavin said. "As my uncle said, justice doesn't raise the dead, it doesn't restore anything, except, we hope, some sense of balance in society. Administering justice takes a toll on everyone, I think. But that's the price of justice. The finality of justice, in this instance, is hard to think about even though Hightower may deserve to die."

Primault shot a quick glance at Gavin. "I don't know if I feel any pity for Hightower," he said. "It's Arlo's family I've been thinking about. It just isn't fair they have to grieve the rest of their lives because some guy didn't want anyone to know his real identity."

"I think I know how you feel," Gavin said. "That man was my friend. I took him to be a scholar. He was a guest in my house and I in his. We worked together for nearly four years. He said all the right words at the right moments, and he was a likeable guy. I trusted him. And what pisses me off the most is that he showed up for Arlo's funeral. But it's not about me, or how I feel. It is about Arlo and his family. I can't disagree with the way it turned out.

"And I think, when we get home, you and I should visit Arlo's folks and tell them what happened here today."

Primault's expression brightened slightly. "Yeah, I'd like that."

"Me, too," Gavin said. "Tell you what, lunch is on me after we get back to the hotel. I've got a call or two to make, and the rest of the day is ours."

"Works for me," Primault agreed. "Thanks."

"Look at it this way. I think Arlo would thank you if he could."

Justin Primault nodded and turned his gaze out the window. From the angle Gavin was looking, he could see the tears welling up in the younger man's eyes.

## ONE HUNDRED TWENTY-THREE

After Gavin turned on his phone, he saw he had several missed calls, but the one that caught his eye was from Gerard. He called back immediately.

"Hey, little brother," Gerard answered. "How's your vacation going?"

"Don't I wish. What the heck time is it there? It's got to be awful damn early."

"Not that early," Gerard said. "It's about seven in the morning. This is a town that wakes up early."

"Okay. What's up?"

"I just wanted to let you know that all the bank transfers are complete. I talked to Loren and Uncle Andrew, and they verified it. So, check your account."

"I will, thanks, bro, for handling all of that."

"Glad to do it. When are you coming back to this side of the pond?"

Gavin heard the knock on the door, walked to it, looked through the security peephole, and opened the door to Primault. He turned back to the conversation.

"Tomorrow."

"Great. How'd it go?"

"Quick and clean," Gavin said. "Hightower's luck ran out."

"As it should have, bro, as it should have. Have a good trip home."

Gavin disconnected the call and stepped over to Justin Primault who handed him a typed note bearing the letterhead of the Judge Advocate General. In his other hand was a sealed envelope.

"This just arrived from Brigadier General Herrold," Primault told him. "He's invited us to witness the hanging, if we choose."

"When?" Gavin asked, tentatively.

"Tomorrow, at seven in the morning."

Gavin shook his head. "I'll pass," he said. "Does he want an answer?"

"There's a number for us to call. If we accept, they'll send a car."

Gavin shook his head again. "Well, I'll go with you, but not to be a witness. I don't want the last image of someone who was a friend to be of him dangling from a rope."

Primault nodded, "I understand." He handed the sealed envelope to Gavin. "This came for you."

The same logo was on the envelope, Gavin noticed, as he sliced it open with his room key card. It was also from the judge.

> Dr. Lone Wolf:
>
> Sir, the prisoner has adamantly requested to speak with you before his sentence is carried out. If you choose to do so, it can be scheduled for 0615 tomorrow. Please call the number at the bottom of this page if that is the case.
>
> Cordially,
>
> Lieutenant Maeve Hinckley
>
> Office of JAG

Gavin felt his jaw clench as he reread the note.

"What is it?" Primault asked.

"Hightower wants to talk to me before they hang him."

"Damn! You're not obligated to do that."

Gavin gestured toward the door. "I don't know about you, but I'm hungry. Can we talk about this over lunch?"

The hotel concierge recommended a historic pub two blocks away. Walking was a welcome distraction.

Gavin ordered roast beef and Primault decided to try the shepherd's pie. While they waited for their food and sipped their bitters, Gavin brought up the letter from the judge.

"You're entitled to be a witness. You certainly built a strong case, and I'm confident that if it had gone to trial at home in federal court, Hightower would have been found guilty. But witnessing an execution is not an everyday occurrence, even for police officers. It's the kind of thing that will stick with you."

"Yeah, I know you're right. I've seen dead bodies. I was the second officer on scene after the call about Arlo came in. I saw him dead, and I can't get it out of my mind. I didn't know him when he was alive. So, ah, in a strange kind of way, I sort of feel like I should be a witness for Arlo and his family."

"Right, I understand. I know you have those tobacco ties in your pocket, and you have sage. So tomorrow, smudge yourself, especially afterwards. My Uncle Andrew told me that Hightower knows he's going to die, so his spirit is turning dark and reaching out. We have to protect ourselves, both of us."

"I will, thanks." Primault glanced around the interior of the pub, at the furnishings and the other diners. "I've been out of the country only once," he said. "I went to Winnipeg for an international conference on policing.

That's why I got a passport. In that case I knew months before that I was going. This all happened really fast." He paused to sigh and shake his head. "And this morning, in front of that judge, it just didn't seem real. Now I'm having shepherd's pie in a historic English pub. In a couple of days, I'll be standing in line to buy bad coffee at the convenience store in Agency Village."

Gavin chuckled. "Listen," he said, "in a few more days you'll be back home with your wife with great stories to tell. But you want to know what the real story is? It's the fact that you solved a murder."

Primault nodded. "I know, but life goes on. There's any number of cases that are still pending, some have turned cold. We got lucky on this one."

"Luck brought about by hard work and commitment," Gavin pointed out. "Don't forget that."

"And with your help," Primault countered. "By the way, have you decided to talk to him?"

Gavin nodded.

## ONE HUNDRED TWENTY-FOUR

As before, a car arrived precisely on schedule, but this time it took them to Basilton Prison. Gavin was escorted to the holding cells and into a room where Hightower was already sitting at a table, with a uniformed guard positioned behind him. Gavin paused a moment before he took the empty chair on the opposite side of the table. On the table, standing upright, was a small voice-activated recorder with a blinking green light.

Gavin didn't know what to say.

"Good morning, my one-time friend," Hightower said hoarsely.

Gavin nodded once.

"I'm glad you came," Hightower went on. "This is not for frivolous reasons, so you should regard this as—as a death-bed confession." He pointed to the recorder. "I asked for that and for it to be given to you, when our meeting is concluded."

Gavin glanced up at the guard, who nodded affirmation. "What do you want to tell me?" he asked, looking directly at Hightower.

"I'm sorry about Arlo, I truly am. If I had been a man, he would be alive."

Gavin held Hightower's intense gaze. "What do you mean?"

"It wasn't just me," he said. "There was someone else."

"You mean an accomplice?"

"Most definitely."

Eleven minutes later Gavin's incredulous gaze remained fixed on Hightower, even as a shiver crawled up his back. His first instinct was to believe every word he had just heard.

"Thank you for telling me," he said.

"Certainly. All my life I've been a follower, pushed or led around. That's why I joined the army, to let someone else decide for me what to do, how to do it."

Five minutes later a second guard escorted Gavin to a large room on the first floor, where he rejoined Primault. The voice recorder with its astonishing recording was tucked into his coat pocket. The last image of Hightower he would always have would be of the tiny spark of satisfaction in his blue eyes and maybe even a flicker of hope for peace.

## ONE HUNDRED TWENTY-FIVE

Gavin waited in an anteroom after Primault had been taken to a viewing room fifteen minutes before the appointed hour. There were others who also waited in the anteroom, and the overall mood was somber.

They could hear nothing of the proceedings, though they could watch the hands of a large clock on the wall. At seven twelve Primault returned to the anteroom, his mouth set in a hard line. He walked slowly across the room and stopped when Gavin stood to meet him.

He glanced at Gavin and nodded once. "He—if there's a hell, I hope that's where he is," he said softly. "I'm ready to leave this place."

No further mention was made of Hightower or the execution. Primault was quiet during the ride back to the hotel.

"So," he finally said at breakfast, "I don't know about you, but I'm ready to go home."

"Me, too, not least for the reason that the English language here is so different than our reservation English."

Primault laughed.

"There is no official American language," Gavin asserted, "just North American versions of the English spoken here. Most people don't know that there were possibly two thousand different indigenous languages on

Turtle Island before it was labeled North America. Now there are about one hundred sixty indigenous languages in the U.S., around sixty in Canada, and a lot in Mexico and Central America."

Primault nodded slowly, as a pensive expression filled his eyes. He glanced up at Gavin. "You know, I saw him—Hightower—drop when the trapdoor opened. That took me by surprise. There was a hood over his head, and the rope tightened, and his body turned slightly to one side. The only other movement was his right foot, it jerked, and then it was still. They waited for a minute or so before they took him down. I left before they pronounced him dead, but I knew he was. I guess that's what justice looks like."

Gavin looked at his young friend. "Yeah, it isn't always pretty," he agreed. "I think I would like to take you into a cleansing ceremony with my uncle. The sooner the better."

"Yeah, okay by me. Thanks."

After a quiet moment, Gavin spoke again. "At Arlo's funeral, I remembered a story my dad told me, something he saw and heard when he was a boy. I remembered it when I heard the women crying for Arlo. My dad saw a bird, a killdeer, and heard her crying. When he got close it didn't run, and he saw that her nest had been torn apart, and there was blood. Her chicks had been killed, probably by a fox or a coyote."

Primault nodded.

"She was grieving for her chicks," said Gavin. "Well, I tell you what, from now on every time I hear a killdeer I'll think of Arlo."

After a moment, the CI leaned back in his chair. "How was the meeting with Hightower?"

Gavin shook his head slowly and took a deep breath. Reaching into his coat pocket he pulled out the voice recorder and turned it on.

Ten minutes later, it was Primault's turn to be shocked.

"So, now Henry Berkin's behavior makes sense because he was afraid Hightower would out him as his accomplice. And that's what got Berkin killed. Damn, Hightower did hire Caruth to do that. Why do you suppose Hightower waited so long to confess?"

"I don't know, maybe because he could, because he had nothing to lose. Now we can turn this tape over to the feds. If a federal court believes it, Caruth is toast."

Four hours later they were at Heathrow International Airport, taking their seats on the airplane bound for Minneapolis.

# ONE HUNDRED TWENTY-SIX

Dating back to 1900, The Gray Grass Community Cemetery was in a wide meadow, not far from a stream called Corn Creek. The newest grave still did not have a headstone. The dirt atop it was no longer dark and fresh, but there were still flowers. Standing next to it were Darrell Berkin and his mother Mavis.

Justin and Sandra Primault approached, holding hands. Primault put the vase of fresh daisies and a bundle of gray sage in the middle of the pile. Turning back, he and Sandra shook hands with the boy and his mother. Darrell pointed to a photograph among all the bouquets and vases. Picking it up, Justin stood and gazed at the portrait of a smiling young man resplendent in a roach headdress and traditional Lakota dance regalia.

"Is that him?" Sandra asked.

Darrell nodded. "Yeah, this is Arlo."

"A handsome young man," she said, wistfully.

"Graduated magna cum laude from Smokey River University," Primault said, "and would have taken his master's degree with high honors as well—about two months ago. He is the only son of Agnes and Raymond High Crane and younger brother to Anna. He was a traditional dancer, historian, and Lakota speaker. He would have made a difference."

Sandra gazed at the photograph, took her husband's arm, and glanced at Darrell Berkin. "Well, then I guess we must do that for him, where we can."

Darrell nodded as the tears ran down his face. He wiped them away as Primault put the photo back among the flowers. From his pocket, Primault took out a sheaf of papers. "This is a copy of the transcript from the hearing in England," he told them. "This is where the judge said he would not grant clemency to Hightower because of what he did here, to Arlo. So, we did manage to get justice for him. Gavin's uncle, Andrew No Horn, said to burn the pages, here, at his grave. That way the smoke will carry the message to Arlo."

Primault took out a disposable lighter, cleared a space among the flowers, put the folded papers down, and set them on fire. At that moment, the breeze paused, and the smoke rose quickly upward, leaving a small pile of blackened ashes. Suddenly the breeze sprang up and whirled the ashes into the sky, carrying them higher and higher until they were gone from sight.

"Sir," Darrell said to Primault, and pulled out his cell phone. "I want to show you something."

"My name is Justin," the CI said. He and Sandra leaned in as the young man brought up a video on his phone, the sound of drums coming from it.

"This is from the pow-wow last summer at the tribal fairgrounds," Darrell said. "I took this of Arlo competing in the men's traditional contest." He pointed to one of four dancers in the video. "That's him, in the mainly blue regalia. He's got the best eagle-feather bustle I've ever seen. He won first place."

They watched as Arlo High Crane moved precisely in time with the drum, mimicking the movements of the *siyo*, the grouse, that still danced on the prairies. It was a performance of precise rhythm and movement, ending in perfect unison with the last beat of the drum.

"That's the way I'll always remember him," Darrell said, wiping away a tear.

"Thank you," Justin said, putting his hand on the young man's shoulder. "I'd really love a copy of that video."

Darrell nodded. "No problem. I'll text it to you."

In a few minutes they turned and walked slowly back to their cars. From a distance came a muted cry. At first Justin thought it was a flute.

Ka-ree-ka-ree-kar-ee

Everyone paused and Primault held up a hand.

"What is that?" Sandra asked.

The cry came again, nearer this time.

Justin smiled, hugged his wife, and turned to Darrell and Mavis Berkin.

"That's a killdeer," he said. "Gavin Lone Wolf told me a story of a killdeer crying for her chicks that were taken from the nest. Every time I hear that from now on I'll think of that story and remember Arlo."

Darrell Berkin nodded, wiping away a tear. "That's cool, the remembering part, I mean."

Primault nodded. "And you know what else? We shouldn't dwell so much on how he died. I think we should remember how he lived and how he danced."

The boy nodded and smiled through his tears. "That's even cooler," he said.

Mavis Berkin stepped forward and shook the CI's hand. "Thanks for inviting us here." She turned to Sandra. "Thank you, too, Sandy."

"Of course. You take care, both of you."

Sandra waited with her husband as they watched Darrell and his mother walk back to their car. "So, Henry Berkin was in on Arlo's murder?"

"Yeah, I'm afraid so. I'm not surprised. But it's the one piece of evidence we decided not to reveal, for their sake."

Primault returned Mavis's wave.

They watched the car turn left onto the gravel road and started back toward theirs. "My heart goes out to them," Sandra said.

## ONE HUNDRED TWENTY-SEVEN

Avery and Primault sat on either side of the table in the conference room. Primault had his laptop open and attached a speaker. "Are you ready?" he said to the Chief.

Avery nodded.

Primault touched Enter on the keyboard and a few seconds later they heard Hightower's voice:

> (Hightower) I need to tell you how it happened, and I'm not asking for forgiveness. Forgiveness won't save my soul. I took Arlo out to the dam. I forced him to drive out of town, then I tied him up with tape, and forced him into the trunk. I knew the area, I fished there a few times. Henry Berkin met me at the dam. It was his idea and we planned it together, and he lives near there, which is why we picked Flat Butte Dam. I shot him, I shot Arlo, with my cap-and-ball pistol. You figured that out. After I did it I threw the gun into the dam. After that I left and he rode home, on his horse.
> (Lone Wolf) I see. There's something I'm not clear about. What was your connection to Henry Berkin?
> (Hightower) He was blackmailing me, two thousand dollars a

month. Berkin was on the committee that interviewed me. He was on staff at the university at the time. As you know, he's a former cop. It seems he did a background check, made inquiries to Durham University, and figured out I was impersonating my brother. If I didn't pay the money, he threatened to reveal my real identity.

(Lone Wolf) I see. How did the two of you figure out that Arlo High Crane was in contact with the University of Durham as well?

(Hightower) Ah, it seems that Arlo, after he got a letter from the university, he told his friend Darrell about it. Apparently then Darrell mentioned it to his father, after that.

(Lone Wolf) Did you and Henry talk about what to do?

(Hightower) Yes. He said we had to eliminate the problem. It was my idea to switch cars.

(Lone Wolf) When and how did all this planning happen?

(Hightower) On May sixteenth, over the phone.

(Lone Wolf) Then what happened?

(Hightower) I abducted Arlo. Henry met us out at the damn. He was there when I shot the boy.

(Lone Wolf) How did Antonio Caruth enter the picture?

(Hightower) I knew him years ago, I worked for his father. They were Italians, a crime family, if you get my drift. Antonio said he would take care of Henry for me. I gave him directions to that old barn where you found Henry.

(Lone Wolf) So Caruth killed Henry Berkin because you asked him to?

(Hightower) Yeah, that's how it went down.

(Lone Wolf) Did Antonio and his dad know you as Caleb, or Carey?

(Hightower) They never knew me as Carey. I told them right from the start I was Caleb.

Primault tapped a key and stopped the audio.

"That is scary to the bone," Avery said.

"No shit. I can make a copy, and then delete most of it and keep only the references to Caruth, from where Gavin asked how Caruth came into the picture."

"Yeah, do that. Mavis and Darrell Berkin don't ever need to know. Hightower is dead and gone, and so are his secrets. That last part, on the other hand, could be trouble for Antonio Caruth."

A knock on the door caught their attention. Patrolman Jason Singer entered with a roll of duct tape in his hand.

"Jason," Primault greeted. "What can we do for you?"

"I just figured something out," he said, smugly. "Remember that strange tire tread, that partial tread?"

"Yeah, I do," Primault said.

"I know how that happened," Singer asserted.

"Well," Chief Avery said, "don't keep it to yourself."

"Duct tape," said Singer. "We found an empty cardboard spool in the trunk of that car, like the one inside this roll of tape." He held up the roll of tape. "Hightower covered the tire treads with duct tape and probably ran out, leaving part of the tread exposed. That's what we found. And because the treads were covered, there were no tracks."

"Damn, that solves that riddle," Primault admitted. "And once he was out of the pasture and onto the road, he yanked off the tape."

"Good work, Jason," Avery said.

Primault closed his laptop, picked up the speaker, and stood. "I guess we can close the books on that one," he said.

## ONE HUNDRED TWENTY-EIGHT

A new van backed into the recently graveled driveway adjacent to the fence at the High Crane residence in Gray Grass. The driver, a young Lakota woman dressed in light green scrubs, stepped down, walked around to the passenger side door, and slid it open. Reaching inside she pulled a lever to activate a ramp and waited for it to slowly swing down from just inside the doorway. When it stopped with a click, it was level with the floor of the van.

The young woman stepped into the van, unlocked the brakes on a wheelchair and rolled it onto the ramp. She pulled another lever and lowered the ramp to ground level, then pushed the chair and its occupant, Anna High Crane, through the gate and up the newly constructed wheelchair ramp leading to the front door.

Agnes and Raymond High Crane watched as the Certified Nurse Assistant pushed their daughter Anna up the ramp and through the open door into the house.

Gavin and his Uncle Andrew had been watching from just inside the yard fence. "So, tell me again what do those, ah, CNAs do?" the old man asked.

"Well, there are two. They both will work four ten-hour days, and they'll overlap one day, so there will be consistent coverage and care, except for the night. Raymond and Agnes are being trained in basic home care, first aid and CPR, since Anna will be home full time now. She won't be at the care center any longer."

"I saw her room and her bed and all the equipment," Andrew marveled. "All this is set up to help her into and out of bed. The new bathroom was built just for her and the front door is new and wide enough for her wheelchair. Pretty fancy stuff you provided, *Tunska*, including that van."

"Except for the home-health care," he told him. "The CNAs are paid through a joint state and tribal program, just for these kinds of situations. Now Anna is home, where she belongs. That's what Arlo wanted."

Raymond approached, smiling happily. "So far so good," he said. "We're getting the hang of it. We can't thank you enough, Nephew."

"No thanks necessary," Gavin said. "I'm only doing what your son would have done."

Raymond nodded. "The two of you come visit anytime," he said.

"We will," Andrew assured him. "We will."

Gavin noticed thunderheads building in the west as he drove toward Kincaid and the university to have a quick chat with President Eagle Shield. Weather-wise it was a typical late summer day on the rez.

Coming from Gray Grass he passed by the pow-wow grounds on the flat above Agency Village. Preparations were in full swing for the annual late August celebration and rodeo. It would be the first time in many years that Gavin would not be dancing in the pow-wow. A year after Grandma Little Turtle's passing, he would dance again. It was customary for a family in mourning to forego public activities for a year after the death of a loved one.

President Eagle Shield had invited him for a quick meeting to report on the establishment of the Arlo High Crane Scholarship, to be awarded annually. The Lone Wolf family had given one-fourth of the proceeds from the sale of the Galand and Sommerville as the initial funding. There were only three stipulations. First, two Lakota students from the reservation, one boy and one girl, would be awarded a four-year scholarship covering tuition, fees, and books. Second, the university foundation would raise matching funds. Three, there would be no publicity whatsoever as to the source of the base funding for the scholarship program.

Gavin decided to stop by for a chat with Ramona. She filled him in on the complete refurbishment of the office Hightower had used.

"The facilities people are almost done painting that room," she told him. "They scraped off the old paint and retiled the floors. As per your uncle's instructions, they demolished and burned all the furniture. He and another medicine man will do a blessing when everything is finished."

Gavin sighed. "Good. What about the workshop in the basement?"

"It was dismantled," she said. "All the walls taken down. It's not even a room anymore."

Gavin paused to gaze up at the lobby wall, at the poster-sized color photograph of Arlo in a red circular frame, the color of honor and the only color the Spirits could see. He was in his traditional dance regalia and smiling.

"That's the photo we all picked," she said. "That's the way I want to remember him, so we can smile and help him dance his way to the other side every time we look at him."

## ONE HUNDRED TWENTY-NINE

On a low bank of the Little White River in the northern part of the Smokey River Reservation, two men sat at a fire sipping coffee and sharing a meal of buffalo meat and wild turnip soup. Behind them their horses grazed.

Gavin glanced at Clayton Lone Hawk for a moment. "I'm not surprised you're not running for re-election," he said. "And I don't blame you."

"If I were ten years younger, I probably would. But I owe it to Veronica since I promised her I would do only one term, beyond finishing Bruneaux's term."

Nearly four years ago Lone Hawk's predecessor had resigned after serious allegations of fraud and ethics violations. The subsequent scandal had nearly caused the Tribal Council to implode. Infighting over appointing an acting tribal president was vicious, but fortunately cooler heads prevailed, and the Legislative Committee had asked Clayton to take the job on an interim basis. But after losing his wife and daughter within a span of three years, politics was the furthest thing from Clayton Lone Hawk's mind. Gavin was one of those who had encouraged his friend to take the job. After the interim year, Lone Hawk had run and won election to a regular term.

"I have a year left on this term," Lone Hawk went on. "And frankly I'm looking forward to retiring, again."

Clayton Lone Hawk had been a teacher and later a school administrator. He and his wife Celia had had one child, a daughter, Autumn. Six years ago, Celia had died of cancer and two years after that Autumn had died after an abortion. She had been raped by a pheasant hunter, a white man from Ohio, and gotten pregnant. When the Redoubt County Sheriff, Cole Trent, had essentially refused to investigate the crime, Clayton had taken the matter into his own hands. Launching his own investigation, he had eventually pursued the man as far as South America to gather evidence. The FBI had finally taken the case and the rapist—a wealthy used car dealer—had been charged, and eventually sent to prison.

An unexpected twist had brought Veronica Streeter into Clayton's life. It had been her estranged husband who had raped Autumn Lone Hawk. Veronica and her two daughters had been shocked, ashamed, and heartbroken after learning of Autumn and Clayton's story. They had traveled to the Smokey River Reservation to apologize to Clayton. Despite the circumstances that had brought them together, there had been instant mutual attraction between Veronica and Clayton. They were married a few months later.

"Life doesn't give too many second chances," Lone Hawk mused. "I have a family, again, a wife and two daughters. I'm a husband and a father again. I want to travel that road."

"And well you should," Gavin affirmed. "You stepped into a tough job and stabilized a bad situation, to say the least. And if the council and the tribal government can't pick up the pieces after that, shame on them."

"Well," Clayton said, smiling slightly. "There is a reason I asked to talk to you today. And I'll get to the point. The Tribal Council needs strong leadership, someone who knows who we were and are and the world we have to contend with. You're one of the few."

"I think I know where you're going with that."

"I'm sure you do. I would like you to think about running for the tribal presidency."

Gavin gazed at the river, at the glistening water as it flowed by. Behind them he heard their horses munching on bunch grass. He sighed. "I'll think about it because you asked," he said. "I've stayed away from tribal politics. It's nasty business, as you know."

"Fair enough." Lone Hawk spoke again, after a moment. "Damn shocking about Henry, isn't it?"

"For sure."

"So, he was blackmailing Hightower for money because he knew the Englishman's real identity."

"Yeah. Then Arlo High Crane also learned, quite innocently, about Hightower. When Henry found that out, he panicked, because he didn't want the cash flow to dry up. He talked Hightower into killing Arlo, and for Hightower there was no choice. A death sentence was waiting for him back in England, and he wanted to protect himself."

Lone Hawk shook his head slowly. "And that boy is dead, Hightower has been hung, and a hit man blew Henry's brains out. And none of that solves any of our problems, does it?" He leaned forward, lifting the coffee pot from the grate over the fire and refilling their cups. "I may be off base, but I think I know part of the reason things are the way they are for us."

Gavin sipped his coffee and waited.

"The voice in Sitting Bull's vision before the Battle of the Little Bighorn warned us. It said, 'do not take anything of theirs.' I mean, I know that's been debated, but, by and large, the 'things' the voice was talking about are the ways and the thinking of Europeans and Euro-Americans. We took on those ways and adopted that thinking, or they were forced on us. Most of us speak English only, we live in square houses, worship their god, live under their laws, and send our children to their schools. I mean, I could go on."

"What do we do about it?" Gavin asked.

"Remember who we are," Lone Hawk replied, immediately. "We revive *our* language, and we go back to *our* ways. That's easy to say and hard to do, but unless we do we'll be what the American Indian Movement was terrified of—apples. We'll be red on the outside and white on the inside. Frankly, that possibility scares the shit out of me, too."

Gavin nodded. "I agree, with everything you said. And I hope that we can understand that no matter how many 'things' we have in this modern life—silverware, computers, cellphones, pickup trucks, and that includes a formal education or being a western-trained physician—it is possible to live by the ways, values, and traditions our ancestors lived by. My sister is half Scottish and half Lakota, is a registered nurse and has a master's degree in public health, but is culturally Lakota."

Lone Hawk nodded in agreement. "Call me cynical, but I'm not impressed because a popular European nursery rhyme is translated into a Native language, because to me that's just another example of colonization. The mainstream society doesn't like that word, and some Native people don't either. It's real and colonization is still happening. I realize that that may sound hypocritical from a Lakota man with a mainstream education married to a white woman, not to mention with two adopted white daughters. On the other hand, I think maybe my family is a guide to the future. My wife and daughters are Lutheran, but they are also tolerant and inclusive. I go to church with them, and they've come with me to Lakota ceremonies. I respect their ways, and they respect mine, without judgment either way. Hell, my wife and my new daughters have taken my name."

"You're a lucky man."

"To say the least. Another thing I've learned from them, from my wife and daughters, is unconditional love and acceptance. That's how we find and create balance in this crazy world."

# ONE HUNDRED THIRTY

Gavin spent a quiet Saturday at home putting the finishing touches on a primitive Lakota bow for a museum. Though he tried his best not to think of Soldier Woman, he couldn't help himself. Their evening at the bar in the Gemini Restaurant had turned out to be quite a conversation. He had enjoyed it and soaked up every moment of her presence. Now he was hundreds of miles and weeks removed from it; yet the memories persisted.

There were other realities, decidedly harsher, that stayed just beyond his awareness until he allowed them to push in. Clayton Lone Hawk was still fighting the self-centered factions on the Tribal Council. There were still homeless on the streets of reservation towns. Too many Lakota women and men, young and old, hollow-eyed, and emaciated, were addicted to every drug and drink that plagued mainstream America. Lakota women and girls were still disappearing. And there were still grandparents raising their grandchildren. Those realities seemed to be multiplying day-by-day, faster than the efforts to fix them.

Gavin tried to set all that aside and spent an hour behind the barn, shooting his Lakota hunting bow to make sure his skills had not diminished. Yet he was sensing that when the leaves fell and the air turned cooler in the mountains, he would not be in them for the chase. This hunting season he would stalk the thickets along the creeks that flowed into the Little White. He preferred to call it *Makizita Wakpa*—Misty Creek—or Smokey River. He would use those ancient game trails as generations of his ancestors had.

He awoke just after dawn the next morning. After meditation and prayer, he went for a three-mile run. After doing the *wahukeza un wicakizapi* (fighting with the lance) routine with his replica war lance, he had a shower and a light breakfast. Chief Avery called just as he finished the dishes.

"Hey, Ben. Don't tell me you're on the job on this fine Sunday morning."

"I'm not, just calling to say you're welcome at the cop shop for coffee anytime."

"Thanks. I'll take you up on that."

Gavin disconnected the call. It had opened the floodgates, releasing a rampage of bottled-up thoughts—most of them connected to Arlo High Crane and "Caleb" Hightower, and now Henry Berkin. All of them connected by death. There was one certainty, a truth that was comforting. Somewhere on the other side Arlo High Crane was soaring, a buoyant spirit carried by the goodness he had shown in this realm. Somewhere, he envisioned, Arlo and Grandma Annie would meet. Hightower and Berkin, on the other hand, were crawling in darkness, burdened by their bad deeds and the evil they had chosen to embrace.

He decided he would ride to Grandma Little Turtle's house to help Loren clean it. In the tack room he grabbed the Australian stock saddle and paused, looking at all the iron bits and heavy leather tack hanging on the wall.

He looked down at his feet, at the pair of rough-out Western boots. "*Hiya* (No)," he muttered and hurried back into the house. Ten minutes later he returned to the barn dressed to fit his mood in the most comfortable pair of blue jeans he owned, a loose-fitting dark-blue sleeveless sweatshirt and Lakota moccasins. A canvas bag and the K-Bar hung from his belt.

The moccasins were plain, one of the last pairs that Grandma Little Turtle had made for him, although she had been a little puzzled that he didn't want them beaded or quilled. He wore them frequently when *wasicu* shoes, sneakers, and boots felt clunky.

Gavin grabbed a thin, braided, soft rope and a halter with a lead rope and walked into the corral where Red Wing and Dancer were waiting. He slipped the rope behind Dancer's ears because he approached first and quickly fashioned a Lakota riding bosal with the soft rope. The halter he put on Red Wing. Opening the gate, he swung up onto Dancer.

"*Hiyupo* (Come on, let's go)," he said, clicking his tongue. The horses responded immediately.

He headed north across the prairies, leading Red Wing. He would ride him coming home. The horses moved eagerly under the early morning sky, as if wanting to play with the cavorting breeze dancing around them. Meadowlarks sang their bright songs, and hawks and eagles rode the high winds.

Grandma Little Turtle's log house was seven miles from his place. On a low hill, beyond the four tall cottonwood trees that guarded the house on the west, was the family cemetery. The newest grave, of course, was Grandma Annie's. The family's plan was to erect a headstone on the anniversary of her passing.

He let the horses walk the final quarter mile to cool down. They had loped at least half the way and made the trip in less than an hour. Uncle Andrew was waiting under the cottonwoods. Dismounting, Gavin turned both horses into the pen next to the small barn where there was water.

"Horses like to be ridden bareback," the old man commented, grinning.

"It just felt like the thing to do this morning, *Leksi*," Gavin said. "Takes me back to when Gerard and I were twelve and didn't have a care in the world. Roaming the prairies on a horse, bareback, was the only way to live." He paused to gaze at his horses. "Maybe I'm just yearning for the innocence of childhood."

"We all do that when we've been through a rough patch," Andrew pointed out. "Those are the kinds of memories that keep us balanced."

"That's all we can strive for, isn't it? Some kind of balance."

The old man nodded.

"*Leksi*," Gavin said. "What do you know about Henry Berkin's family?"

"I knew his dad, Laurence. He worked for the BIA, and he's the one that changed the family name from Bear King to Berkin."

"Why?"

"Didn't want to be Lakota. That's the sad truth," the old man said. "Henry's brother Oliver kept the old name. He speaks Lakota, too."

They heard vehicle noises and turned to watch Morgan and Loren's SUV pull into the yard. Morgan and Thomas began hauling buckets and other cleaning tools into the house, while Loren joined Andrew and Gavin.

"I brought some sage and *wasna*," Gavin told them, pointing at the cemetery.

The two rail-wood fences around the cemetery formed a circle, a reminder that life cycled from birth to death. Eleven graves filled the west half. They walked the outside of the fence, clockwise starting from the east-facing gate. In doing so they touched all four directions—east, south, west, and north.

Stepping inside they left bundles of sage on each grave, starting with Grandma Little Turtle's. Except for hers, simple white headstones marked each. Names were written in Lakota, birthdates and dates of passing in

English. Carved in between the name and the date on each headstone was the sacred medicine wheel. Some of the headstones were noticeably older. Gabriel and Molly McLean Lone Wolf shared one wide granite marker. In thirty-four years, it had yet to show signs of weathering. And it was the only marker that had a Christian cross carved into it, on Molly's side above her name.

They went last to two graves just inside the west quadrant of the fence. The one on the left said *Sina Luta* (Red Shawl) and to the right was *Mayaca Isnala* (Lone Wolf). They stood for several moments, gazing silently at the headstones and the names. There was a large bundle of sage on each grave. Gavin guessed one of their relatives had come to visit.

He took two strings of red tobacco ties out of his canvas pouch and laid one on each grave next to the sage bundles. Red was the color of honor and respect, especially for the matriarch and patriarch of the family. Then he took out two bags of *wasna*, dried and pounded buffalo meat mixed with pounded chokecherries and tallow, and put them down as well for a food offering.

"*Zuya wica tawoecun kin tunkasila na ate unspeunkiyapelo* (We learn the way of the warrior from our fathers and grandfathers)," he said. "*Eyas wooihitike he ina na unci etan unkunspepi* (But we learn courage from our mothers and grandmothers)."

"I wish every Lakota child could grow up learning that," Loren said wistfully.

They stood for a few more minutes until Loren spoke again. "I'll put on coffee and water for tea."

"Good," Gavin said, smiling. "Your coffee's the only reason I got up early this morning."

"Yeah, right," Loren said, returning his smile.

As they walked toward the house, Uncle Andrew sniffed the air and looked around. "It's a good day," he said. "I was here a couple of days ago. I'm glad we decided to rent out Grandma's house. I hate to see it standing empty."

"Yeah, me, too," Gavin said. "The university is always looking for housing for teaching staff, especially those who come from off-reservation. The rent money can go right into the scholarship fund we set up."

Andrew nodded. "Yup, that's a good idea. By the way, my *hankasi* (cousin) Esther Red Thunder called me very early this morning."

"Is she okay?"

"Oh, yeah. She just wanted to tell me she had finally learned how to work her phone."

"Oh, good. That's a big step for her."

As Andrew went into the house, Loren grabbed her brother's arm. "Hey, I like your moccasins."

"Grandma made those for me."

"I remember." She stopped in front of him and took him by the shoulders. "How are you doing, little brother? You've been on a hard road."

"Not nearly as hard as it's been for Arlo's family. I'm good. Funny thing, though, I really miss *Ina* (Mom) and *Ate* (Dad). I wish I could talk to them."

"I know what you mean." She paused and studied his face. "I have another question."

"Sure."

Her gaze searched his face. "Do you still love Katherine?"

He blinked and looked away for a moment, then returned his gaze to hers and sighed. "Yeah, I never stopped loving her."

"I thought so," she said softly. "And she still loves you, too."

"How do you know that?"

"A woman's intuition, but I think you know, too. But she's afraid to ask."

"Ask? About what?"

"Another chance. She's afraid to ask because she broke it off. Life is full of risk and no guarantees. Better to share it with someone you love. Do you understand what I'm trying to say?"

He nodded slowly, gazing out across the prairie. "Yeah, I think so."

"Good. So, what are you going to do about it?"

## ONE HUNDRED THIRTY-ONE

After Gavin finished brushing down the horses from their ride to Grandma Little Turtle's, he turned them loose into the pen. He chuckled as they both immediately rolled in the dirt. Inside, the clock on the kitchen wall said something past six. It was an hour later in Washington DC.

He stood for a moment, remembering Soldier Woman sitting on his couch in black silk pajamas, a cup of tea in her hand. Voices echoed in his head.

*I lost the love of my life to cancer, and you lost yours to human nature. I'll never grow old with the woman I loved more than life. You still have a chance, please don't let it pass you by...*

*Life doesn't give too many second chances.*

*Life is full of risk and no guarantees. Better to share it with someone you love.*

Walking to his desk he pulled out the chair and sat, staring at the landline phone, wondering if he should use it or the cell phone. He sighed.

*You jumped out of a damn airplane at night and you're afraid to pick up a phone to make a simple phone call.*

But perhaps it wasn't so simple; and yet if he had read the signs correctly and if his brother and sister were right, it should be.

With a sigh he stepped to the credenza and picked up the cell phone. He knew exactly what he wanted, to see Soldier Woman sitting on that couch, to ride across the prairies with her, and to see her long hair spilling across the pillow every morning when he opened his eyes. He wanted to be a reason she was happy.

He wanted to share this life with the woman he loved.

He dialed her cell phone, his heart in his throat.

"Hello, Gavin," she answered. Her soft, husky voice sent a shiver though him. "How are you?"

"Good, now that I hear your voice. Got a minute to talk?"

"For you I have all the minutes there are and will ever be."

# EPILOGUE

The White Earth River Valley
Great Sioux Reservation
Moon of Leaves Turning Brown
September 1876

It was near sundown by the time the wagon and its outriders reached the valley where the Smoking Earth River flowed into the White Earth River. They stopped there among the tall cottonwood trees, inside a thicket of oak and ash. After more than a month of traveling and hiding, they were home. Three men, two women, and a small girl comprised the entire group.

Lone Wolf spoke to his brothers. "I will ride back a ways and cover the wagon tracks as much as I can," he said. "I will be back by sundown." He looked around. "Make camp. Our Uncle, Fast Hawk, and his family should still be near here," he said.

White Tail Feather nodded. "We'll watch out for them."

Red Shawl cast worried glances to the west as they worked to hide the wagon with tree branches. Her mother, Blue Corn Woman, and her daughter, Little Shawl, were helping as well.

"I saw no one following," Black Wolf reassured her. "We have seen no sign of people for over eleven days. Don't worry."

White Tail Feather returned with the wagon horses, after watering them, and picketed them nearby to let them graze with the two other horses. Then he pitched in to help finish hiding the wagon.

All of them were dressed in white-people clothing, the men in shirts and trousers and the women, even five-year-old Little Shawl, in calico dresses. Everyone wore a battered hat. Anyone seeing them at a distance would think they were a family of whites. That was the reason for the clothing.

They had traded their lodge covering and lodge poles for the wagon and the two big horses to pull it. Red Shawl had learned to drive the wagon horses, and she and her mother had learned to hitch and unhitch them.

Not three months ago, at the end of the Month When Berries Ripen, they had been in a village of a thousand lodges along the Greasy Grass River.

After the Long Knives had attacked and were defeated, the People had moved south, into the foothills of the Shining Mountains and then into the Powder River country. All the while the old men leaders, such as Sitting Bull of the Hunkpapa Lakota, and the war leaders, such as Crazy Horse of the Oglala Lakota, talked. There was more argument than wise debate. Therefore, there was no agreement as to how best to use the decisive victory over the Long Knives. So, the People disbanded. Sitting Bull and his people went north, while Crazy Horse and his small band stayed near the Tongue River. Hoping to avoid retaliation, those who had come from the Long Knife camp called Fort Robinson in Nebraska Territory to join Sitting Bull and Crazy Horse in the spring went back to Nebraska.

Lone Wolf and his family had been with Crazy Horse, and White Tail Feather and Black Wolf had traveled from the valley of the White Earth River to join the village on the Greasy Grass. As a family they had decided to return to the White Earth River to rejoin their uncle Fast Hawk and his family. It was a place they knew best.

Here the men would hunt with the silent bow and arrow rather than the captured rifles with voices like thunder. Each of the brothers had a rifle but no more than twenty bullets each. The rifles were to be used for defense only.

The heat of the summer lingered and so the nights were warm. There was dried meat so a fire was not needed. Fires were made only in the daylight, because even the smallest fire could be seen from great distances at night.

As the dusk deepened the women rolled out their blankets and robes to sleep in the wagon bed. The men would take turns standing watch during the night.

Red Shawl joined her husband as he sat against the base of a thick oak tree on a rise a stone's throw from the concealed camp. Black Wolf was on the other side of the camp, hidden in a low thicket on a hillside. White Tail Feather was guarding the five horses.

"There are trees and many deep gullies here," Lone Wolf said. "Good places to build shelters that are hidden. And there are still deer along these rivers. I think we shall need to hunt, even in the winter. We have not been able to make meat yet."

"It will be good," Red Shawl asserted. "We will do well here."

"We will live, we will take care of one another," Lone Wolf declared. "We may know hunger times, but we will live as our ancestors did. We will not give in to the whites, as our relatives at Robinson have. We should not give in; we won the battle."

"I am ready."

"Someday, perhaps, our people will gather again," Lone Wolf said, hopefully. "But now, this is our path. We will walk it."

They fell silent and listened to the sounds as the deepening dusk turned to night. Coyotes barked and somewhere a wolf howled. Stars began to appear here and there.

"It was necessary to take the Long Knife rifles," Lone Wolf said in a low voice. "I found mine after we stopped the Long Knives who attacked from the south. All their long guns are the same. That is why the bullets are the same. But the six-shooter I took is different. That is why I could not find bullets."

"Perhaps you should throw it in the river," Red Shawl suggested. "Without bullets, it is useless."

"I will keep it," Lone Wolf said. "Someday I will give it to our daughter. I will tell her the story of how my brothers and I fought, and how I captured it, so she can tell her children. So that what happened at the Greasy Grass will live on after us, so that those yet to be born will know what we did."

# GLOSSARY

*Ate* (ah-the) – Lakota word for "Father" or "Dad"

**BIA** (Bureau of Indian Affairs) – Federal agency within the U.S. Department of the Interior, established in 1824 as part of the War Department to deal with Native tribes; moved to the Interior Department in 1849 as overseer, then later redirected to be (supposedly) an advocate for Native tribes recognized by the federal government

**Ceremony** – Refers to Lakota ancient healing rituals still used by Lakota medicine men

**Drum Group** – Small group of young and old Native men who play traditional songs at *wacipi* (traditional celebrations) and other events

**Honor Song** – Lakota song to honor an individual for a significant accomplishment or achievement, such as being in the military or graduation; often sung at funerals to honor the deceased

*Hunka* (hun-kah) – Lakota word for "the making of relatives," i.e., the ceremony of binding one person to another person to form an extended family network

**IHS** (Indian Health Service) – Established in 1955 to provide health care to members of federally recognized Native tribes through clinics and hospitals located on reservations, recently beset by corruption and ineptitude mainly at the administrative and managerial levels

**Ina** (ee-nah) – Lakota word for "Mother"

**Iyeska** (ee-yeh-skah) – Lakota word meaning "speaks white," often used as a derogatory label toward Lakota individuals of mixed ethnicities; equates to "half-breed" or "mixed-breed"

**Lakota** (lah-koh-tah) – The Lakota, Dakota and Nakota tribes (each of these words means "allies" or "alliance of friends") make up the largest third of the Lakota nation, which consists of seven bands on five reservations

**Leksi** (lehk-kshee) – Lakota for "Uncle," used in reference to one's mother's brother(s) or male cousins of one's father and mother or as a term of respect for an older man of one's parents' generation not related by blood

**Long Knives/Long Knife** or *Mila Hanska* (mee-lah han-skah) – Designation for white soldiers that became the common term for all Euro-Americans

**Medicine Man** or *Wapiya Wicasa* (wah-pee-ya wee-chah-shah "the man who fixes") – A male Lakota traditional healer (a woman healer is wapiya winyan); to be a medicine man or woman one must have extensive knowledge of medicinal plants and the ability to be guided by "the Old Ones" or Spirits

**Medicine Wheel** – Sacred symbol representing spiritual knowledge and a connection to everything in the universe in which the four quadrants symbolize the four cardinal directions, four seasons, and various entities

**Mniconju** (mnee-koh-joo) or the Cheyenne River Sioux – Fourth largest of the seven bands of the Lakota, whose ancestral territory was west of the Missouri in the north central portion of what is now South Dakota

**Pow-wow** – Derivative of an Algonquin word that now is widely used in reference to Indian or Native cultural celebrations and dances

**Regalia** – Refers to the various types of dance costumes used by both Lakota male and female dancers corresponding to traditional, grass, jingle, and fancy dancing

**Sicangu** (see-chan-guh) – Third largest of the seven bands of the Lakota, whose ancestral territory was the south-central portion of what is now South Dakota, referred to in English as the Rosebud Sioux

**Smudge** – To burn any of the four sacred plants—sage, flat cedar, sweet grass, or medicine root—while praying to invoke a blessing or protection

**Sun Dance** – The most sacred ritual and observance among the traditional Lakota, performed in the Middle Moon, from late June to mid-July, in which men dance for four days from sun up to sun down staring at the sun while praying, and get pierced through the skin on their chests by chokecherry wood skewers that are inserted and attached to a cord bound to the center cottonwood tree; the dancer tries to break free of the cord by pulling back, causing the skewers to break through his skin in a sacrifice of pain on behalf of his people

**Sweat or** *Inipi* (ee-nee-pee "to live again")– Term used to describe the "rebirth" ceremony, which consists of four rounds of songs and prayers by the participants and is conducted by a medicine man in a sweat lodge, essentially a wet sauna, with water poured over hot coals inside a small, enclosed lodge

***Tahansi*** (tan-han-shee) – Lakota word for male cousin of a male

**Tobacco Ties** – Small amounts of tobacco tied into squares of colored cloth as prayer offerings attached to a string for the purpose of a ceremony

**Tunska** (tun-shkah) – Lakota for "nephew" used by both male and female speakers in reference to one's siblings' son(s), or to someone taken (chosen) as a relative (see hunka)

**VFR** – Visual flight rules

**Victory Song** – A traditional song performed and sung by drum group to commemorate a past victory or to draw attention to a victory attained by a contemporary Lakota individual or group

**Vision Quest or** *hanbleceya* (han-bleh-cheh-yah, "cry for a vision") – Refers to the act of seeking a vision for guidance in which the vision seeker is placed alone on a hill or butte in an isolated location for up to four days and four nights without food and water to meditate and pray for a vision for guidance

**Wasicu** (wah-shee-chuh) – Lakota for "fat takers or "fat stealers," a word used for white people

# ABOUT THE AUTHOR

**Joseph M. Marshall III**
Award-winning Sicangu Oglala Lakota author and historian, Joseph M. Marshall III, PhD, is one of the most prolific Native writers in the United States. Raised by his maternal grandparents in a traditional Native household on the Rosebud Indian Reservation in South Dakota, he has written eighteen historical fiction and nonfiction books and narrated his own audio books. He is best known for award-winners *The Lakota Way*, *The Journey of Crazy Horse*, and *The Day the World Ended at Little Bighorn*. His work is informed by his background as a Lakota craftsman, who makes his own Native Lakota bows and arrows; a skilled archer; and specialist in wilderness survival. The accounts of real historical figures along with the events that he experienced on the reservation and heard as a child from his grandparents and their generation of oral storytellers figure prominently in his books. His Native name, given to him at age five is *Ohitiya Otanin*, which means "his courage is known."

Marshall's accomplishments include co-founding Sinte Gleska University on the Rosebud Reservation; teaching; public speaking; mentoring of indigenous youth; and serving on the Board of Directors of Lakota Youth Development, Inc. He has been a teacher at the high school level and a professor at several colleges and universities, where he taught Native culture, Lakota language and history. He often lectures and speaks on Native issues and topics. In 2022 he received the Crazy Horse Memorial® Foundation Educator of the Year Award for his lifelong leadership in education and the impact that he continues to make on Indigenous youth and communities.

Marshall has served as a cultural and historical consultant and technical advisor on films, television series and documentaries. He has also appeared as an actor in two television mini-series *Return to Lonesome Dove* and *Into the West* as well in documentaries and film. In 2023, Marshall was inducted into the Western Writers Hall of Fame, and he received the Owen Wister Award by Western Writers of America for lifetime contributions to Western literature. Previous honorees include Pulitzer Prize winners N. Scott Momaday and Louise Erdrich.

Marshall's "Smokey River Suspense Series" represents his first contemporary fiction. His latest novels are based on current issues facing Lakota people, including crime and the interface between tribal government, the Bureau of Indian Affairs, and the FBI, and the ongoing epidemic of Missing and Murdered Indigenous Women that has largely been ignored by the American public and media. After spending many years in Santa Fe, New Mexico, Marshall has once again returned home.

Printed in the USA
CPSIA information can be obtained
at www.ICGtesting.com
CBHW061804081024
15571CB00049B/1127